PRIVATE
ARMY

DEDICATION

This book is dedicated to my uncle Carl A. Hobbs. A decorated captain in the 29th Infantry Division, he was wounded outside St. Lo, and while minor, it must have been spectacular. The incident has been described in at least four WWII books. A later wound by an MP-40 at point blank range nearly killed him.

Carl was a 33rd Degree Mason, a long-time political operative (he served as the finance director for U.S. Congressman J.J. 'Jake' Pickle and did the same work for President Lyndon Johnson in Travis County) and he retired as the Postmaster of Austin, Texas.

Growing up, my family consisted of the Hobbs, Larys and Wards who all started out Depression Era broke but became successful, and the children were all told we could be anything we wanted to be but I don't think anyone actually believed that.

On Christmas at Carl's house, whichever of my cousins who had distinguished themselves was allowed to sit at the adult table. I got there twice… the year I made Eagle Scout, then when I was nineteen and one of the youngest officers to graduate from the U.S. Army Ranger School.

Took a lot to impress Uncle Carl.

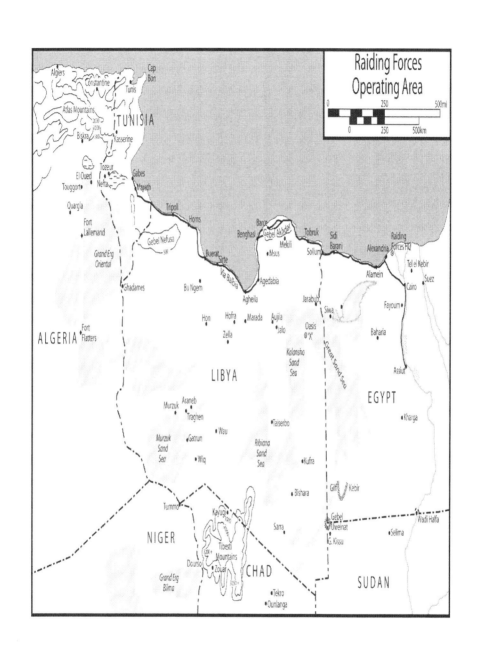

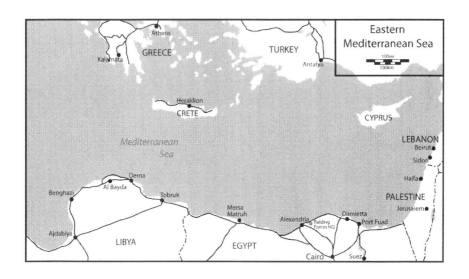

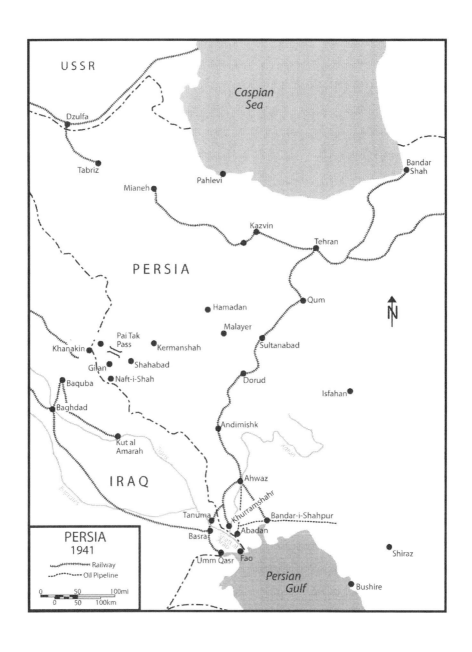

USSR

Caspian
Sea

Dzulfa

Tabriz

Bandar
Shah

Mianeh

Pahlevi

Kazvin

PERSIA

Tehran

Qum

Hamadan

N

Malayer

Pai Tak
Pass

Khanakin

Kermanshah

Sultanabad

Gilan

Shahabad

Baquba

Naft-i-Shah

Dorud

Baghdad

Isfahan

Andimishk

Kut al
Amarah

IRAQ

Ahwaz

Khurramshahr

Tanuma

Bandar-i-Shahpur

Basra

Abadan

Umm Qasr

Fao

Shiraz

Persian
Gulf

Bushire

PERSIA
1941

——— Railway
- - - Oil Pipeline

0   50   100mi
0   50   100km

PRIVATE ARMY

PHIL WARD

Contents

DUKW

The DUKW makes its appearance in Private Army. Since the story is set in mid-1941 I may be early on when it could have actually arrived in Middle East Command through the Lend Lease Program.

Some state D stands for "Designed in 1942", U stands for "Utility", K stands for "All Wheel Drive", W stands for "Dual Rear Axel".

If that is true the DUKW could not have made it to Africa as early as Private Army.

However at least one military historian claims the 'D' stands for Duplex, which opens the door for the DUKW to have been designed before '42.

And, another source asserts 1942 was the date of the "final production design". If true the original design could have been made earlier, submitted to the U.S. Army for tests, rejected (as actually happened) and the dozen test vehicles dumped on the British.

Who knows…that's what makes writing the Raiding Forces Series so interesting. It's all true except the parts I make up or get wrong.

Phil

ACRONYMS
PRIVATE ARMY

Adv. HQ. A-Force—Advanced Headquarters, Airborne-Force

AO—Area of Operation

AP—Armor Piercing

AVG—American Volunteer Group

DDOD(I)—Deputy Director Operations Division (Irregular)

DRW—Desert Raiding Wing

DZ—Drop Zone

GHQ—General Headquarters

HQ—Headquarters

HQME—Headquarters Middle East

IP—Initial Point

KORR—King's Own Royal Regiment

KRRC—King's Royal Rifle Corps

LCA—Landing Craft Assault

LCT—Landing Craft Tank

LCVP—Landing Craft Vehicle Personnel

LLY—Lancelot Lancers Yoemanry

LMG—Light Machine Gun

LRDG—Long Range Desert Group

LUP—Laying Up Position

OCS—Infantry Officers Candidate School

ORP—Objective Rally Point

PLAN A-R—(Anti-Rommel)

PLF—Parachute Landing Fall

PWE—Political Warfare Executive

RAF—Royal Air Force

RAN—Royal Australian Navy

RFDP—Raiding Forces Desert Patrol

RFDS—Raiding Forces Desert Squadron

RFHQ—Raiding Forces Headquarters

RFSS—Raiding Forces Sea Squadron

RIN—Royal Indian Navy

RM—Royal Marine

RN—Royal Navy

RNR—Royal Navy Reserve

RNPS—Royal Navy Patrol Service

1SAS Brigade—1Special Air Service Brigade (SAS)

SIM—Servizio Informazioni Militare, Military Intelligence Service (Italian)

SIME—Security Intelligence Middle East

SOE—Special Operations Executive

SOP—Standard Operating Procedure

TO&E—table of organization and equipment

W/T—wireless/telephone equipment

RANDAL'S
RULES FOR RAIDING

Rule 1: The first rule is there ain't no rules.

Rule 2: Keep it short and simple.

Rule 3: It never hurts to cheat.

Rule 4: Right man, right job.

Rule 5: Plan missions backward (know how to get home).

Rule 6: It's good to have a Plan B.

Rule 7: Expect the unexpected.

PRIVATE ARMY
LIST OF CHARACTERS

Ace

Amal Atrash

Benito Mussolini

Brandy Seaborn

Brig. George Davy

Brig. Joe Kingstone

Brig. Raymond J. 'R.J.' Maunsell

Brig. Robert Lochner

Capt. A.W. "Sammy" Sansom

Capt. "Geronimo" Joe McKoy, OBE

Capt. Hawthorne Merryweather

Capt. James J. (Jimmy) Roosevelt

Capt. Jane Seaborn, OBE, RM

Capt. Jeb Pelham-Davies, DSO, MC

Capt. Michael Crichton-Steward,

Capt. Patrick "Paddy" Leigh-Fermor

Capt. Pip Pilkington, MC (Bar)

Capt. "Pyro" Percy Stirling, DSO, MC

Capt. Roy "Mad Dog" Reupart

Capt. Taylor Corrigan, DSO, MC Horse Guards

Cdr. Mallory Seaborn, RN

Chief-of-Surgery Dr. Stephen Milam

Col. Ouvry Roberts

Col. Ralph Bagnold

Count László Almásy

Cpl. Basio Thurgood

Cpl. Bernard H. Holms

Cpl./ Sgt. Ned Pompedous

ex-Captain Travis McCloud

ex-Technical Sergeant Hank W. Rawlston

Flanigan

Flight Lieutenant Dicky Cleaver

FM Claude Auchinleck

FM Erwin Rommel

FM Sir Archibald Wavell

Frank Polanski

Gen. Eduard Dietl

Gen. Louis Spears

Guido "GG" Grazinni

Guns

Joker

King

Lana Turner

Lovat Scout Lionel Fenwick

Lovat Scout Munro Ferguson

Lt. Alexandra (Mandy) Paige

Lt. Butch "Headhunter" Hoolihan, DSO, MC, MM, RM

Lt. Dick Courtney

Lt. Fraser Llewellyn

Lt. Jeffery Tall-Castle, MC

Lt. Karen Montgomery

Lt. Mark Hathaway

Lt. Martin Gibbs,

Lt. Pamala Plum-Martin, OBE, DFC w/bar

Lt. Penelope "Legs" Honeycutt-Parker, RM

Lt. Randy "Hornblower" Seaborn, DSC, RN

Lt. Roy Kidd

Lt. Westcott Huxley, MC (Bar)

2nd Lt. Billy Jack Jaxx

Lt. Col. Dudley Clarke

Lt. Cdr. Ian Fleming, RN

Lt. Col. John Randal, DSO (Bar), MC

Maj. Clive Adair

Maj. Edward "Ted" Everett

Maj. Jack Black

Maj. Norman Crockatt

Maj. Sir Terry "Zorro" Stone, KBE, DSO, MC

Maj. Gen. Charles Harvey

Maj. Gen. Frank Messervy

Maj. Gen. James "Baldie" Taylor, OBE

Maj. Gen. Neil M. Ritchie

Maj. Gen. William "Bill" Slim

Club

Diamond

Heart

Spade

Zargo

Nigel Davidson

P.J. Pretorius

RAdm. Gholam Ali Bayandor

Red

Rikke /Rocky Runborg

Rita Hayworth

S/Lt. / Skipper Warthog Finley, OBE

Sgt. Maj. Mike "March or Die" Mikkalis, DSM, MM

Sherry Auchinleck

Sqn. Ldr. Paddy Wilcox, DSO, OBE, MC, DFC

The Great Teddy

VAdm./DDOD(I) Sir Randolph "Razor" Ransom, VC, KCB, DSO, OBE, DSC

Veronica Paige

Waldo Treywick, OBE

1
GUTSHOT

To: Lieutenant General Claude Auchinleck
Subject: Special Forces, Middle East Command
Classification: SECRET

Raiding Forces Desert Squadron (RFDS) can best be used to affect the enemies' morale. Their use against airfields, administrative establishments and the like can and does engender very considerable uneasiness in the mind of the enemy.

> Major General Neil M. Ritchie
> Deputy Chief of Staff
> Middle East Command

JAMES "BALDIE" TAYLOR READ THE MEMORANDUM SILENTLY AND handed it back to Colonel Dudley Clarke. "I say, Dudley, the Deputy Chief of Staff does not appear to have a clear understanding of the actual mission Raiding Forces has been assigned."

"Wavell is out. Auchinleck is in," Col. Clarke said. "The Long Range Desert Group and Raiding Forces Desert Squadron are currently much in vogue at General Headquarters, being our only success stories in Middle East Command of late."

Jim said, "Every other enterprise since Sidi Barrani and the liberation of Abyssinia has certainly ended in failure."

"A-Force shall have to take pains to ensure that the great ones do not become confused by *our* misinformation campaign," Col. Clarke said, "The purpose of the exercise being to mystify and mislead Rommel, not ourselves."

"Raiding Forces," Jim said, "is tasked to operate against the Via Balbia road system along the Mediterranean coastline and isolated enemy installations in remote locations in the Western Desert. We search out soft targets that are lightly guarded. The idea is to arrive unannounced and unexpected, with the intention to destroy enemy fuel carriers, motor transport and other military materiel that is difficult to replace.

"RFDS's secondary objective is to draw off and tie down Axis fighting troops by keeping them occupied, guarding against future motorized and/or amphibious attacks that may never come."

"Classic guerrilla tactics," Col. Clarke said, "modified to our enemies' current military environment in the Western Desert at the end of a long, tenuous supply chain."

Jim said, "RFDS's mission is most definitely *not* to attack enemy headquarters, airfields or any other hardened target that could escalate into sustained combat, resulting in the loss of any of our highly trained personnel or precious equipment for marginal gain.

"We need this clarified straightaway, Dudley."

"Agreed," Col. Clarke said. "I understand that General Auchinleck cabled Lady Jane, asking her to act as his social secretary since he is an Indian Army officer. He does not know his way around the Cairo scene and did not bring his wife, Sherry, with him to Egypt. Jane had Phantom message her acceptance and is flying out as we speak.

"We can count on her to champion Raiding Forces—Colonel Randal famously being her pet project."

"Outstanding," Jim said. "Lady Jane has always been our staunchest advocate. She shall help set this right."

"And I shall take pains to clarify the exact nature of the RFDS mission with the 'Auk' at our first A-Force briefing later this week," Col. Clarke said, "to ensure there will be absolutely no confusion."

"Our operators are highly trained hit-and-run specialists," Jim said, "Handpicked small-scale raiders who operate independently behind the lines … not in business to make anyone uneasy, though it's perfectly all right with us if the enemy is constantly looking over his shoulder."

"Randal's band of cutthroats makes *me* nervous," Col. Clarke said.

The fact that Jim was saying "we," "our" and "us" was not lost on Col. Clarke. He had never heard the senior MI-6 officer do that with any other operation he ran.

Jim said, "We have to protect Raiding Forces from being misused by the GHQ armchair commandos—the Short Range Shepard's Patrol set who have no understanding of our true capabilities or inherent limitations.

"We do not want our people frittered away on missions that more conventional units can accomplish."

"You are singing to the choir, Baldie," Col. Clarke said.

"Raiding Forces are the professional's professionals," Jim said. "Casualties are something we can ill afford."

LIEUTENANT COLONEL JOHN RANDAL, DSO, MC, WAS LYING BESIDE HIS gun jeep—shot. Violet Patrol was returning to base at Oasis X after a successful three-week war patrol…its first. Out of nowhere, an Italian Macchi C.202 fighter strafed the column as the jeeps were winding through an area of cone-shaped desert mounds common to that part of the Western Desert.

Trouble comes hard and fast out of the blue. The dirt-colored enemy aircraft made a single thundering gun run and was gone. The only person hit was Lt. Col. Randal.

He never even saw the Macchi.

Brandy Seaborn, who had been driving, was out of the vehicle and on the ground cradling him, crying and calling for help.

"Don't die, John …"

Jeeps were revving their engines, men running, shouting—there was mass confusion.

Lieutenant Penelope "Legs" Honeycutt-Parker, RM, arrived first. She ripped open Lt. Col. Randal's khaki blouse. There was not much blood. It took a moment for her to locate the wound—a purple through-and-through gunshot on the right side.

The problem was, there were no trained medical personnel attached to Violet Patrol to evaluate the injury.

What to do?

The patrol first aid kit contained alcohol, mercurochrome, packets of sulfur powder, field dressings, a pair of scissors and not much else.

Violet Patrol was 300 miles from Oasis X, but there was no doctor located there either. Two Zar Cult priestesses, Rita Hayworth and Lana Turner, were in residence, but no one was giving magic ritual much consideration at the moment.

The girls might have to be pressed into service later if all else failed.

"John," Brandy pleaded, "please be all right."

Waldo said, "Let's haul the man over in the shade."

Lieutenant Roy Kidd and ex-Captain Travis McCloud dragged Lt. Col. Randal over to the shadow cast by the gun jeep and propped him up against the right front wheel of the Bantam. The soldier of fortune who went by King took the Colonel's cut-down bush hat and placed it behind his head like a pillow.

"Get these vehicles dispersed," Lt. Col. Randal ordered, through gritted teeth.

Lt. Honeycutt-Parker was jabbing him with two of her fingers, working her way around the entry wound, "Feel anything, John?"

"Just you poking me."

"Lean forward to allow me to look at your back," Lt. Honeycutt-Parker ordered, continuing her inspection.

"I think the bullet missed your ribs."

"Wop seven-point-seven full metal jacket," Waldo said. "The exit ain't any bigger than the entry … 'bout the size of a No. 2 pencil."

"Always preferred No. 3s myself," Lt. Col. Randal said. "Harder tip. Have one of those Italian cigarillos left, Mr. Treywick?"

Brandy giggled through her tears. Lt. Col. Randal might be dying, but he had not lost his sense of humor.

"I do," Waldo said. "Had me a pile custom rolled before we pulled outta Cairo. Stick a handful in your pocket, Colonel."

The ex-ivory poacher was enjoying the prerogatives of his newly-acquired wealth, which he had earned from the treasure he had smuggled out of Abyssinia.

"Our major concern," Lt. Honeycutt-Parker said to no on one in particular, as Lt. Col. Randal fumbled to produce his battered U.S. 26th Cavalry Regiment Zippo, "is infection. We do not want the wound channel to turn septic."

"Mercurochrome is all we have to prevent it," Brandy said. "Suitable for scratches—"

"We could dip some on a piece a' gauze," Waldo said, "stick it on the end of a gun rod and run it through there."

"Care to hold *my* hand, Mrs. Seaborn?" Lt. Col. Randal said, blowing on the glowing tip of one of Waldo's cigarillos. Earlier in the patrol, she had turned down a similar request from a wounded ex-Capt. McCloud, on the grounds that he was only scratched.

Lt. Col. Randal locked eyes with Brandy.

Then he touched the cigar to the bullet hole in his side—cauterizing it—for what seemed like a long time. Everyone gathered around could smell the burning flesh. Nobody said a word. You could have heard a pin drop in the sand. If anyone had dropped one.

Brandy gasped.

Lt. Col. Randal had not felt a thing when he was hit, only realizing what had happened when he saw the small patch of blood on his jacket. The cigar hurt. He thought he might pass out from the pain.

"I saw Randolph Scott do that trick," ex-Capt. McCloud said, "in a Western movie."

"Yeah," Lt. Kidd said. "I did too."

"OK, Parker," Lt. Col. Randal said. The Zippo flamed again as he struggled to relight the crushed tip of the cigarillo; he got it going, handed the little cigar to the leggy Royal Marine, then rolled over sideways so she could get at the wound in his back—out of his reach.

"Showtime ... let's do this."

When Lt. Honeycutt-Parker stabbed the scorching cigarillo into the puckered exit wound, Brandy squeezed his hand with both of hers for all she was worth.

Lt. Col. Randal was glad she did.

• • •

THE TWIN ENGINE ANSON, WITH THE VARGAS GIRL-LOOKING PILOT, Lieutenant Pamala Plum-Martin, OBE, DFC, RM, at the stick, and Lieutenant Colonel John Randal in the right seat, made a perfect three-point landing at Cairo International Airport. The glamorous special operations pilot taxied to where an ambulance and Captain the Lady Jane Seaborn's white Rolls Royce were parked.

"What the hell?" Lt. Col. Randal said.

The ground crew wheeled a short ladder up to the Anson when Lt. Plum-Martin cut the engines. Brandy Seaborn, Lieutenant Penelope "Legs" Honeycutt-Parker, Lieutenant Mandy Paige, RM, and King disembarked first, followed by Lt. Col. Randal, who had his 9mm Beretta MAB-38 submachine gun in one hand and a lightweight parachute container he used as a travel bag in the other.

Captain the Lady Jane Seaborn, OBE, RM, was waiting with a pair of nurses in starched white uniforms. Lt. Col. Randal had not known she was in Cairo. He thought Lady Jane was home in England patching up her marriage—her estranged husband had asked for reconciliation.

"What's this?" Lt. Col. Randal asked.

"Get in, John," Lady Jane ordered by way of a greeting. "You are going to the hospital."

"I'm not riding in any ambulance ..."

Drop-dead gorgeous Lady Jane turned on him like a magnificent lioness, eyes flashing. "GET IN THE AMBULANCE!"

Lt. Col. Randal got in the ambulance.

The ride to the hospital was at full speed, with the siren wailing. Lady Jane and Lt. Mandy (no one called her Lt. Paige) rode in the back with the two nurses who immediately started checking Lt. Col. Randal's vital signs. Flanigan, now serving as Lady Jane's bodyguard/chauffeur, and the rest followed in the Rolls.

Lt. Col. Randal was lying on a stretcher. King had relieved him of most of his weapons—the visible ones. He was glad to see Lady Jane, but it was hard to talk with a thermometer stuck in his mouth. She had never looked more beautiful.

The truth was, he had not expected her back.

In the Six Hundred—the power elite families who control Great Britain through their enormous wealth, vast land holdings and political connections—it generally takes more than the odd affair with a snow-blond Norwegian bombshell to break up a marriage.

The fact that Lady Jane was here in the ambulance gave Lt. Col. Randal something to think about.

When they reached the hospital, the driver raced up to the Emergency Entrance. A muscular male nurse was waiting outside with a wheelchair.

"Do not even think about it," Lady Jane said.

Lt. Col. Randal sat in the wheelchair.

The nurse ran through the corridors of the hospital pushing the wheelchair, scattering people out of the way. They arrived at the surgery theatre, where the chief-of-surgery, Dr. Stephen Milam, was on standby, waiting for their arrival.

The doctor was a prominent surgeon with a distinguished civilian medical career, a volunteer out from Great Britain for the duration. His civilian practice consisted primarily of members of the Six Hundred or high-ranking politicians.

Like most brilliant medical professionals who are at the apex of their career, Dr. Milam was a no-nonsense, take-charge type who had a sense of humor—but you had to be smart yourself to recognize it. He was a surgeon's surgeon with—his colleagues claimed—the best hands in the business.

To demonstrate that the claim was true, Dr. Milam liked to perform a party trick. Holding a cigarette lengthwise in his left hand with his trigger finger on one tip and his thumb on the other, he would slice lengthwise through each of the three thin layers of cigarette papers encasing the tobacco, one at a time, with his scalpel-sharp pocketknife, peeling them off layer by layer until all that was left was a stalk of tobacco. Then he would blow on the stalk while a crowd of suitably impressed onlookers watched it disappear into a puff of dust.

The staff at the hospital treated Dr. Milam like he could walk on water. And, he expected no less.

Lady Jane insisted on going into the examination room with Lt. Col. Randal, while the rest of the entourage waited in the lounge.

The doctor noted that the injured Commando officer acquiesced.

Dr. Milam did not know the nature of their relationship; however, he did know Lady Jane, and he knew her husband, Mallory.

Normally, he saw patients alone or with immediate family only. Virtually never did he perform examinations with an unrelated witness present. But it did not require genius to realize that there was more going on here than a wounded officer being brought in for a checkup.

The emergency call from Lady Jane to clear the deck for a VIP patient who had suffered a gunshot wound to the body was all the information the surgeon had received in advance.

Dr. Milam said, "Remove your blouse, Colonel, and let's have a look."

Lt. Col. Randal was sitting on the edge of the examining table. He removed his lightweight khaki Chatterley's Military Tailors jacket. He was not wearing a shirt.

"Nearly eaten by a big cat fairly recently," Dr. Milam said. "The scar on your face … get that at the same time?"

"Roger."

"Took one round above the heart," Dr. Milam said. "Half an inch lower and we would not be here now, looking at these two brand-new bullet holes.

"Appears you have had a colorful war, Colonel."

"Had its moments," Lt. Col. Randal said.

"How long ago was this last wound incurred?"

"Five days."

"Seems quite an extended time to have to wait to be evacuated," Dr. Milam said, examining the entry in front and then inspecting the exit in back.

"Coming in after I was patched up," Lt. Col. Randal said, "we decided to swing by an Italian radio relay installation to put it out of action."

"Not in any hurry to seek medical attention?" Dr. Milam said.

"It was on the way."

"Who cauterized these?"

Lt. Col. Randal said, "I did the one in front …"

"Parker," Lady Jane said, "repaired the wound on John's back."

"Penelope did this?" Dr. Milam said, studying the little round scar. "Steady hand."

Lt. Col. Randal said. "I couldn't reach it."

"From a medical perspective," Dr. Milam said, "if you have a through-and-through gunshot wound from a bullet that does not fragment, hit any bones, major arteries or vital organs, the bullet simply zips straight through—everything closes right back up behind the round as it passes, and you are good as new.

"Colonel, what did you use to cauterize the entry and exit?"

"Cigar."

"Randolph Scott performed the same procedure in a cowboy film I attended at the open-air cinema the other evening," Dr. Milam said.

"Slapped a little mud on his. You do that too?

"Negative."

"One weeks' rest, then return to duty. No jumping out of airplanes or slitting any throats for a full seven days.

"Lady Jane, I am placing you in charge of ensuring Colonel Randal follows my instructions to the letter. Understood?"

"Right after I murder him, Doctor."

"Whatever for?"

"Causing me so much emotional distress."

"In the future, Colonel," Dr. Milam said, "a little sulfur powder sprinkled in the bullet hole will work as well as a burning cigar—probably hurt less."

Lt. Col. Randal said, "I didn't know that."

"Bet you wished you had."

2
LIGHT DUTY

STRETCHED OUT ON A LOUNGE CHAIR FOUR HUNDRED YARDS FROM THE pyramids, Lieutenant Colonel John Randal was at the shallow end of the private pool attached to—and for the exclusive use of—the secluded suite Captain the Lady Jane Seaborn had reserved for them at the Mena House Hotel. It was day one light duty.

He was alone.

Lady Jane and Lieutenant Mandy Paige were in Cairo shopping for Oasis X.

Brandy Seaborn and Lieutenant Penelope "Legs" Honeycutt-Parker were inside getting dressed for a meeting in town with Brigadier Raymond J. Maunsell, who liked to be called "R. J." The two adventuresses were working with MI-5, counterintelligence, trying to trap László Almásy, the master desert-savvy spy.

Lieutenant Pamala Plum-Martin was having a drink with a fighter pilot at Shepard's Hotel. And King had gone to the Raiding Forces Headquarters (RFHQ) compound to obtain a report on the status of the remaining RFDS patrols slated to take the field.

Veronica Paige (Lt. Mandy's mother) walked out in a black swimsuit—dark tan, athletic horsewoman, *very* attractive. She dove into the far end, swam the length of the pool underwater, surfaced, walked up the steps while sweeping her shoulder-length chestnut hair back with both hands and stretched out on the lounge next to Lt. Col Randal.

She said, "Frogspawn."

• • •

"MAJOR NORMAN CROCKATT, CHIEF OF MI-9, SENT A MOST SECRET Officer-Only message to my office through Phantom at Raiding Forces Headquarters, Middle East," Veronica said, "marked EXPEDITE URGENT.

"Major Stone is away. His family's regiment, the Lancelot Lancer Yeomanry, part of Kingcol under Brigadier Kingstone, has been participating in the invasion of Syria out of Iraq.

"Kingcol had Palmyra as its objective. Royal Air Force support was not available to provide air cover for the column. En route, it came under intensive air attack from German aircraft flying off of Vichy French airfields in Syria.

"Unfortunately, both Brigadier Kingstone and Sir Terry's brother, who was in command of the Lancers, suffered nervous breakdowns from battle fatigue and have been evacuated.

"Both men require institutionalization."

Lieutenant Colonel John Randal said, "Must have been some air attack."

"Major Stone has gone out to resume command of the regiment," Veronica said. "He plans to turn the unit's Rolls Royce armored cars over to the 2nd Life Guards attached to the regiment as lorried infantry and bring the Lancers back here to RFHQ to take up duties with Raiding Forces."

"Good."

"Problem is," Veronica said, "Major Crockatt's communiqué was addressed to Sir Terry. Since he was absent, it landed on my desk.

"While I have clearance for all MI-9 material, when I read the communiqué I had no idea what to do, so I took the message directly to Colonel Clarke because in Middle East Command, MI-9 is a function of A-Force…Section N to be exact.

"He read it, said MI-9 was attached to Raiding Forces for direct-action missions, and that I should bring it to your immediate attention."

"Dudley's a world-class delegator," Lt. Col. Randal said.

"While we were in the midst of our conversation, Jim arrived," Veronica said. "Colonel Clarke showed him Major Crockatt's message. He informed Jim that Raiding Forces worked for him; therefore, it was Jim's responsibility to oversee the mission.

"To be candid, Colonel," Veronica said, "I am more than a little confused about who MI-9 and Raiding Forces actually *do* work for."

"Me too," Lt. Col. Randal said. "You ever find out, let me know.

"What's the dispatch say?"

"You—and it specifies you by name, Colonel—are to meet 'an agent or agents known to you' on the island of Crete," Veronica said.

"You are ordered to retrieve a highly classified item of signals equipment and its crypto secret operator."

"The Germans hold Crete," Lt. Col. Randal said. "You're kidding, right?"

"Actually, no."

"When?"

"Tonight."

JAMES "BALDIE" TAYLOR DROVE UP TO RFHQ AS THE MENA HOUSE limousine was dropping off Lieutenant Colonel John Randal and Veronica Paige. As the three stood talking in the drive, a cab arrived with Lieutenant Pamala Plum-Martin in back.

The compound was like a ghost town compared to the last time Lt. Col. Randal had been there. Raiding Forces Desert Squadron (RFDS) was in the field on operations. Raiding Forces Sea Squadron (RFSS) had relocated to Tobruk to conduct amphibious Commando pinprick raids against the Via Balbia.

The only troops in residence were a team of specialists from the Vulnerable Points Wing providing security. Royal Marines from Captain the Lady Jane Seaborn's hand-picked detachment provided staffing for the Operations Center, which was open around the clock and performing the administrative tasks that are the lifeblood of any fighting organization. The group also included a Phantom section to operate the long-range radio network linking RFHQ, Oasis X and Seaborn House in England, and a small rear-area vehicle maintenance section desert-izing the last of the new jeeps. There were also a few men out from Seaborn House waiting to be assigned to either RFDS or RFSS.

Captain Roy "Mad Dog" Reupart—the man who had trained Raiding Forces at No.1 Parachute School and who had later volunteered to become a member of the unit—was conducting a selection course for the local volunteers who had applied for Raiding Forces, but they were off somewhere on exercises.

All together, Raiding Forces Middle East, including the female Royal Marine detachment, did not number more than 200 personnel, about the size of a standard line infantry rifle company.

While small in actual troop strength, Raiding Forces had responsibility for Middle East Command's direct-action missions theatre-wide. High priority operations could, and did, come up with little or no advance warning. The men and women of Raiding Forces were never discomfited when that happened – it was a common occurance.

Commander Ian Fleming, RN, was waiting in the Operations Room. He had arrived from England. The normally debonair Naval Intelligence officer looked like he had been sleeping under a bridge.

"Flew out in the belly of a Lancaster bomber, bloody dreadful trip. I do not recommend the experience."

Cdr. Fleming knew everyone present except Veronica.

"Fleming, Ian Fleming," he said, oozing charm. "You must be the MI-9 officer …"

"Time is short, Commander. We need to sort out this mission," Jim interrupted.

"Colonel, has Mrs. Paige briefed you on the MOST SECRET rocket from Major Crockatt?"

"She has," Lt. Col. Randal said. "Didn't have much actionable intelligence."

"I can provide a few additional details," Cdr. Fleming said. "However, at the end of the day we have very little information to work with."

"Colonel Randal has been away on deep desert operations for most of the past month," Jim said. "Let me give him a big picture briefing on what has taken place in theatre during that time. Then, Commander, you can chime in and tell us what you know about this specific mission."

"Capital," Cdr. Fleming said, taking out his elegant silver cigarette case. "This is a rush job for me as well. Afraid I have not been paying much attention to the Middle East Command lately.

"All I know is that the news from out here is all bad all the time."

"When I last saw you, Colonel," Jim said. "RFDS was taking the field in support of OPERATION BATTLEAX, an offensive by Middle East Command to relieve the Port of Tobruk.

"Field Marshal Wavell did not believe his troops were in any condition to engage in a major campaign. The famed 7th Armored Division 'The Desert Rats,' for example, had become a shell organization … a maneuver unit in name only. All, and I do mean all, of the division's tanks were worn out. The 7th's veteran tanker troops had nearly all been transferred out to other divisions that *did* have tanks, and many key division officers given other jobs elsewhere.

"When Prime Minister Churchill learned about the deficiency in armor, he took a gamble—sent out a special convoy to Egypt, devoid of air support, carrying brand-new Lend-Lease tanks from the U.S. The convoy was a juicy target but it got through.

"Unfortunately, the reconstituted Desert Rats had no experience with the new model tanks. The tanks had arrived straight from the factory, were not modified for desert conditions, and the U.S. Stuarts—the troops call them 'Honeys'—turned out to be no match for the Afrika Korps Panzer Mark IIIs.

"Churchill ordered BATTLEAX to proceed regardless. Wavell objected again and was overruled again. The attack went in.

"Initially, Wavell met with some success," Jim said. "Then our generals, sensing victory, overplayed their hand. They charged Rommel's anti-tank screen … our tanks were decimated.

"Then and there, the difference in Allied vs. Axis tactics became painfully evident.

"The Desert Fox employs a combined arms team integrating his artillery, tanks and infantry with close air support—Stuka dive bombers in the role of aerial artillery," Jim said.

"His favorite tactic seems to be to lure our tanks onto his anti-tank artillery, which consists of anti-aircraft 88s employed in the anti-tank role. Then, when the British armor has spent itself, Rommel launches a vicious armored counterattack characterized by wide-ranging flanking maneuvers conducted at high speed, supported by clouds of Stuka dive bombers.

"Our generals tend to view their tanks as armored cavalry," Jim said. "They ride to the sound of the guns in large mobile formations looking to do battle, leaving the infantry to fend for itself without the benefit of artillery or air support—charge straight at the Afrika Korps positions where they find them, only to be shot to pieces.

"Lesson learned: You do not use tanks to attack fixed positions.

"Our army was out-generaled in BATTLEAX," Jim said. "And, the RAF refuses to fly air-to-ground combat support missions.

"Only quick thinking by Frank Messervy of Gazelle Force fame in Abyssinia—now promoted to major general—saved us from total defeat.

"At the moment, the only thing standing between Afrika Korps and where we are sitting right this minute is Tobruk, a hellish port where our troops are surrounded and besieged.

"The good news is, the Germans are spent," Jim said. "Rommel does not have the logistical capability to continue sustained operations this deep into Egypt … yet.

"Meanwhile, in Lebanon and Syria," Jim said, "OPERATION EXPORTER has ground on. The Vichy French are putting up more resistance than anyone dreamed possible. In fact, the campaign is not over yet, and we have already taken more casualties fighting the French than we did the Germans in BATTLEAX.

"On Crete," Jim said, "prior to the invasion, the Nazis had lost the element of surprise. Our side knew they were coming, and we outnumbered them—but somehow managed to lose that one too.

"The 7th Flieger Division parachuted in and captured airfields located in the interior of the island," Jim said. "Then the German 5th Mountain Division air-landed on those strips.

"The Allied command on Crete imploded.

"While the Commonwealth troops fought hard, inflicting horrendous casualties on the Nazi's airborne forces, our soldiers were badly served by their senior commanders.

"The Royal Navy attempted yet another Dunkirk-type evacuation, but in large part failed, leaving thousands of troops and untold equipment marooned on the beach. Finally, the men surrendered.

"And that," Jim said, "brings us to where we are now—with orders for you, Colonel, to travel to Crete tonight and rendezvous with 'an agent or agents known to you.'"

"The purpose of the exercise," Cdr. Fleming said, "is to retrieve a single piece of highly-classified signals equipment that should have been brought off the island before the battle began or destroyed instantly once the first enemy parachute cracked open.

"I am here to confirm that the machine you bring out is indeed the item Intelligence wants back safe and sound."

"We need a pinpoint coordinate, signals, contact information," Jim said.

"I have the grid coordinates of a location on a remote beach where a Special Operations Executive stay-behind officer advising the Cretan guerrillas will be waiting tonight," Cdr. Fleming said.

"He has with him a man known to you, Colonel Randal. One cannot simply hand an item of this magnitude over to a complete stranger, what?

"The signal is a red light from the shore. That is to be responded to with a green light blinking three dots followed by three dashes: SO.

"Col. Randal goes ashore, retrieves the package—about the size of a suitcase—and the technician who operates it."

"That's it?" Jim said.

"Should for any reason a complication arise getting the operator out," Cdr. Fleming said, "Colonel Randal is to terminate him immediately."

"Be perfectly clear," Jim said. "Colonel Randal is authorized to kill a British soldier."

"Preventing the gadget *or* the technician who operates it from falling into enemy hands is a matter of national security," Cdr. Fleming said. "Prime Minister Churchill sanctioned tonight's mission. These orders were delivered to me verbally, in person, by the PM.

"Should there arise the slightest problem extracting the operator, the least problem at all—kill him."

"Anything you want to contribute to the conversation, Colonel," Jim said, "now would be the time."

Lt. Col. Randal said. "I'm on light duty."

It took about ten minutes to develop a plan. Commander Ian Fleming showed them the pinpoint on the map. Lieutenant Pamala Plum-Martin studied the location and measured the distance.

"Approximately 200 miles by air," Lt. Plum-Martin said. "Put the Seagull down off shore. You will have to paddle ashore, John."

"I'll need King," Lieutenant Colonel John Randal said, "and a Lifeboat Serviceman."

"Naturally, chaps," Cdr. Fleming said, producing a cigarette and tapping it on his silver case, "my presence is required on board the aircraft to confirm the package the moment it comes aboard.

"Orders strictly prohibit me from going ashore."

"This is our maiden MI-9 mission in Middle East Command," Veronica said. "I should like to come along to observe."

Lt. Col. Randal said, "As long as you agree to stay on board the Seagull with Fleming."

"Thank you, Colonel."

"Takeoff 2000 hours," Lt. Plum-Martin said. "That should give you plenty of time to go ashore, make the pick-up, return to the airplane and allow us to arrive back here before sunrise."

"I plan to monitor the mission from RFHQ," Jim said.

"Anyone not here at 2000 hours," Lt. Col. Randal said, "gets left. Let's do it."

Lt. Plum-Martin rode back to Cairo with Lt. Col. Randal and Veronica in the Mena House limousine.

"Jane is going to kill you, John," Lt. Plum-Martin said.

"Yeah," Lt. Col. Randal said. "She's already threatened me in front of a witness."

"Better come up with a plan," Lt. Plum-Martin said. "Fast."

Lt. Col. Randal leaned forward and gave the driver a change of destination … to the hospital.

Dr. Stephen Milam was not expecting to see Lt. Col. Randal when he walked into his office accompanied by Veronica and Lt. Plum-Martin.

The doctor had been in surgery most of the day and was bone-tired and irritable. While not overjoyed to have visitors simply drop in, Dr. Milam could not help but admire Lt. Col. Randal's habit of traveling with uncommonly attractive women.

"Doctor," Lt. Col. Randal said, "what I'm about to tell you is classified."

Dr. Milam listened silently.

He said, "Know what I hate most about being a doctor? When I work harder on my patient's health than they do."

"I hear you," Lt. Col. Randal said, "loud and clear."

3
KILL EVERYONE

LIEUTENANT PAMALA PLUM-MARTIN HAD THE ENGINE OF THE SEAGULL ticking over when Lieutenant Colonel John Randal, Commander Ian Fleming, Veronica Paige and Jim Taylor arrived at the dock. King was loading their personal gear, while a Lifeboat Serviceman was lashing a Goatly dory to the floats.

"Your contact," Jim said, "is Captain Patrick "Paddy" Leigh-Fermor. SOE says he operates in disguise as a shepherd named 'Michalis.' The 'agent known to you' is an evader who linked up with him, a King's Royal Rifle Corps corporal."

"SOE has no direct knowledge of who he is."

"You will either know him or not," Jim said. "If it turns out you do *not* recognize the corporal, consider him a German intelligence operative, the mission blown and act accordingly."

"What's that mean," Lt. Col. Randal asked, "exactly?"

"Recover the equipment," Jim said. "Then kill everyone and come home."

"Including the SOE guerrilla leader?"

"Everyone standing except King."

"You hear that, King?" Lt. Col. Randal asked.

"Affirmative," the Merc said.

"Colonel," Jim said, "you have no business going out tonight. If this mission were not of national strategic importance—and I have confirmed it is—I would refuse to allow you to participate.

"How did Lady Jane take the news?"

"Doesn't know yet," Lt. Col. Randal said. "Had to run over to General Auchinleck's to go over the invitation list for a dinner party."

"Mandy's going to tell her when Jane gets back to our hotel."

"Oh, no!" Jim said. "Lady Jane will storm RFHQ like an avenging angel when she finds out."

"Better you than me," Lt. Col. Randal said. "Mandy was bad enough. Joining the Marines has had a negative influence on her vocabulary."

"Lady Jane will come for my scalp," Jim said. "Had I not been threatened with imprisonment in the Tower of London or worse if I even fantasized about strap-hanging the mission, I would go with you.

"No matter what you run into on Crete, things are guaranteed to take a bad turn here."

"Roger that," Lt. Col. Randal said. "Have a nice night."

LIEUTENANT PAMALA PLUM-MARTIN LIFTED OFF, BROUGHT THE Seagull to approximately fifty feet altitude and made a beeline for the pinpoint on Crete. She was a natural pilot, personally tutored by the ace Squadron Leader Paddy Wilcox, DSO, OBE, MC, DFC, and by now one of the most experienced Special Operations aviators in the world.

Lt. Plum-Martin had cut her teeth flying high-risk night amphibious missions. The Royal Marine pilot probably did not realize how good she was.

Tonight's assignment was about as simple as missions came for her. The Seagull could fly a straight line across the Mediterranean Sea to the target and back, approximately 200 miles each way. She was going to splash down offshore, let the Lifeboat Serviceman paddle Lieutenant Colonel John Randal and King to the pinpoint and wait—bobbing silently until they returned.

Waiting was the hard part. But tonight she had Veronica Paige and Commander Ian Fleming to keep her company.

The low flying was by choice, not necessity. There was very little chance the Germans had set up radar installations on Crete at this early stage of their occupation. The Nazis had yet to completely secure the island.

There were no reports of Luftwaffe night fighters stationed on the island. However, why take a chance? The idea was to sneak in and sneak out.

Lt. Plum-Martin liked to fly low when sneaking. Screaming along skimming the tops of the waves in the moonlight was a real adrenalin rush. Especially when flying into enemy territory.

Veronica Paige sat up front in the co-pilot's seat with Lt. Plum-Martin.

Lt. Col. Randal rode in the back with Commander Ian Fleming, King and the Lifeboat Serviceman. The men went over the mission, trying to think of every possible contingency, but finally gave it up as a wasted exercise. Other than the sequence of exiting the aircraft into the Goatly dory and the light signals with the contact ashore, there was not enough intelligence for them to make any plausible plans.

Finally, Lt. Col. Randal tilted his cut-down bush hat over his eyes and went to sleep. He was cradling his 9mm Beretta MAB-38 submachine gun. The stubby weapon was like a natural appendage.

Cdr. Fleming looked at King and shook his head in disbelief. The Naval Intelligence officer was not going ashore and he was nervous as a cat. No chance of him taking a nap. The Merc looked back, devoid of expression—a scary individual.

King took out his Fairbairn knife. He started stropping it on the leather strap on his 9mm Beretta MAB-38. The soldier-of-fortune seemed to be oblivious to the perils of the mission ahead.

Cdr. Fleming sat pondering his predicament. He was a Naval Intelligence staff officer, employed by the admiral in charge of Naval Intelligence. By all rights, he should be sweating out this mission at the posh Mena House Hotel with the ravishing Lady Jane and a decanter of martinis—shaken, not stirred. Not here on board a flying relic amphibian that looked like it belonged in the Stone Ages, flown by a glamorous Vargas Girl pilot, en route to an enemy-occupied island, watching a killer fondle his knife while the mission commander slept like a baby.

There was one simple reason Cdr. Fleming was on board and not at the Mena House by the Pyramids with Lady Jane.

The signals equipment Lt. Col. Randal was being sent to recover was a Typex Mark III (portable) cypher machine. It was the British equivalent to the Nazi Enigma encoding and decoding device. The machine was the single most highly-classified Allied apparatus in existence. Period.

Cdr. Fleming's assignment was to confirm that what was brought out was, in fact, a Typex Mark III, not a ringer substituted by the German Abwehr while the Nazis kept the original to attempt to reverse engineer it.

The debonair Naval Intelligence officer was one of only a handful of people who could identify the device.

THE PITCH ON THE ENGINE CHANGED. LIEUTENANT COLONEL JOHN Randal's eyes came open instantly. King put away his Fairbairn knife.

"Splashdown one minute," Lieutenant Pamala Plum-Martin said over the intercom. "I have a small, solid red light in sight."

King checked the green-filtered flashlight he had on his webbing, flicking it on and off. He would be the bowman in the Goatly dory—responsible for signaling SO: three dots and three dashes in Morse Code.

The Lifeboat Serviceman would exit first to launch the dory. King would be second out, followed by Lt. Col. Randal, who was just a passenger tonight. The pinpoint was a remote, rugged, rocky point—not a place anyone would anticipate British Commandos to come calling. A fair degree of skilled boat handling was necessary to make a safe landfall.

Lifeboat Servicemen are the best small boat handlers in the world.

Captain the Lady Jane Seaborn had originally suggested they be recruited—back in the early days—to solve the seemingly insurmountable small boat problems Raiding Forces was experiencing. Those accepted went through all the training—No. 1 British Parachute School, Achnacarry Commando School, etc.—as any other member of the unit. Once qualified, the Lifeboat Servicemen made excellent Special Forces operators.

And Raiding Forces no longer experienced small boat problems.

The Seagull splashed down. The Lifeboat Serviceman stepped out on the strut while the plane was still moving. King was right behind him.

Lt. Col. Randal ducked into the pilot's compartment.

"Two hours, Pam," Lt. Col. Randal said. "If we're not back by then, go home."

Lt. Plum-Martin had received similar orders from him before. She had not liked them then; she did not like them now. She did not argue. However, there was absolutely no chance the Seagull would be taking off in two hours without the team on board.

She was the plane's captain.

Lt. Col. Randal swung out onto the float and stepped into the Goatly dory. Within seconds, the little boat had glided away silently into the night.

Watching it disappear, Cdr. Fleming was aware of something about Lt. Col. Randal even he did not know. The Raiding Forces commander was carried on the rolls of the Special Operations Executive as an agent. Had been ever since Lady Jane hooked Raiding Forces up with SOE at about the same time both were being formed.

SOE had designators for its agents, which consisted of two, or sometimes three, parts. Usually it was a combination of a letter and one or two numbers. The idea was to have a way to identify the agent in writing or over the radio without having to use his or her name.

The designators almost always started with a letter that matched the first letter of the area the agent operated in.

For example SOE agents in West Africa were assigned a letter designator of *W*, those in East Africa an *E*, etc.

The next part of the designator was a number for a specialty, in the event the agent had one. For those agents who had completed training at one of the SOE "killing schools" or an army equivalent, like the Commando Depot at Achnacarry, the first number was a zero, indicating that the agent was trained/authorized to use lethal force.

The second number simply displayed the SOE sequence of when an agent had been assigned to a certain area. For example, the fifth SOE agent assigned to East Africa would have a designator of E.5. If that agent was qualified and authorized to use lethal force then the designator would be E.05.

Because Special Operations Executive originally sponsored, trained and provided certain equipment to Raiding Forces, Lt. Col. Randal had been issued a secret personal designator before he came to Africa.

Because he had been diverted to carry out an SOE operation (which, in fact, was an MI-6/Naval Intelligence mission using SOE as cover) in the English Channel to capture a German E-boat off the coast of France before traveling out to the Gold Coast on another clandestine operation, and because the idea was for Raiding Forces to be able to go where needed, Lt. Col. Randal had been issued an area designator that was nonspecific.

Instead of a letter his was a neutral number: zero.

As a graduate of Achnacarry who had also attended several SOE "finishing schools," (much of the firearms training had been taught by Captain "Geronimo" Joe McKoy), Lt. Col. Randal was authorized to use lethal force. So, the first number in his designator was a zero.

And, finally, because he was the first SOE agent to be given a zero neutral country designator, his third number was a 1.

Lt. Col. Randal was referred to in SOE secret interagency communications as agent 0.01. The designator meant he was licensed to kill worldwide. Only Lt. Col. Randal knew nothing about any of that.

No one had ever informed him.

CRETE IS COMPOSED OF AN INCREDIBLY RUGGED TERRAIN. A SERIES OF snow-capped mountain ranges run across the island. Scattered between the mountains are freefall gorges, deep valleys, razor-sharp ridgelines and high plateau saddles.

Not that Lieutenant Colonel John Randal and King were going to get to see any of it. The moon was down by the time the Lifeboat Serviceman gave the command "Make way together," and started paddling to the pinpoint. In the distance, the red light was visible.

When the Goatly dory was approximately 400 yards offshore, King flashed the signal: three green dots and three green dashes. The red light onshore responded by clicking off.

If it came back on, that was a wave-off—they were not to land.

The Lifeboat Serviceman brought the dory in through the swell up against a jagged rock. King leaped ashore, holding a line to secure it for Lt. Col. Randal.

The moment Lt. Col. Randal made his way onto the rock, King pitched the line back aboard the boat. The Lifeboat Serviceman rapidly began back-paddling, backing and turning the dory. He disappeared in the direction of the Seagull.

The plan called for him to take up station 200 yards offshore, then wait for the green light signal notifying him to come in and extract the team, the technician and the super-secret, suitcase-sized gadget.

Captain Patrick "Paddy" Leigh-Fermor and two men were waiting on the far side of the rock. They had a suitcase with them. Lt. Col. Randal slipped his 9mm Beretta MAB-38 submachine gun off his shoulder and silently clicked off the safety.

"King," he said.

The Merc shined his light on the three, illuminating their faces. Lt. Col. Randal clicked the safety back on. He recognized the King's Royal Rifle Corps corporal in the trio from Calais, Swamp Fox Force. The man—he could not remember his name (if he had ever known it; things had been moving fast at the time)—had been a private then.

"We're good," Lt. Col. Randal said. King turned off the light.

"Corporal Holms, sir. Bernard H.," said the "agent or agents known" to Lt. Col. Randal. "I was with you in Swamp Fox Force at Calais."

"I remember you," Lt. Col. Randal said.

"Assigned to the 10th Battalion, KRRC, after we returned from France, sir," Cpl. Holms said. "The battalion shipped out to Greece in time to move up, fight one battle, then turn around and start our retreat. We evacuated to Crete right before the Germans invaded."

"Bad timing," Lt. Col. Randal said.

"Our lads killed a lot of Fallschirmjägers, sir, but they kept coming, and the battalion disintegrated. I did what you taught us in Swamp Fox Force—never gave up.

"Headed for the hills. Linked up with Capt. Leigh-Fermor eventually, sir."

Lt. Col. Randal said, "Had yourself a hard war."

"Most of it fighting backward, sir," Cpl. Holms said. "Any way for you to take me off the island?"

"No problem," Lt. Col. Randal said. "We've got room for one more on the ride back."

"Time is short," Capt. Leigh-Fermor said. "My party needs to travel high into the mountains a long way from here before daylight.

"I have something for you, Colonel."

Capt. Leigh-Fermor handed over a thick, heavy case that looked like a typewriter carrier. In a way, it was.

"Is he the operator?" Lt. Col. Randal asked, as he passed the case to King, indicating the third man in Capt. Leigh-Fermor's party. "I've orders to bring the technician out with the suitcase."

"Actually," Capt. Leigh-Fermor said, "no."

"Captain," Lt. Col. Randal said, "you were ordered to meet me here with the signals equipment and the operator."

"Understood, sir," Capt. Leigh-Fermor said. "The technician got drunk on raki. Left him behind because otherwise we could not make the rendezvous in time. The fool was smashed."

"How far?"

"Thirty minutes, but it is a pretty steep climb from here," Capt. Leigh-Fermor said. "He is in a house on a remote sheep farm."

"Signal the Lifeboat Serviceman to come in, King," Lt. Col. Randal said. "You take the suitcase out to the Seagull. Inform Commander Fleming of the situation. Tell Lieutenant Plum-Martin to put takeoff on hold for another hour."

"Negative."

"What?"

"I am not leaving you, chief," the Merc said. "Send Holms out to the Walrus with the package. He can do the explaining."

"King …"

"Risk facing Lady Jane without you in tow, Chief? Who do you think writes my paycheck?"

"*You* work for Jane?"

"Ancillary contract," King said. "Made me an offer I couldn't refuse."

"Brief Corporal Holms, then," Lt. Col. Randal said. "Escort him to the dory. We'll move out as soon as you're back."

"Roger."

"Corporal," Lt. Col. Randal said. "You lose this suitcase between the beach and the Walrus and I'll have you air-dropped back over Crete. Is that clear?"

Cpl. Holms said, "I'm not a qualified parachutist, Colonel."

"Let anything separate you from the case, Bernard," Lt. Col. Randal said, "and lack of training's not going to be a problem. You won't be wearing a parachute."

"Sir!"

"Captain," Lt. Col. Randal said, "be ready to move out the instant King is back."

"Yes, sir."

THE CLIMB WAS ALMOST VERTICAL UP A PATH A MOUNTAIN GOAT would have had difficulty negotiating. Lieutenant Colonel John Randal was in trouble within minutes. He was accustomed to operating in mountainous terrain. Crete was not any steeper than Abyssinia, but this part of the island was treacherous. It was solid jagged rock.

Apparently, his wound had taken more out of Lt. Col. Randal than he thought.

Captain Patrick "Paddy" Leigh-Fermor pulled King aside and whispered, "I read the Colonel's book, *Jump on Bela*. He's supposed have a capital *S* on his chest, a man of steel.

"Is he going to be able to make it tonight?"

"The Chief was shot recently."

"When?"

"Last week," King said. "Restricted to light duty."

"If this is what you Raiding Forces people call light duty," Capt. Leigh-Fermor said, "I would not care to endure full service."

"This is the easy part," King said. "His problems start when he arrives back at Mena House."

"Cairo?"

"Lady Seaborn is going to tear him limb from limb."

"Lady Jane Seaborn?" Capt. Leigh-Fermor asked.

"Colonel Randal's girlfriend."

Capt. Leigh-Fermor said, "Thought she was married."

"Married or not, Lady Seaborn is with the Colonel," King said. "The Chief came on this mission without telling her.

"My standing orders are not to let anything happen to him."

"From what I know of Colonel Randal's reputation," Capt. Leigh-Fermor said, "you jolly well have your work cut out."

The guide called a halt.

"The farm is a stone's throw," Capt. Leigh-Fermor said. "In a glen over the edge of the cliff, approximately fifty yards.

"We are miles from the nearest village or any known enemy encampments. Things should be as we left them, but my man will go ahead and verify everything is safe to be double sure."

"Good idea," Lt. Col. Randal said. He needed a break from the climb. While not in pain, he was exhausted.

"Afraid we cannot afford the time to go back down the cliff with you, sir," Capt. Leigh-Fermor said. "You and King are on your own when it comes to getting the operator to the pickup point."

"Fair enough," Lt. Col Randal said. "You've done your job. When we reach the farm, confirm the identity of the technician to me, then take off."

"Wilco."

The guide came back and had a whispered conversation with Capt. Leigh-Fermor.

"We have a situation, sir," Capt. Leigh-Fermor said. "A patrol from the 22nd Air Landing Division has arrived at the farm. The troops are bivouacked in the barn.

"The officer is sleeping in the house."

"What about our man?" Lt. Col. Randal said.

"Hidden in the attic," Capt. Leigh-Fermor said. "The Germans are not aware of his presence.

"The farm owner slipped out to warn us off."

King said, "I can neutralize the troops in the barn with grenades, Colonel."

"Negative," Lt. Col. Randal said. "We don't want anyone to know we've been here after we leave.

"Take up position outside the barn, King. Don't do anything unless firing breaks out in the house. In that case, light it up. Otherwise, when you hear two claps of my hands, fall back here."

"Roger."

Captain Patrick "Paddy" Leigh-Fermor, the farmer and Lieutenant Colonel John Randal slipped into the farmyard. They entered the ancient stone house by the back door. Pitch dark inside.

The entrance to the attic was located in the hall outside the kitchen by way of a concealed fold-down ladder that pulled down hidden inside a rectangle entry. The farmer took a stick with a small metal hook on the end, reached up and pulled down the ladder.

Capt. Leigh-Fermor quietly unfolded the shaky ladder, then crept up and peeked in the attic. Lt. Col. Randal was right behind him, looking over his shoulder.

Snoring was coming from a pile of quilts.

Lt. Col. Randal shined his flashlight at the sound. He saw an empty bottle of raki next to the pallet on the floor. A figure raised up drunkenly, shading his eyes from the beam of light.

"That him?"

"Yes, sir," Capt. Leigh-Fermor said.

Whiiiich, Whiiiich. Lt. Col. Randal's silenced .22 High Standard Military Model D made a sound no louder than a pair of matches being struck.

A pair of thumps—sounding like those a grocery shopper would make to check to see if a watermelon was ripe—followed the shots. Two holes appeared in the technician's forehead.

He fell back dead.

"Bloody hell!"

Lt. Col. Randal said, "We were never here."

Back outside ... down the goat path at the cliff ... in the Goatly dory ... paddling hard ... then scrambling back on board the Seagull.

Lt. Col. Randal handed the technician's identification disc to Commander Ian Fleming.

"Problem resolved?" The debonair officer asked, casting an eye at the bloodstain on the cord.

"Affirmative," Lt. Col Randal said. "Let's get the hell out of Dodge."

4
THREE BEARS

Lieutenant Colonel John Randal was sunning on a lounge out by the pool at the private suite Captain the Lady Jane Seaborn had reserved for them at Mena House Hotel. It was day two of light duty.

He was alone, but King was posted at the front door. It was not clear whether the mercenary was stationed there to keep people out or to keep Lt. Col. Randal in. Lady Jane had not been amused by his escapade on Crete.

Women of her class were trained from birth to never show any emotion other than joy in public. She must have flunked that part. The stormy reception by Lady Jane on the dock at Raiding Forces Headquarters when the Seagull landed following the MI-9 mission could best be described as a hurricane.

For reasons he could not quite put a finger on, Lt. Col. Randal felt guilty for causing her to be so upset. He was thinking it would be a good idea to take the remainder of his week of rest and recuperation more seriously.

Brandy Seaborn walked out to the pool in a white, French-cut swimsuit, lay down on the lounge next to him and started oiling her perfect golden legs.

"I'm never going to recover," Lt. Col. Randal said.

"I am here to make things right between you and Jane," Brandy said. "Is it true that you had the doctor write a note giving you permission to travel in light aircraft and small boats?"

"No comment."

"Are you aware," Brandy said, "that you and Jane have an anniversary coming up?"

"Negative … what anniversary?"

"A year since you two met," Brandy said. "At least that long since you and I had our private dinner at the Bradford and became such friends after."

"Seems longer," Lt. Col. Randal said.

"Actually, that is true, but totally irrelevant," Brandy said. "You have to give Jane the perfect gift."

"What might that be?" Lt. Col. Randal asked.

"Something personal she will cherish forever."

"Jane is having my ivory quirt from Abyssinia with the lion's tail modified so it can be converted into an officer's walking-out stick," Lt. Col. Randal said. "I asked her to have her jeweler melt down some Fat Ladies to make a coin silver knob with a high relief 'J' engraved on the end.

"Jane thinks it's for me but I'm planning to give it to her."

Brandy started laughing.

"Just a thought," Lt. Col. Randal said.

"You are having Jane create her own surprise present. Priceless," Brandy said. "I love you, John. You are a one-of-a-kind original."

"I don't have any way to give an expensive gift," Lt. Col. Randal said. "I live on my army salary."

"That is where you are wrong, hero," Brandy said, reaching into her bag and taking out the black velvet pouch last seen on board the Iraqi Air Marshal's yacht on Lake Habbaniyah after they had broken into his hidden safe.

"I consulted with father on the subject of war prizes. According to the Admiral, the rule of thumb on plunder is that if you can carry it in your knapsack and as long as it does not have any intrinsic military intelligence value—finders keepers," Brandy said.

"We British are open-minded about loot as long as it is legitimate capture. To the victor go the spoils. Many of the great fortunes in England got their start from a pocket full of rubies pilfered from some rebellious maharaja."

"Buccaneering's still legal?"

"Absolutely," Brandy said. "This bag contains a fortune's worth of investment-grade diamonds. Plunder, taken fair and square from an enemy combatant during an active campaign. Blood was spilled."

"Fits in your purse," Lt. Col. Randal said.

"Jane will love the ivory walking-out stick," Brandy said. "Do it, by all means. She steals everything of yours she can get her hands on anyway.

"However, a cane will not do to get you out of your current jam. A light duty secret mission—what were you thinking?"

"Your situation requires a special present."

"Like what?" Lt. Col. Randal said.

"Jane is a difficult person to gift," Brandy said. "Has everything. Inherited enough jewelry to open a store and almost never wears any except her wedding ring, which you may have noticed she has not put back on since Mallory returned from the dead, thanks to you."

"Never realized that."

"Jane has her own timeless style," Brandy said. "Simple elegance."

"That, I have noticed."

"What she does not own," Brandy said, "is a pair of round, brilliant cut, 2-karat diamond ear studs mounted in 18-karat white gold settings. And I am positive she would love a pair."

"What would something like that cost?" Lt. Col. Randal asked.

"The price of the mounting," Brandy said. "We have a bag full of diamonds. Pick out a pair of firecrackers, John. This present has to come from you."

"I don't know anything about jewels," Lt. Col. Randal said.

"All one need know about diamond ear studs," Brandy said, "is that 3 karats are too big and 1 karat is too small."

"Like the 'Three Bears'," Lt. Col. Randal said.

"A quick learner." Brandy laughed. "That's 2 karats per ear, by the way. A single, perfect stone in each."

"I see," said Lt. Col. Randal.

"Engle's in Cairo graded these. Each stone is magnificent, worth a king's ransom," Brandy said. "You cannot go wrong with any of them."

"That good, huh?"

"Trust me. Once you give Jane 2-karat studs made out of these exquisite stones, you will be off the hook," Brandy said. "The exact perfect gift—you captured the diamonds. Oh my!"

Lt. Col. Randal said, "Show me one that's 2 karats."

Brandy poured out the contents of the pouch on the small glass-topped table between their lounges. The result was a large pile of sparkling diamonds.

The rocks flared in the Egyptian sunlight.

She professionally sorted out the 2-karat stones with the edge of a nail file. There were only a few of them. The rest of the diamonds were larger, a lot larger.

Lt. Col. Randal could not tell one from the other. They all looked the same. He selected two at random.

"Fabulous," Brandy said. "I shall have King run these beauties over to Engle's straightaway ... incredible artisans.

"I took the liberty of having the white gold mounts already made. All Engle's has to do is mount the stones while King waits. He can bring the finished pieces back within the hour, and you give the pair to Jane at dinner tonight.

"What fun!"

"Thanks, Brandy," Lt. Col. Randal said.

"My pleasure, handsome," Brandy said. "Now, this will be the *last* surprise present you ever give Jane. Understand?"

"No," Lt. Col. Randal said, "I don't."

"Men believe that simply because they go to the trouble to pick out a gift for a woman, she will automatically adore it," Brandy said. "Big mistake."

"From now on, tell Jane what you would like to give her, as a birthday present for example, and then the two of you go out together and you allow *her* to pick it out … never go wrong, John.

"Roger," Lt. Col. Randal said, "got it."

"The exception being," Brandy said, "you can always consult with me."

CAPTAIN THE LADY JANE SEABORN WAS DUE BACK AT ANY MOMENT. Rita Hayworth and Lana Turner were frolicking in the shallow end of the swimming pool, having flown in on the Hudson out of Oasis X. Brandy had left to meet Lieutenant Penelope "Legs" Honeycutt-Parker at MI-5 to discuss how to neutralize the elusive German desert spy, Almásy.

Lieutenant Colonel John Randal was beginning to enjoy light duty.

Lieutenant Mandy Paige came out of the glass doors of the suite in a swimsuit that would have gotten her arrested at any public establishment.

She dove in and swam the length of the pool under water, surfaced, and walked up the steps in the shallow end, sweeping her brunette hair back with both hands. Dark tan, spectacularly good-looking, she lay down on the lounge next to Lt. Col. Randal.

Lt. Mandy said, "Frogspawn."

"Not a chance, Mandy," Lt. Col. Randal said. "Whatever it is, I'm not doing it, negative."

"John …"

"Why don't you go find Pam and round up a couple of fighter pilots to entertain yourselves?"

Lt. Mandy said, "I broke a date to come spend the afternoon here after I saw Brandy, and she told me you were alone."

"Really?"

"I like spending my time with you," Lt. Mandy said. "We have hardly seen each other in over three months. Surely you missed me."

Lt. Col. Randal said, "I don't think this is a social call."

"Started out as one," Lt. Mandy said. "R. J. asked me to deliver a confidential message when he found out where I was going. Jane has banned anyone from Mena House on army business until you are off light duty."

"R. J. as in Brigadier Maunsell?"

"I have been working with Sammy and Mr. Zargo on the counter-intelligence program at Oasis X … love it," Lt. Mandy said. "'Spying spies,' as Sammy says.

"R. J. is going to allow me to attend the MI-5 qualification courses."

"Running with a cold-blooded crowd, Mandy," Lt. Col. Randal said. "Known to kill people."

"You are their favorite triggerman," Lt. Mandy said. "Have a reputation, John."

"Don't listen to them," Lt. Col. Randal said.

Lt. Mandy changed subjects. "Any idea where I could obtain one of those Baby Colt .22s that Pam and Red wear under their skirts on their garter belts?"

"I'll see what I can do," Lt. Col. Randal said.

"What's R. J.'s message?"

"Rikke Runborg," Lt. Mandy said, "wants you to call her."

"I don't have her phone number," Lt. Col. Randal said.

"R. J., Sammy and Baldie need to drop by and talk to you," Mandy said. "Promise to only occupy fifteen minutes of your time.

"Then you and I will be free to enjoy the rest of the afternoon by the pool together until Jane arrives.

"I *know* you missed me."

Lt. Col. Randal said, "We better hope Jane doesn't come back and catch us having a meeting. I'm in deep enough trouble."

"Don't worry. Lady Jane will be unavoidably detained in town," Lt. Mandy said. "Jane definitely does not have a 'Need to Know' about you calling Rocky."

"Roger that."

Lt. Mandy went inside to use the phone. Within minutes, Captain A. W. "Sammy" Sansom appeared at the back gate. Jim Taylor came through the glass doors of the suite, followed in less than a minute by Brigadier Raymond J. "R. J." Maunsell.

All three men were wearing dark glasses, slacks and sports shirts.

Lt. Mandy did not return to the pool. Apparently she was not cleared for the details the three intelligence officers wanted to discuss.

That is how "Need to Know" works: A person is allowed only as much knowledge as necessary to fulfill a role in an operation. Nothing else.

"Thank you for seeing us on such short notice, Colonel," Brig. Maunsell said. "We shall be brief."

Jim said, "We are not having this conversation."

"Sure we are," Lt. Col. Randal said.

"No, we are *not*, Colonel," Jim said. "What I am going to tell you is classified; it is a matter of national security, and no one other than the four of us has the Need to Know anything said here today.

"No signals intelligence is involved, or it would not be possible to discuss even the sketchy details I am about to relate."

"In fact," R. J. said, "the story may not be true, but three reliable agents not known to each other have confirmed it independently. MI-6, the British Secret Intelligence Service, want the facts run to ground. Passed the request to us with their highest expedite priority."

"Make it quick, gentlemen," Lt. Col. Randal said. "We don't want Jane catching us."

"No, we do not," Jim said.

"In 1940, General Auchinleck, then commander of VI Corps fighting in Norway, was winning the campaign, had German General Eduard Dietl on the ropes. The Nazi was so desperate he was contemplating crossing the border into neutral Sweden and allowing himself and all his troops to become interned for the remainder of the war," Jim said.

"Then a beautiful Norwegian spy, reported to be a former member of the Russian Ballet—who was either the lover of, married to, or divorced from a Russian officer— opened a ballet school in Oslo. Now in the employ of the German Abwehr, she infiltrated Auchinleck's headquarters at Tromso to attempt to learn the details of his plan of attack.

"The female agent was successful," Jim said. "She obtained a copy of VI Corps Operations Order and delivered it to Dietl. The Nazi was able to shift his defenses in time to defeat Auchinleck's assault, which had the ripple-down effect of the British Expeditionary Force eventually having to abandon Norway."

"There are no known photographs of the spy," R. J. said. "Her name is believed to be Marina Lee."

"We are of the opinion you know the woman as Rocky," Jim said. "She wants a phone call."

"Be interested to know why, Colonel," Capt. Sansom said. "The lady refuses to talk to anyone else."

"Terry was going to contact her," Lt. Col. Randal said. "I gave him the phone number."

"Zorro struck out," Jim said. "We have run every good-looking officer we have at her and a couple of red-hot women—failed."

"Has Lady Jane," R. J. said, "ever mentioned anything to you about what her husband Mallory had to say concerning his escape with the woman in question prior to your extracting them from France for MI-9, Colonel?"

"Jane never talks to me about her husband," Lt. Col. Randal said.

"Lady Jane is divorcing the bounder. Clearly in love with you, yet does not indulge in disparaging pillow talk," R. J. said. "Commendable, but not helpful."

"Do you think you could pump her for information?" Capt. Samson asked.

"No."

"Naval Intelligence," Jim said, "never has believed Commander Seaborn's story, nor has Counterintelligence or the Secret Intelligence Service.

"How did he and Rocky meet? How did the two of them get from Norway to France? A long way through Nazi-controlled territory.

"The Commander's standard answer to every question put to him has been to claim amnesia from the trauma of the sinking of his destroyer, which he also says he does not remember," Jim said.

"As a result," R. J. said, "the Royal Navy decided to put him in the 'cooler.'"

"What's the cooler?" Lt. Col. Randal asked.

"Command of a naval supply depot," R. J. said, taking a Player's out of his silver case and tapping it. "Located on a barren, semi-artic Shetland island without a tree on it, so small you can stand in the middle and see all the way across in every direction. There is not a woman within 300 miles."

"What do you want from me, sir?" Lt. Col. Randal said.

"Call Rocky."

LIEUTENANT COLONEL JOHN RANDAL AND LIEUTENANT MANDY PAIGE were sunning on the lounges by the pool. The three intelligence officers were gone. Rita and Lana were throwing a big red-and-white blow-up ball back and forth in the shallow end.

"King showed me the diamond ear studs," Lt. Mandy said. "Perfection. He said you took them off a beautiful Nazi SS spy you shot in Istanbul."

"Don't believe everything you hear," Lt. Col. Randal said.

"Where did you get them, John? Had to cost a fortune."

"Won 'em in a strip poker game in Manila," Lt. Col. Randal said. "Russian émigré claimed she was a member of the czar's royal family."

"Jane is going to die when you give her the diamonds," Lt. Mandy said. "Might want to leave out the strip poker story."

"Let me ask you a question, Mandy," Lt. Col. Randal said. "You think those sparklers will be enough to keep me out of trouble with Jane if I have to jump Rocky's bones in the line of duty—for King and Empire?"

"Not on your life," Lt. Mandy said.

LIEUTENANT COLONEL JOHN RANDAL FINISHED PUTTING ON HIS KING'S Royal Rifle Corps dining-out uniform: short jacket, no decorations—jump wings only—green beret with the Rangers Regiment Crest and 9mm Browning P-35 tucked in around the back. Captain the Lady

Jane Seaborn was dressed in a simple black sheath—dark tan, walnut hair, sea green eyes, drop-dead gorgeous.

King discreetly slipped him the little blue box containing the diamond ear studs.

In the Rolls Royce, Lt. Col. Randal gave Flanigan a change of destination. Lady Jane appeared mildly surprised, then settled back in the seat and curled up next to him. She did not care where they dined.

Flanigan drove to an exclusive Nile River floating restaurant. They boarded and were escorted to a small private dining compartment on the upper deck reserved for the two of them. The paddleboat cast off shortly.

Lt. Col. Randal nodded to the attendant standing by the door, and the man departed the room. He produced the box from his pocket and handed it over.

"A trinket."

Lady Jane said, "No one has ever given me a *trinket*!"

When she opened the box the desired effect was achieved, instantaneous and immediate. A lightning strike; one shot—one kill.

Lady Jane was laughing, almost hyperventilating, eyes glittering as bright as the stones.

"Absolutely stunning, John," Lady Jane said. "Most exquisite I have ever laid eyes on … never taking these off."

Clearly a hit.

The attendant wheeled in a full-length mirror and departed.

Lt. Col. Randal had never seen a woman have so much fun. For someone with as hard an edge as he had, tonight had turned into a rare, fine evening.

It occurred to him that Lady Jane might not be the larger-than-life figure people made her out to be. The rule of British Society was: "It's not what you know but who you know."

Lady Jane knew everyone, which made her a social lioness in the eyes of most.

Tonight, when it was only the two of them alone, Lady Jane was simply a girl playing with her new earrings. Allowing him to share in the pleasure of the moment.

And it felt like an honor.

Lt. Col. Randal had no idea how love worked. He only knew he had never liked any woman better.

Lady Jane did not trust many people. The number could be counted on one hand. She had chosen to include him in that circle—not something to be taken lightly.

He did not intend to.

"Jane," Lt. Col. Randal said, "what I'm about to tell you is classified. "*You* do not have a Need to Know …"

5

MAROONED

"So," Sergeant Major Mike "March or Die" Mikkalis said, "blue Patrol laagered for the night. Lt. Huxley and I took a jeep and drove to within a half mile of a German convoy's remain overnight position along one of the secondary roads paralleling the Via Balbia."

He and Lieutenant Colonel John Randal were sitting by the pool at the suite at Mena House Hotel. Captain the Lady Jane Seaborn had relented and was allowing visitors on day three of light duty—possibly swayed by 4 karat's worth of diamond ear studs.

"We proceeded on foot to do a reconnaissance of the enemy truck park, then once we had the intel we needed, returned to where we had our vehicle concealed in a small wadi.

"Jeep had a flat tire," Sgt. Maj. Mikkalis said. "No spare because the only one we had blew out the day before. There we were, fifteen miles or more from Blue Patrol, a flat, no spare, and no way were we going to walk off and leave the Nazis a perfectly operational gun jeep—except for a bad tire."

"Hate it when that happens," Lt. Col. Randal said.

"Lt. Huxley said 'wait here'," Sgt. Maj. Mikkalis said. "Then he started back toward the German camp."

"I asked him, 'Where do you think you are going, Lieutenant?'"

"'To borrow an air pump,' Lt. Huxley said. 'I speak German like a Bavarian.'"

"Huxley said that?"

"In a little while he comes back with one," Sgt. Maj. Mikkalis said. "We pump up the tire. Then Lt. Huxley walks off in the dark again—planning to take the bloody pump back.

"I put a stop to that, Colonel."

"No kidding," Lt. Col. Randal said. "What happened next?"

"We drove to the laager position, picked up Blue Patrol, went back and Lt. Huxley led a beat-up of the German convoy … the same one he was going to take the air pump back to.

"Knocked out maybe a dozen trucks. Hard to get an exact count, sir."

"Nice going, Mike."

"RFDS need additional spare tires, sir," Sgt. Maj. Mikkalis said. "Like Capt. McKoy says, 'Too many ain't enough.'"

"Get with Rawlston," Lt. Col. Randal said. "Have him design some way to mount more spares on the outside of the jeeps. Maybe on the hood?"

"As you know, sir, our gas cans are prone to leakage," Sgt. Maj. Mikkalis said. "We captured some German cans, what the troops call 'Jerrycans.' They have built-in handles, which make them easy to work with, and they absolutely do not leak.

"I advised Captain Corrigan that RFDS needed to make it a priority to replace all our issue gas cans with captured Jerrycans as soon as we can lay hands on them."

"If the Jerrycans don't leak, it could increase the range of our patrols by at least 25 percent," Lt. Col. Randal said.

"Anything else?"

"Implement a policy of never sending out a single jeep alone—asking for trouble, sir," Sgt. Maj. Mikkalis said. "RFDS should always travel in pairs."

"Will do," Lt. Col. Randal said. "Each jeep needs its own air pump too.

"Can't keep borrowing from the bad guys."

James "Baldie" Taylor arrived shortly after Sergeant Major Mike "March or Die" Mikkalis departed for RFHQ to consult with ex-Technical Sergeant Hank W. Rawlston.

"Change of plans last night?" Jim said. "Decided on a cruise down the Nile?"

"If Jane and I had showed up at the restaurant where we had our original reservations," Lieutenant Colonel John Randal said, "We wouldn't have been dining alone—would we?"

"Had the place bugged," Jim said, "wall to wall."

"Mallory has never talked to Jane about his destroyer being sunk," Lt. Col. Randal said, "how he was rescued, or any of the details of making his way to the coast of France.

"Told Jane he doesn't remember a thing."

"Sticking to his story," Jim said.

"Jane's not inclined to believe Mallory," Lt. Col. Randal said, "in part because she's always sensed he was holding back on account of Rocky."

"You informed Lady Jane," Jim said, "about Rocky?"

"Yeah," Lt. Col. Randal said, "I did."

"Do not tell anyone else."

"Understood," Lt. Col. Randal said.

"Commander Seaborn is either being truthful and does not remember a thing," Jim said, "or he deserted his ship alone in the only lifeboat to make it off before the destroyer went down with all hands and wants to cover up the fact he's a coward, or he was intentionally helping a German spy infiltrate Great Britain.

"In fact, Colonel," Jim said, "the man could be guilty of any number of combinations of those possibilities."

"Jane's not involved," Lt. Col. Randal said.

"No one ever even considered that likelihood," Jim said. "Our hope was that Mallory might have said something to her that could help us cipher this out … wanted to hear it from her lips."

"Never happened," Lt. Col. Randal said. "Jane says he claims amnesia."

"Unfortunate," Jim said. "If Rikke Runborg is, in fact, Marina Lee, and there is any way for us to turn her—then play her back at the Nazis, Rocky becomes a priceless British intelligence asset.

"The kind that, under the right circumstances, might be manipulated to alter the outcome of the war."

Lt. Col. Randal said, "What makes Rocky so valuable?"

"The story is that Marina Lee is known to both Stalin *and* Hitler," Jim said. "Any idea what British Intelligence could do with that kind of access? Possibilities only limited by one's imagination."

"You're after *her*, then," Lt. Col. Randal said, "not Seaborn?"

"The Commander is a little fish," Jim said. "The Navy marooned him. Now, MI-5 has the luxury to sort out the details of what precisely he is guilty of, if anything, at their leisure. In the unlikely event Seaborn is completely innocent, well … someone has to command that depot.

"Rocky is the prize."

JAMES "BALDIE" TAYLOR SHIFTED TO ANOTHER SUBJECT, SORT OF. THE fact that Lieutenant Colonel John Randal had briefed Captain the Lady Jane Seaborn about Rikke Runborg might work to an advantage. Having been read into the operation to run the spy Marina Lee to ground, Lady Jane might now be open to letting her boyfriend off restricted light duty early.

An urgent mission had come up.

Colonel Dudley Clarke's deception organization, A-Force, had been working around the clock. The name of his command had lately been formalized and, like everything else, even the unit's name was a deception.

The idea was for Col. Clarke to set up shop in the Middle East Command as a notional airborne brigade, 1Special Air Service Brigade (1SAS). Since 1SAS was supposed to be secret, it might be too obvious to call his unit the Advanced Headquarters, 1SAS Brigade. So, the world's master military hoaxer settled on A-Force. On paper, officially Advanced Headquarters, A-Force (Adv. HQ. A-Force).

The hope was the Nazis would figure it out: "A" stood for "Airborne." The name was not very deceptive, but sometimes in military intelligence when you wanted the other side to know something, it did not hurt to help them.

Col. Clarke was currently engaged in a deception with an even less subtle title, PLAN A-R (Anti-Rommel). Another name the master military deceiver intentionally designed for the Nazis to figure out.

PLAN A-R's goal was to cause the German general to divert precious battle troops to protect his supply lines. As all good deceptions need to be, it was part true, part fiction. The story was that the British and Free French intended to carry out a series of attacks on Afrika Korps communications lines from Tobruk to Tripoli. That was true.

An amphibious landing by British Commandos supported by a special assault ship dispatched from England would be made on the coast of the Gulf of Sirte to set up a blocking force. The Commandos and ships were real, the landings "notional," which in the world of military deception meant imaginary/not true.

Photos of M-3 Stuart tanks advertised as "air-conditioned desert capable" somehow slipped past censors and appeared in the newspapers. The M-3s were reported being delivered from the U.S. under Lend-Lease to make an attack on Tripoli possible during the "hot months," as it was known that the Germans, with their limited experience in desert warfare, believed that tank crews could not operate in the intense summer heat.

The notional—meaning it existed only on paper—10th Armored Division, reinforced by notional air-conditioned tanks, was being brought in overland by transporters from Nigeria via Fort Lamy, and staging in Libya to attack Rommel's desert flank.

Talkative 10th Armored Division troops flooded the local bars bragging about what they were going to do to the Desert Fox in their luxurious new air-conditioned tanks.

Meanwhile, non-notional Free French troops supported by RFDS were slated to make long-range raids on Afrika Korps' lines of communication.

The Free French troops would strike across the Sahara from French Equatorial Africa, which was possibly true—the plan was actually under consideration. At the same time, RFDS would be conducting raids from secret bases deep in the Great Sand Sea, which was true. Actual RFDS missions were being launched from Oasis X.

The presence of the American Volunteer Group (AVG) was "accidently leaked" to the press.

To add to the big lie, a notional electronic mine field claimed to have been built in 1940 south of Mersa Maruth that could be detonated by remote control had been added to the story mix to give the Germans something to think about.

Brigadier Raymond J. "R. J." Maunsell's Security Intelligence Middle East (SIME) aided Col. Clarke in the dissemination of the PLAN A-R deception. Rumors in the bazaars, "press leaks," and "indiscretions" were simultaneously orchestrated in Cairo, Istanbul, Athens, Palestine, Lisbon and at the Free French HQ in West Africa.

The bars and coffee houses were buzzing with the story.

Dummy gliders were publicly marshaled, and a mixture of actual (RFHQ supplied a handful of real jumpers) and notional parachutists (consisting of duffel bags filled with sand) were dropped near Cairo in full view of the city.

The PLAN A-R deception was in full swing, diverting Rommel's Afrika Korps and his more numerous Italian allies, when Col. Clarke received an urgent call from Field Marshal Sir Archibald Wavell. Greece had fallen, as had Crete.

His services were required.

The fear at Middle East Headquarters was that Cypress would be the next domino. A-Force was tasked with devising a deception to delay the anticipated German invasion by two weeks until reinforcements could be rushed to the island.

When Lieutenant General Claude Auchinleck replaced FM Wavell, one of his first orders was for Col. Clarke to implement the Cypress deception.

What to do? First, he had to come up with another name for his deception that made it easy for the Nazis to figure out. No problem. He christened the operation CYPRESS DEFENSE PLAN.

Next, Col. Clarke decided to turn the actual 4,000 troops currently stationed on Cypress into a full, semi-notional division of 30,000 troops, plus a notional regiment of the 1SAS Brigade.

Then he spread the word, telling the Germans what he had done—leaving out the word "notional.'

Orders went out to rename the command on Cypress "7th Division" and for the brigadier on the island to assume the local rank of major general. A fake division Headquarters was requisitioned, office space commandeered, phony signs posted and a blizzard of sham messages flew back and forth between Headquarters Middle East (HQME) in Cairo and 7th Div. HQ on the island.

The customary rumors were floated in the bars, bazaars and coffee houses of the capitals around Middle East Command.

A squadron of dummy tanks was shipped to the 7th Division.

Now, Jim and Col. Clarke had come up with the final two pieces of the deception.

A phony defense plan to include order of battle and maps of the island's defensive positions was to be placed on an agent known to be a German operative (Rocky, provided she could be persuaded to cooperate).

And, a notional regiment of the equally notional 1SAS Brigade was scheduled to make an actual, highly publicized daylight parachute drop on Cypress to reinforce the garrison.

Raiding Forces was the only parachute unit in the Middle East Command.

"Any chance, Colonel," Jim asked, "Lady Jane could be persuaded to spend two weeks with you and a few friends on a Mediterranean island?"

"She might like that," Lt. Col. Randal said.

CAPTAIN "GERONIMO" JOE McKOY AND WALDO TREYWICK WERE smoking cigars by the pool at a table under an umbrella with Lieutenant Colonel John Randal at the suite at Mena House. Rita and Lana were playing badminton. Captain the Lady Jane Seaborn, Lieutenant

Penelope "Legs" Honeycutt-Parker, Lieutenant Mandy Paige and Brandy Seaborn were sunning on lounges.

The women were admiring Lady Jane's new diamond ear studs.

Capt. McKoy and Waldo were giving Lt. Col. Randal a report on the patrols that had come in from the desert after he had been medically evacuated. Everyone reported some degree of success. The combination of the jeeps' mobility, the skill of the AVG drivers and the hard target intelligence from Mr. Zargo's team, "Murder Inc.," was proving to be deadly effective.

"We done good, but we ain't goin' to be able to keep the tempo up," Capt. McKoy said. "Not at the rate you started us out on, John.

"We need us nine patrols, minimum. Three a-operating, three traveling to or returning from their Area of Operation and three being refitted at X at all times."

"Should have all six RFDS patrols in the field by now," Lt. Col. Randal said. "Terry is attaching the Lounge Lizards to Raiding Forces, so that's three more.

"There's your nine, Captain."

"Be a big help," Capt. McKoy said. "Those Lancer boys have a lot of mobile combat experience. Should take to deep-desert patrolling like ducks to water."

"Major Adair finally cut a deal with the LRDG. Got us a half-dozen navigators so we're good on that end."

"Probably take six weeks," Lt. Col. Randal said, "to get Terry's people fully amalgamated."

Capt. McKoy said, "Setting up an operating base at an oasis no one ever heard of in the middle of nowhere was no small thing. Raiding Forces hit the ground running. Pretty impressive, John.

"You got you some good patrol leaders too, unusual mix—complement each other. We're going to make life miserable for that Desert Fox Nazi."

"I'm ready to get back," Lt. Col. Randal said.

"The life of a nomad guerrilla raider," Capt. McKoy said, "kinda gets in a man's blood, don't it, John."

"Colonel," Waldo said, "if me and Joe had a-known you was plannin' to custom-build diamond earrings for Lady Jane, we'd a-felt honored to donate a couple o' eye popper rocks the size of walnuts to the project.

"Too bad ya had to settle for 'em little chips."

"When it comes to diamond ear studs, Mr. Treywick," Lt. Col. Randal said, "3 karats are too big, and 1 karat is too small.

"Jane's are 2 karats each."

"Like the Three Bears," Capt. McKoy said, rolling his cigar between his fingers.

"Learn somethin' new every day," Waldo said. "I thought with diamonds, bigger was better."

"Not always, Waldo," Capt. McKoy said. "There's more ways to choke a cat than by feeding it butter."

LIEUTENANT COLONEL JOHN RANDAL AND CAPTAIN THE LADY JANE Seaborn were reclining on lounges by the pool. She was very fit, tanned tawny gold. Royal Marines exercise a minimum of one hour per day— at least she did.

Everyone was gone except Rita and Lana, who were in the water floating on air mattresses. King was on duty at the door. Flanigan was keeping him company.

"John," Lady Jane said, "Have you ever heard of a DUKW?"

"A duck?"

"No ... a DUKW."

"Negative."

"Amphibious truck. It can swim," Lady Jane said. "Ten of them appeared on the Lend-Lease manifest today.

"No one has any idea what to do with a seagoing two and a half-ton truck. Navy turned their nose up at them. The army has no use for trucks that float."

Lady Jane said, "Raiding Forces can have the full consignment."

"I don't know what to do with a swimming deuce and a half either," Lt. Col. Randal said. "But maybe Sea Squadron can think of something—we'll take 'em."

"You and I have been offered the opportunity to go on an island holiday," Lady Jane said. "Did Jim mention it?"

Lt. Col. Randal said. "What island?"

"Cypress."

"What's on Cypress?"

"Well, you and I will be," Lady Jane said.

"Good enough for me."

"We are allowed to invite a few people, stay in a private villa on the beach," Lady Jane said. "Fly over in the Hudson."

"When?"

"As soon," Lady Jane said, "as you make contact with Rikke Runborg."

6
ROCKY

Lieutenant Colonel John Randal, Captain the Lady Jane Seaborn and Lieutenant Mandy Paige were in the back of the white Rolls Royce with Flanigan at the wheel. All three were wearing swimsuits. They were headed to the Gezira Sporting Club.

Lt. Col. Randal had arranged to meet Rikke Runborg poolside. She had specified a public place.

"Here's the Baby Colt .22 you asked for," Lt. Col. Randal said to Lt. Mandy. "You'll have to ask Pam how the garter belt holster trick works. She's never demonstrated it to me."

"Thanks, John."

"Try not to shoot yourself."

Flanigan pulled up outside the club. Security started at the curb. One of Captain A. W. "Sammy" Sansom's men was pulling duty as the valet. He signaled to park the car right in front, then opened the door for them to exit.

In the front, Flanigan had Lt. Col. Randal's cut-down 12-gauge Browning A-5 concealed under a newspaper on the seat.

Lt. Col. Randal and the two girls walked through the lobby to the pool out back—the largest in Cairo. Both women had handguns in their shoulder bags (in addition to Mandy's new deep concealment Colt .22). In her purse, Lady Jane was also carrying Lt. Col. Randal's

9mm Browning P-35 for him and the engraved Walther PPK he had captured from the German panzer general on Raiding Forces' first Commando raid and given to her.

Brigadier Raymond J. "R. J." Maunsell was sipping a drink from his table that offered a clear view of the pool.

Capt. Sansom was leaning against the wall in a corner with an equally good view of the pool, reading a racing sheet.

Neither man seemed to notice the trio as they passed through the lobby. They were the only men in the room who failed to.

Up on the second story balcony, Colonel Dudley Clarke and Jim Taylor shared a table by the railing that looked down on the pool. Lt. Col. Randal caught a glimpse of them in his peripheral vision as he walked toward three lounges strategically prepositioned to allow a very public private conversation.

Two men and a woman who were occupying the lounges, Capt. Sansom's operatives, stood up and drifted to the outside bar.

Lt. Mandy broke off and continued to the poolside glass-topped table where Lieutenant Pamala Plum-Martin was chatting up two more MI-5 men.

She walked past Lieutenant Penelope "Legs" Honeycutt-Parker and Brandy Seaborn, who were sitting on the edge of the pool dangling their legs in the water.

King was in the lifeguard stand.

The Clipper Girl/MI-6 agent Red was stretched out on a towel.

Rita Hayworth and Lana Turner danced by, tossing a beach ball back and forth.

Veronica Paige was doing yoga on a mat on the grass.

Everyone was armed. In fact, there was enough firepower poolside to fight off a panzer platoon.

Lt. Col. Randal and Lady Jane reclined on two of the now-vacant lounges.

Rikke Runborg appeared right on time and took the third lounge.

Lt. Col. Randal made the introductions.

Rocky was very self-assured. The snow-blond Norwegian did not seem the least ruffled to find Lady Jane, the wife of the lover with whom she had traveled through enemy-occupied France, present.

She went straight to the main point.

"I am an agent of the Abwehr, the foreign intelligence gathering agency of Germany. While I agreed to be recruited, my intent has never been to spy for the Nazis.

"I have always planned to turn myself in to the British Secret Service once I arrived in England.

"My desire is to offer myself as a double agent to work against the Hitler regime."

"Why," Lt. Col. Randal asked, "are you talking to me and not MI-5?"

"I require a sponsor," Rikke said. "A patron who can safeguard me, and you are the only Englishman I can trust."

"I'm an American."

"Counterespionage officers can be cruel," Rikke said. "I require a protector. Someone who can guarantee that MI-5 will not subject me to torture, execute me or play me back to the Nazis and then intentionally compromise me so they can kill me.

"Mallory was supposed to fulfill that role, but he was under a cloud almost immediately after you rescued us. He has not been able to protect himself."

"Why me?"

"You are Special Forces," Rocky said. "Your command is under the control of British Intelligence. That much is known to the Abwehr.

"And, you saved my life," Rocky said. "Hopefully you will wish to do so again."

"Can we make the guarantee?" Lt. Col. Randal asked Lady Jane.

"We can."

Lady Jane reached into her handbag and took out a pair of oversized tortoise shell sunglasses and put them on—signaling to the watchers the meeting had been satisfactorily concluded.

"Brigadier Maunsell will evaluate your offer to work with British intelligence," Lt. Col. Randal said.

"Likes to be called R. J."

"I was not sleeping with Mallory out of love," Rocky said. "My relationship with him was merely an arrangement of convenience."

"As was mine," Lady Jane said.

Lt. Col. Randal said, "Glad you two could get that settled."

THE HUDSON WAS EN ROUTE TO THE ANCIENT ISLAND OF CYPRESS. Lieutenant Pamala Plum-Martin was at the stick, getting a check ride from Squadron Leader Paddy Wilcox. The idea was for her to be certified to pilot the multi-engine aircraft.

Lieutenant Colonel John Randal and Captain the Lady Jane Seaborn were sitting on the two seats on the port side. Jim Taylor had the aisle seat on the starboard side. He was leaning across the aisle talking to Lt. Col. Randal.

Lieutenant Mandy Paige was sitting next to him reading a movie star magazine. Brandy Seaborn and Lieutenant Penelope "Legs" Honeycutt-Parker were directly behind with Major Sir Terry "Zorro" Stone, KBE, DSO, MC, and Red across the aisle.

Captain "Geronimo" Joe McKoy and Waldo Treywick were also on board, as were Rita and Lana.

Captain Hawthorne Merryweather, the Political Warfare officer, had arrived in Cairo from Seaborn House at the last minute and been invited along.

Everyone on board was jump-qualified.

With the exception of Jim, none of the passengers were aware that they constituted the advance party of the notional 1ˢᵗ Special Air Service Brigade or that they were playing a starring role in A-Forces deception, CYPRESS DEFENSE PLAN.

Only Jim had any idea that Cypress was the next domino in the Nazi Mediterranean master plan. They did know they were going to do a flyover of the island and parachute in—show the flag with a demonstration jump.

"Kenya has been holding what is being called the 'Trial of the Century,' Colonel," Jim said. "Broughton got off of killing Lord Hay, the Earl of Erroll … 'the world's greatest pouncer.'"

"Found not guilty."

"That's good," Lt. Col. Randal said, "since he didn't do it."

Lady Jane giggled. She had been present on the dark country road the night the Earl of Erroll was shot.

"Man did not make it easy for himself," Jim said. "Admitted the crime to at least three people, including the jailers holding him for trial."

"Really?" Lt. Col. Randal said. "Broughton did that?"

"Probably a good idea if you never go back to Kenya, or at least to Nairobi," Jim said. "The authorities believe Broughton did it. The police are not looking for any other perpetrator, but why take a chance?"

"Roger that."

"The Iraqis have signed a treaty with Great Britain," Jim said. "The Golden Square is kaput. But there is a provision in the accord that stipulates we have to return any national treasure captured.

"Want their gold back."

"What'd you tell 'em?" Lt. Col. Randal asked.

"What gold?"

"Are they buying that?"

"No," Jim said. "The Air Marshal believes you stole it. In the future, Colonel, you should make a point of not going to Baghdad either."

"How did I get involved? You took the gold."

"All those diamonds," Jim said.

"Untraceable ... the Air Marshal's yacht conveniently exploded in the middle of Lake Habbaniyah, so you have no problems on that score.

"The Air Marshal is of the opinion the stones were blown to kingdom come, but the Iraqis are angry about the stash of gold—known to hold a grudge."

"All I need."

"R. J.'s first interview with Rocky was wrapping up as I was leaving to catch the Hudson," Jim said. "She admits to being a German agent. Willing to work for us. Denies knowledge of anyone named Marina Lee."

"German spies turning themselves in like she did," Lt. Col. Randal said. "Is that normal?"

"Happens all the time," Jim said. "Most Nazi operatives arrive in England, then go straight to the nearest police station and give themselves up."

"Why?"

"German spies are convinced that MI-5 is so efficient they will be caught immediately," Jim said. "Most claim they never intended to do any spying, they only wanted to get out of Germany."

"Nazi spies paddle ashore from a U-boat, then give up," Lt. Col. Randal said. "Just like that?"

"Just like that," Jim said. "Those deemed worthy are taken on by one intelligence agency or another and played back at the Abwehr.

"We have something MI-5 calls the XX Committee—the double cross, to run the double agents. Those spies deemed of no value are imprisoned. Hardcore Nazi zealots who do not turn themselves in and are caught or who turn back on us as triple agents are executed.

"Rocky has been on British soil for close to a year," Jim said. "Our question is why she waited so long to come forward."

"What's her excuse?"

"Claims it took her a while to realize Commander Seaborn would not be able to protect her." Jim said. "After that she says she has been trying to locate you.

"Rocky does not trust MI-5 without a benefactor," Jim said. "At least that's her story."

"Are you buying it?"

"Not entirely," Jim said. "Rocky is dissembling. I have the feeling the lady is a highly-skilled operative.

"Russia trains their spies for up to ten years before putting them in the field. If Rocky is Marina Lee, that makes her a Russian agent planted on the Germans who—unaware of what she was—trained her again before sending her to spy on Auchinleck in Norway, then England.

"In that case, we have a professional on our hands," Jim said. "Breaking Rocky's story down to where we can believe it, trust her, then run her back at the Third Reich may prove daunting."

"Says she's not Marina Lee," Lt. Col. Randal said.

"That's right."

"Then who is she?"

THIRTY MINUTES OUT, LIEUTENANT PAMALA PLUM-MARTIN CAME ON the intercom and announced the estimated time of arrival.

Lieutenant Colonel John Randal stood up and ordered, "Chute up!"

The passengers began the ritual of putting on their parachutes.

The British military did not permit women to participate in direct combat, though they were allowed to be in active war zones. MI-6, the Secret Intelligence Service, used female operatives, but it really preferred not to.

Special Operations Executive and A-Force had no such inhibitions. They sent women to the exact same schools their men attended and on the same missions behind enemy lines carrying out dangerous operations where capture meant torture followed by a brutal death.

Every single person on the Hudson worked for MI-6, SOE or A-Force, whether they realized it or not. Colonel Dudley Clarke had not given it a second thought when he and Jim came up with the idea to drop them on the island as part of the CYPRESS DEFENSE PLAN deception.

At the last minute, Jim had decided to come along on the trip. He was feeling guilty, not wanting to send people someplace he was not willing to go. Cypress was not unlike the situation at RAF Habbaniya before hostilities commenced.

German airborne forces could arrive at any moment.

No matter how often it has been done before, inflight rigging is always an intense exercise. The airplane is hurtling toward the Drop Zone (DZ). There is just so much time to get the parachute on, buckled up and the jumpmaster inspection completed before the green light.

All the passengers would be jumping except Lt. Col. Randal. He was still on light duty. Today he was the static jumpmaster. He had a busy half hour ahead of him.

First off, he helped Captain the Lady Jane Seaborn into her X-type parachute. She would get a pre-jump jumpmaster inspection like everyone else, but Lt. Col. Randal first carefully checked every strap on her legs and shoulders and then ran his hands under the parachute pack to make sure nothing was knotted or twisted. Made sure the snaps on the quick release were set, locked and the safety clip firmly in place.

Last he traced her static line, which was draped over her left shoulder, then hooked it above the quick release. When the order to "Hook Up" came she would unsnap it and hook it to the steel cable running down the length of the roof of the Hudson.

Lady Jane was as cool as ice. She liked jumping out of airplanes. Lt. Col. Randal had always been impressed by how fearless she was—he was less than casual about jumping himself, being afraid of heights.

Once the parachute was on, Lady Jane sat back down on the edge of the seat, leaning back against the parachute pack.

Lt. Col. Randal helped Jim into his chute, then left him to strap it on. Lieutenant Mandy Paige was the least-experienced jumper onboard. He pulled her out into the aisle to help her chute up.

If the girl was scared, she did not show it. It would be fair to say Lt. Col. Randal was considerably more worried at the moment than she was, and *he* was not going to jump.

"Better than sex," Lt. Mandy said.

Lt. Col. Randal tugged on her leg straps until she gasped. "John!"

Once everyone was chuted up, Lt. Col. Randal began his jumpmaster inspection. He took his time, but did not waste any, working his way from the front to the rear of the aircraft, not knowing what he was expecting to find during his inspection but always looking for something out of place.

A jumpmaster inspection is half visual, half like reading braille, with a portion of extra sensory perception thrown in. The jumpmaster can see some things; others he has to check by touch; some require pure instinct.

The jumpmaster inspection accomplishes two things. The jumper is inspected to make sure the parachute has been put on properly. And, it instills confidence in both the parachutist *and* the jumpmaster, who is worried about everything. It is no small thing to be responsible for putting people out the door of an aircraft in flight.

Every parachutist enjoys the jumpmaster inspection.

It is a serious exercise. While being inspected, the parachutist remains in a semi-position of attention and stares straight ahead, never looking directly at the jumpmaster. Even so, the inspection provides a chance for the jumpmaster and each jumper to exchange a few words.

When he ran his hands around and under Lieutenant Penelope "Legs" Honeycutt-Parker's leg straps, she drawled, "Enjoying yourself, John?"

"Roger that."

When Lt. Col. Randal came to Brandy, he said, "I didn't realize until today you were parachute qualified."

"Took the Short Course with Parker," Brandy said. "We used to go down to No. 1 Parachute School to straphang extra jumps. Made over fifty…love the balloon."

That gave Lt. Col. Randal something to think about. No. 1 Parachute School was not in business to train civilians.

"Glad you're back," Lt. Col. Randal said to Major Sir Terry "Zorro" Stone.

"Ten minutes," Lt. Plum-Martin said over the intercom. The red jump light came on.

Lt. Col. Randal went to the back of the cabin and opened the door and locked it down. The wind outside howled like a banshee. When the jump door opened, tension inside the aircraft ratcheted up.

Lt. Col. Randal ran his hands around the edges of the door, feeling for burrs or any sharp edges. He took out a gray roll of tape and taped the trailing edge of the door from top to bottom.

Locking his fingers in the interior edges of both sides of the door and wedging his canvas-topped raiding boots on each side of the door, Lt. Col. Randal arched himself outside of the aircraft. He was not wearing a parachute (Lady Jane did not want him to *accidentally* fall out after all the jumpers had exited), but he was hooked up to a safety line.

Up ahead he could see the island of Cypress glimmering in the distance.

He swung back inside, glanced at his Rolex and, without waiting for Lt. Plum-Martin's announcement, ordered, "SIX MINUTES!"

Every eye in the passenger compartment of the Hudson was on him now. Tension ratcheted to the pressure cooker level. It was happening.

Lady Jane and Lt. Mandy made their way to the back of the airplane doing the "airborne shuffle"—not picking up their feet to eliminate any chance of tripping.

Lady Jane was going to lead the stick out. Lt. Mandy was the least experienced jumper. Lt. Col. Randal wanted her to jump number two so he could keep his eye on her during the series of pre-jump commands.

Locking his left arm across the door so she could not fall out, with his free hand Lt. Col. Randal physically moved Lady Jane into the position where he wanted her to stand.

Then Lt. Col. Randal turned back to the door, gripped the interior edges on each side with his fingertips again and arched outside again. The Hudson flew over the beach. He was looking for a checkpoint called Initial Point (IP).

He swung back inside.

Lt. Col. Randal looked down the line of jumpers. They were all ready. Everyone was focused.

Good.

"HOOK UP!"

He watched Lady Jane as she clicked her snap-link onto the steel cable—snap side away from the skin of the aircraft—and jerked on it to make sure it was seated. Then she doubled up the yellow static line and grabbed it in her right fist in the approved technique so she could not accidently pull it prematurely. Last, she took the safety wire dangling down on a nylon string and poked it through the tiny hole on the snap-link and bent it down on the far side with her finger.

Lt. Col. Randal noted she never missed a beat. Hitting the pin-sized hole was a tricky process when encased in a parachute and getting ready to jump out of an aircraft in flight that was bucking its way through the sky.

He gave her a wink.

Lady Jane ignored him, totally absorbed in the process, strictly professional. An Olympic-class equestrian, she was focused on preparing for her jump.

Lt. Mandy was fixated on Lt. Col. Randal looking over Lady Jane's shoulder—she winked back.

"CHECK STATIC LINE!"

There was the sound of metal on metal rattling as the jumpers vigorously shook their static lines back and forth to make sure their snap-hooks were firmly attached to the steel cable.

"CHECK YOUR EQUIPMENT!"

Today was what paratroopers call a "Hollywood jump." They were not carrying any equipment except their personal side arms. And, unlike combat jumps, if anyone found anything wrong with their parachute or equipment, Lt. Col. Randal would either correct the deficiency or sit the jumper down.

No one would be taking any chances—other than those inherent in all parachute operations.

"SOUND OFF FOR EQUIPMENT CHECK!"

"OKAY, OKAY, OKAY, OKAY …"

"ALL OK …" Lady Jane shouted, giving him one of her patented heart attack smiles, which did not make him feel better about not jumping with the stick.

Lt. Col. Randal swung back outside the aircraft. He could see orange smoke on the DZ ahead. The Hudson flashed across a road: his final checkpoint.

"ONE MINUTE!"

"Lt. Col. Randal mentally started counting off the seconds. He did not want his first jumper, Lady Jane, standing in the door for longer than a few seconds.

"CLOSE ON THE DOOR!"

Lt. Col. Randal again had his left arm locked across the door, and his eyes were locked on Lady Jane as the rest of the stick shuffled forward, all pressing tightly together. Jumpers are keyed up at this point. All they want to do is get out of the aircraft.

He did not want the second jumper, Lt. Mandy, to bump Lady Jane and make her think she had felt the customary slap on the leg that signaled "go."

Lt. Col. Randal knew a jumpmaster had to be careful at this stage of a drop or he would find himself watching his stick of paratroopers shuffle out the door before the green light came on.

It had happened before.

"STAND IN THE DOOR!"

On a combat jump, this command is not given because the jumpmaster leads the stick out the door. However, today Lady Jane was leading the way, and Lt. Col. Randal would be landing aboard the Hudson.

She shuffled up to the door until the toe of her lead raiding boot was halfway over the edge. Lady Jane reached outside the aircraft then slapped her hands wide, pressing them against the skin of the airframe, knees slightly bent.

Keeping his left arm locked across the door holding her back, Lt. Col. Randal checked to see that Lady Jane's static line was draped over her shoulder. Not around her neck. The light on the weld on the tail blinked green.

"GO!"

Lady Jane went, feet and knees together, chin down on her chest, elbows in, arms crossed on her chest, leaning back—the perfect tuck position. Lt. Mandy was right behind her, followed by Captain "Geronimo" Joe McKoy, Waldo, Rita, Lana and the rest of the stick as fast as they could charge out the door.

The last jumper, Jim Taylor, pushing the stick, cleared the aircraft. Then Lt. Col. Randal swung outside to make sure none of the parachutists were being towed—a jumpmaster's worst fear.

He already knew they were not. Had there been, one of the static lines, the one towing the parachutist, would be down at the bottom of the door. All of them were at the top trailing the Hudson.

Following procedure, he checked anyway. Behind the airplane he could see the parachutes swimming open like octopuses.

Everything was copacetic.

Lt. Col. Randal hauled in the static lines, a task that was a lot harder than it looked. Then he went up to the cockpit.

Lt. Plum-Martin was lining up on the airfield in the distance. The Vargas Girl-looking Royal Marine seemed very relaxed. She was very much in command of the aircraft.

Squadron Leader Paddy Wilcox, flying co-pilot, had his eye-patch pulled up. Lt. Plum-Martin was his prize pupil. He was watching her every move like a hawk.

Sqn. Ldr. Wilcox said over his shoulder, "There is a priority message waiting at the airfield, Colonel."

"Any idea what it's about?"

"Negative," Sqn. Ldr. Wilcox said. "Only that the General Officer Commanding is standing by at the airfield to deliver it to you personally upon touchdown."

"Wonder who we hacked off this time?"

"General Auchinleck."

7
AIN'T FOR THE FAINT-HEARTED

LIEUTENANT PAMALA PLUM-MARTIN BROUGHT THE TWIN-ENGINE ANSON down on the landing ground at Oasis X. Lieutenant Colonel John Randal, Captain the Lady Jane Seaborn, Lieutenant Mandy Paige, Captain "Geronimo" Joe McKoy and Waldo Treywick disembarked.

Raiding Forces policy was for the Ansons to fly in pairs on desert flights. As soon as Lt. Plum-Martin taxied off the strip, the second plane—flown by one of the Hawaiian-shirted, cowboy-booted, Ray-Ban-wearing Canadian bush pilots who had operated out of Camp Croc in support of Force N—landed.

Captain Hawthorne Merryweather, Veronica Paige, King, Rita and Lana were on board.

The vacation to Cypress had been one of the shortest on record. When Lieutenant General Claude Auchinleck discovered Lady Jane was part of a deception on an island expecting to be invaded at any moment by German Airborne Forces, he ordered their part of the mission to stand down.

Immediately.

The deceivers of 1SAS Brigade spent the afternoon at the beach and flew home the next morning. By the time the party arrived back in

Cairo, Lt. Col. Randal was off light duty. He flew out to Oasis X the same day.

Lady Jane and Lt. Mandy went along to continue organizing the Raiding Forces Headquarters at the oasis.

Capt. Merryweather wanted to spend time with Mr. Zargo to investigate possibilities for psychological warfare in the Jebel.

Veronica needed to meet with Mr. Zargo to discuss setting up a desert escape line for downed RAF pilots and aircrew.

Lt. Col. Randal was going to take to the field immediately upon arrival, on a five-day raiding patrol.

Major Sir Terry "Zorro" Stone was bringing the Lancelot Lancers overland to the oasis on their maiden jeep expedition through the Great Sand Sea. The Lancers had formed three patrols—Gecko, Chameleon and Iguana—continuing their proud Lounge Lizard tradition. Their eighteen jeeps all had the same turquoise silhouette stenciled on the front bumpers: a lizard that looked like it had been run over by a road grader.

Each patrol had two of the U.S. volunteers attached—veterans of RFDS patrols—to teach desert driving techniques and to familiarize the Lancers with their new gun jeeps.

If all went as planned, by the time Lt. Col. Randal's Violet Patrol returned from its five-day raiding patrol, the Lancers would have arrived at X. A major reorganization of RFDS would take place at that time.

Mr. Zargo met Lt. Col. Randal at the landing strip. He had four tough-looking men with him. Each one had a playing card with the numbers trimmed off pinned to his faded khaki bush jacket. Every card was a different suit: spades, diamonds, clubs and hearts.

"Colonel," Mr. Zargo said, "I wanted you to have an opportunity to meet another element of my team coming in to reinforce our current intelligence operators. The crew I have in the field will be overextended now that we are increasing the number of RFDS patrols.

"My people will work two men per AO. One operative will be collecting, evaluating and conducting target reconnaissance of intelligence, while the other serves as guide for the RFDS patrol operating in the area.

"They are going to live in their assigned AO and switch off with each other when the patrols rotate back and forth to X. Patrols can link up with them as they travel out and drop them off on the way in."

"Mr. Spade, Mr. Diamond, Mr. Club and Mr. Heart," Lt. Col. Randal said. "If you men are as good as your counterparts, this is going to get interesting."

"You will not be disappointed, Colonel," Mr. Zargo said.

"Expect not," Lt. Col. Randal said. "Which one of you is going to be working with Ace?

The man with the spade pinned to his blouse said, "That would be me, Colonel."

"Will you be traveling with Violet Patrol when we pull out?"

"Affirmative."

"Link up with Lieutenant Kidd to get squared away. You can ride with me," Lt. Col. Randal said. "Mr. Treywick will hook you two up.

"If you require anything in the way of weapons or equipment, King should be able to arrange for what you need."

Captain Taylor Corrigan, DSO, MC, drove up in a jeep. Lt. Col. Randal, Lady Jane and Lt. Mandy stowed their gear in the back and climbed onboard. Rita and Lana squeezed in.

"I'm going to want a quick briefing on your operations during my absence, Taylor," Lt. Col. Randal said.

"Violet's pulling out within the hour."

LIEUTENANT CLONEL JOHN RANDAL HAD VIOLET PATROL ON THE move. The patrol was of short duration: five days. The idea was to cross the Great Sand Sea at its narrowest point, pick up Ace, then attempt to get to the hardball strip of the Via Balbia and find a location from which to attack enemy transports traveling along it.

There were problems associated with the plan.

Tobruk was in their AO. It marked the far end of the right boundary on the coast. The Afrika Korps was closed up on it, besieging the port. The Luftwaffe was active in the area.

And, the Via Balbia was not a simple single black-topped road running along the coast, although it was the only paved highway in Afrika Korps' entire line-of-communications and had only a single hardball strip. A series of secondary dirt roads, tracks and trails paralleled the Via Balbia for up to twenty-five miles inland.

German and Italian convoys ranging from one vehicle up to fifty trucks used these lesser roads. This close to the fighting front, convoys often ran at night to avoid being attacked by marauding RAF fighter sweeps.

To reach the hardball along the coast, Violet Patrol would have to cross the dirt roads, tracks and trails. This meant a stealthy infiltration dodging the bad guys, followed by an ambush of enemy transport, then a hell-for-leather exfiltration—most likely with the enemy in hot pursuit.

Violet Patrol had to be able to lose itself in the Great Sand Sea and be in a hide position under camouflage before daylight. The Luftwaffe was the biggest threat, and the German's fighters would be coming for them.

The Italian Air Force, the Regia Aeronautica, was also active in the region, and it could do real execution when it had a patrol pinned down in the desert.

But enemy air was not the only danger.

This close to the front, Italian and German armored cars patrolled the roads and tracks. While Axis armored cars did not normally operate off-road in the desert, they were capable of pursuit if they chose, particularly the Nazi Sd. Kfz. 222 light armored cars.

All of that was running through Lt. Col. Randal's mind as Violet Patrol's jeeps climbed up the escarpment and moved out above Oasis X.

The composition of the patrol varied from the last mission. Captain "Pyro" Percy Stirling, DSO, MC, was no longer with it. He had formed his own patrol, the Railroad Wrecking Crew II. There were only two rail lines available to Afrika Korps in this part of the world.

The Death or Glory Boy had orders to reduce that number to zero.

A navigator from the LRDG, Corporal Basil Thurgood, was aboard. The Corporal had nearly a year's experience navigating deep desert patrols. He was chafing under the restriction against shorts and sandals.

Lieutenant Fraser Llewellyn was in command of a jeep to bring the number of gun jeeps in Violet Patrol to six, so that it could conform to Lt. Col. Randal's new Standard Operating Procedure (SOP) that jeeps always operate in pairs. His jeep carried the mortar, which brought Violet Patrol's firepower up to the same standard as the other RFDS patrols.

At Lt. Col. Randal's suggestion, Lt. Llewellyn switched places with Spade in the command jeep for the first part of the day.

"Fraser, I'm going to use you as my training officer when the Lounge Lizards arrive," Lt. Col. Randal said. "The regiment has a lot of combat experience, and they've spent time in desert terrain—but nothing like the Great Sand Sea."

"Yes, sir."

"Do good," Lt. Col. Randal said. "You'll be first in line to get your own patrol after Travis McCloud gets his."

"Frankly, sir," Lt. Llewellyn said, "I am rather surprised you allowed me any chance at all in Raiding Forces considering the LRDG patrol, under my temporary command, was strafed the way it was."

"What'd you do wrong?" Lt. Col. Randal said, lighting a cigarette one-handed with his old U.S. 26th Cavalry Regiment Zippo as he drove.

"Failed to relocate to an alternate position once we were spotted by the Arabs on horseback, sir."

"Why didn't you?"

"If we had moved, your party would not have known where to find us," Lt. Llewellyn said.

"Also, sir, LRDG tends to trust the nomadic desert Arabs. Their appearance was not a cause for alarm."

"What would you do differently next time, Fraser?"

"Shoot the bloody Arabs the instant they tried to ride away from our camp," Lt. Llewellyn said. "Happens again, I shall."

"Roger that," Lt. Col. Randal said. "Never take a chance when the security of your troops is at risk."

69

"My big mistake was not shifting to a predestinated fallback position and leaving a guide behind to show you to our new laager when you arrived, Colonel."

"You won't ever make that mistake again," Lt. Col. Randal said.

"No, sir."

"You'll make a *different* one next time, Lieutenant," Lt. Col. Randal said. "Learn, adjust, then move on."

"I will, sir."

"Being in command," Lt. Col. Randal said, "ain't for the faint-hearted."

VIOLET PATROL DID NOT MAKE IT OUT OF THE GREAT SAND SEA BEFORE sundown. The patrol laagered and began the SOP activities it carried out each evening: vehicle maintenance, cleaning weapons, radio checks, etc.

Lieutenant Colonel John Randal got with Corporal Basil Thurgood to study the map. While the Corporal was the patrol navigator, the Raiding Forces Commander made it a point to know at all times where he thought the patrol was on the map. By necessity, his navigation was fairly rough dead reckoning.

The Corporal's was expected to be dead on.

"We are here, sir," Cpl. Thurgood said, pointing to a blank spot on the map. The patrol had approximately thirty miles to go before they broke out of the Great Sand Sea.

Lt. Col. Randal was secretly pleased to see that he was not more than a few miles off in his estimate of their position. Not bad navigation without the benefit of contour lines on a virtually blank map, while on the move driving a jeep. He was beginning to get a feel for the desert.

"You won't have time to do your normal checks tonight," Lt. Col. Randal said. "We're going to keep moving as soon as the patrol finishes their details and GG serves chow."

"Travel at night, sir?" Cpl. Thurgood said. "The LRDG never move under cover of darkness unless performing a reconnaissance of a point type target or conducting a raid on one that is known.

"Night movement is dangerous, sir."

Lt. Col. Randal said. "So's getting caught on the move in daylight by enemy air."

"Point taken, sir."

Lt. Col. Randal held a commander's call with ex-Captain Travis McCloud, Lieutenant Roy Kidd, Lieutenant Fraser Llewellyn, Waldo Treywick and Corporal Ned Pompedous, the acting patrol senior NCO.

Each man gave him a brief report on the status of the jeep they commanded. Fuel consumption, mechanical problems, personnel matters such as injuries, etc. There was not a lot to discuss.

No major problems.

Violet Patrol was on its third patrol. The men considered themselves veterans, and they were performing like old desert hands. Each vehicle had been reconfigured so that it met the individual standards of its commander and crew.

The troops loved their jeeps.

Considering the late start in the day, Violet Patrol had made excellent time. Lt. Col. Randal was glad to be back in the field, on the move. He enjoyed the pace of being a patrol leader.

In Lt. Col. Randal's career, he had led horse cavalry patrols with the US 26th Calvary Regiment and small foot patrols deep into the jungles of the Philippines chasing Huk guerrillas, motorcycle patrols at Calais and mule cavalry patrols in Abyssinia.

It had not taken long to appreciate how much flexibility the quarter-ton gun jeeps gave him. Men got footsore, horses and mules could be temperamental, and motorcycles did not carry much firepower. Jeeps were heavily armed and kept on going—provided they had tires, fuel and water.

If supplied by airdrops or from a clandestine RFDS supply dump, patrols could stay in the field indefinitely.

There were two things Lt. Col. Randal wanted to establish. Could a jeep patrol move through the desert at night, then hide by day? And, how difficult would it be to penetrate to the black-topped road on the coast, carry out an attack in the vicinity of Tobruk and exfiltrate?

"We'll be pulling out in two hours," Lt. Col. Randal said. "Have your men ready to go."

King had a blanket spread over a makeshift table. He and Spade were cleaning their weapons. Lt. Col. Randal joined them and went to work on his pistols with an oily rag and a shaving brush.

He started with the Colt 1911 .38 Supers. The weapons had been custom-built by Captain "Geronimo" Joe McKoy, as had his 9mm Browning P-35 and the .22 High Standard Military Model D. The work had been slight—it not being desirable to make extreme modifications to fighting pistols.

The triggers broke like glass rods. All the moving parts were hand-polished. The actions cycled like they ran on ball bearings.

The sights on the four pistols were of Capt. McKoy's own design, simply being oversized versions of the sights John Browning had originally designed. The front sight had a large gold bead mounted.

Lt. Col. Randal did not buy into the current school of thought on snap shooting from the hip being taught to SOE operatives and British Commandos. He liked to call his shots.

That said, Lt. Col. Randal would be the first to admit that in a close-range pistol fight he almost never saw the sights.

Spade said, "Raiding Forces is a strange outfit, Colonel."

"What makes you say that?"

"Old men, beautiful women, teenage officers, mercenaries, even a former enemy combatant," Ace said.

"Anyone can join. Everyone fights. Where do you recruit them?"

"They just turn up," Lt. Col. Randal said.

"It's what characterizes Raiding Forces," King said. "The Chief puts round pegs into round holes and square pegs into square holes."

"In my military experience," Spade said, "that *is* strange."

• • •

VIOLET PATROL PULLED OUT RIGHT ON TIME. THE MOON WAS RAT cheese round. It reflected blue off the sand. Visibility was about as good as it ever would get at night.

Lieutenant Colonel John Randal had substantial cross-country driving experience during the hours of darkness. As a teenager he had hunted coyotes from an old, jacked-up Model A convertible on his grandfather's ranch in California. He would chase them, shooting his pistol with one hand while he drove.

In the Great Depression, domestic livestock like chickens, lambs and calves were too valuable to be lost to predators. Weekends, his job had been to hunt down and exterminate the coyotes by whatever means.

That night work was good training for what lay ahead. And it gave Lt. Col. Randal reason to believe that, with practice, Violet Patrol could operate in the desert at night.

The difference was that when he had been chasing coyotes, his Model A had its lights on.

Behind enemy lines as they were, the jeeps could not afford that luxury. Unless they used German cat's eye running lights. He made a note to check with Lieutenant Wescott Huxley, MC, on the status of his project of having cat's-eye running lights made for Raiding Forces.

The patrol moved closed up tight in column. While the jeeps did not have their headlamps on, Lt. Col. Randal could signal to the vehicle behind him with his brake lights by tapping his brakes. Each driver had orders to tap his brakes immediately when the brake lights on the car in from of him flashed.

Rear-end collisions were a real possibility in the dark.

It soon became apparent that Violet Patrol needed to have a guide on foot leading the way. That was going to dramatically reduce the speed it could travel, but it would avert tragedy.

King led off.

After an hour, Spade replaced him. The two Mercs rotated the assignment—one riding; one walking.

The night patrol was man and machine against the terrain. The patrol had to get acclimated to operating jeeps under cover of darkness. After a while, a rhythm developed. Starting, stopping as the guide came back to strategize about an obstacle, shifting gears, going around things, dodging drop-offs or soft sand, up and over sand dunes … constantly attacking the terrain.

At times, Lt. Col. Randal had to dismount and go forward to inspect an obstruction and decide the next move.

Engines raced, tires spun, and the little convoy inched its way forward. Movement was jerky, stop and start. The night was liquid warm and full of dust thrown up by the spinning tires.

The moon was a Chinese lantern and the sky clear.

Lt. Col. Randal had to exercise iron discipline not to give in to the temptation to drive faster than the distance he could see ahead, identify a hazard and stop. The impulse to accelerate when the opportunity presented itself was almost overwhelming. That is where his nights spent chasing coyotes paid off—he knew that to do so guaranteed eventual disaster.

Violet Patrol traveled at a snail's pace, moving in lurches, drivers straining to see, fighting the wheel, inching forward; hurry up and wait. Men dismounted and walked beside the quarter tons at times, pushing at others. Hard, dusty, hot work, but the jeeps were making headway.

As the sky paled and began to show signs of brightening, the patrol broke out of the Great Sand Sea.

Lt. Col. Randal signaled the column to come on line as they drove into the limestone brush country. Each jeep chose its own path. Due to this simple tactic, any enemy aircraft spotting their single-file trail through the soft sand would see it suddenly vanish into thin air.

On Violet's first combat patrol it had operated during the hours of darkness in the limestone and brush country along the coastal belt. With that experience under their belts, the drivers found the going considerably easier this trip.

Lt. Col. Randal selected a good location in a wadi five miles out of the soft sand and laagered for the day hidden in thick brush under camouflage netting.

The sun burned down hot. GG began a meal. Vehicle maintenance and weapons cleaning commenced.

The troops were exhausted, but felt like they had accomplished something significant. Everyone was dialed-in, focused on the mission—functioning like a well-oiled machine.

Violet was on a war patrol. The Raiders intended to draw blood.

VIOLET PATROL MADE ITS WAY TO THE COAST, LYING UP BY DAY UNDER camouflage netting and traveling at night. When they came to a dirt road or a track, instead of crossing it, the patrol would drive down it until they came to a likely spot. Then one at a time the drivers would individually turn off the road and drive into the desert in a rough, on-line formation and continue on azimuth.

That way they left no visible sign they had ever been there.

The more the patrol operated at night, the better they became at it. But it was never easy and always challenging. As they closed in on the Via Balbia, it became evident that there was a lot of enemy traffic moving toward Tobruk. They skirted Afrika Korps rear area supply points and long-range field artillery positions. They lay in hiding and watched as convoys rolled past on the dirt roads.

During the day there was substantial enemy air activity overhead.

Lieutenant Colonel John Randal could have raided the supply points, artillery positions or ambushed the convoys they encountered, but that was not the object of the exercise. He wanted to reach the hardball Via Balbia.

On the third night, Lt. Col. Randal smelled the ocean. Not long after, he drove out of the limestone gravel desert floor onto a paved roadway. Violet Patrol was on Rommel's highway—at the moment the most strategic road in the entire world.

Immediately, Lt. Col. Randal came to a halt. The patrol turned around and drove back into the desert for fifty yards. He dispatched two gun jeeps under Lieutenant Roy Kidd to drive a mile in one direction and two jeeps under Waldo Treywick to drive one mile in the other direction to investigate the possibility of there being a convoy laagered anywhere near—or even better—a roadhouse they could raid.

Lt. Col. Randal kept ex-Captain Travis McCloud's jeep with him and waited for the two reconnaissance patrols to come back with their reports. He glanced at his Rolex: 0247 hours. Sunrise was approximately 0530 hours. If they were going to hit a target, it would have to be soon.

Getting caught traveling by daylight was not an option.

From the left came the sound of engines. A convoy of German trucks with their cat's eye running lights on rumbled past. There were fourteen vehicles in the column.

A few minutes later Waldo's two jeeps rolled up, following the enemy convoy.

"We seen 'em comin'," Waldo said. "Slid off t' the side, let 'em drive by."

"We'll tag on the end of the convoy," Lt. Col. Randal said. "Keep your eyes peeled for Roy. Follow my lead."

A quarter of a mile down the Via Balbia, they met Lt. Kidd's two-jeeps element coming back in their direction. Lt. Col. Randal braked to a halt. He and Lt. Kidd were about six inches apart sitting behind the wheels of their two jeeps facing in opposite directions.

"Swing in behind, Roy," Lt. Col. Randal ordered.

Violet Patrol caught up to the rear of the German convoy about a mile farther down the road. As soon as he saw the trucks, Lt. Col. Randal slowed down and followed at a distance.

"Stand by ready, Mr. Spade."

"Guns up, sir."

"King?"

"Affirmative, chief."

Lt. Col. Randal accelerated and caught up to the tail end truck in the convoy. Then he pulled around into the oncoming lane passing it. The German trucks were closed up, running about thirty miles an hour. It was nighttime, there was no chance of being attacked from the air, and the convoy was in Axis-controlled territory.

The truck drivers had nothing to fear except falling asleep at the wheel—they thought.

The first the drivers knew about the jeeps was when they pulled up alongside and drove past. The little quarter-ton cars, driving with their lights off, were virtually impossible for the Germans to see in their rearview mirrors.

It was not unknown for one Axis convoy to try to pass another on the Via Balbia. Hauling supplies is long, dull work. A little jockeying now and again to see who got to the next roadhouse first livened things up for the bored truckers.

In the dark and fog of war it was easy for the German drivers to confuse the jeeps with Kübelwagens.

Violet Patrol drove up level with the middle of the German convoy. The drivers they had passed looked down at the little column pulling by, took notice, started honking their horns to signal the lead truck to speed up, and the race was on.

Lt. Col. Randal laid his 45mm Brixia shoulder-fired mortar up on the hood of the jeep as he drove. He adjusted the twin Vickers K .303 machine guns mounted on the hood in front of him so they were angled at the German convoy. Then he put the accelerator to the metal.

The Germans were running closed up. Violet Patrol was spaced fifteen yards apart between gun jeeps. That made the two columns almost equal in length.

When Lt. Col. Randal pulled up to where he could see the lead vehicle traveling five trucks ahead, he raised the 45mm Brixia to his shoulder, aimed at the point truck, and triggered the weapon one-handed. Then he immediately grabbed the firing handle of the twin Vickers K .303s and opened.

Several things happened all at once.

The world exploded right in Violet Patrol's face. The lead truck must have been carrying artillery or ammunition because when the mortar round slammed inside its rear cargo compartment and detonated, it went up in a massive fireball. The second truck crashed into it and it exploded.

Simultaneously, thirty-five machine guns commenced hammering the convoy (thirty-four Vickers K .303s and one Breda 20mm) as one. The Germans began slamming on their brakes to avoid hitting the two exploding trucks—piling up in a massive collision. Tortured tires were screaming on the pavement.

Some truckers managed to steer off the road. Several trucks flipped over, rolling at speed when their tires hit the sand. Others crashed into each other. Tracers slicing through canvas truck covers caused a few to catch fire.

Lt. Col. Randal was stunned and momentarily blinded by the flash of the first and second trucks blowing up. Driving by instinct, he steered around the conflagration, fighting the wheel while somehow managing to keep the jeep on the pavement.

Then Violet Patrol was past the enemy convoy, guns going silent as jeep after jeep drove by their last visible target—a violent ripple effect followed by deafening silence.

Behind them, burning trucks were cooking off.

Immediately ahead over the next rise in the Via Balbia was the roadhouse where the convoy had been intending to stop. Trucks were parked next to it. Surprised Germans were streaming outside to see what was causing the explosions down the road.

Lt. Col. Randal never slowed down, "Let 'em have it."

He fired his twin Vickers Ks but only got in one short burst. Spade and King were leaning into their guns, fighting hard. The rest of the jeeps in Violet opened up as soon as their machine guns came to bear.

Men were screaming, tracers ricocheting off steel truck bonnets, hand grenades tossed from the speeding jeeps rocked the night: *KAAAAABOOOOM, KAAAAABOOOOM, KAAAAABOOOOM!*

In an instant, Violet Patrol raced past and was swallowed up in the night.

8
HARD INTELLIGENCE
SOFT TARGETS

JAMES "BALDIE" TAYLOR WAS ENJOYING THE VIEW AS HE SAT ON THE deck of Lieutenant Colonel John Randal's bungalow, which was carved out of solid white stone on the face of the cliff at the top of Oasis X. Major Sir Terry "Zorro" Stone was there. Captain the Lady Jane Seaborn and Lieutenant Mandy Paige were also present.

Major Clive Adair, Phantom Squadron N Commander/the "Mayor of X," and Captain Taylor Corrigan, RFDS's commanding officer, arrived. Ex-Captain Travis McCloud followed closely behind.

Freshly shaved and wearing a clean uniform, Lt. Col. Randal walked out, feeling the best he had felt since being wounded.

"Fantastic patrol, Colonel," Jim said. "Really stirred up a hornet's nest. Y-Service intercepts indicate Afrika Korps has gone glasshouse crazy at the idea British Forces were able to penetrate around behind Tobruk.

"The Operations staff at Grey Pillars is ecstatic."

"Yeah, well," Lt. Col. Randal said, "we won't be doing that again."

"Operations wants more and more," Jim said. "The moment he read Violet Patrol's report, Brigadier Davy authorized three additional desert raiding units like LRDG and RFDS to be raised when the men and equipment can be spared."

"Fine," Lt. Col. Randal said, "let them do it."

"I fail to understand," Jim said.

"The Via Balbia corridor in AO Don is a deathtrap," Lt. Col. Randal said. "At least the last fifty miles to Tobruk is.

"No place for RFDS to operate."

"Chock full of targets," Jim said. "I would have thought it was exactly what RFDS was looking for."

"Tell him what happened, Travis," Lt. Col. Randal said.

"Our patrol drove for five nights total—to and from—had to hide by day," ex-Capt. McCloud said. "We were in action for less than five minutes."

"A productive five minutes," Jim said.

"With the exception of knocking out a few enemy trucks," Lt. Col. Randal said, "which we could have done a lot easier somewhere else, Violet Patrol did not accomplish anything to justify the risk of the mission."

"I must be missing something, Colonel," Jim said. "Your patrol infiltrated the target area covertly. Hit and ran exactly the way you spelled out in Raiding Forces' mission statement ..."

"Soft targets, General," Lt. Col. Randal said. "Hard intelligence—soft targets.

"RFDS specializes in dirty deeds done quick ... and *easy*. Patrols arrive unannounced and unexpected, a long way from anywhere, preferably with no one around.

"We do what we need to do, then vanish into thin air," Lt. Col. Randal said.

"Rommel is forced to divert men to remote regions to guard isolated installations that he doesn't want to guard and we don't intend to raid again unless we change our mind. Tie down a lot of enemy troops twisting in the breeze doing absolutely nothing that way.

"And, we don't take unnecessary risks."

"The 'King's Own Pencil Pushers' at GHQ are hard at it planning more targets for you, Colonel," Jim said. "Staff fancies themselves special operations masterminds now that you provided them something to crow about."

"You don't use small-scale special forces like ours to fight conventional actions," Lt. Col. Randal said. "An armored car platoon could have accomplished the same mission."

"Not going to like it," Jim said. "The Operations staff are virtuosos at moving pins around on a map, drafting orders for someone else to carry out. Then dropping by the Long Bar at Shepard's for a cool one later on, exhausted from all that planning."

"Not Raiding Forces," Lt. Col. Randal said.

"How are they to ever earn an OBE without our patrols to do their bidding?" Jim asked.

Lt. Col. Randal glanced at Lady Jane. Perfectly straight poker face, no hint of a smile, very beautiful. She would be having a private conversation with Lieutenant General Claude Auchinleck in the near future.

"Our mission is to interdict Rommel's fuel supply, degrade his truck transport and tie down his troops," Lt. Col. Randal said.

"If GHQ attempts to dictate our patrol target selection from Grey Pillars, I'll go back to Seaborn House or return to my regiment."

"No need to get hasty, Colonel," Jim said. "You can count on me to run interference at the 'Puzzle Palace.' Everyone who works there seems chronically puzzled."

"Thanks, General."

"Nevertheless, you pulled off a spectacular raid—made Rommel scream."

"We got lucky."

"I need to get out on patrol," Jim said, "develop a better feel for what RFDS is experiencing on the ground."

"Anytime."

There was something of a problem. And it was a big one.

Normally Jim would refer the issue of GHQ meddling to Colonel Dudley Clarke. The A-Force commander would take steps. That would be the end of it. Unfortunately, he could not do that.

Colonel Clarke had vanished.

No one knew where he had gone, when he had left, or why. For all practical purposes, the Colonel was missing in action. His staff was concerned.

A-Force was intended to mystify others, not itself.

LIEUTENANT MANDY PAIGE, WITH HER CONSTANT BODYGUARD RITA Hayworth tagging along, took Jim Taylor on a tour of Oasis X. She briefed him on the state of the counterintelligence operation that Captain A. W. "Sammy" Sansom, Cairo Chief of Counterintelligence, had helped put in place while he was on site vetting the natives at the oasis.

Lt. Mandy and Mr. Zargo were engaged in a tiny but intense spy vs. spy campaign.

"The Italians have a wretched track record as a fighting force," Lt. Mandy said. "However, their intelligence agency the Servizio Informazioni Militare is reportedly well-organized and highly effective. SIM has paid operatives throughout the Western Desert."

Jim said, "I believe SIM to be more capable than the Abwehr—highly dangerous—not to be taken lightly."

"Mr. Zargo thinks so too," Lt. Mandy said. "He says while most Arabs do not like the Italians, the Blackshirts have a reputation for paying for information in gold."

"It's of vital importance, Mandy," Jim said, "for you to prevent anyone at X from providing intelligence to SIM."

"Capt. Sansom and Mr. Zargo are of a mind that it is only a matter of time until someone gives in to the temptation to strike it rich," Lt. Mandy said.

"In a place as small and isolated as X, it's impossible to keep a secret," Jim said, "especially where money is involved. Anyone spying for the Italians—you will find them out."

"Retribution," Lt. Mandy said, "will be swift and terminal."

"That's the spirit," Jim said.

"When it happens," Lt. Mandy said, "do you think John might loan me his .22 pistol with the silencer?"

LIEUTENANT COLONEL JOHN RANDAL, MAJOR SIR TERRY "ZORRO" STONE, Major Clive Adair, Captain Taylor Corrigan and ex-Captain Travis McCloud were discussing a reorganization of RFDS. Captain the Lady Jane Seaborn was sitting in on the meeting.

"I've been thinking about the Lancelot Lancers," Lt. Col. Randal said. "They've earned their regimental status on the battlefield. We don't want to do anything to take away from that."

"Thank you," Maj. Stone said. "The Lancers are down to less than sixty effectives. The lads have been hard used the past nine months."

"Here's my idea," Lt. Col. Randal said. "Change the name of Raiding Forces Desert Squadron to Raiding Forces Desert *Patrol*—RFDP. It'll consist of the patrols we have now, plus the Lancelot Lancers formed into three new patrols.

"RFDP will be under your command, Terry," Lt. Col. Randal said. "Pick one of your Yeomanry officers to command the Lancers or maybe offer the job to Jack Black."

"I shall take Major Black," Maj. Stone said.

"Good choice.

"Taylor, you continue in command of Desert Squadron, but we're going to need a new name for it. Something that sounds bigger," Lt. Col. Randal said.

"I'll assign Jeffery Tall-Castle's patrol to the Lancers since he's a Yorkshire Dragoon Yeomanry officer. Be a good fit.

"Dick Courtney's Gold Coast patrol will go to you, Taylor.

"When you get your patrol, Travis," Lt. Col. Randal said, "since your AVG has already been badged into the Lancers, you'll be there."

"Horney Toad Patrol," ex-Capt. McCloud said.

"Get it organized," Lt. Col. Randal said. "Sergeant Rawlston should have your jeeps ready."

"Roger that, sir!"

"We'll move U.S. people around to your patrol. You can recruit volunteers from the new troops Mad Dog has been training or a combination of both. Your call—you pick the men."

"Yes, sir."

"Percy's Railroad Wrecking Crew II will belong to you, Terry, as a RFDP asset, not part of the Regiment."

"Roger," Maj. Stone said.

"Violet Patrol stays independent," Lt. Col. Randal said. "A Raiding Forces asset. Since the Wing patrols are all named after colors, it's going to need a name change to avoid confusion.

"New officers and NCOs will be required to do a mission with me before being assigned."

"What do you want to call your outfit, Taylor?" Lt. Col. Randal asked.

"How about Desert Raiding Wing—DRW—sir?" Capt. Corrigan said. "No one will have any idea what that means."

"I like it," Lt. Col. Randal said, "The Regiment and the Wing."

"Ingenious," Maj. Stone said. "I can stay in titular command of the Regiment while commanding Desert Patrol, with Veronica Paige running MI-9 reporting to me.

"Even Father should approve for once."

"We'll refine the organization as we go," Lt. Col. Randal said, lighting a cigarette with his hard-used Zippo.

"Clive, you continue as Mayor of X in command of Phantom. Report to me."

"Yes, sir," Maj. Adair said.

"Clive," Lt. Col. Randal said, "when you brief me on a problem, brief me on the recommended solution at the same time."

"Understood, Colonel," Maj. Adair said.

"In fact, effective right now, that's Raiding Forces First Commander's Standing Order," Lt. Col. Randal said.

"Bring me a problem, bring me the solution."

WHILE THE RAIDING FORCES REORGANIZATION MEETING WAS TAKING place, a flurry of messages arrived in the Signals Center at Oasis X.

Lieutenant Colonel John Randal was directed to proceed at his own due speed to meet Vice Admiral Sir Randolph "Razor" Ransom, VC, KCB, DSO, OBE, DSC, at Raiding Forces Headquarters Middle East.

Jim Taylor was ordered to report in person to the Inner Allied Intelligence Bureau.

Captain the Lady Jane Seaborn received a request to return to Cairo.

Lieutenant Pamala Plum-Martin was notified to get the planes ready. The two Ansons were airborne within the hour. After a long flight, they landed back in Cairo.

Lt. Col. John Randal went straight to Raiding Forces Headquarters to find VAdm. Ransom, recently arrived in Egypt from Seaborn House; his grandson, Lieutenant Randy "Hornblower" Seaborn, DSC, RN, in from Tobruk; and ex-Technical Sergeant Hank W. Rawlston conducting an inspection of a line of ten weird-looking vehicles.

A Royal Engineer captain was giving the two a briefing.

"Called the DUKW," the RE officer said. "Bloody Yanks rejected them for service but sent these out to us under Lend-Lease.

"Then, the U.S. Army changed their mind. Decided to adopt the DUKWs after a U.S. Coast Guard ship ran aground in a storm that blew up unexpectedly during an amphibious demonstration with high-ranking dignitaries present. One of these amphibious trucks putt-putted out and rescued the crew in rough seas and high winds when Coast Guard cutters in the area were unable to reach it.

"What you are looking at, gentlemen, is a bloody swimming, two-and-a-half-ton GMC truck."

"What's the U.S. Army intend to do," Lt. Col. Randal asked, "with amphibious trucks?"

"No one has the vaguest idea," the Royal Engineer said. "We have no earthly use for them.

"Ten were listed on the manifest; however, a dozen arrived. We believe the Yanks dumped all they had in inventory on us to get rid of the beasts before the melodramatic rescue caused the U.S. Army to reconsider."

"What do we plan to do with swimming trucks?" Lt. Col. Randal asked.

"I need some way to carry out short- to intermediate-range raids along the coast," Lt. Seaborn said. "We want to use our two MAS boats for longer strike missions, sir."

"I see," said Lt. Col. Randal. Which meant he did not have any idea what his young naval officer was talking about.

"Commando is a bad word at Middle East Headquarters for some unfathomable reason," VAdm. Ransom said. "Operations staff does not seem to grasp the vulnerability of Rommel's exposed Mediterranean flank to small-scale, amphibious, pinprick raiding.

"The Prime Minister has tried in vain to get Middle East Command to employ the splendid Commando Brigade he had shipped out here—Layforce. GHQ simply refused to comply. Thought the PM was interfering.

"Frittered away the highly trained Commando troops in penny packets on fool's errands. Layforce has been disbanded."

"Heard about that, sir," Lt. Col. Randal said.

"GHQ's attitude on the subject is about to change," VAdm. Ransom said. "The Admiralty has seen fit to appoint me to a newly created position, Deputy Director Operations Division (Irregular)—DDOD(I). Which means I am now in charge of all private navies worldwide.

"Since Randy has his own private navy, he works for me. Actually, I work for him. My mission is to make sure he has the means to carry out his mission."

"Congratulations, Admiral," Lt. Col. Randal said. "Right man, right job."

"When Randy messaged me through Phantom about these new amphibians, I caught the first flight out," VAdm. Ransom said.

"We mean to figure out how to put them to use."

"No one seems to know the first thing about DUKWs," Lt. Seaborn said. "The amphibious trucks are large enough for a single one to transport a complete raiding party if we so choose.

"The drawback is the DUKWs do not have the sea speed to ingress and egress the target area in the time we have to carry out a raid if the point of departure is our Sea Squadron advanced base at Tobruk.

"One of the problems we have encountered is that the Via Balbia does not run right along the coastline. In places it cuts several miles inland," Lt. Seaborn said.

"Raiders have to go ashore, do a forced march overland, mine the road, march back, return to the boat and be gone before daylight.

"You reckon, Colonel," ex-Sgt. Rawlston said, "we could fit a jeep in the back o' one a' those deuce and a halves?"

"Take a crane to lift it in," Lt. Col. Randal said.

"DUKWs come with a fittable lift device, sir," the Royal Engineer captain said, "Only has to be mounted.

"Designed to load and off-load supplies. We believe the Yanks are thinking the amphibious trucks can deliver supplies ship-to-shore—a miniature sea shuttle cargo hauler."

"Why would you wish to put a jeep—whatever the devil that is," VAdm. Ransom asked, "in the back of a DUKW?"

"A jeep is a small, open-topped car, Admiral," Lt. Col. Randal said. "Four-wheel drive, loaded with machine guns. We use 'em for desert patrolling.

"If Sergeant Rawlston is able to piggyback our gun jeeps on the DUKWs—and you and Randy can find some way to ferry the jeeps behind enemy lines—our Sea Squadron operators will have the ability to land the jeeps on a deserted beach, drive to their target and back, sir."

"Understood," VAdm. Ransom said. "Original thinking there, Sergeant Rawlston. Extraordinary! Any more bold thoughts? Do not hold back, man."

"They'll fit, Colonel," ex-Sgt. Rawlston called from where he had climbed up on the DUKW to measure the bed of the truck with a steel tape.

"Barely squeeze 'em in—inches to spare. But we can do it. No sweat, sir, if we have a crane."

"How do we transport the DUKWs to the target area, grandfather?" Lt. Seaborn asked. "Enemy air starts at daylight at Tobruk. We cannot be caught at sea returning from a mission."

"There is a monstrosity called a Landing Craft Tank, or LCT," VAdm. Ransom said, "used for the first time in the evacuation from Crete. Proved rather less than seaworthy. Wallows like a drunken whale.

"Navy hates the thing … redesigning it.

"Which means," VAdm. Ransom said, "we can have one of the original LCTs if we want it. If the craft is capable of shipping armored tanks, it will be able to hold quite a lot of two-and-a-half-ton trucks—nine or ten.

"Park it off shore like a floating island."

"In that case, Admiral," Lt. Col. Randal said, "we can station a full six-jeep patrol on board—or maybe two smaller four-jeep patrols."

"I shall arrange to have an LCT assigned to Raiding Forces straightaway, Colonel," VAdm. Ransom said.

"Randy, sea trials begin immediately."

"We need specialists from the States to come out and demonstrate how to operate these DUKWs," Lt. Seaborn said. "Certainly the company who builds them has technicians they can send."

"Amphibious Jeep Commandos," VAdm. Ransom said. "Revolutionary."

"Craziest idea Raiding Forces has come up with yet," Lt. Col. Randal said.

9

THE LAND OF DARKNESS

JAMES "BALDIE" TAYLOR ARRIVED AT RFHQ AS THE INSPECTION OF THE DUWs was winding down. When Lieutenant Colonel John Randal saw the look on the MI-6 man's face, he immediately clicked on. They had worked together a long time and didn't always need words to communicate.

In Lt. Col. Randal's (and Captain the Lady Jane Seaborn's) private quarters on the third floor, Jim immediately launched into what amounted to an abridged Warning Order.

"Target Persia," Jim said, "also known as Iran—sometimes called the 'Land of Darkness'—neutral, but friendly with Germany.

"The Nazi's intentions are to transform Persia into a power base from which to penetrate the Near and Middle East. To that end, they have provided German 'civilians' to work in key positions in the Persian National Telephone Company and the Persian State Railroad—3,000 of them, by best estimates.

"The German invasion of Russia has been a walkover so far. The Nazis are driving hard on Moscow. The Russians are surrendering by the millions. And that, Colonel, is no exaggeration," Jim said.

"What it means to us in Middle East Command is this: if the Russians collapse, the Germans will have enormous numbers of troops available to divert to Egypt, Palestine and Syria through Persia.

"The Chiefs of Staff have concluded that the loss of the Anglo-Persian oilfields and the Abadan refineries would make it problematic—read impossible—for our side to carry on the war in the Middle East," Jim said.

"With only two German divisions, the 21st Panzer Division and the 5th Light Division—which is currently in the process of being reconfigured into the 15th Panzer Division—acting as stiffeners to the Italians, Rommel's Afrika Korps has run rings around our army and made fools out of our current crop of Allied generals.

"Imagine what the Desert Fox could accomplish with a massive infusion of German troops, tanks and aircraft," Jim said.

"I'd rather not," Lt. Col. Randal said.

"Four days before OPERATION BARBAROSSA, Hitler's invasion of Russia, Turkey and the Nazis signed a treaty of mutual friendship and nonaggression. Before the ink was dry, the Germans blitzed almost all the way to the capital of Russia.

"The Turks see the handwriting on the wall. *They* are the next domino. Now Turkey has expressed a desire to initiate a secret dialogue with the UK.

"Politicians never learn," Jim said. "Always imagine they can come to terms with Hitler rather than deal with him by strength. It is impossible to negotiate away danger with a madman, especially one backed by an evil regime devoid of any semblance of morality. Force is the only thing that works."

"A dead Nazi," Lt. Col. Randal said, "is no threat."

"Right you are, Colonel," Jim said. "England is preparing a preemptive joint invasion of Persia in company with the Russians so that we can be in position to fight the Germans when they come.

"You have been requested, by name, to be the Special Operations Commander."

"I'm getting a lot of practice," Lt. Col. Randal said, "attacking countries that don't know we're at war with 'em."

"What will Persia make? Three?" Jim asked.

"Four," Lt. Col. Randal said, "if you count the Portuguese Protectorate of Rio Bonita invaded by Raiding Forces one dark night."

"How could I forget?"

• • •

Lieutenant Colonel John Randal and Captain the Lady Jane Seaborn were sitting at a table in Groppi's. They were in a corner at the back of the room having lunch. Lady Jane was entertaining him with stories about her day's adventures, as she always did. He was half listening to her, half distracted by visions of gun jeeps, DUKWs, Landing Craft Tanks (LCTs) and the upcoming invasion of Persia that kept dancing in his head. He was enjoying being there with her, alone, in a room full of people.

There was a raucous party of officers gathered at the bar where the center of attention was a slim, black-haired girl seated on a stool.

Lt. Col. Randal could not get a clear view of her but she seemed familiar.

"Amal Atrash," Lady Jane said. "A local singer. At the age of thirteen she married the Druze Emir. He fell madly in love with her, but she eventually divorced him to come to Cairo to pursue her music."

"Became the toast of the town."

"A singer," Lt. Col. Randal said, remembering where he had known her. Different name then, no mention of singing or any emir.

He was under the impression she was a contract employee of Special Operations Executive. Or at least had been when SOE used her as one of the women who vetted him for a security clearance he did not need before his mission into Abyssinia.

"Before OPERATION EXPORTER was carried out against Syria," Lady Jane said, "Amal was dispatched by SOE with goatskin bags stuffed with gold sovereigns to bribe her ex-husband into ordering his people not to resist our troops when we crossed the Jebel Druze territory on the way to Damascus."

"Goatskin bags?"

"Not quite sure what Amal actually did with the gold," Lady Jane said. "Nevertheless, the Druze did not oppose us."

"She and the emir remarried. As a reward for keeping the Druze on the sideline, he was appointed defense minister of the provisional Syrian government.

"Amal celebrated by riding into Damascus clad in traditional Arab dress escorted by a troop of Druze horsemen clattering through the streets to the Grand Serail."

"Some story," Lt. Col. Randal said, lighting a cigarette with his U.S. 26th Cavalry Zippo.

"Gets better," Lady Jane said. "As a good, or maybe not so good, Druze girl, she hated the French because of their occupation of her tribal lands. She and her husband lobbied for an independent Druze nation.

"No luck. We did not want to antagonize the French ..."

"Antagonize?" Lt. Col. Randal said. "I blew up one of their bridges, and Middle East Command invaded Vichy French Syria. We sure wouldn't want to make anybody mad."

"True," Lady Jane laughed. "To continue, John, the Abwehr contacted Amal and invited her to Ankara to discuss Druze autonomy. By this time, she and the emir were divorced for the second time.

"Perhaps he was not providing her with the requisite funds. It is said she 'spends money like a rain cloud scatters water,'" Lady Jane said. "So, Amal was off to strategize with the Nazis."

"Really?"

"Alas, her departure was observed by MI-5," Lady Jane said.

"Nigel Davidson, the 9th Army liaison officer to the Free French who knew Amal, boarded the train at the last station before the railroad crosses into Turkey. He took her off and turned her over to the French Security Service, the Deuxième Bureau.

"Eventually the French deported Amal to Jerusalem."

"Sounds like she gets around," Lt. Col. Randal said.

"Major General Louis Spears, the general officer commanding the Syrian mission to the Free French, was certainly taken with her," Lady Jane said.

"He told me Amal was one of the most beautiful women he has ever seen, with 'eyes the color of the sea you have to cross over to reach … Paradise.'"

"Gen. Spears said that?"

"Yes, John."

"Well, that's word for word the way I described you to the General, Jane, at a cocktail party," Lt. Col. Randal lied, "when I was making the rounds pretending to be the commander of 1 SAS Brigade for Dudley."

As best he could remember, Lt. Col. Randal had never met the commander of the Syrian Mission, Maj. Gen. Spears.

Brigadier Raymond J. "R. J." Maunsell appeared at their table in time to suffer collateral damage from the heart attack smile Lady Jane was beaming at Lt. Col. Randal.

Lady Jane knew, for a fact, that Lt. Col. Randal had never met the commander of the Syrian Mission. Also, she had read Amal's confidential report on him.

Lt. Col. Randal did not know that Lady Jane had read Amal's confidential SOE report.

"A blind man could see he was interrupting," R. J. said. "Duty calls. I shall be brief."

"Are you aware," Lt. Col. Randal asked, "you have a German agent sitting at the bar, sir?"

"Amal Atrash," R. J. said, taking a seat and producing his elegant silver cigarette case. "Recently ejected from the St. David Hotel for arranging 'orgies' in her suite.

"Back in Cairo now, lucky us. Bowls over British officers with the speed and accuracy of a machine gun."

"Orgies?"

"Her ex, the emir, did me the professional courtesy of sending a note saying he was planning to dispatch someone to 'put her down.' The old boy is taking his ex-wife's antics personally, stain on the family name, what?"

Lt. Col. Randal said, "A hit man?"

"Would have made things simpler if he had done it. Naturally, I had no other choice but to respond that His Majesty's Military Government took a dim view of murder."

"John thought I was embellishing the story," Lady Jane said.

"Difficult to exaggerate," R. J. said. "Unfortunately, I fear the girl is not long for this world.

"Why?" Lady Jane asked. "She seems so full of life."

"The Germans want Amal dead because she worked with the British. The French want her dead because she collaborated with the British, the Germans, and plotted against France for an independent Druze state.

"Her ex-husband wants her dead for reasons of the heart.

"Oh, and Captain Sansom wants her dead for all the above. Feels it would be bad form to arrest the emir for murder. Thinks we would be doing everyone a favor if we eliminated her.

"Once a spy, always a spy in Sammy's eyes."

"The war," Lt. Col. Randal said, "is a lot simpler on the sharp end of the stick."

"Cairo," Brig. Maunsell said, "is a snake pit—why I want a word with you, Colonel.

"A complication has developed involving our favorite *femme fatale* you may be able to help me resolve.

"Rocky?"

"Miss Runborg has been standing by, waiting for the Abwehr to deliver a long-range radio to her apartment," R. J. said.

"The Nazi desert specialist, Count Almásy, whom Parker and Brandy are trying to figure a way to capture, is supposed to ferry an agent with the radio from Tripoli across the Great Sand Sea to the outskirts of Cairo, who will then deliver it to Rocky here in town.

"We have been staking out her apartment building, but no joy," R. J. said. "Without the set, Rocky does not have any means of making contact with her handlers in Berlin.

"Since she is now working for Security Intelligence Middle East—meaning me—it is paramount for her to have access to a wireless in order to transmit the messages *we* want passed to the Abwehr," R. J. said.

Lt. Col. Randal said, "I can see that might be a problem."

"I went to the Signals Division at GHQ. Asked if they could build a radio of a type Rocky could explain away as having obtained illicitly on the local black market here in Cairo," R. J. said.

"Signals listened politely, said that they were in the business of ensuring enemy operatives did *not* have radio transmitters to send messages to their masters, were not inclined to make one for a known Nazi spy. And they sent me on my way."

"Sometimes, R. J.," Lt. Col. Randal said, "I get the impression that we're not taking this war seriously."

"Agreed," Lady Jane said.

"Perhaps," Brig. Maunsell said, "you might be persuaded to prevail on Major Adair to have Phantom construct a transmitter for Rocky so we can put the Great Game in play."

"Love to," Lt. Col. Randal said.

LIEUTENANT COLONEL JOHN RANDAL AND CAPTAIN THE LADY JANE Seaborn were in the back of her Rolls Royce, en route to Raiding Forces Headquarters. Colonel Ouvry Roberts, the Chief of Staff of the 10th Indian Division, was flying in to brief Raiding Forces on their role in OPERATION COUNTENANCE, the invasion of Persia.

Time was short. The Colonel was flying back out as soon as his briefing was completed.

"The Prime Minister had been growing increasingly dissatisfied with Field Marshal Wavell for some time," Lady Jane said. "When OPER-ATION BATTLEAX failed, the PM felt it was the excuse he needed to relieve him—even though Archibald had recommended against the operation."

"Doesn't sound right," Lt. Col. Randal said.

"The Field Marshal *was* tired," Lady Jane said. "Even so, Churchill did him an injustice.

"To provide political cover, the Prime Minister came up with an elegant political solution. Rather than simply fire him, the PM had

Archie switch jobs with the Commander-in-Chief of India Command, Lieutenant General Claude Auchinleck.

"Archie goes off to a quiet theatre for a rest cure, and the Middle East gets a new commander."

"Pretty slick," Lt. Col. Randal said. "But bringing in the best-qualified commander would have been a better idea."

"Agreed," Lady Jane said. "Claude is an Indian Army man. He has not been well-received at GHQ or by the Regular Army officers commanding the large maneuver elements."

"Why not?" Lt. Col. Randal said.

"Indian Army officers and some regular officers who have spent much of their service in the colonies are thought only capable of handling native troops," Lady Jane said.

"That kind of short-sighted thinking is a fact of life in a military system where a man can be judged by the cut of his buttonhole."

"Colonel Roberts is an India Army man," Lt. Col. Randal said. "I'd put him up against any officer I've ever served with."

"We British have a habit of prejudging based on a rigid pecking order: schools, clubs, regiments," Lady Jane said.

"As a demonstration of confidence, the Prime Minister is promoting Claude to Field Marshal. Not that it will change anything.

"My brief association with the new Field Marshal has confirmed my impression that the Prime Minister made a blunder," Lady Jane said.

"Blunder?"

"The Middle East Command is over Claude's head," Lady Jane said. "Claude is very likeable, but he did allow his battle plans to fall into the hands of the Nazis in Norway—let the side down."

"We'll see how General Auchinleck does," Lt. Col. Randal said, "when Raiding Forces invade the 'Land of Darkness.'"

"Actually not," Lady Jane said. "In a bizarre twist, Persia falls under India Command.

"Instead of a rest cure, now Archie has a new war to fight. Poor man, he deserved a quiet duty station for a change."

"What do you want to bet," Lt. Col. Randal said, "we're about to be informed by Colonel Roberts that Persia is the most strategically important piece of real estate on the planet. Unfortunately, there aren't enough troops, tanks, airplanes or ships to guarantee success of the mission …"

"Not taking that wager, John."

COLONEL OUVRY ROBERTS HAD ARRIVED AT RAIDING FORCES Headquarters by the time Flanigan pulled up.

Lieutenant Colonel John Randal, Captain the Lady Jane Seaborn, Vice Admiral Sir Randolph "Razor" Ransom, James "Baldie" Taylor, Major Jack Black, Captain Hawthorne Merryweather, Captain "Geronimo" Joe McKoy, Waldo Treywick, Lieutenant Randy "Hornblower" Seaborn, ex-Captain Travis McCloud, Squadron Leader Paddy Wilcox, Lieutenant Pamala Plum-Martin and Sergeant Major Mike "March or Die" Mikkalis—all the senior Raiding Forces people who happened to be at RFHQ at the moment, for one reason or the other—filed into the briefing room.

King took up a position at the door.

VAdm. Ransom said to Lt. Col. Randal as they were taking their seats, "We have our LCT, Colonel. Navy was glad to be rid of one of the monstrosities.

"No crew … we shall be forced to improvise."

"Maybe Randy can recruit Sea Rover Scouts again, sir," Lt. Col. Randal said, "or Girl Guides."

"Not for this assignment," VAdm. Ransom laughed.

"The Sea Rover Scouts worked out well, sir," Lt. Seaborn said. "One of my better ideas, actually."

"Landing Craft Tanks are a different proposition than small craft," VAdm. Ransom said. "Over 150 feet in length, a range of a 1,000 miles with a crew of two officers and ten ratings—require specialist's skill sets. In high seas, LCTs are difficult craft to handle.

"The skipper is going to have to be a seafaring man."

"Don't tell Brandy, sir," Lt. Col. Randal said. "She'll want the job."

"With a top speed of eight knots," VAdm. Ransom said "LCTs travel too slow to be of interest to my daughter.

"There is a pool of unemployed sailors on the beach whose ships were sunk off Crete. May be possible to press-gang a few—most likely no officers or senior ratings will be available," VAdm. Ransom said.

"Those, I have no idea where to find."

"You'll think of something, Admiral," Lt. Col. Randal said.

Standing in front of the briefing room, Col. Roberts uncovered a map on a three-legged stand. "OPERATION COUNTENANCE/ BISHOP, the invasion of Persia—also known as Iran, 'land of the Aryans.'

"With Nazi armies fast approaching the outskirts of Moscow, it has become alarmingly apparent the Russians are on the point of total capitulation. If that should take place, the Germans will be able to pivot and strike into the Middle East through Persia, Turkey, Syria, etc.

"The oil refinery located on Abadan Island is a strategic asset that must not be allowed to fall under Nazi control. Great Britain is dependent on Persian oil production.

"The Trans Persian Railway has to be kept open so that U.S. Lend-Lease war material can be shipped overland from the Persian Gulf to Russia, the only point on the globe where that is possible."

Lady Jane nudged Lt. Col. Randal with her riding-booted-knee and whispered, "Genie reader."

"From a strategic perspective," Col. Roberts said, "we urgently need to establish a British blocking force in Persia to prevent either of those things transpiring."

Col. Roberts pointed to the map. "The scheme of maneuver has not been finalized, even though the operation is set to launch in seventy-two hours. The newly-promoted Commander of Ground Forces Major General William Slim, commander of 10th Indian Division, has only recently been designated ground commander though he has yet to lay eyes on the plan. He is away from the division and is en route to rejoin as we speak.

"What I can tell you about the order of battle is that there will be a three-pronged attack by 10th Indian Division, 8th Indian Division, and an *ad hoc* cavalry brigade that is being reinforced to division strength striking out of Iraq.

"A naval force will be coming in from the Persian Gulf, styled OPERATION BISHOP.

"A *coup de main* contingency plan, OPERATION DOVER, is being drawn up to seize Abadan Island in advance of the main attack, should it become necessary.

"Persia is strategically located between Russia and India—ancient enemies the Persians have played against each other for centuries and who now are united in a death struggle against the Nazis.

"The Shah has fallen under the influence of the Nazis ... possibly due to the Aryan connection. It is reported that he lives in terror of offending Hitler.

"He may either not understand the nature of the British Russian Alliance, or he may not be receiving a true picture of the situation due to palace intrigue from the sycophants advising him. The Shah does not seem to comprehend that Persia is going to be invaded by either the Allies or the Axis. The only question is which one does it first.

"Needless to say, the tipping point has been reached; diplomacy exhausted, we are going in. This is a joint operation with the Russians who will be attacking overland with three armies.

"However, there are complications.

"We do not have the ability to communicate with the Russians at the tactical level, so we do not have any idea what their intentions are. Persia is one of the most undeveloped countries in the world. Their internal road network is virtually nonexistent, which means our forces will be moving cross-country.

"The 8th Indian Division received its Warning Order three weeks ago. Unfortunately, the 8th was a division on paper only at that point in time, consisting of a single brigade.

"In an extraordinary feat of staff work and logistics, the division has been brought up to strength by the addition of two more brigades and an artillery regiment and by transferring in individual troops to make up shortages in the under-strength battalions.

"Unfortunately, the reconstituted 8th Division has never conducted so much as a single training maneuver as a unit.

"Finally, General Slim has yet to see the final operational plan, much less approve it," Col. Roberts said.

"When the General found out he had been nominated to be the ground commander, acting on my recommendation, he cabled Field Marshal Auchinleck to request that Colonel Randal be loaned to OPERATION COUNTENANCE to serve in the capacity as its Special Operations Commander.

"FM Auchinleck graciously acceded," Col. Roberts said. "Unfortunately, there is no Special Operations Plan. We need one.

"Colonel Randal, we want you to focus your attention on the southwestern quadrant of Persia—specifically Khuzestan Province. The island of Abadan and the port of Bandar Shahpur are specific targets we could use your help securing."

"Roger," Lt. Col. Randal said.

"Elements of the Royal Navy, Royal Australian Navy, the Royal Indian Navy, plus some odd navy reserve units I have never personally heard of before—the Royal Navy Patrol Service—transporting two battalions of Indian troops will make the assault, striking out of the Gulf. A number of German, Italian and Persian vessels berthed at both locations will have to be boarded.

"It is my understanding that Raiding Forces has experience taking down enemy ships."

"None," Lt. Col. Randal said, "we care to admit to, sir."

"An airborne landing is wanted at Haft-l-Khel to seize control of the oilfield and to evacuate the British nationals who operate it," Col. Roberts said.

"Colonel Randal, you are tasked with planning, organizing and executing that mission.

"This concludes my briefing," Col. Roberts said.

"To summarize, the purpose of OPERATION COUNTENANCE/ BISHOP is to secure strategic oil production and safeguard the Trans Persian Railway for Lend-Lease.

"For *public* consumption, we are not 'invading Persia.' We are simply 'pre-positioning' British troops to protect the Persians and to shield Turkey from the evil Nazis.

"Col. Randal, any questions or comments you wish to make before I have to depart?"

"The Turks escorted me out of their country—invited me to never come back," Lt. Col. Randal said.

"Best not mention I'm involved."

10
OPERATION COUNTENANCE

LIEUTENANT COLONEL JOHN RANDAL WALKED COLONEL OUVRY Roberts out of Raiding Forces Headquarters. Ex-Technical Sergeant Hank W. Rawlston was standing by to drive him to Cairo, where he was immediately flying out to Iraq to link up with Major General William "Bill" Slim at the 10th Indian Division.

"There is something you should be aware of," Col. Roberts said. "OPERATION COUNTENANCE has been scheduled and postponed several times. I am afraid we have lost the element of surprise—the Persians know we are coming."

"Any chance, sir," Lt. Col. Randal said, "we're attacking with overwhelming force?"

"You do have a sense of humor," Col. Roberts said. "The Persian Army will likely outnumber us as much as the Iraqis did at Habbaniya.

"Persia has a sizable air force, which we supplied and trained.

"And our sea component—on which we are relying heavily—can only be described as a heterogeneous fleet of mismatched craft of several classes, hastily thrown together from three different navies with soldiers—instead of Royal Marines or Commandos—on board acting as our landing parties."

Lt. Col. Randal said, "I would like to borrow some of the men from the Strike Force we had at Habbaniya, if that's possible, sir."

"The 1st King's Own Royal Regiment has seen hard service," Col. Roberts said. "The battalion commander, Lt. Col. Everett, was grievously wounded and two company commanders killed. The troops suffered heavy casualties in the fight to take Baghdad and then the follow-on operations into Syria.

"Afraid the KORR is not in any condition to participate in COUNTENANCE.

"You should know, Colonel," Lt. Col. Randal said, "Raiding Forces is going to find it difficult to pull together more than a token force on this short notice. Any of the old Strike Force men you can let me have will be a big help."

"I shall send out a call for volunteers," Col. Roberts said. "Do not count on much."

"We'll take what men you can give us, sir."

LIEUTENANT COLONEL JOHN RANDAL REASSEMBLED THE PEOPLE WHO had attended Colonel Ouvry Roberts' briefing. Everyone present was a professional. The tension in the group was palpable.

"Raiding Forces is on alert for an operation," Lt. Col. Randal said. "Only, other than the airborne assault on Haft-l-Khel, we did not get an actual assignment."

"The Mission Statement left something to the imagination," James Taylor said. "As I understood it, you are authorized to develop your own, Colonel."

"Well, that could be a problem, General," Lt. Col. Randal said.

"RFDP has its patrols scattered from here to the 'Shores of Tripoli'; Sea Squadron is at Tobruk, and there are no other British paratroop units to carry out an airborne drop."

Jim said, "Makes it challenging."

Captain the Lady Jane Seaborn said, "India Command must actually believe A-Force's misinformation campaign about Airborne Forces in Middle East Command. If Dudley was anywhere to be found, he would be delighted to hear it's working … at least against our side."

"What I took away from Colonel Roberts' briefing," Vice Admiral Sir Randolph "Razor" Ransom said, "is that Raiding Forces needs to plan for three components of OPERATION COUNTENANCE/ BISHOP.

1. The drop on Haft-l-Khel;
2. Boarding enemy ships moored at Abadan and Bandar Shahpur;
3. Special Operations of our own choosing."

"We may already be involved with BISHOP," Lieutenant Randy "Hornblower" Seaborn said.

"How might that be?" Lt. Col. Randal said.

"The second Sea Squadron troop finally arrived from Seaborn House. 'Headhunter' Hoolihan's troop was scheduled to rotate back to RFHQ for rest and to refit after months of nonstop raiding," Lt. Seaborn said.

"Before they could depart Tobruk, Captain Pelham-Davies received an urgent request from the Royal Australian Navy for experienced Commandos to conduct a hostile ship-boarding training program.

"Butch took his whole troop. They flew out of Alexandria to an undisclosed location on the Persian Gulf aboard two RAN Catalinas over a week ago."

"Admiral," Lt. Col. Randal said, "can you find out what that's about?"

"Has to be BISHOP," VAdm. Ransom said. "If there were ever a perfect operation for the Deputy Director Operations Division (Irregular) to cut his teeth on, this would be it. Expect my fullest cooperation."

"We're going to need every bit of target information we can get our hands on," Lt. Col. Randal said.

"In progress," Jim said. "While you were walking Col. Roberts out, I was working the phone.

"Couriers should begin arriving from every intelligence organization operating in the Middle East Command within the hour, containing everything available on Persia."

"Perfect," Lt. Col. Randal said.

"We can hope. The country is called the 'Land of Darkness' for a reason … it's a mysterious place. The nickname has its roots in a fable, but the fact is, we do not know much about what goes on there," Jim said.

"Information about Haft-l-Khel, Abadan and Bandar Shahpur should be available because British subjects work in the oil industry. It's a given some of them will be clandestine intelligence operatives on our payroll."

"Randy," Lt. Col. Randal said, "if it turns out Butch is involved with BISHOP, I want you to get over there as fast as you can and act as Raiding Forces liaison to the Royal Australian Navy or whoever will be running the naval side of things."

"Yes, sir,"

"Paddy," Lt. Col. Randal said, "you're responsible for planning the air portion of the drop on Haft-l-Khel. Raiding Forces is the only airborne unit in Africa, and we're never going to be able to assemble in time to organize a large enough team to conduct the mission."

"Wilco," Squadron Leader Paddy Wilcox said.

"The 1st KORR, the only British battalion to have ever carried out a tactical air-landing," Lt. Col. Randal said, "isn't available either."

"You just answered my first question," Sqn. Ldr. Wilcox said. "Trying to make this difficult, aren't they?"

"Think of something," Lt. Col. Randal said.

"Yes, sir."

"Travis," Lt. Col. Randal said, "you assist Paddy. The tactical ground plan is your responsibility. We'll see if you learned anything teaching Airborne Operations at the Infantry School."

"Roger."

"Jack," Lt. Col. Randal said, "I'm designating you COUNTENANCE Operations Officer. Hand off your other duties upon conclusion of this meeting. Take charge of mission planning and get this show organized."

"Yes, sir," Major Jack Black said. "Are you going to want duplicate map boards in your private quarters, as usual?"

"Same way we always do it," Lt. Col. Randal said.

"Sir!"

"What's the status of the Lancelot Lancers, Sergeant Major?" Lt. Col. Randal asked.

"In the field, training," Sergeant Major Mike "March or Die" Mikkalis said. "Mrs. Seaborn and Lt. Parker have been introducing the lads to the mysteries of soft sand driving techniques in their new gun jeeps.

"Maj. Stone is supposed to arrive in the next few days to lead the regiment to Oasis X."

"Don't let them depart RFHQ," Lt. Col. Randal said, "under any circumstances. They're the only parachute unit we can assemble in the time we have before H-hour.

"Alert the Lancers for a combat jump. Have Mad Dog initiate pre-jump refresher training immediately."

"Sir!"

"Pam," Lt. Col. Randal said, "you're mission Air-Officer. I need you here to advise me—not off flying."

"Absolutely, John."

"I'll draw up a list of key Raiding Forces personnel and prioritize it," Lt. Col. Randal said, "You'll need to figure out how to locate the men wherever they are and have them flown back here to RFHQ.

"Aye aye, sir."

"Jane," Lt. Col. Randal said, "we're going to be shuffling people and equipment around. Probably need to requisition or do things no one has thought about yet ..."

"Awkward, John, we shall not be able to call on Middle East Command. COUNTENANCE is not their operation," Lady Jane said.

"India Command is far too distant to be of help in the time we have before Raiding Forces has to go into action."

"Do your magic," Lt. Col. Randal said. "We're going to need the right people in the right place, with the right gear."

"Agreed," Lady Jane said. "Leave the arrangements to me."

"Hawthorne," Lt. Col. Randal said, "time to break out your bag of dirty tricks. COUNTENANCE seems like it's perfect for the old para-chutes-weighted-down-with-blocks-of-ice stunt."

"Yes, sir."

"We want the Persians shifting troops to places where the only thing they'll find is damp parachutes," Lt. Col. Randal said.

"My thought precisely, Colonel," Captain Hawthorne Merry-weather said. "Amazing, the fear and despondency a handful of silk canopies can instill in the opposition."

"Let me hear your tactical deception plan as soon as you have one," Lt. Col. Randal said. "Get with Pam to work out the air assets to execute it."

"A pity," Capt. Merryweather said, "we shall not be able to utilize your orange squirrel gag. Love to have that one on my resume."

"Jane," Lt. Colonel Randal said, "where's Karen?"

"Lt. Montgomery and a party of her riggers are in Kenya touring the parachute training facilities we built for Force N," Lady Jane said.

"Mad Dog is planning a class for the new Raiding Forces people who are not airborne qualified."

"We'll need Karen to rig the parachutes for the drop on Haft-l-Khel and for Hawthorne's diversion/deception operations," Lt. Col. Randal said.

"Get her back here."

"Straightaway," Lady Jane said.

"One last thing, people," Lt. Col. Randal said. "Col. Roberts has informed me COUNTENANCE has lost the element of surprise—the bad guys know we're coming."

The announcement was met with silence. It was the last thing any of the military professionals in the room wanted to hear. Surprise is *the* essential element of Special Operations.

"Don't let that bother you," Lt. Col. Randal said. "Surprise is what you make of it. We'll craft a plan so crazy the Persians would never expect anyone to try it."

"They'll be surprised."

"Hot damn!" Captain "Geronimo" Joe McKoy said. "This is gettin' good."

"Maybe not," said Waldo.

RAIDING FORCES HEADQUARTERS WAS A BEEHIVE OF ACTIVITY. TIME was short and information nonexistent. Planning, for the most part, was on hold.

Couriers began arriving at RFHQ with their intelligence dossiers. A picture of the target, meaning the southern quadrant of Persia, started to emerge.

The thing that leapt out first was that Raiding Forces was a long way from its objective. Persia was almost 1,000 miles from RFHQ. The best place to marshal for OPERATION COUNTENANCE appeared to be Basra, in southern Iraq.

Captain the Lady Jane Seaborn volunteered to fly there to locate a secure site for Raiding Forces to set up an advanced base to launch from.

"Negative," Lieutenant Colonel John Randal said. "I want you close, Jane. Who else can we send?"

At that moment, Veronica Paige arrived. She had learned Raiding Forces was on alert and immediately came to volunteer her services where needed.

The timing could not have been better.

"Pack your bags, Veronica," Lady Jane said, "you are off to Basra. Make sure to carry your Most Secret credentials. You shall need them."

Abadan, it turned out, was the name of a town thirty-three miles upriver from the Persian Gulf situated on the bank of the Shatt al-Arab in addition to being the name of the island it was built on.

The Anglo-Persian Oil Company had its company headquarters and a private air strip there.

The A-P Refinery on Abadan had produced the largest output in the world in 1938, the last time it had been possible to compare numbers.

Roughly nine miles north upriver, at the junction of the Shatt al-Arab River, was the Persian Naval Headquarters and the radio station located in the town of Khurramshahr—sort of.

Khurramshahr and the military radio station were on the west bank, while the naval barracks, said to house 1,500 Persian sailors, was on the east bank.

The Persian Navy had two sloops and four gunboats moored at Khurramshahr in what was best described as a "restricted waterway."

One hundred air miles, more or less, from Basra across the border in Iraq was Haft-l-Khel. The oil field was relatively isolated in the middle of nowhere. India Command had decided for unknown reasons (oil fields were scattered all across Persia) that an airborne operation to secure the Haft-l-Khel oil field and protect the British subjects working there should be a priority mission.

Bandar Shahpur was a small port at the head of the Persian Gulf. Since the beginning of the war, a number of Axis merchant ships had been lying up there, interned. Five were German ships, the *Marinfels, Strumfels, Hohenfels, Wildenfels* and *Wiessenfels*. Three were Italian, the *Caboto, Bronte* and *Barbara*. The latter two were tankers.

The picture was beginning to swim into focus. A three-pronged land invasion out of Iraq by the 8th and 10th Indian Division plus a reinforced cavalry brigade (division strength) would be accompanied by a double-pronged naval attack from the Persian Gulf—the Russians would be coming in from Russia, but no one had any idea what their strength or intentions were.

No one said so, but Lt. Col. Randal could tell from looking at the map that the idea was to hit the Persians hard and fast in a number of different places simultaneously and hope their military would deflate like a machine-gunned hot air balloon.

Vice Admiral Sir Randolph "Razor" Ransom, Captain "Geronimo" Joe McKoy, Waldo Treywick and Lady Jane were in Lt. Col. Randal's (and Lady Jane's) private quarters watching Jim Taylor mark the map as new information arrived.

"Colonel Randal informed me that Persia will make the fourth time he will have carried out an operation against people or a place that did not know it was at war," Jim said as he labeled the map.

"Did you count the pistol fight you was in, John," Capt. McKoy said, sticking a long, thin cigar between his front teeth, "on that French submarine? That'd make five."

"Negative," said Lt. Col. Randal.

"Six, then," said Lady Jane. "Bela was a private island not at war with anyone until you dropped in."

"Yeah," Lt. Col. Randal said, "that's true."

"World record," Waldo said. "Gotta be."

• • •

WHILE THE MAP OF THE TARGET WAS BEGINNING TO FILL UP, IT WAS mostly names on a blank page. There was little actionable intelligence. The clock was ticking. (In fact, down in the operations center, Major Jack Black had marked the number of hours until H-hour on a blackboard, and one of Captain the Lady Jane Seaborn's Royal Marines was detailed to erase it and write in a new, smaller number every hour.) Very few people had ever visited Persia … including agents of the British Secret Intelligence Service, MI-6.

"Time spent on reconnaissance," Captain "Geronimo" Joe McKoy said, "is rarely wasted."

"That is a fact," Lieutenant Colonel John Randal said.

"I better go take a look," Capt. McKoy said. "We're burning daylight."

"Try to stay out of trouble, Captain."

"Absolutely, John … low profile," Capt. McKoy said. "Discretion's what I'm all about … clandestine."

"That's very comforting," Lt. Col. Randal said.

After everyone had departed the suite, Lt. Col. Randal continued to study the map.

"You already know," Lady Jane said, "what Raiding Forces is going to do."

Lt. Col. Randal said, "Pretty much."

11
LET'S TALK US SOME OIL

THE HUDSON THAT DID NOT EXIST—BECAUSE IT HAD CRASHED IN Abyssinia supporting Force N guerrilla operations (that was the official story)—lined up on its final approach to the private Anglo-Persian Oil Company airstrip located on Abadan Island. It was flying out of Shaibah, Iraq, where it had made a stop to refuel. The towers of the refinery rose out of the flat delta like skyscrapers.

The aircraft had a black square with a white circle inside and a large, red, five-pointed star with a green T in the center freshly painted on the nose—Texaco Oil Company.

A Lone Star Texas flag was stenciled on the side of the plane.

Standing by on the tarmac to meet the flight was the vice president in charge of A-P operations and the Persian Army colonel in charge of the customs station on the island.

There was also a small ground crew with a mobile ladder for the passengers to use to disembark.

The ground crew had orders to refuel the Hudson, which would be taking off immediately.

The twin-engine aircraft made a perfect landing. Clearly, the pilot was a skilled professional. The plane taxied to the waiting group and cut its motors.

When the door of the Hudson opened, a stunning red-headed flight attendant in rolled-up khaki shorts and a pair of peewee cowgirl boots stepped out on the deck of the landing ladder. As she did, an empty bottle of Old Crow rolled past her out the door.

The colonel in charge of customs cast a disapproving eye on the bottle as it tinkled down the steel steps of the ladder the crew had rolled up to the aircraft. Alcohol was strictly forbidden in Persia. Fortunately, he was in the pay of the British Secret Intelligence Service, MI-6, through the good services of the operations division of the A-P Oil Company.

Captain "Geronimo" Joe McKoy came out of the door wearing a ten-gallon Stetson, a white Mexican shirt that hung down to mid-thigh (concealing a Colt 1911 Model .38 Super at his waist), and whipcord pants that were tucked into his yellow alligator cowboy boots.

Obtaining a visa to visit Persia was virtually impossible for most people. It was a land of mystery that did not welcome outside visitors, but a Texas oilman with a United States passport was the exception.

He was carrying a cased fishing rod.

"Howdy, boys," Capt. McKoy said. "Let's talk us some oil."

"Reckon the fish is bitin'?"

The pilot, in a skin-tight black flight suit, walked out behind Capt. McKoy. Long, snow-blond hair cascaded down when she pulled off her black baseball cap with the Texaco logo stitched on the front.

"Haul your tack off my airplane, cowboy," Lieutenant Pamala Plum-Martin said. "You men get this ship turned around.

"Today is payday, and I'm headed to Cairo to spend my cut."

So much for clandestine.

KING LET WALDO INTO LIEUTENANT COLONEL JOHN RANDAL'S SUITE. Lt. Col. Randal was studying the map board of Persia and leafing through a thin sheaf of papers when he arrived.

"You lookin' for me, Colonel?"

"Roger that, Mr. Treywick," Lt. Col. Randal said.

"Admiral Ransom is flying to the Persian Gulf to link up with the naval force that'll be carrying out OPERATION BISHOP, the seaborne attack on Abadan and Bandar Shahpur.

"I'd like you to travel out with him."

"If you say so, Colonel," Mr. Treywick said. "But I ain't a navy man or no admiral's dog robber."

"Maybe not," Lt. Col. Randal said, "but you're the best river reconnaissance operator we have in Raiding Forces ... scouted out the German cruiser *Königsberg* up the Rufiji with P. J. Pretorius in the last one."

"That's true," Waldo said, "but the Admiral's a blue water sailor. I'm a brown water man."

"After completing your mission of locating the cruiser," Lt. Col. Randal said, "you went back out in a rowboat, sounded the river, and then marked a channel that Royal Navy gunboats could use to navigate in range to take her under fire with their high angle guns."

"Some reason," Waldo asked, "you been checkin' on my bona fides, Colonel?"

"Abadan is about forty miles up the Karun River, and Bandar Shahpur is farther than that, up a fairly narrow waterway called the Khoum Moor at the head of the Persian Gulf," Lt. Col. Randal said.

"Butch is out there now, teaching Australian and Indian sailors how to board the enemy ships moored in those two harbors. They have to get there to do it. When BISHOP goes in, my guess is the 'Headhunter' will be leading the way.

"I'd feel better, Mr. Treywick, if you were along to make sure Butch stays out of trouble," Lt. Col. Randal said.

"There's a Phantom radio team standing by ready to go with you."

"Take about ten minutes," Waldo said, "to get my gear together."

FORCES PERSONNEL WHO HAD BEEN IN THE FIELD ON PATROL out of Oasis X began arriving at RFHQ. Major Sir Terry "Zorro" Stone, No. 1 on the priority list, flew in first. He reported to Lieutenant Colonel John Randal immediately.

Lieutenant Westcott Huxley, the No. 2 man on the list, was with him. Captain "Pyro" Percy Stirling, Captain Jeb Pelham-Davies, DSO, MC, Captain Taylor Corrigan and Lieutenant Roy Kidd were en route. Every man in RFDP who had participated in OPERATION

LOUNGE LIZARD, the cutting-out operation on Rio Bonita off the Gold Coast, was being flown back to participate in the upcoming invasion of Persia.

Also, certain other Raiding Forces personnel were being tapped for assignment.

It was a challenge to locate the men and the patrols in their area of operations, then dispatch aircraft to fly to their location, land and pick up the designated personnel. The distance was vast. RFDP was scattered across the length of the Western Desert, carrying out small-scale hit-and-run raids.

Since Lieutenant Pamala Plum-Martin was away flying (originally she had been ordered to say at RFHQ to advise Lt. Col. Randal), Lieutenant Penelope "Legs" Honeycutt-Parker had taken over the duties of tracking down the desired personnel and arranging to have them flown in from the field.

The clock was ticking. Time was short.

Lt. Col. Randal ordered Maj. Stone, "Relocate your regiment to Shaibah, Iraq.

"There's an airfield we can use to marshal. Be prepared to conduct a combat jump within the next forty-eight hours on a target somewhere in Persia—to be specified later—25 August 41.

"Questions?"

"A bit light on details, old stick," Maj. Stone said.

"Yes, it is," Lt. Col. Randal said. "Move out, Terry."

"This shall be interesting," Maj. Stone said. "All up, the Lancelot Lancers Yeomanry total thirty-one souls available for duty, not counting the Americans we badged into the Regiment ... not that it matters. None of the AVG happens to be airborne-qualified, with the exception of Travis McCloud.

"The remainder of the Regiment is detached observing patrols, some away on leave, and a few on light duty recovering from wounds. The LLY is the smallest Territorial cavalry regiment in the army, as you are aware; one under-strength squadron, and it took casualties in the Syrian Campaign."

"A platoon is about all we have the air assets to drop anyway, Terry," Lt. Col. Randal said. "I'll brief you on details as soon as I figure them out.

"Get with Jane, she's organized air transport for the Lounge Lizards to Shaibah. Veronica Paige is there now, awaiting your arrival. Initially we planned to marshal at Basra. Shaibah's a better airfield."

"Making it up as you go?"

"Terry, that's a blank map."

"Noticed that, old stick," Maj. Stone said. "Press on."

Lt. Huxley, a 10th Lancer who had problems pronouncing his 'R's', was waiting, talking to King as Maj. Stone was leaving.

"Clear your social calendar, Westcott," Lt. Col. Randal said. "I need you to organize a team tasked with marking a landing zone for a company-sized tactical air-landing at Haft-l-Khel. The objective is to secure the oil field there.

"Here's a list of available men. Pick five. You know the drill."

"Will you be leading the pathfinduws, suw?"

"Negative," Lt. Col. Randal said. "You are, lieutenant. Report to Squadron Leader Wilcox; he and Captain McCloud are the airborne mission planners.

"You're making a night jump on Persia in less than forty-eight hours. Don't waste any of 'em."

"Woj … I mean Wilco, suw!"

LIEUTENANT PENELOPE "LEGS" HONEYCUTT-PARKER STUCK HER HEAD IN the door. "Zargo radioed a request to be put on the manifest to fly here to take part in the Persian operation."

"Negative," Lieutenant Colonel John Randal said. "He's mission critical to Desert Patrol. Murder, Inc.'s intelligence is the magic sauce.

"Message Mr. Zargo back that I said I'm not risking him on a Commando raid."

"Will do, John."

Vice Admiral Sir Randolph "Razor" Ransom was shown in by King. He was preparing to depart for the Persian Gulf aboard a Royal

Navy Sunderland flying boat. In his capacity as Deputy Director of Operations Division (Irregular), he intended to be on hand for OPER-ATION BISHOP.

"I'm off," VAdm. Ransom said. "Randy and Waldo will be traveling with me. The Phantom radio team was a splendid idea, Colonel. We shall put it to good use.

"I'd like to fly out to inspect Lt. Hoolihan's troop, but there's no time," Lt. Col. Randal said. "Keep your eye on my people for me, Admiral."

"My pleasure," VAdm. Ransom said. "BISHOP, the navy phase, is pure eighteenth-century-style buccaneering at its finest. Sail in, board the enemy ships, land the Marines ashore—or in this case Indian Army troops consisting of A and D Companies from the 3/10 Baluch Regiment—and seize the ports."

"I've sent Lieutenant Hoolihan orders to break down his men into teams when they've completed their training mission," Lt. Col. Randal said.

"Raiding Forces personnel from his troop of Sea Squadron are to be spread out on every ship to act as stiffeners for the Indian and Australian sailors who make up the boarding parties."

"Jolly good," VAdm. Ransom said. "The boarding parties are the weakest link in as motley a Royal Navy armada as has ever joined together to sail the Seven Seas.

"I intend to travel in the headquarters' vessel for the expedition, the armed merchant cruiser HMRA *Kanimbla.*

"You shall be able to contact me aboard her."

"Roger," Lt. Col. Randal said.

"Sir, my Raiders' orders are to lead the boarding parties. Their mission is complete once the ships have been seized.

"I don't want my people going ashore engaging in house-to-house or street fighting. That's a job for infantry. Raiding Forces are too valuable to lose in a battle they're not trained or equipped to conduct."

"Understood," VAdm. Ransom said, "loud and clear. I will personally see to it that Raiding Forces personnel are not misused. Lt.

Hoolihan's men will be withdrawn and flown out by flying boat the moment the Axis ships they board are under our control."

"Perfect."

"Where are your plans, Colonel?"

Lt. Col. Randal walked over and tapped the map.

"I'll be at this location with a few of my men in advance of H-hour. What do you think, sir?"

"Strategic planning," VAdm. Ransom said. "*Very* good, young Colonel."

"Seems," Lt. Col. Randal said, "like the thing to do."

Ex-captain Travis McCloud came upstairs to see Lieutenant Colonel John Randal.

"When the American Volunteer Group was formed," ex-Capt. McCloud said, "there were two officers in the unit."

"Where's the other one?" Lt. Col. Randal said.

"Just arrived," ex-Capt. McCloud said, "2ⁿᵈ Lieutenant Billy Jack Jaxx."

"What took him so long?"

"He was on trial at Fort Benning," ex-Capt. McCloud said. "Homicide."

"Really," Lt. Col. Randal said.

"Lt. Jaxx has a colorful past, sir."

"Well," Lt. Col. Randal said, lighting a cigarette with his hard-service Zippo, "let's hear it."

"Grew up on a small ranch west of Fort Worth, sir," ex-Capt. McCloud said. "His father is an independent oil wildcatter … away from home most of the time.

"His grandfather, a famous Texas lawman, the sheriff of the county, helped raise him. From the time he was fifteen years old, the sheriff took Jack along as backup when he served warrants.

"Big county, not many people live there, only two full-time deputies, lots of criminals hiding out or passing through, to or from the Dallas/Fort Worth area.

"When he graduated high school, Jack received a football scholarship at the University of Texas. Punt and kickoff returns were his specialty. Ran one back against Baylor for 102 yards."

"No kidding," Lt. Col. Randal said.

"In the middle of his freshman year, there was a panty raid on the Tri-Delta House," ex-Capt. McCloud said. "A photo appeared in the *Austin Statesman* of Jack waving a pair from the second-story balcony.

The judge's granddaughter was a Delta Delta Delta pledge, and he gave Jack a choice. "'Marine Corps or this new army outfit called U.S. Paratroops … Take your pick or we'll set a trial date.'

"Billy Jack went Airborne.

"'Come back in four years,' the judge said, 'when your enlistment's up and my granddaughter's graduated. Help us beat the hell out of Texas A&M.'"

"Generous of the man," Lt. Col. Randal said.

"Assigned to the 501st at Fort Benning, Jack completed jump training and joined a company, but the commander was a rabid Oklahoma Sooner who did not want any ex-UT football players in his outfit, sir," ex-Capt. McCloud said.

"He ordered the First Sergeant to get rid of him.

"No problem, a call for volunteers for Infantry Officers Candidate School (OCS) had come down. Jack found himself transferred to the Infantry School on the other side of the post in OCS," ex-Capt. McCloud said.

"Ninety days later, after maxing the leadership, tactics and marksmanship portions of the training and having slept through most of the rest of the classes, 2nd Lt. Jaxx reported back to the Five-O-One wearing a shiny new gold bar—the youngest officer in the outfit.

"The Tri-Delts were impressed."

"Bet they were," Lt. Col. Randal said.

"On his first day of duty, Jack was detailed to escort an officer prisoner from the Phoenix City jail to the stockade at Fort Benning," ex-Capt. McCloud said.

"As he was signing for the required Government Model .45 pistol and seven rounds of ammunition, the armorer repeated the military myth that's been floating around since Valley Forge:

"Lose a prisoner, you have to serve out the rest of his sentence."

"I've heard that," Lt. Col. Randal said.

"The prisoner turned out to be a 2nd Armored Division captain, one of Georgie Patton's boys, big guy—played guard for Michigan State—about twice Lt. Jaxx's size," ex-Capt. McCloud said.

"The tanker was under arrest for statutory rape ... a thirteen-year-old who could drink like a fish, sir."

"Thirteen?"

"With the body of an eleven year old," ex-Capt. McCloud said. "Man was in serious trouble.

"The minute the two walked outside, the 2nd AD Captain knocked Lt. Jaxx down, then took off at a dead run.

"Jack rolled over, drew his issue .45, tapped the magazine, racked the slide, shouted 'HALT' and shot the prisoner before he made it off the courthouse lawn.

"Provost Marshal pressed charges for murder."

"Doesn't seem right," Lt. Col. Randal said.

"Several witnesses stated that Lt. Jaxx's actions didn't take place in the sequence described, sir," ex-Captain McCloud said.

"Some dispute over which came first: the command to halt or the pistol shot. Everyone was in full agreement that it all happened fast. Lt. Jaxx got off at the court martial.

"He is well-liked by the troops, Colonel."

"That's good," Lt. Col. Randal said.

"The men call him 'Jack Cool.'"

JAMES "BALDIE" TAYLOR AND LIEUTENANT COLONEL JOHN RANDAL were standing in front of the map of Persia.

Jim said, "I will make this short and simple.

"Enemy Forces: nine Persian Infantry Divisions, five Independent Infantry Brigades, one Independent Mechanized Brigade and an Armed

Gendarmerie of seven Regiments and fifteen battalions. The police are for internal security, but they can fight. Their units are classified as 'mixed use', which means they are mobile—mostly truck transport.

"Estimates are 126,000 Persian regular army troops plus the auxiliaries."

"That's a lot of bad guys," Lt. Col. Randal said.

Jim said, "We've got one standing division, one hastily cobbled together division, and one cavalry brigade with attachments that bring it up to division strength—but that doesn't make it a real division."

"The Persians," Jim said, "have a poor reputation for military planning."

"And we have a good one," Lt. Col. Randal said. "What about BATTLEAX?"

"I am merely repeating the line GHQ is postulating," Jim said.

"The Persian Army has 100 Czecho-Morvaska 7.5- and 3.5-ton tanks—the 3.5s only come out of their armories for ceremonial parades. There is a difference of opinion on how many serviceable tanks the Persians can field. Some sources claim the count may be as low as sixteen."

"How many tanks do we have?" Lt. Col. Randal asked.

"Less than that," Jim said.

"The Persian Air Force consists of 200 British manufacture aircraft: twenty-five fighters, 100 general purpose planes and seventy-five training aircraft. But as you know from experience at RAF Habbaniya, even trainers can be armed up and expected to give a good account of themselves."

"Sounds like serious enemy air," Lt. Col. Randal said, lighting a cigarette with his battered U.S. 26th Cavalry Regiment Zippo.

"The fighters," Jim said, "are a concern."

"I can see how they would be."

Jim said, "The ground campaign will be a three-pronged invasion with Slim's 10th Indian Division in the north, the cavalry in the central part of the country and Harvey's 8th Indian Division south against Abadan Island to the Persian Gulf."

"Total British troop strength in the attack—nineteen thousand men with fifty armored fighting vehicles of all classes; armored car, light and medium tanks.

"What is your thought, Colonel?"

"Well, the odds don't sound good, General," Lt. Col. Randal said. "And Slim's the ground commander. We both saw what happened to him at Gallabat when the numbers were in his favor."

"Yes, we did," Jim said. "However, someone must think he has the right stuff. Slim keeps being promoted when other men would have been relieved long ago."

"Maybe getting shot in the ass in Abyssinia," Lt. Col. Randal said, "has had a motivating effect …"

"Perhaps we should hold those thoughts," Jim said. "What are your intentions?"

"Raiding Forces will be in and out of Persia," Lt. Col. Randal said, "before the real shooting starts."

"Sensible," Jim said. "COUNTENANCE has all the elements of an operation that could turn ugly."

12

OPERATION BRAIN-DEAD

RAIDING FORCES MARSHALED AT AN ABANDONED IRAQI AIRFIELD AT Shaibah, not far from the Persian border. Lieutenant Colonel John Randal assembled everyone who had made it in an empty hangar.

Not everyone who had been on his priority list was there. But time had run out.

Lt. Col. Randal was holding a pointer as he stood by a large map of Persia, preparing to issue the most convoluted Operations Order he had ever given. In fact, he was not certain that *he* knew all the details. The invasion of Persia was an improvised campaign.

OPERATION COUNTENANCE had a lot of moving parts. A number of different missions would be taking place more or less at the same time during the initial phase. Not one of them had adequate men or equipment to accomplish their mission, and not one of them had been given enough time to rehearse.

Lt. Col. Randal said, "Situation: The Germans are driving on Moscow. The Russian Army is surrendering by the millions. Over 3,000 Nazi operatives have infiltrated Persia, with the intention of taking over the communications system, railroads and oil refineries.

"Hitler's intent is to secure the world's largest producing refinery at Abadan, then use Persia as a springboard to launch into Africa once

Russia collapses. In such an event, the Wehrmacht will have massive tank armies freed up to drive through Persia, Iraq and on to Egypt.

"Enemy forces: The Persian Army consists of 126,000 regulars, 100 light tanks—Renault FT-6s and Panzer 38(t)s—though intelligence has indicated that less than twenty are serviceable—La France TK-6 armored cars and an air force of 200 aircraft, some twenty-five of which are fighters.

"The Persian Navy, commanded by Rear Admiral Gholam Ali Bayandor, who is also the military commander of the southern Khuzestan Province in which Raiding Forces will be operating, has a royal yacht, two sloops and four gunboats. All Italian-built and crewed by Blackshirt sailors on contract to the Shah.

"Distribution of enemy ground maneuver units: 27,000 of the Persian troops and all the armor are concentrated in Khuzestan Province.

"Friendly forces: The 10th Indian Army Division, the recently formed 8th Indian Army Division and a reinforced Cavalry Brigade—brought up to division strength by the addition of attachments—supported by elements of the Royal Navy, the Royal Australian Navy, the Royal Indian Navy and the Royal Air Force, totaling approximately 16,000 men.

"Mission: In order to prevent the German Army from trespassing into Persian territory, British Forces will launch a preemptive three-pronged ground attack out of Iraq simultaneously with a two-pronged naval assault at the head of the Persian Gulf with the objective of establishing an Allied blocking force. Prior to the invasion, the RAF will do a massive drop of leaflets over the major cities that state, "YOU ARE NOT BEING INVADED."

"Execution: 10th Indian Division will attack to the north. The Provisional Cavalry Division to the center. 18 Brigade, 8th Indian Division out of Basra—consisting of the 1/2 and the 2/3 Gurkhas and 5/5 Marhattas Light Infantry—will conduct an amphibious movement in boats out of Iraq down the Tigris River to Khurramshahr.

"Simultaneously, 24 Brigade—consisting of the 2/6 Rajputana Rifles, 1 Kumaon Rifles and 3 Field Regiment Royal Artillery—will be following 18 Brigade with the two infantry battalions in another convoy of boats, while the artillery advances overland to the bank of the

Shatt al-Arab River where it will take up firing positions. 24 Brigade's objective is to capture Abadan Island.

"While this is taking place, elements of the Royal Navy will be sailing up the Shatt al-Arab River from the head of the Persian Gulf to support the 24 Brigade attack on Abadan, then continue upriver to Khurramshahr to assist the 18 Brigade attack on the Persian Naval Headquarters.

"Other elements of the navy will simultaneously be entering the port of Bandar Shahpur, with the idea of boarding and capturing the eight enemy ships moored there, then landing A and D companies of the 3/10 Baluchis, serving in the role of Royal Marines, to capture the town.

"Meanwhile, the RAF will be carrying out bombing missions on the same towns it had advised we are not invading.

"Concept of the operation: Raiding Forces will drop a six-man pathfinder team—commanded by Lieutenant Huxley—at Haft-l-Khel oil field to mark a landing zone in order for C Company 3/10 Baluchis, reinforced by a 12-man party of air landing advisors from the 1st King's Own Royal Regiment, to conduct a tactical air assault in six Vickers-Valentia troop transports. The C Company mission is to secure the oil facilities and to safeguard British subjects in the area.

"Lieutenant Huxley's pathfinder team and the KORR airborne advisors will extract on the transports that fly in the Baluchis.

"The Lancelot Lancers Regiment, commanded by Major Stone, will conduct OPERATION LEAPING LIZARDS—a night parachute drop on the Island of Abadan in advance of 24 Brigade's attack. The Lancers' mission is to safeguard the approximately 1,000 British and 1,500 Indian employees of the Anglo-Persian Oil Company located on the island.

"Immediately after 24 Brigade arrives on Abadan Island and assumes control of the British subjects, Major Stone's Lancers will assemble on the A-P Oil Company airfield, then be flown back to the departure airfield to await return to RFHQ Cairo.

"Jumping in with Major Stone to conduct OPERATION BRAINDEAD will be a six-man special mission team under my personal command. Once on the ground, it will move upriver to Khurramshahr by boat, attack the radio station located on the west bank of the Shatt al-Arab River, destroy the military communications system inside, then be extracted by amphibious aircraft prior to 18 Brigade's assault on the town.

"While the Abadan/Khurramshahr/LEAPING LIZARDS/BRAIN-DEAD phase of OPERATION COUNTENANCE is taking place, other elements of Raiding Forces Sea Squadron will be serving as stiffeners for the boarding parties participating in OPERATION BISHOP taking down the eight enemy ships berthed in the port of Bandar Shahpur.

"Administration and logistics: To be briefed by Major Stone, Lieutenant Huxley and myself at the time we issue our individual Mission Orders.

"Command and signal: To be briefed.

"What are your questions?"

No one had any questions—at least they did not ask them if they did. Lt. Col. Randal had just given a Warning Order of a type that would normally be issued by an army commander to his senior subordinate maneuver element commanders—not the honcho of a small Special Operations outfit.

And not one person pointed out the absurdity of a hastily assembled, three-division British "blocking force" being placed in the way of gigantic Nazi panzer armies expected to come slicing out of Russia.

With the exception of the two American volunteer officers, everyone in the briefing who would be taking part in the invasion was an experienced Special Forces Commando.

The Raiders knew to a man that the operation was a roll of the dice.

OPERATION COUNTENANCE was going up against an enemy who outnumbered them, who knew they were coming and who knew where at least one of the ground forces out of Iraq would be attacking.

OPERATION BISHOP, the naval action, was hoped to be a surprise.

The scheme of maneuver was complicated. It called for a night combat parachute jump, a tactical air-landing behind enemy lines, a pair of long, amphibious river-flanking approaches from opposite directions utilizing small boats, and a river crossing against an entrenched enemy, with the Royal Navy simultaneously attacking thirty-three miles up a constricted waterway—the Shatt al-Arab—noted for the silt that accumulates below the confluence of the Tigris and Karun Rivers and hampers navigation.

The raid on the radio station, OPERATION BRAIN-DEAD, was high-risk at best.

Other than the navy, aided by Lieutenant Butch "Headhunter" Hoolihan, DSO, MC, MM, RM, and his Sea Squadron troop, having trained the boarding parties at sea eleven miles offshore in the Persian Gulf, there had been no rehearsals.

The invasion of Persia did not conform to Raiding Forces' Rules for Raiding. The scheme of maneuver was not "Short and Simple." There was no "Plan B." There was no way to cheat—well—maybe a little.

No reinforcements were to be had.

The only way home was to defeat the Persians.

H-Hour was 0400 on D-Day 25 Aug 41—tomorrow morning. The Lancelot Lancers and Lt. Col. Randal's team would be dropping at 0200—two hours in advance of the invasion.

The forced entry by Raiding Forces and the 8th Indian Division's 18 and 24 Brigades would be taking place under the cover of darkness, following a complicated series of amphibious river and ground troop movements in the middle of the largest date palm forest on earth, an estimated eighteen million trees—one-fifth of all the date palms in the entire world.

What could possibly go wrong?

C COMPANY 3/10 BALUCHIS ARRIVED BY TRUCK AT THE DEPARTURE airfield. With them were twelve volunteers from the King's Own Royal Regiment—veterans of the first strategic airlift the British Army had ever conducted and a tactical air assault into Iraq. They were to accompany the Baluchis in the role of air assault advisors.

Six ancient Vickers-Valentia troop transports flying out of RAF Habbaniya landed. Three of the Valentias would drop the Lancelot

Lancer Yeomanry Regiment on the private Anglo-Persian Oil Company airstrip on Abadan Island.

Two would drop parachutes attached to blocks of ice on selected drop zones as a diversion to create an army of phantom parachutists.

The Valentias would return to the departure airfield, land and link up with the aircraft that had dropped the pathfinder team at the Haft-l-Khel oil field.

Then all six aircraft would embark C Company, fly back to the oil field, land the troops and bring out Lieutenant Westcott Huxley's pathfinder team.

Lieutenant Karen Montgomery had one section of her Royal Marine rigger section issuing the X-type parachutes for the night drop.

Another section was organizing the worn-out parachutes flown in from RAF Habbaniya aboard the Vickers-Valentias that were to be used by Captain Hawthorne Merryweather for his phantom parachutist diversion/deception plan.

Capt. Merryweather made arrangements for blocks of ice to be delivered to the departure airfield to weigh down the parachutes.

Ex-Captain Travis McCloud (Special Mission Team), Lt. Huxley (pathfinders) and the three Lancelot Lancer jumpmasters were detailed to inspect the jump aircraft.

James "Baldie" Taylor was updating the map as more intelligence became available. He also posted aerial photos of Abadan Island and the radio station located in Khurramshahr that Red had taken when she and Lieutenant Pamala-Plum Martin dropped off Captain "Geronimo" Joe McKoy at the A-P Oil Company airfield.

Veronica Paige laid on a hot meal for the troops.

A liaison officer arrived from the 5/5 Matthias Light Infantry. He met with Lieutenant Colonel John Randal to establish signals between the 18 Brigade and the Raiding Forces team, should the brigade arrive at Khurramshahr before the Special Mission Team departed the area.

Lt. Col. Randal said, "We'll have pulled out before you make your attack. In the unlikely event the radio station is still standing when you arrive, *DO NOT* allow your troops anywhere near the building or the pier. They will be wired for demolitions and are going to blow."

Raiding Forces Lancelot Lancer personnel were broken down into sticks. They linked up with the individual aircraft that would be dropping them, to be introduced to the aircrews. Then they returned to their team assembly areas to allow C/3/10 as much time as possible to conduct drills loading and unloading the Valentias under the guidance of the veteran air assaulters from the 1st King's Own Royal Rifles.

The 3/10 Baluchis were neither airborne-qualified nor volunteers. A lot was being asked of them.

Lt. Col. Randal and ex-Lieutenant Billy Jack Jaxx strolled over to the edge of the airfield to a makeshift range to test-fire their weapons. As was his practice, Lt. Col. Randal was keeping his newest officer close as Raiding Forces prepared for their night drop.

Under normal circumstances, a new member of Raiding Forces of untested quality would not be included on a small team assigned to carry out a high-risk mission within a hazardous operation.

However, nothing about the invasion of Persia could be considered "normal." Lt. Col. Randal had not been able to assemble all the men he requested, and he had no time to plan in-depth or rehearse. Ex-Lt. Jaxx was a former U.S. Army Paratrooper. He was going to make his first combat jump—ready or not.

When given the opportunity to select his personal weapon for the mission, ex-Lt. Jaxx had opted for a .45-caliber Thompson submachine gun. He claimed he'd been using one since he had been twelve years old. His grandfather, the Texas sheriff, had two in his department's armory.

Test-firing was done before each mission to ensure that every Raider's weapon was functioning properly. It was not done for score. Sometimes not even against any kind of a target—simply fired down range.

That was the case this evening. All the two needed to do was to double-check that everything worked. And, Lt. Col. Randal wanted to see how Billy Jack performed.

He need not have worried. Ex-Lt. Jaxx handled the Thompson like a virtuoso.

"What's that pistol you're carrying?" Lt. Col. Randal asked.

"A Colt Ace .22 on a 1911 Government Model .38 Super frame," ex-Lt. Jaxx said. "My grandfather had the slide cut back from five inches to four and one-fourth and threaded the exposed barrel for a silencer."

Lt. Col. Randal said, "You used silencers in law enforcement?"

"My job as a reserve deputy, sir," ex-Lt. Jaxx said, "was to eliminate guard dogs when we served warrants. Lots of crooks keep them around their hideouts."

"Dangerous?"

"Best not miss, sir," ex-Lt. Jaxx said. "I'd shoot 'em with the silenced .22 when they attacked or the barking was giving away our approach. Then the Sheriff would move in with his Winchester 351 self-loading carbine and make the arrest.

"Do that often?"

"Most every Friday, Saturday and Sunday from the ninth grade, sir," ex-Lt. Jaxx said. "Friday nights during football season we'd go serve warrants after my games.

"I brought my .22/.38 Super conversion out here because Captain Roosevelt told me Raiding Forces carried .38 Supers, sir."

"Quite a few do," Lt. Col. Randal said. "I let the men carry what they like."

"Back home," ex-Lt. Jaxx said, "when Grandfather and I were chasing crooks, sometimes we had to shoot out the motors on their cars. A .38 Super round will penetrate completely through an engine block, sir."

"I've heard that," Lt. Col. Randal said. "If you're chasing a car, Jack, how do you hit the motor?"

"Texas heart shot, sir," ex-Lt. Jaxx said. "Fire one up the tailpipe; see what happens.

"What rig should I bring tonight, Colonel?"

"The quiet .22," Lt. Col. Randal said. "You and I are going to clear the radio station. Since it's located in the center of the Naval HQ complex at Khurramshahr, surrounded by 1,500 enemy sailors, probably not a good idea to advertise."

"Clear?" ex-Lt. Jaxx asked. "What does that mean exactly, sir?"

"We're going to walk in about 0340," Lt. Col. Randal said, "and shoot every bad guy in the place.

"OK with you, Lieutenant?"

"That's a rodge, sir."

Ex-Lt. Jaxx was what the troops claimed… *cool.*

Captain the Lady Jane Seaborn and Lieutenant Mandy Ppaige flew in just before dark. Lady Jane had been waiting at Raiding Forces Headquarters to see if any more of the personnel on Lieutenant Colonel John Randal's priority list arrived.

No joy. Sandstorms, lack of suitable landing areas to make pick-ups, aircraft engine problems and a litany of other troubles all contributed to making assembly of the men impossible in the short time before the mission launched.

The only person to show up was Lt. Mandy, and she had not been on the list.

Raiding Forces would have to make do with the personnel it had.

Major Sir Terry "Zorro" Stone had a total of thirty-one Lancelot Lancers present for duty. The Lancers were reinforced by Captain Hawthorne Merryweather, who would be responsible for creating a diversion to increase the appearance of the size of the regiment.

The happy psychological warrior would be jumping in with several door bundles of pyrotechnic devices that would enable him to create the illusion of, he claimed, a division-sized airborne force in action.

Additionally, a huge resupply of tracer ammunition for the Lancers' weapons would be air-dropped in with them—enough for the troops to keep up a continuous rate of fire to complete the deception until the 18th Brigade, 8th Indian Division arrived to relieve them.

Lt. Col. Randal would be leading OPERATION BRAIN-DEAD, a Special Missions Team made up of Captain "Pyro" Percy Stirling, ex-Captain Travis McCloud, Lieutenant Roy Kidd, ex-Lieutenant Billy Jack Jaxx and King. Captain "Geronimo" Joe McKoy would be waiting at the drop zone—the Anglo-Persian Oil Company airstrip.

Capt. McKoy would mark the DZ, then provide a motorboat to transport the team the 18.4 miles up the Shatt al-Arab to raid the radio station at Khurramshahr.

Red's aerial photos, taken when Lieutenant Pamala Plum-Martin had made a pass over Khurramshahr in the Hudson after dropping off Capt. McKoy, showed one of the Persian gunboats berthed at the dock on the west side of the river where the Raiding Forces team intended to land.

Capt. Stirling and King had a plan to deal with it. King would silently eliminate the sentries on the boat. Then Capt. Stirling would go aboard and place a prepared explosive device timed to blow it out of the water at 0400: H-Hour for 18 Brigade's attack on Khurramshahr.

Capt. McKoy and Lt. Kidd would take out any sentries on the dock and/or outside the radio station, then provide security for the entry team.

Lt. Col. Randal and ex-Lt. Jaxx would enter the building and secure it so that Capt. Stirling, following behind, could come in and place explosive charges while they rendered the signals equipment inoperable.

By knocking out its means to communicate, Raiding Forces intended to paralyze the Persian military machine during the initial phase of the invasion.

Once the explosives were set, the team would leapfrog back to the motorboat being secured by ex-Capt. McCloud, then withdraw downriver to where Lt. Plum-Martin would be waiting around the first bend in a Walrus to fly them back to the departure airfield.

That was the plan.

"*BRAIN-DEAD*!" Lt. Mandy said to Lt. Col. Randal when she heard it. "Parachuting into the heart of the Land of Darkness in the middle of the night. Are you crazy?

"Persians are depraved. They strangle people with silk scarves.

"Whoever thought this idea up *is* brain-dead."

13

WARNING SHOT

THE HUDSON LINED UP ON ABADAN ISLAND (FORTY-TWO MILES LONG BY two and a half miles wide) with three Vickers-Valentia troop transports in trail formation behind. Persia was not at war. The island was not blacked out, though at zero hour for OPERATION BRAIN DEAD / LEAPING LIZARDS, what few lights were showing were in the town of Abadan off in the distance.

Squadron Leader Paddy Wilcox was flying the left seat, with Lieutenant Pamala Plum-Martin as co-pilot. She flipped the red light on.

In the troop compartment, Lieutenant Colonel John Randal ordered, "SIX MINUTES. STAND UP. HOOK UP."

The jump commands and timing of the red light had been modified for this drop; the red light normally came on ten minutes out.

Six Raiding Forces paratroopers, augmented at the last minute by James "Baldie" Taylor who had demanded to come along, struggled to their feet, clicked their snap hooks on the steel cable running down the length of the cabin—the hook facing away from the skin of the airframe—and jerked down on it to make sure it was seated and locked. Then each man inserted the safety wire dangling on its string through the tiny hole in the snap hook, bent it down on the far side with his trigger finger, pulled the static line down, then looped it back up again—creating an oversized fist full of yellow cord folded in the palm of his right hand.

Now the jumper could hang on to his static line to balance himself without fear of deploying his parachute inside the aircraft.

"CHECK STATIC LINE."

The cabin was filled with the metal-on-metal sound of snap links being rattled back and forth on the steel cable.

"CHECK EQUIPMENT."

The Raiding Forces team ran their hands over their equipment even though it was too late to do anything now if anyone found something out of place. Everyone was going to jump.

"SOUND OFF FOR EQUIPMENT CHECK."

"Okay, Okay, Okay, Okay, Okay," starting from the back of the stick.

"ALL OKAY," ex-Lieutenant Billy Jack Jaxx shouted at Lt. Col. Randal, even though they were only standing about six inches apart at the door.

Lt. Col. Randal grasped both sides of the top of the doorframe with his fingertips, wedged his rubber-soled raiding boots on both sides at the bottom and arched himself outside the Hudson. The wind whipped and tore at his uniform … distorted his face. Up ahead he could see the private Anglo-Persian airfield. Incredibly, it lit up. The strip, their DZ, was now outlined in landing lights.

He had not expected that.

Looking back, Lt. Col. Randal could see the Vickers-Valentias carrying the Lancelot Lancer Regiment thundering along behind the Hudson with deadly purpose. He swung back inside the aircraft. The Hudson was rocking, being buffeted by the heavy tropical night air and skidding from time to time.

The troops had their knees bent, riding with it.

"ONE MINUTE."

Lt. Col. Randal swung back outside for one last look. There was no need to check for his final point as a reference. He knew where the airplane was in relationship to the drop zone.

They would go on green.

The DZ was lit up better than any training exercise Raiding Forces ever conducted. No one had envisioned invading a country at zero dark thirty with the drop zone outlined in electrical landing lights.

"CLOSE ON THE DOOR."

Lt. Col. Randal braced his right arm across the door in front of ex-Lt. Jaxx as the stick shuffled forward until every jumper was jammed up tight against each other. He did not want the Lieutenant exiting too soon, this being his first combat jump.

Mistakes happen.

The Hudson was pounding toward the DZ. Lt. Col. Randal took up his position in the door, counting off the seconds in his head while watching the outside jump light which was weld-mounted on the tail wing. The light was glowing red. It flashed green at the same time he reached sixty.

"LET'S GO."

He launched himself outside the aircraft in the prescribed parachute school position—tight tuck, head down, chin on his chest, feet and knees together almost in a sitting position, elbows in. This was a low-level jump, 400 feet. The idea was to get down quick before anyone noticed the parachutes.

It might work.

The trade-off was that the jumpers were going to come in hot. Major Sir Terry "Zorro" Stone's Lancelot Lancers, *aka* Lounge Lizards, were all airborne-qualified, but not experienced paratroopers. Most only had their initial qualifying jumps under their belt.

The low-level exit was a calculated risk.

Lt. Col. Randal's parachute cracked open. He looked up, saw that there were no blown panels, the lines were not twisted and he was not oscillating.

Whaaaam! He was on the ground, having come in backward, never actually seeing it. The momentum of the parachute landing fall (PLF) flipped him over so that he hit all five points of contact: balls of the feet, side of the calf, thigh, side of the hip and small of the back automatically without trying ... or even thinking about it. Training paid off.

The landing hurt, but he was not injured.

The violence of the PLF carried him all the way over backward so that he automatically bounced into the upright standing position. Lt. Col. Randal popped the quick-release safety snap off and hammered the device with his fist, causing his parachute harness to fall off into a pile on the ground at his feet. The lines and risers were stretched out straight on the tarmac with the silk occasionally rippling in the breeze like a dying octopus.

Lt. Col. Randal glanced up and saw that his BRAIN-DEAD team was already on the ground recovering their chutes, with the LEAPING LIZARDS coming down fast under their canopies.

Quickly he did the arms stretched figure eight maneuver, wrapping up his chute; then he stuffed it into his parachute bag, zipped it shut and popped the snaps. The jumpers needed to move their parachutes off the runway. The airstrip had to be cleared so that it could be used later for the aircraft to return and land.

Captain "Geronimo" Joe McKoy appeared from out of nowhere.

Maj. Stone came trotting by with a cluster of his troopers carrying their parachute bags. They were heading toward their assembly area where they would be picked up by Anglo-Persian Oil Company personnel in company trucks and driven to their objective: the Abadan oil refinery.

Maj. Stone's orders were to "seize and hold until relieved," the classic airborne mission.

King picked up Lt. Col. Randal's parachute bag and jogged off the airfield with it. Within minutes, the Raiding Forces Special Missions Team had dropped off their parachutes, assembled, and were ready to follow Capt. McKoy to the boat that would be taking them upriver to their objective: the radio station at Khurramshahr.

OPERATION LEAPING LIZARDS / BRAIN-DEAD was underway. No serious jump injuries. No shots fired.

So far, so good.

• • •

THE SHATT AL-ARAB RIVER IS FORMED BY THE CONFLUENCE OF THE Tigris and Euphrates Rivers out of Iraq, with the Karun out of Persia as a tributary. It is a dirty river that ranges from 750 to 2,500 feet wide. And it runs through the world's largest date palm forest—which some claim is a remnant of the Garden of Eden.

At night, the river is a dark, spooky place.

Captain "Geronimo" Joe McKoy had a thirty-foot inboard pleasure craft belonging to the Anglo-Persian Oil Company standing by; it was topped off, ready for the run upstream to Khurramshahr.

As the Raiding Forces team boarded the boat, King handed Capt. McKoy the 9mm Beretta MAB-38 submachine gun with the ammunition pouch he had jumped in for him.

Once the boat shoved off, the team members passed Captain "Pyro" Percy Stirling the extra ten pounds of Nobel 808 plastique explosives that each one of them had jumped in, to add to the forty pounds he had brought to blow the Persian Radio Station building and the gunboat docked at the pier leading to it.

The 18.4-kilometer trip up the river was uneventful. Soft, velvet quietness shrouded the riverbanks in the dark. Persians stayed off the waterway after nightfall.

The only craft they sighted the entire way was Lieutenant Pamala-Plum Martin's Walrus bobbing next to the bank near the last turn in the river before they reached Khurramshahr.

When the Hudson returned to the departure airfield to pick up Lieutenant Westcott Huxley's pathfinder team for their drop at Haft-l-Khel, Lt. Plum-Martin had transitioned to the Walrus and flown back to the Shatt al-Arab—only a short hop.

Everyone on board waved as the boat motored by. But in the poor light, no one could see for certain whether Lt. Plum-Martin waved back.

Capt. McKoy briefed Lieutenant Colonel John Randal during the run up the river.

"Made this trip last night, John," Capt. McKoy said. "There's five "T" piers at Khurramshahr. A Persian Navy sloop, the *Babr,* is docked at one of 'em on the north bank near the naval barracks.

"At the radio station on the south bank, a gunboat's tied up at the pier—pretty big, 'bout a hunert feet's worth. No sentries posted on the dock. Can't say 'bout on board. I didn't see any when I walked by.

"There was a couple of sentries on duty outside the radio station, though."

"Town lit up?"

"Like a Christmas tree," Capt. McKoy said. "The Persians ain't acting like they're expecting trouble."

Lt. Col. Randal said, "That's how we like it."

Khurramshahr swam into sight around the bend in the river. As advertised, the military installations and civilian parts of the town were not blacked out. However, it was late ... or more accurately, early—0330—and there were not many lights showing.

The only lights on the pier were those at the far end. Low-wattage bulbs were illuminating the exterior of the Radio Station in a pale yellow glow. All the palm trees made the place look more like a remote jungle outpost in a Tarzan movie than the military headquarters of a province in a Middle Eastern country.

Capt. McKoy eased the boat in with the motor almost idling. No one was on the dock. The arrival of the Anglo-Persian Oil Company pleasure boat did not invite attention.

Ex-Captain Travis McCloud leaped up on the dock and tied off on one of the log stanchions. He was responsible for staying with the boat to secure it. That was part of Raiding Forces' Rules for Raiding: "Know how to get home."

When ex-Capt. McCloud returned to the boat, Capt. McKoy turned the wheel over to him, leaving the motor burbling.

Capt. McKoy and Lieutenant Roy Kidd went up on the pier and strolled toward the single-story radio station at the far end on the bank of the river. Both men were wearing oversized Hawaiian shirts with a giant green and black flower motif that made excellent night camouflage and concealed Capt. McKoy's Colt .38 Super and Lt. Kidd's pair of 9mm Lugar P-08s.

Capt. McKoy was wearing his Stetson.

He had a silenced .22 High Standard Military Model D behind his back in one hand. Lt. Kidd had a silenced .22 Colt Woodsman behind his. They took their time getting to the end of the dock.

While they were making their way toward the mellow light bathing the radio station, King was slipping aboard the Persian gunboat. The boat was crewed by Italian sailors on contract to the Shah. They were legitimate enemy combatants. However, with the exception of one guard who was fast asleep in a hammock, the rest of the crew was ashore.

King silently dispatched the sailor with his Fairbairn, then moved on to search the rest of the gunboat to make sure no one else was aboard.

Capt. Stirling waited on the dock until King signaled him all clear. He proceeded below deck and placed ten pounds of Nobel 808 plastique explosives behind the fuel tanks. A quarter pound would have been plenty.

Then he set a time pencil fuse to detonate the charge in thirty minutes: OPERATION COUNTENANCE's H-hour: 0400 hours. That was when 18 Brigade, 8th Indian Division was scheduled to hit Khurramshahr.

Special Missions Team intended to be gone by then.

Lt. Col. Randal and ex-Lieutenant Billy Jack Jaxx stepped up on the dock. They strolled toward the radio station at the end of the T pier. Lt. Col. Randal had his silenced .22 High Standard in one hand down at his side. He was wearing both of his Colt .38 Supers, with his 9mm Browning P-35 around back in a skeleton holster.

Ex-Lt. Jaxx had his .22 Colt Ace in his hand hanging down behind his right leg, walking about a step behind Lt. Col. Randal to his left.

Up ahead, Capt. McKoy and Lt. Kidd reached the radio station. Outside the front door, sound asleep in their chairs, were two sentries wearing distinctive mustard-colored Persian uniforms.

"On three," Capt. McCoy mouthed, pointing to Lt. Kidd's target. "One, two, thr... *whiiiiich, whiiiiich, whiiiiich, whiiiiich.* Two rounds to the head for each man—in accordance with Lt. Col. Randal's policy for using .22 caliber weapons to take out enemy personnel.

Both of the guards slumped over, never knowing what hit them.

Lt. Kidd slipped around behind the radio station. There was a back door with a weak light bulb encased in a wire cover mounted over it. No one was on guard. He took up a position in the shadows and stood ready.

Capt. Stirling stepped off the gunboat. He picked up the heavy pack he had left when he went aboard to place the demolition charge. It contained the rest of his explosives. Slinging the straps over one shoulder, he followed Lt. Col. Randal and ex-Lt. Jaxx up the dock.

Capt. McKoy was waiting outside the radio station when Lt. Col. Randal and ex-Lt. Jaxx arrived. He had a long, thin, unlit cigar clenched in his teeth. The sentries no longer posed a threat. The arched door was standing open.

"All yours, John."

The silver-haired cowboy would provide rear security while they made the entry.

Lt. Col. Randal brought up the .22 High Standard automatic, holding it in both hands, barrel parallel to his face. He made eye contact with ex-Lt. Jaxx, then walked inside, taking a half step to the right to allow the ex-Lieutenant a clear field of fire. The room was full of men on duty wearing uniforms of all three branches of service—Army, Navy and Air Force—from both Italy and Persia.

Whiiiiich, whiiiiich, whiiiiich, whiiiiich. Lt. Col. Randal shot the two radio operators closest to the door.

Pandemonium erupted. The room became a blur of movement. Three men dashed for the back.

The others momentarily froze.

Whiiiiich, whiiiiich. Ex-Lt. Jaxx dropped one of the running sailors.

Whiiiiich, whiiiiich. Lt. Col. Randal shot a soldier who was reaching for a rifle.

Whiiiiich, whiiiiich, whiiiiich, whiiiiich. Ex-Lt. Jaxx took out the two remaining signalmen left in the room who, no longer paralyzed, were trying to crawl under their desks. Then he changed magazines on his pistol.

The two Raiding Forces officers were shooting fast, not having the luxury of time to follow the rule of "three to the body" and not chancing head shots on moving targets.

There was an office to the right and another across the main room. Lt. Col. Randal swung into the one closest. Ex-Lt. Jaxx moved to clear the other.

The office Lt. Col. Randal entered was empty. He did a quick check under the desk to make sure no one was hiding, then went to back up ex-Lt. Jaxx.

On the way, he passed six people sprawled on the floor—more than he would have expected to be on duty at this time of day. And at least two more had made it out the back door.

"Capt. McKoy …"

The Captain responded immediately. He came in, walked around and put an insurance round in each of the "dead bad guys" with his silenced .22 High Standard.

Capt. McKoy did not want anyone "playing possum."

Lt. Col. Randal stepped into the room ex-Lt. Jaxx had disappeared into—a palatial mad dream of a private office decorated in scarlet and gold, plush rugs with a sparkling crystal chandelier.

Seated behind a desk the size of a battleship, with flags planted on both sides of it, was the commander of the Persian Navy and Khuzestan Province, Rear Admiral Gholam Ali Bayandor.

He was pointing a CZ-27 7.65 caliber pistol at ex-Lt. Jaxx.

The profusely engraved handgun was a token of eternal friendship from Benito Mussolini. Il Duce had selected it, aware of RAdm. Bayandor's preference for Czechoslovakian small arms. The gift was a thank-you present for the Admiral purchasing Italian-built ships and contracting Blackshirt sailors as crews.

Ex-Lt. Jaxx was staring at the beribboned naval officer over the sights of his .22 Colt Ace, with his finger on the trigger.

"I was explaining," RAdm. Bayandor said to Lt. Col. Randal in flawless English (his wife was British), "that you are my prisoners. Surrender or I shall kill one or possibly both of you. I am quite the excellent marksman and will not submit."

"Colonel," ex-Lt. Jaxx said, "do you know what a warning shot is?"

"Negative," Lt. Col. Randal said.

"Neither do I, sir."

Whiiiiich. Ex-Lt. Jaxx shot RAdm. Bayandor center of mass. The bullet made a little puff on the Admiral's beautifully-tailored uniform blouse precisely where his heart was located.

Jack Cool.

Whiiiiich, whiiiiich. Lt. Col. Randal put two more rounds in the Admiral's brain to make sure. Even so, as he slumped over, the CZ-27 discharged into the highly-polished desktop.

The only round fired by the opposition this night so far.

Capt. McKoy, Capt. Stirling and James "Baldie" Taylor, who had arrived to search the radio station for documents while it was being prepared with explosives, came in fast with weapons at the ready when they heard the report of the small-caliber handgun.

"Throw'd a monkey wrench in the opposition's C and C," Capt. McKoy said.

"Ain't nobody to issue any commands now. And when Pyro gets finished, there ain't gonna be no control, neither."

Jim began ransacking the Admiral's desk. The office was a potential treasure trove of intelligence.

Ex-Lt. Jaxx slipped the CZ-27 into his pocket.

Capt. Stirling went back out in the main room and started unpacking his demolitions.

King came up the pier, rolling a fifty-five gallon steel drum of fuel he had found stacked on the deck of the gunboat. He manhandled it inside the Radio Station.

"Additional accelerant," he said to Capt. Stirling. "Never hurts to cheat."

"P for Plenty," Capt. Stirling said. "Set it right over there."

Lt. Col. Randal walked out the front door, went around the side of the building and called out softly "Brain-Dead." For simplicity, the password for the evening was the same as the name of the Special Missions Team's operation.

"Those two bad guys sure are, sir," Lt. Kidd said.

Two dead men stitched with .22 rounds were sprawled on the steps in a pool of weak yellow light cast by the bulb in the cage over the back door.

"Not a great idea to head for the nearest exit," Lt. Col. Randal said, "when you're part of a security detail that comes under fire. Someone like you, Roy, might be waiting out back."

"Wondered who these men were, sir," Lt. Kidd said. "Heavily armed for simple sailors. Those are Czechoslovakian ZK-383 9mm submachine guns they were carrying."

"Admiral Bayandor was inside. Jack shot him," Lt. Col. Randal said. "Be ready to pull out in zero five. I'll come get you."

"Roger," Lt. Kidd said. "I'll bring the ZK-383s."

"FIRE IN THE HOLE!" CAPTAIN "PYRO" PERCY STIRLING SHOUTED. "SHORT fuse, Colonel. You said 0400—ten minutes from now. Not only is this place and the boat about to blow, but 18 Brigade is probably out there in the dark right now moving into position."

"Rally," Lieutenant Colonel John Randal ordered. He went outside to the back of the radio station while the others cleared out of the building.

"Let's go, Roy."

The team leapfrogged back down the pier. Ex-Captain Travis McCloud was revving the engine on the Anglo-Persian inboard. The Raiders piled into the boat in no particular order.

"Last man," Lt. Col. Randal said when he reached the end of the dock. "Give me a count, Travis."

"All present and accounted for," ex-Capt. McCloud reported. "Seven men including you, sir."

Lt. Col. Randal leapt aboard. The boat pulled away from the dock, making a power turn, and headed downriver, kicking up a rooster's tail in its wake.

In minutes they were around the bend and pulling up beside the bobbing Walrus. Lieutenant Pamala Plum-Martin had the engine ticking over.

Captain "Geronimo" Joe McKoy pitched an anchor overboard. Hopefully it would hold the A-P Oil Company boat until it could be recovered later.

The men clambered onto the float and inside the aircraft. All the interior seats had been removed for ease of loading, so they sat on the floor. Lt. Col. Randal boarded last.

He climbed into the vacant co-pilot's seat.

"Let's do it, Pam."

"Buckle up, John," Lt. Plum-Martin said as she taxied out into the middle of the river to begin her takeoff run. The little amphibian leapt into the air.

When it gained altitude, Lt. Col. Randal could see Abadan Island had erupted into a massive fireworks display to the south. He glanced at the lime green hands on his Rolex: 0400 on the dot.

Flares were up, tracers crisscrossing the dark sky and the occasional cluster of aerial pyrotechnics exploding in starbursts—looking like something you would expect to see on the Fourth of July.

It seemed like a major battle was in progress—exactly what Major Sir Terry "Zorro" Stone's Lancelot Lancers were supposed to be simulating.

As Lt. Col. Randal watched, the west bank of the river lit up along the length of Abadan Island as the 24 Brigade, 8th Indian Division began its attack right on schedule, complete with artillery support.

Two battalions, 2/6th Rajputana Rifles and 1st Kumaon Rifles, had traveled down the Shatt al-Arab in an mixed collection of boats with one battery of 3rd Field Artillery Regiment, while the other two batteries moved overland to the bank of the muddy river opposite Abadan and took up firing positions.

The eclectic little amphibious convoy was escorted downriver by the sloop HMS *Shoreham* (transporting the Headquarters Company and two platoons of 3/10 Baluchi Regiment), the armed yacht HMY *Seabelle*, the Auxiliary Patrol *Lilavati*, river paddle steamers *Ishan* and *Zenobia*, five Eureka assault boats and four dhows.

LEAPING LIZARD was in full swing with the cavalry (meaning 24 Brigade) riding to the rescue.

Lt. Plum-Martin banked right and headed for the departure airfield in Iraq. Out the right window, Lt. Col. Randal saw the radio station detonate. Then the gunboat exploded in a massive fireball. The troops in the back started chanting, "Pyro, Pyro, Pyro …"

Still no sign of Brigadier Robert Lochner's 18 Brigade moving up the Karun to attack Khurramshahr. The brigade was running ten minutes late. This was understandable since it was attempting a complicated, double pincers movement, having made a river crossing across dhows lashed together side by side with planks laid across mid-ships, traversing a stretch of desert, then negotiating the largest date palm forest in the world—all the while in the dark.

The 1/2ⁿᵈ Gurkha's and 2/3ʳᵈ Gurkha's—crammed aboard a motley collection of civilian watercraft and barges escorted by sloops HMS *Falmouth* and HMS *Yarra*—were traveling down the Tigris River to the confluence with the Karun, then turning back upriver to Khurramshahr, while the 5/5ᵗʰ Mahatmas Light Infantry with A Squadron, 10ᵗʰ Guides Cavalry (mounted in armored wheel carriers) and a battery of field artillery looped around through the desert to flank the town.

Neither 18 or 24 Brigades plan of attack at Abadan or Khurramshahr conformed to Raiding Forces' Rule to "Keep It Short and Simple," but at least the part Lt. Col. Randal was most concerned about—the relief of the Lancelot Lancers—was right on schedule.

The Walrus was flying as fast as it could, and BRAIN-DEAD was "getting the hell out of Dodge."

Mission accomplished.

14
ONE-MAN ARMY

D-DAY—25 AUGUST 1941. THE INVASION OF PERSIA KICKED OFF AS THE Special Missions Team was touching down at the Raiding Forces departure airfield at Shaibah, Iraq, having completed its mission.

An oddball collection of Allied ships steamed up the Persian Gulf toward their objective, closing the distance to Bandar Shahpur. The naval and army units taking part in OPERATION BISHOP were known as Force B.

A pair of tugboats belonging to the Anglo-Persian Oil Company, designated Tug A and Tug B and temporarily being commanded by Royal Naval Patrol Service Skippers, preceded the Force B Headquarters' vessel and troopship for the expedition, the Armed Merchant Cruiser *Kanimbla*. Vice Admiral Sir Randolph "Razor" Ransom, Deputy Director Operations Division (Irregular), was on board the *Kanimbla* to observe the operation.

Astern of the Armed Merchant Cruiser came the RIN sloop *Lawrence,* the corvette HMS *Snapdragon* and the ex-China Yangtze River gunboat *Cockchafer.*

Last in the column was the ex-Milford Haven trawler *Arthur Cavanagh* of the Royal Naval Patrol Service. The RNPS was as unorthodox a navy outfit as one could imagine. With no age limit to join, it consisted mostly of fishermen, yachtsmen and the like—reservists who had been called to active duty at the outbreak of the war. Trawlers had quit fishing one day, stowed their gear, received some hastily-installed new equipment, and begun mine-sweeping patrols the next day.

The Patrol Service was a private navy within the Royal Navy with their own badge and a Headquarters/Training Center called the Sparrows Nest—named after the man who had originally owned the property—not the bird. Nevertheless, when the students graduated and were assigned to their ships, it was said that they "flew the nest."

The RNPS fell under the umbrella of VAdm. Ransom's irregular naval empire. The Patrol Service had seen constant sea duty from the first day of the war, providing anti-U-boat convoy escorts and mine sweeping patrols—but today was their maiden invasion in Middle East Command.

Traveling in front of the flotilla was a motorized native craft, Dhow 8, manned by a scratch crew of RNPS sailors disguised as Arabs under the command of Lieutenant Randy "Hornblower" Seaborn.

Waldo Treywick and the Phantom radio team, clad in local costume, were aboard to perform reconnaissance, sound the channel and provide timely communications to the Force B commander on the *Kanimbla*.

Following Dhow 8 was a Royal Air Force Air Sea Rescue Boat #80 with a party of heavily armed Australian Blue Jackets aboard. They were led by a pair of Sea Squadron Raiding Forces Raiders prepared to act as a quick reaction force if the dhow ran into trouble.

Both Dhow 8 and RAF #80 were equipped with a supply of hurricane lanterns they intended to attach to any unlighted buoys in Khor Musa Channel.

Eight boarding parties, consisting mostly of Royal Australian Navy sailors, were spread out across the Force B armada—each stiffened by a pair of Raiding Forces Sea Squadron Commandos. Their mission was to go aboard and capture the German, Italian and Persian Navy ships moored in Bandar Shahpur.

The Baluchis aboard the *Kanimbla* chanted war songs; the Gurkhas whetted their kuris until they were sharp enough to shave with; the Australian Blue Jackets in khaki battledress oiled their weapons and double-checked rappelling hooks and boarding ladders. All glanced in wonder at the Raiding Forces Commandos who would be leading them; they were taking a last-minute snooze before the battle commenced.

At the tail end of the eclectic little fleet, aboard the RNPS trawler *Arthur Cavanagh,* Lieutenant Butch "Headhunter" Hoolihan reviewed his orders.

First the trawler was to move alongside the Italian tanker *Bronte,* which was lying in the Khor Musa Inlet, and he was to board her. After she had been captured, RNPS personnel would transfer to the ship to take it under control.

When the sailors came on board, Lt. Hoolihan and his Blue Jackets would return to the *Arthur Cavanagh,* move on to the *Barba* and board her in turn.

Lt. Hoolihan and the Raiding Forces "stiffeners" were looking forward to the mission.

It was a relief for them to be out of Tobruk.

There, Raiding Forces had been under constant enemy artillery fire and air attack during the day and running "quiet" missions at night. Going ashore from Sea Squadron's pair of fast Italian MAS boats, Raiding Forces Commandos were stealthily planting mines on the Via Balbia, then pulling out, deliberately avoiding enemy contact.

Most days, Sea Squadron patrols arrived back at their base in Tobruk just as the morning air attacks resumed. The Raiders seldom got any real rest. The living conditions were primitive. The food was bad.

And they almost never had the satisfaction of witnessing the results of their road mining expeditions.

OPERATION BISHOP was a welcome break from the grind of the sun, sand, and incoming fire of Tobruk. Today, Sea Squadron would not be avoiding contact. The Raiders were going to take it to the bad guys, witness the outcome up close and personal, and they did not have to be stealthy.

The only curb placed on the Raiders in their rules of engagement was to capture the ships intact. There was no restraint placed on how they were to take down the enemy sailors. No one much cared if they were damaged goods.

Raiding Forces planned to execute their mission with "extreme violence of action." Lt. Hoolihan made that clear in his Mission Statement.

• • •

As force b was steaming up the Khor Musa channel, Lieutenant Westcott Huxley and his team of pathfinders were exiting their ancient Vickers-Valentia aircraft, jumping over the oil field at Haft-l-Khel. The drop zone was a straight stretch of road that serviced the Anglo-Persian Oil Company facility.

Lt. Huxley and his men were tasked with marking the road with flares for an air landing by C/3/10 Baluchi Regiment. They had one hour to accomplish their mission. Then at sunrise, six Vickers-Valentia troop transports would fly in to land the C Company troops.

This was only the fourth time a tactical air landing to insert British troops behind enemy lines had been attempted—and that was if you counted Lieutenant Colonel John Randal's raid to take out the Iraqi artillery battery firing into RAF Habbaniya. Lt. Huxley had played a role in three of the four operations.

Raiding Forces was still working on the technique of what it was beginning to call "pathfinder" missions. But the young 10th Lancer was now the most experienced pathfinder in the British Army.

A crucial component of this pathfinder mission was finding at least a half-mile stretch of straight road that did not have excessive potholing. The team was armed with picks and shovels to fill in any potholes they discovered.

This was a new technique Raiding Forces had never tried before.

Lt. Huxley made a soft PLF in the faded, salmon-colored sand beside the road. Sergeant Major Mike "March or Die" Mikkalis came down a few yards away, followed by the other four Raiders in the team.

The desert was empty.

First thing, all six men recovered their X-type parachutes. They would be bringing them out when the team extracted back to Shaibah on the Vickers-Valentia troop transports, after dropping off the company of Baluchis. Lieutenant Karen Montgomery, Raiding Forces

Chief Rigger, had made it clear she wanted them back—parachutes were in short supply in Middle East Command.

Sgt. Maj. Mikkalis took charge of assembling the pathfinder team. The men immediately shook out their weapons and moved out, patrolling in the direction of the road, which was only twenty-five yards away.

Lt. Huxley led the way, pulling point.

When the team reached the road, Lt. Huxley stood fast while Sgt. Maj. Mikkalis continued down the road with the patrol, dropping off a man every 150 yards. Each man was equipped with a pair of railroad flares. On signal they would ignite them and place one on each side of the right of way—the signal to execute was a green Very pistol flare fired by Lt. Huxley.

When Sgt. Maj. Mikkalis dropped off the last man, he continued on for another 150 yards and placed his parachute bag in the middle of the lane to mark the position. Then he returned to where Lt. Huxley was waiting.

The two strolled back down the road again inspecting it. There were only a few small potholes in the right of way, and the Raiders were already busy filling them. When they reached Sgt. Maj. Mikkalis' parachute bag, Lt. Huxley turned to return to his position.

"Pewfect, Sawgeant Majuh," Lt. Huxley said.

Standing on a road in enemy territory in the middle of nowhere as the sky brightened was a lonely proposition. Would a Persian motorized patrol arrive before the Vickers-Valentias with the Baluchis?

What to do if it did?

Lt. Huxley broke out his Very pistol. He plunked a fat flare round in the short stubby barrel of the pistol with a bore so big it looked like it was designed for shooting dinosaurs and snapped it shut.

Then, he stood by, ready.

Time seemed to stop moving; at least the hands on his watch did, which did not make a lot of sense unless it was broken, considering daylight was coming fast. In the distance, blue lights twinkled on the tops of the oil derricks.

The wait was lonely. The night was still. Not a sound was to be heard.

Operating deep behind enemy lines is not for everyone.

As the sky turned rose, then burnt orange, the sound of airplanes could be heard approaching from the direction of Iraq—that was good. Lt. Huxley looked at his Patek Philippe wristwatch. It was working. The yellow luminous hands were pointing straight up 0500 hours. Right on time.

Lt. Huxley fired a flare straight up.

The little parachute cracked open and the flare dangled down, fizzling green. The Raiders swung into action igniting their brilliant red, sparkling railroad flares to mark the landing ground.

Then, per the plan, Sgt. Maj. Mikkalis walked up the road rolling up the pathfinder team as he came.

When the party reached Lt. Huxley, he moved them a safe distance into the desert. The Raiders did not want to be standing too close when the big troop transports came in for landing.

Six Vickers-Valentias flew into sight. The first aircraft touched down on the road between the sparkling flares, immediately followed by the second, third, fourth and fifth. Men began discharging from the aircraft while they were still rolling.

The sixth aircraft came in hot. The pilot misjudged. The airplane reversed engines. The pilot stood on the brakes. While Lt. Huxley's team watched, transfixed, it ploughed into the transport that had landed in front of it.

Luckily, the troops on the fifth airplane had all disembarked and cleared the area by the time the collision occurred.

Urged on by the King's Own advisors shouting "Go, go, go," the Baluchis on plane six disentangled themselves after the crash and began deplaning on the double. By some miracle, all the troops made it off before both aircraft burst into flames.

In the blink of an eye, three men were dead. The pilot and co-pilot of plane six died, as did one of the aircrew on plane five. There was no way to get the RAF men's bodies out of the burning troop transports before the airplanes were engulfed in flames.

Lt. Huxley ordered, "Follow me."

He led the team toward the first Vickers-Valentia to touch down. The King's Own air-landing advisors double-timed up the road to join them.

Sgt. Maj. Mikkalis counted the troops aboard.

"Good count, sir," Sgt. Maj. Mikkalis said. "All personnel accounted for."

Lt. Huxley was last man on. The RAF pilot did not waste time. Sitting on the ground in the middle of Persia with a war getting ready to start was not his idea of a good time.

The troop transport was taxiing for takeoff before the door was slammed closed. The obsolete airplane, a model long overdue for the boneyard, lumbered into the air. As the plane banked to head back to Iraq, down below three Vickers-Valentias could be seen taking off. Two others were blazing furiously.

Mission accomplished—at a price.

THE PASSAGE UP THE KHOR MUSA WAS UNEVENTFUL, WITH DHOW 8 AND RAF Air Sea Rescue boat #80 out front. They were followed by the Armed Merchant Cruiser *Kanimbla,* leading the invasion fleet with Tugs A and B on either bow.

Kanimbla reached buoy 13, the final checkpoint, at 1310 and fell behind in accordance with the plan. Astern of her were the *Cockchafer,* the *Lawrence,* the *Snapdragon* and the *Arthur Cavanagh.* The ebb tide was at least two knots. All units were signaled to proceed to the objective at ten knots.

At this point, Waldo Treywick transferred from Dhow 8 to Tug B, and Lieutenant Randy "Hornblower" Seaborn transferred to Tug A, there being no further role for the unarmed dhow in OPERATION BISHOP.

Waldo was particularly happy to be on Tug B because its orders were to "take up a position in the middle of the harbor and not engage." The tugboat was to stand by on call to shift enemy prizes if and when needed.

When he came on board still in costume wearing native garb, Waldo immediately went up on the bridge to introduce himself to the captain. There, the first thing he noticed was a target in a big frame under glass posted outside the wheelhouse: a K created by bullet holes.

Addressing the tug's captain, Royal Navy Patrol Service Temporary Acting Probationary Skipper, Sub-Lieutenant Warthog Finley, OBE, Waldo said, "Only two men that coulda shot that—"Geronimo" Joe McKoy or Colonel Randal."

"*Major* Randal shot that K for me," Skipper Finley said. "Stands for *King Kong,* my old tug back on the Gold Coast."

"Who are you supposed to be, Waldo? Lawrence of bloody Arabia?"

"I was workin' undercover," Waldo said. "How do you know Colonel Randal?"

"We was doing something real crazy I can't talk about," Skipper Finley said. "Three of us tugboat captains was in a briefing when we met and we wasn't real impressed. Tried to stare the man down."

"So, how did that work for 'ya?" Waldo said.

"I don't think he noticed," Skipper Finley said. "Wish Randal was here. I'd be a lot more confident."

"The Colonel's in on this," Waldo said. "Done been here and gone by now. We ain't got nothin' to worry about, Warthog."

"Only got assigned yesterday, so I ain't up to full speed on all the details of BISHOP," Skipper Finley said. "You say Raiding Forces is part o' this?"

"The Colonel knocked out the Persian's military communications complex about ten minutes ago by my watch," Waldo said. "Right about now, those carpet merchants ought to be figgerin' out they ain't got no way to talk to each other."

"Well, that's good," Skipper Finley said.

"Gonna' find a confused bunch a' ragheads afloat," Waldo said, "when we hit that bay, Warthog."

"Ain't that too bad," Skipper Finley said.

RAF Launch #80 and the *Arthur Cavanagh* were unable to keep up with the ten-knot pace. The *Lawrence* now forged ahead, overhauling Tug A, Tug B and the *Cockchafer.*

At 0415, the *Lawrence* pulled into the lead and entered the inlet at Bandar Shahpur. The German ships were anchored in the stream nearest the entrance. The Italians were moored in a line nearest the town of Bandar Shahpur. Two Persian gunboats were positioned between the two groups of Axis merchantmen.

The *Marinfels* was the first to be captured by a boarding party of Blue Jackets, who swarmed aboard the enemy ship. Task-organized into two teams, as all eight boarding parties were—upper deck and engine room. Each team was led by a Raiding Forces Commando. The takedown went fast and easy—at least for the boarding party personnel.

However, the quick success was a signal for trouble.

All the Axis ships were prepared, to some degree, for scuttling in the event the inlet was ever attacked. Lengths of fuse were run, and kerosene and tar buckets strategically placed about, ready to be fired on command. The crews had been drilled to open the main valve and to detonate high-explosive charges in the holds. On some ships, electronic detonating cord had been run to prepared explosives.

Seeing their sister ship being boarded, the *Wiessenfels'* crew promptly executed their orders to scuttle, and the tanker burst into flames.

A machine gun began firing from the *Strumfels* when the *Snapdragon* slid in beside her.

While this was happening, the *Lawrence* proceeded alongside and boarded the Persian gunboats *Karkas* and *Chabraz*. Seeing the Armed Merchant Cruiser *Kanimbla* looming astern the sloop, the two Persian Navy craft, commanded and crewed by Italians, opted for discretion over valor.

They surrendered.

Ignoring the fireworks going on all around, the *Arthur Cavanagh,* with Lieutenant Butch "Headhunter" Hoolihan in command of the ship's boarding party, proceeded boldly on toward the Italian tanker *Bronte.* As the RNPS trawler edged in alongside her quarry, fire broke out amidships on the enemy deck.

Nevertheless, Lt. Hoolihan ordered, "After me, lads!"

The rugged Australian Blue Jackets stormed over the side onto the Italian ship, swinging ax handles and enthusiastically carrying out their young Commando leaders' order to "execute the mission with extreme violence."

Blackshirt sailors went down like ten pins. The crew was quickly subdued. Realizing they were burning the ship out from under themselves, the Italian sailors, not being stupid, pitched in and helped bring the fires under control.

As per the plan, Lt. Hoolihan and his men promptly returned to the *Arthur Cavanagh* and moved off to attack their second target—the tanker *Barba*. The Australian Blue Jackets had their blood up now and were raring for more action.

Even though the Italian ship was blazing when the RNPS trawler arrived alongside, the boarding party went over, battered the Fascist sailors into submission with the ax handles, then forced them to form firefighting parties.

Things were touch and go on the *Barba* for a while, but eventually, with the help of additional reinforcements from the *Arthur Cavanagh,* they were able to extinguish the fires and save the ship.

Lt. Hoolihan had accomplished a Royal Marines fantasy: two successful contested boarding actions in a single morning.

On board Tug B, Waldo was standing next to Skipper Finley in the wheelhouse. Both men were smoking cigars. They had front row seats to the invasion of Persia. Action was going on all around them. The tugboat was a passive observer. Her complement had instructions not to fire on any of the ships in the inlet because they might hit the friendly sailors in the boarding parties.

The two men were enjoying the show when, without warning, an armed Axis tug towing a barge took Tug B under machine gun fire.

"Those bloody bastards," Skipper Finley said as splinters flew off the wheelhouse, "are doing a real bit of target practice, Waldo."

The Italian crewmen operating the Persian tug were shooting off the upper deck and from out of the portholes.

As Skipper Finley was the captain of Tug B, he had the ultimate responsibility for the safety of his command. A ship's captain is a king when it is underway. No one outranks the captain. And that is especially true when the ship is imperiled.

"Stand by to board, Waldo," Skipper Finley ordered.

"*What?*"

"Pick any four of my ratings," Skipper Finley said. "Make it snappy—we're going alongside in about thirty seconds."

Waldo knew better than to argue. He ran down the stairs to the deck screaming, "Get me the four biggest, meanest sons-a-bitches on this boat!"

Four men stepped forward, armed with Enfield Mark III rifles with sword-type bayonets fixed. They were civilian tugboat sailors, employees of the Anglo-Persian Oil Company. Not one of them had the advantage of as much as a single day's military training.

Waldo looked at the men in horror. All four had cigarettes dangling from their lips. They were the least intimidating sailors he had ever laid eyes on. He was afraid they were going to accidentally stick each other with the bayonets.

Before Waldo could issue a single instruction, Skipper Finley slammed Tug B into the side of the barge.

Clutching his prized Rigby 7X57 in both hands, Waldo jumped for all he was worth. While he was in mid-air, the tug bounced off the old tires strung along the side of the barge and was carried clear.

Three Blackshirts standing on the barge were blazing away at him with Gilisenti 10.35mm revolvers, and snipers were firing from the enemy tugboat as he came sailing over. The four Tug B sailors with the Enfields failed to make it across.

Unintentionally, Waldo was storming the barge all by himself.

The beneficiary of army training back in the last one when he was scouting with P. J. Pretorius in East Africa, Waldo braced his fall with the butt of the Rigby's stock, rolled, and got off a couple of quick shots faster than he would have ever believed possible with a bolt-action magazine rifle, knocking down two of his assailants.

The third Italian dropped his pistol, threw his hands up and surrendered, wondering why a crazed Arab was single-handedly attacking his ship.

Having more immediate concerns, Waldo ignored him. A furious fire was coming from the enemy tug. To reach better cover, he ran across the barge—which was as flat as a pool table—and climbed up on the enemy tugboat.

Skipper Finley came back alongside the barge.

He was bellowing, "Get aboard her, you worthless lubbers!"

The four sailors in the scratch Tub B boarding party, more terrified of Skipper Finley than the enemy sailors, made it on their second try. One butt-stroked the Italian (who was attempting to surrender) with his Enfield, having seen that move at the cinema—life imitating art.

Then the A-P Oil Company tugboat men ran after Waldo.

Since most of the enemy firing was coming out of the portholes, the Tug B sailors quickly climbed up on the enemy tug's deck, moved aft, slammed down the hatch and bolted it shut.

Leaving one man to stand guard, the boarders then proceeded straight to the watertight doors leading to the forward hold and bolted it shut also.

Now they had the Italians completely isolated down below— trapped like rats, though they could still shoot out of the portholes at other ships if they chose.

Realizing their predicament, the Italians down below ceased fire.

Skipper Finley ordered across the last three of his sailors he could spare to help Waldo's men secure the enemy tug.

Firing broke out again when the Tug B men moved up the stairs to the upper deck. The Italians and the boarding party were blazing away at each other from point-blank range, neither side doing any damage to the other.

"Break out the grenades, boys!" Waldo shouted. No one had a hand grenade, but the Blackshirts had no way to know that.

The Italian crew instantly threw down their weapons, then stood up with their arms raised.

With their surrender, Raiding Forces' role in the Anglo-Soviet invasion of Persia came to an end. Sea Squadron flew out one hour later on a Catalina PBY provided by Vice Admiral Sir Randolph "Razor" Ransom.

"You trying for the Victoria Cross, Mr. Treywick?" Lt. Hoolihan said on the seaplane, after listening to Lt. Seaborn's recital of the boarding action he had witnessed from Tug A.

"Not me, Butch," Waldo said. "The Colonel says "it don't count when you're savin' yourself." And that right there is a gilt-edged fact."

"Sounds like," Lt. Hoolihan said, "you were a one-man army."

15
WHAT'S A DUCK?

"I know you will be changing the name now that desert patrol is being reorganized, but is it true, John," Captain the Lady Jane Seaborn asked, "that you named your jeep patrol Violet because it's my favorite color?"

"Negative," Lieutenant Colonel John Randal said. "I named the patrol after the color of your eyes."

"My eyes," Lady Jane said, "are green."

"Oh," Lt. Col. Randal said. "Maybe it was Brandy's."

"Hers are golden." Lady Jane laughed.

"Well, it was someone's eyes."

"Better not be."

The two were waiting on the tarmac at the departure airfield in Iraq. Major Sir Terry "Zorro" Stone and his regiment, the Lancelot Lancers, were airborne inbound, having completed their mission at Abadan.

Lieutenant Butch "Headhunter" Hoolihan and his Sea Squadron troop had flown in from the Persian Gulf earlier, after playing their role as stiffeners for the boarding parties in OPERATION BISHOP. Lieutenant Westcott Huxley's pathfinders were already back. Raiding Forces were assembling for the return trip back to Cairo—it was a gathering of eagles.

While the Special Missions Team and Lt. Huxley's pathfinders had not suffered any casualties, the Lancelot Lancers experienced "minor scrapes and abrasions"—some not so minor—from their low-level jump. And the Sea Squadron troop had reported two boarding party men wounded, though both were expected to recover. However, Lt. Col. Randal was not experiencing the euphoria normally associated with the conclusion a successful operation.

He was feeling guilty.

One glance at Lt. Hoolihan had put him on notice that he had been derelict in his duties as a commander. The young Royal Marine looked ten years older than he had the last time Lt. Col. Randal had seen him, before his troop departed RFHQ for Tobruk. Clearly, Lt. Hoolihan and his men had seen hard service.

Lt. Col. Randal had been so fixated on organizing Desert Patrol that he had violated a basic principle of command. He had failed to go to Tobruk in person to see, firsthand, what the operating conditions were like.

Sea Squadron had been left to fend for itself.

Lt. Col. Randal realized he had not honored two primary principles of leadership he demanded from his Raiding Forces officers—"take care of your troops" and "lead from the front." He did not intend to allow that to stand.

Now that Captain Jeb Pelham-Davies had his second Sea Squadron troop out from Seaborn House, it was long past time for Lt. Col. Randal to travel to Tobruk to see how they were faring.

As the word went round that the Lounge Lizards were inbound, more and more Raiding Forces personnel drifted out to the airstrip to watch the aircraft come in. Raiders returning from a mission always drew a crowd. Everyone liked to be on hand to see the troops arrive—better than any parade.

Only there would not be any cheering, waving of flags or band playing.

The three troop transports appeared in the distance, circled round and came in for a landing. The Lancers began to disembark as soon as the aircraft rolled to a stop. The troops moved across the tarmac with the easy confidence of hardened combat veterans.

Maj. Stone's men had fought across 1,700 miles of Abyssinia, crossed 1,000 miles of uncharted desert to relieve RAF Habbaniya, attacked into Baghdad, then invaded Vichy French Syria. Now they had completed OPERATION LEAPING LIZARD—their first combat parachute drop.

The Lancelot Lancers may have been the smallest regiment in the British Army, but they had seen as much action as any.

When Maj. Stone walked up, he said, "Brought Raiding Forces a present, old stick."

Eight of his men were carrying four long, wooden boxes by rope handles affixed on each end. 'SKODA WORKS' was stenciled on the sides.

"Each crate contains a dozen brand new .303 Bren Mark 1 guns still in the Cosmoline," Maj. Stone said. "Originally called the ZGB/30 I believe."

The Bren was the *one* arm Raiding Forces had never been able to obtain. They were the most sought-after weapons in Middle East Command.

Though classified a Light Machine Gun (LMG), a Bren was actually a magazine-fed automatic rifle, arguably the best of class in any army. Having one gave a tremendous boost in firepower to a small unit like an infantry squad, a boat team of Commandos, or a dismounted gun jeep crew.

"The Royal Small Arms Factory manufacture our Brens under license, though I rather doubt we are paying the fee now to the Germans, who are turning them out as fast as they can in 7.92 Mauser for the Wehrmacht," Maj. Stone said.

"These are straight out of Czechoslovakia for the Shah's Navy, stamped 1938."

"Outstanding," Lt. Col. Randal said. "How'd it go, Terry?"

"Once the fireworks started," Maj. Stone said, "Persian soldiers began tearing off their uniforms and fading into the civilian population. We only had a few brief exchanges of gunfire.

"Other than two A-P Oil Company employees killed by an RAF airstrike because they disobeyed instructions to stay indoors, there were no casualties unrelated to the drop on our side.

"Never be another mission like this one."

"Good job," Lt. Col. Randal said.

LIEUTENANT COLONEL JOHN RANDAL WAS HOLDING COURT IN THE BACK of the Hudson that was winging its way to Raiding Forces Headquarters. Vice Admiral Sir Randolph "Razor" Ransom, Major Sir Terry "Zorro" Stone, Captain "Pyro" Percy Stirling, ex-Captain Travis McCloud, Captain "Geronimo" Joe McKoy, Waldo Treywick, Lieutenant Butch "Headhunter" Hoolihan, Lieutenant Roy Kidd, Lieutenant Randy "Hornblower" Seaborn and ex-Lieutenant Billy Jack Jaxx were sitting on the wooden crates of Bren guns the Lancelot Lancers had captured.

"When we get back," Lt. Col. Randal said, "I want to dial in on our primary mission—destroying German and Italian motor transport. That's where Rommel's most vulnerable.

"We've taken our eyes off the ball shooting up airfields and roadhouses.

"Arriving unannounced, unexpected, in the dark of night with all guns blazing, rolling out with the place in flames is a lot more glamorous than picking off supply trucks in ones and twos. But trucks are our primary target.

"Time for Raiding Forces to get back to basics.

"Terry, I originally gave you six weeks to have the Lancelot Lancers amalgamated into Desert Patrol," Lt. Col. Randal said. "Try to do it in four."

"I shall get with Jack Black," Maj. Stone said. "We should be able to accelerate the conversion from armed cars to gun jeep patrols—provided the jeeps are ready, old stick."

"Travis," Lt. Col. Randal said, "I want your new patrol ready to roll when the Regiment becomes operational."

"Roger that," ex-Capt. McCloud said. "I've decided on most of the men, sir."

"Capt. McKoy, I'd like you to take a look at fine-tuning our tactics for the Boys .55s. The Lovat Scouts haven't been doing enough sniping. They're way too valuable not to maximize their potential."

"Can do," Capt. McKoy said. "We need to think small in a big way, John. Ain't necessary to destroy the trucks. Have the Scouts plink an armored piercing round through the engine housing from a mile or so out—that'll get the job done."

"Exactly," Lt. Col. Randal said.

"Nickel and dime 'em to death," Capt. McKoy said. "Damage enough Axis trucks in the middle a' nowhere, we overload the opposition's recovery and maintenance system."

"In a nutshell," Lt. Col. Randal said, "that's how we hurt the Afrika Korps—thinking 'small in a big way.'"

Waldo said, "I met a friend a' yours, Colonel. Warthog Finley."

"Where did you run into Capt. Finley?"

"Skipper of Tug B," Waldo said. "Had the craziest rank I ever heard: Actin' Provisional Temporary Royal Navy Patrol Service Skipper Sub-Lieutenant or somethin' like 'at.

"Warthog said to tell you hello."

"There's the LCT commander we're looking for, Admiral," Lt. Col. Randal said. "Can you arrange a transfer for Captain Finley?"

"Yes I can, if you believe he is the man for the job," VAdm. Ransom said. "The RNPS fall under my authority.

"The Patrol Service recently established a base outside of Alexandria at a place called Sidi Bishr, shipped 5,000 men out here from the Sparrows Nest. The Royal Navy is refusing to use them on some of their ships.

"We can have our pick."

"Warthog was on OPERATION LOUNGE LIZARD off the Gold Coast with us, Grandfather," Lt. Seaborn said. "He skippered the lead tug boat—decorated with an OBE for his actions."

"In that case, I shall organize travel to Sidi Bishr the moment we get back to Cairo," VAdm. Ransom said, "transfer Skipper Sub-Lieutenant Warthog Finley to Raiding Forces, then let him select his own RNPS crew to man the LCT.

"You can use a few more sailors for your two MAS boats, Randy. Fly out with me and recruit the ratings you need.

"Care to come along, Colonel?"

"I have to go to Tobruk, sir, but I'd like you to take Lieutenant Kidd," Lt. Col. Randal said. "Roy doesn't know it yet, but he's slated to command the gun jeep patrol we're going to station afloat aboard the LCT."

"Congratulations, Lt. Kidd," VAdm. Ransom said. "A plum assignment."

"Thank you, sir," Lt. Kidd said, not having a clue what they were talking about.

Lt. Col. Randal said, "Roy, I'll give you Frank Polanski for your patrol sergeant if you want him. He was a U.S. Marine, so Frank thinks amphibiously, knows his way around the navy.

"You can have any man in Raiding Forces within reason—a light patrol, six jeeps, two Raiders per."

Lt. Kidd did not know what a Landing Craft Tank was, and he had no idea why Lt. Col. Randal planned to station a gun jeep patrol at sea on a ship that sounded like it was a tank.

"Sir, why do we want a jeep patrol afloat?"

"To ride in the DUKWs."

"What's a 'duck,' sir?"

"DUKW," Lt. Col. Randal said. "A two and a half-ton swimming truck. Possible to load nine of 'em on an LCT. If you lift it in with a crane, a gun jeep will fit in the truck bed.

"The LCT with the DUKWs and gun jeeps on board can rove up and down the coast over the horizon, running parallel to the Via Balbia, Roy. At night, the DUKWs will launch, ferry your jeeps to a deserted beach and drive 'em up on the shore.

"Your patrol will unload, proceed inland, mine the road, shoot up a roadhouse or raid a truck park, return to the beach, load back in the DUKWs, cruise out to the LCT, re-embark, then sail away over the horizon to do it all over again somewhere else the next night.

"At least that's the idea," Lt. Col. Randal said. "You'll have to work out the details."

"Colonel," Lt. Kidd said, "if I hadn't been with you at RAF Hab-baniya, I'd think you were making this up."

"Well, I am, Roy," Lt. Col. Randal said, "but you still have to do it."

"Understood, sir," Lt. Kidd said, "loud and clear.

"Why me, Colonel?"

"You're the stud who tackles man-eating leopards. A graduate of the Commando School, and you've been understudying me," Lt. Col. Randal said. "You're ready."

VAdm. Ransom said, "Who is to operate the DUKWs, Colonel—soldiers or sailors?"

"I have no idea, sir," Lt. Col. Randal said.

"Since the DUKWs only need to make it from the water's edge up on shore, getting them from the LCT to the beach is the greater challenge.

"Why not recruit Patrol Service coxswains to captain the DUKWs?"

"Admiral Ransom," Lt. Col. Randal said, "I'll leave that decision up to you, Randy and Roy, sir."

"This LCT enterprise is more than a little interesting," VAdm. Ransom said. "A lot of combinations to work with. I had no idea Special Operations offered the commander so many possibilities.

"Best war I ever served in."

LIEUTENANT COLONEL JOHN RANDAL, VICE ADMIRAL SIR RANDOLPH "Razor" Ransom, Captain "Geronimo" Joe McKoy, Waldo Treywick and ex-Lieutenant Billy Jack Jaxx were still in the back, sitting on the Skoda Works' weapons crates and smoking Waldo's cigars. The others had returned to their seats on the Hudson and were fast asleep.

"Billy Jack," Capt. McKoy said, "you related to Sheriff Marlin Jaxx by any chance?"

"Yes, sir," ex-Lt. Jaxx said, "he's my grandfather."

"Hardcase," Capt. McKoy said. "Two-gun sheriff carries a pair of big, ivory-gripped .357 Smith & Wesson Triplelocks. Used to strap the bad men he'd shot to the fenders of a Pierce Arrow he'd confiscated from a bootlegger and drive 'em in to the county seat.

"Marlin still do that?"

"We brought one in," ex-Lt. Jaxx said, "the week I left to join the army."

"You was a football player?"

"Six man squad in high school, sir. I played quarterback—which meant I was the running back too," ex-Lt. Jaxx said. "Coach mostly used me for punt returns and kickoffs at UT."

"Heard you had yourself a Tri-Delt' problem," Capt. McKoy said.

"What's a Tri-Delt'?" Waldo asked.

"A college sorority made up of the best-looking girls in Texas," Capt. McKoy said. "Which means the world, Waldo.

"Daddies is all rich ranchers, oilmen, land barons ..."

"Yes, sir, that's a Rodge," ex-Lt. Jaxx said. "I did have a Tri-Delta problem."

"Bein' a university man, Lieutenant," Waldo said, "I'd 'a figured you'd know ..."

"Know?"

"The problem is the solution," Waldo said. "Got yourself a problem, say it out loud, and the solution pops right out at ya—hey, presto! Like magic. They teach that in college."

"I don't think it works, Mr. Treywick," Lt. Col. Randal said, "when women are in the mix."

LIEUTENANT COLONEL JOHN RANDAL AND CAPTAIN THE LADY JANE Seaborn were seated at a table in Groppi's in the far back of the room, as usual, in a corner almost hidden behind a tall, potted fern. Lady Jane insisted on taking him out to dinner alone after the Hudson arrived back at Raiding Forces Headquarters.

Brigadier Raymond J. "R. J." Maunsell and Captain A. W. "Sammy" Sansom walked in and spoke to the *maître d'*, who pointed in their direction. The two officers surveyed the room, spotted them and made a beeline for their table.

"Congratulations are in order, Colonel," R. J. said, "on a job well done.

"Initial intelligence reports, while sketchy, indicate the Persian military has imploded. Our ground troops are making rapid advances everywhere.

"Seems the Persian communications system has broken down. The Shah has the vapors. The senior command appears to have disintegrated. It is not clear who—if anyone—is directing the Persian forces."

Lt. Col. Randal said, "I promised Jane no business tonight, but that's good news."

"Forgive the intrusion," R. J. said. "I only wanted to stop by to advise you we shall not be needing Phantom to build the radio we discussed after all."

"Why might that be?"

"The German Intelligence Service came through," R. J. said. "Rikke Runborg's wireless arrived at long last."

"And how," Lady Jane asked, "did the Nazis arrange delivery?"

"Amal Atrash," Capt. Sansom said, "hand-carried the Abwehr's set to Rocky's front door."

Lt. Col. Randal said, "Uh-oh!"

"Better late," R. J said, "than never."

Lady Jane said, "Not for Amal."

16
RATS OF TOBRUK

THE WALRUS WAS FLYING UP THE COASTLINE, FIFTY MILES SHORT OF Tobruk. Lieutenant Pamala Plum-Martin was scanning the ocean ahead, looking for the Raiding Forces MAS boat. Lieutenant Colonel John Randal was riding in the co-pilot's seat, helping her search.

It was possible—but risky—to fly directly into Tobruk during the hours of daylight. Doing so meant trusting to the friend/foe identification skills of trigger-happy anti-aircraft gunners, many of whom had no formal training. Cooks, clerks—anyone available—were pressed into service, assigned an anti-aircraft machine gun position to stand to and provided unlimited ammunition.

The general rule of thumb at Tobruk being, "If it flies, it dies."

Why take a chance?

The better plan was to rendezvous with the MAS boat, land the Walrus and have Lt. Col. Randal transfer to it for the remainder of the journey to inspect Raiding Forces Sea Squadron. Lt. Plum-Martin would wait, anchored offshore, until he returned.

Lt. Col. Randal was in the camp of *there is no such thing as friendly fire when it's coming at you.*

Up ahead he spotted a speck. Lt. Col. Randal was not skilled in ship identification. However, Lt. Plum-Martin was, and she saw it almost at the same time.

"There's your taxi, John," Lt. Plum-Martin said, "dead ahead."

The Walrus landed. A Lifeboat Serviceman picked Lt. Col. Randal up in the MAS's dinghy and rowed him to the torpedo boat. Lt. Plum-Martin was wearing her swimsuit under her flight suit. She slipped it off, climbed out and reclined on one of the floats with a book.

The captain was a young Royal Navy Reserve lieutenant Lt. Col. Randal had never met before, Lieutenant Mark Hathaway. A friend of the Seaborn family, he had volunteered for special service in order to serve with Lieutenant Randy "Hornblower" Seaborn and had gone through all the training necessary to qualify, to include the Commando School at Achnacarry.

That made him a priceless addition to Raiding Forces.

Lt. Hathaway pushed the beautiful Italian-built MAS boat hard. It pounded along the coastline. Then, ten miles out, the motor torpedo boat made a wide loop to sea. Afrika Korps had Tobruk completely surrounded, so they did not want to pass by close in sight of the Axis shore positions.

"Colonel," Lt. Hathaway asked as the MAS boat cruised into Tobruk Harbor, "does your pilot look as spectacular up close as she did through my binoculars? For a moment I thought I was seeing a real live Vargas Girl."

"Lt. Plum-Martin's better-looking," Lt. Col. Randal said, "than any Vargas drawing I've ever seen."

"Any chance I could impose on you for an introduction, sir," Lt. Hathaway said, "when I go on leave in Cairo?"

"I'll see what I can do," Lt. Col. Randal said. "Pam specializes in fighter pilots, Mark, but she's been branching out lately."

The MAS boat began passing wrecked ships. Lt. Hathaway avoided an anchored, snow white hospital ship with huge red crosses painted all over it, anchored in the middle of the harbor.

"Tobruk Harbor, sir," Lt. Hathaway said, "where Rommel ran out of steam. For the last four months, the Desert Fox has turned the full brunt of his Luftwaffe, Panzers and German eight-wheeled armored cars against us. Our forces—consisting mostly of the Australian division—have rebuffed him.

"And now our infantry are beginning to launch fighting patrols at night—going out picking their way through the mine fields to raid the German and Italian positions surrounding the perimeter."

"Lord Haw-Haw calls you the 'Rats of Tobruk,' as in trapped," Lt. Col. Randal said. "How do the troops feel about that?"

"Trapped rats we may be, sir, but the lads are fighting hard," Lt. Hathaway said. "We have taken everything the Luftwaffe has to bring against us, and now the garrison is not getting the Axis ground attacks like we used to. Seems the siege is turning more and more into an artillery duel.

"One thing for certain, the Afrika Korps advance has been stopped dead in its tracks here at Tobruk, sir. There is no way around. The Great Sand Sea protects one flank; the Mediterranean the other. If Rommel wants to drive on to Cairo he has to come straight down the Via Balbia through the port.

"No one here plans to let him do it."

"What are living conditions like?" Lt. Col. Randal asked.

"No women, picture shows, ice, fresh vegetables or entertainment of any kind other than shooting at dive-bombing German and Italian airplanes," Lt. Hathaway said.

"Did I mention no women, sir?"

"Yeah," Lt. Col. Randal said, "you did."

"The troops play cricket and swim, sir," Lt. Hathaway said. "We live underground in bunkers.

"Sea Squadron collects old pieces of abandoned Italian cannon and ammunition, sir, which is scattered around everywhere—inside and outside the perimeter.

"The lads do not have any precision sights and would not likely know how to use them if they did, so they poke their heads up the barrels to sight the gun before the charges are placed in the breech. Elevation is accomplished by adding or subtracting a rock from the base of the gun, sir," Lt. Hathaway said.

"When everything 'looks right,' the gunners let fly.

"No one has any idea what they are doing, sir. But our boys have been so enthusiastic, the commanding general has officially recognized the Raiding Forces 'battery' by giving us a place in the line alongside the Royal Artillery.

"We do not have any dedicated anti-aircraft weapons either, sir, so the lads simply blaze away with their Tommy guns and Beretta MAB-38s at everything that passes by in range. Claimed a handful of kills, too.

"We hate this bloody place, Colonel," Lt. Hathaway said. "But Raiding Forces is giving as good as it takes, maybe better. Same as everyone else, sir."

"Sounds like it," Lt. Col. Randal said.

"That's what we do during the day, sir," Lt. Hathaway said. "Under cover of darkness, Sea Squadron sails forth to raid the Via Balbia. We look forward to nightfall."

"How would you say the troops are holding up?" Lt. Col. Randal asked, surveying the war-ravaged seaport as the MAS boat slowly motored in.

Everything he saw looked broken.

Tall columns of black, oily smoke were rising here and there in the distance within the perimeter. Everywhere there was bomb damage. The place was a pile of rubble.

The inescapable impression was of sailing straight into hell.

In the distance, the mushy *cruuumph* of sporadic incoming artillery rounds could be heard detonating from time to time, followed occasionally by the flatter thunder of outgoing cannon fire—it took a trained ear to know the difference.

"Our lads are lucky, sir. They get to go out nights and hit back," Lt. Hathaway said. "I would say Sea Squadron is doing well, all things considered.

"Everyone in this place is bomb-happy, sir."

"I can see how they might be," Lt. Col. Randal said.

The MAS boat docked alongside a bombed-out merchant ship, the *Urania,* which had been put out of action by bombs for'ard. Lt. Col. Randal and Lt. Hathaway had to go through the hole in her side to reach shore.

"Careful, sir," Lt. Hathaway said, indicating a piece of enemy ordinance they had to negotiate.

Lt. Col. Randal stepped over an unexploded 500-pound aerial bomb ... not a good feeling.

The two officers came out the other side of the merchantman, walked down a plank and stepped on to dry land, where Captain Jeb Pelham-Davies, Sea Squadron's commanding officer, was waiting.

"Welcome to scenic Tobruk, sir," Capt. Pelham-Davies said.

"Sorry," Lt. Col. Randal said, "I took so long to get here."

"You have no idea what you have been missing, Colonel," Capt. Pelham-Davies said.

"When the Luftwaffe attacks, the crane on the jetty starts spinning around with each bomb blast, looking something like the training dummy on a swivel at bayonet practice. There is a Nazi big gun called 'Bardia Bill,' sir. When it opens on the port, we have to move the MAS boats to another part of the harbor.

"Sounds like an incoming freight train when the shell comes over.

"Sea Squadron did not have anti-aircraft weapons," Capt. Pelham-Davies said, "so we used rum to bribe the 40mm Bofors crew up on the hill to fire at any plane coming for our position or the MAS boats. Quite an extortion racket the gunners are running, sir.

"The other day, some of the lads grew more bored than usual and went on a scrounging patrol outside the wire. Found an abandoned Italian 20mm Breda. They brought it in. A relay of patrols went back out to retrieve the ammunition.

"The men are convinced the Breda is superior to our Oerlikon, makes a fine anti-aircraft weapon, sir."

"We have them mounted," Lt. Col. Randal said, "on one jeep in each of our patrols."

A siren started wailing.

"Here they come," Lt. Hathaway said pointing. "Stukas."

Raiders started running to man the 20mm Breda. Others rushed outside their bunkers carrying their personal weapons, hoping for a chance if one of the planes flew close enough.

Up high, a flight of four Stukas winged over and went straight for the hospital ship. Furious, every ship in the harbor, every gun crew around the port and anyone else who felt like it, commenced firing at the Luftwaffe dive-bombers.

The Stukas came straight down with their dive sirens screaming, adding to the bedlam. One plane was hit immediately, the tip of a wing blown off. The Nazi bomber started spinning around and around as it came down with a withering vector of tracers converging on it.

Even after the plane crashed into the water, enraged gunners continued to fire at the scattered wreckage.

Screaming down, another Stuka began trailing smoke. It jettisoned its bombs, managed to pull out of its dive, banked around, skimming the water, and flew low over Lt. Col. Randal's head, barely pulling up in time to avoid crashing into the cliffs behind the harbor.

Everyone was firing at it with submachine guns, rifles, side arms—whatever they could lay hands on. Some of the infuriated Australian infantrymen jumped out of the slit trenches along the top of the cliff and threw their boots, helmets and even rocks at the intruder as it flashed over.

Out in the harbor, a pair of bombs exploded, straddling the clearly-marked hospital ship. Tall geysers of water went up on both sides. Miraculously, the white ship with the giant red crosses managed to escape being hit.

So much for the Germans honoring the Geneva Convention.

Ordnance expended, the two remaining Stukas rolled out and streaked for home, chased on their way by streams of green and white tracers.

Watching the departing planes, Lt. Col. Randal had a flashback to the bridge at Calais. He had not thought about it in a while. The Luftwaffe pilots had intentionally slaughtered fleeing civilians, men, women and children.

Best not forget.

"Never a dull moment, sir," Capt. Pelham-Davies said, "except for the all-consuming boredom."

"You men hold tight," Lt. Col. Randal said. "I'm working on a plan."

THE LCT WAS HOVE THREE MILES OFF THE BEACH BEHIND RFHQ OUT-SIDE of Cairo. Skipper Sub-Lieutenant Warthog Finley was standing on the bridge. The K shot in bullet holes by then-Major John Randal before the raid on Rio Bonita was mounted outside the wheelhouse in a position of honor—only now it stood for *King Duck*.

The newly christened LCT was without question the most ungainly craft on the Royal Navy list, but Skipper Finley did not see it that way. To him, the *King Duck* was a thing of beauty, a ship-of-war. He had fulfilled his life's ambition—command of a Royal Navy fighting vessel.

Skipper Finley shouted an order, spoke to his Number One, then hurried down the ladder and climbed behind the wheel of the final DUKW in the column of vehicles on board the LCT, just below the bridge. Waldo Treywick was already in the amphibious truck, riding shotgun. There was a jeep stacked in the bed behind their bench seats, with Captain Hawthorne Merryweather sitting in it.

Up at the bow of the *King Duck*, Lieutenant Colonel John Randal was at the wheel of the lead DUKW. He had one of Waldo's unlit cigars clenched between his front teeth. Captain the Lady Jane Seaborn was sitting next to him.

High in the driver's seat of the gun jeep in the DUKW's bed behind him was ex-Technical Sergeant Hank W. Rawlston, effecting an air of detached boredom as only a seasoned U.S. Army NCO can do when in the company of a party of officers.

Next to the Sergeant was Lieutenant Mandy Paige. Rita Hayworth and Lana Turner were perched in the back of the jeep.

Everyone was wearing floatation devices.

On Skipper Finley's order, the ramp in front of Lt. Col. Randal was lowered with a splash. The lime green hands on Lt. Col. Randal's Rolex read 2125 hours.

There were a million sparkling stars in the Egyptian sky, but a few feet ahead the water was black.

"Hang on," Lt. Col. Randal said, putting the DUKW into low gear and letting out the clutch. He tried to square up the blunt nose of the amphibious truck on the dancing ramp. Not easy—it was being buffeted by the waves and the rocking motion of the *King Duck*.

The engine revved as they started down, head first into the water. Tension aboard the DUKW shot straight up, sky high.

Lt. Col. Randal's chest got tight. Right about now, driving a two and a half-ton truck into the ocean seemed like a really bad idea.

Out of his peripheral vision, drop-dead gorgeous Lady Jane was not laughing for once—which had the usual effect of making her look even more beautiful.

"We are all going to die," Lt. Mandy said.

"Slow and easy, Colonel," ex-Sgt. Rawlston said.

"Ease her in gradual—too fast, we could nose-dive—DUKW's an amphibian, not a submarine, sir."

The Sergeant had the benefit of a week's instruction from the two General Motors Corporation technical representatives who had been flown in from the United States to demonstrate the mysteries of the DUKW to Raiding Forces.

One of his men was stationed on each truck in tonight's exercise to act as onboard advisor.

SPLAAAAASSSSSSSSH!

The DUKW plowed into the choppy waves with a resounding smack—shuddered, struggled to swim, then righted itself.

"Little too fast, sir," ex-Sgt. Rawlston said. "Okay, now shift to water drive."

Lady Jane turned and gave Lt. Col. Randal one of her patented heart attack smiles. All was right with the world. No one was going to drown, at least not yet.

Lt. Col. Randal experimented with the steering and accelerator. The DUKW was a tub. It took a little getting used to, but once he got the hang of it, the truck was not all that difficult to maneuver.

The trick seemed to be small adjustments. No hard turns or heavy acceleration. Point the DUKW in the right direction and let the truck's water-drive propeller do the work.

The rest of the DUKWs followed him off. Vice Admiral Sir Randolph "Razor" Ransom was at the wheel of one; Brandy Seaborn was in the driver's seat of another, with Lieutenant Penelope "Legs" Honeycutt-Parker and Veronica Paige onboard. Next came ex-Lieutenant Billy Jack Jaxx, with Lieutenant Pamala Plum-Martin in the passenger seat and Lieutenant Karen Montgomery in the back. Lieutenant Randy "Hornblower" Seaborn brought up the rear of the column, with Captain Roy "Mad Dog" Reupart and Sergeant Major Mike "March or Die" Mikkalis.

Tonight was a familiarization exercise to demonstrate the capabilities of the LCT and the DUKWs to Raiding Forces personnel who, most likely, would rarely if ever travel in one. The purpose of the exercise was to allow them to experience first-hand what their new military toys could or could not do.

Lt. Col. Randal liked to include as many Raiding Forces people as possible in as many of the outfit's activities as possible. It built unit cohesion. And there was no way to know when one of tonight's participants might dream up an idea the Raiders could put to use later.

His original thought was that DUKW'ing might be fun.

Tonight might be their last chance. Lieutenant Roy Kidd had the six gun jeeps, which he had named Duck Patrol, out in the desert. He was concluding a shakedown run prior to embarking on the patrol's first combat cruise aboard the *King Duck.*

Duck Patrol had already completed sea trials.

Sea Squadron's newest raiding element would be going to war shortly. Their motto was: "No beach out of reach."

Soon the DUKWs were all circling the *King Duck* exactly like a bunch of baby ducks.

"Let's do it, Jane," Lt. Col. Randal said as the DUKW came back around landward.

"Starboard a bit," Lady Jane said, checking the luminous dial on the lensatic compass resting on her knee. She had the azimuth to the beach at RFHQ pre-dialed in on the bezel.

"Steady on course."

Away they went. The *King Duck* immediately vanished astern. The DUKW bobbed and wobbled like a cork.

It rode low, very low—scary low—in the water. The waves were less than a foot below Lt. Col. Randal's elbow, rolling, heaving, swelling, threatening to swamp the tiny craft, but never quite doing it.

Lt. Col. Randal stared through the spray-wet windscreen at the razor-thin black line in the far distance which he imagined was the shore. To the left was the faint blue glow of Cairo. The city was on wartime blackout restriction but in a city with a population of two million people who never seemed to sleep and traffic that never stopped, zero light was impossible to achieve.

Most drivers took the covers off their headlights despite the restriction. Driving at night in Cairo was tantamount to involuntary manslaughter.

The other DUKWs snaked along behind in an undulating formation at a steady six knots per hour. The amphibious trucks were uncommonly seaworthy, but they swayed and dipped inches from disaster. The dangling road wheels created drag, making it necessary for Lt. Col. Randal to constantly work the steering wheel to keep the craft on course and the bow square to the waves.

The heaving seas made the passengers in the DUKW feel small and alone when they were down in a trough and giddy and adventurous when they were skating across the top of a wave.

A red light glowed from the dashboard indicating all was well. The windshield wipers swished back and forth constantly. Lady Jane called out course adjustments from time to time.

"Breakers ahead, Colonel," ex-Sgt. Rawlston said. "Careful not to broach, sir."

"Port five degrees," Lady Jane said.

"*Broach?*" Lt. Mandy said.

Straight ahead without warning, a thin line of foaming white waves breaking on the shore became visible through the arch in the windscreen cleared by the hard-working wipers.

Events began to pick up speed.

Lt. Col. Randal steered onto Lady Jane's adjustment in course. The sound of the breakers swelled to a roar. The DUKW was bucking, crabbing … skidding here one instant, there the next, like a piece of flotsam.

"Square up, Colonel," ex-Sgt. Rawlston said, not sounding quite as bored as he had been up to this point in the trip.

The DUKW floundered in a trough, then a mountainous wave from behind snatched it up on its crest and flung it toward the shore.

"*SQUARE IT UP, SIR!*"

Lt. Col. Randal fought the wheel, but nothing happened. The DUKW was unresponsive. They were at the mercy of the surf. The amphibian made a precipitous drop into a deep trough. The waves towering high overhead on both sides seemed the size of snow-capped mountains.

Then a powerful surge of water popped the DUKW up on the crest and shot it at the beach.

Lt. Col. Randal was fighting the steering to no avail but did manage to remember to switch into wheel drive. The DUKW's wheels started spinning, catching the sand.

Then, with the waves lapping gently around the tires, the amphibious truck drove up on the beach exactly like it was supposed to.

Lady Jane's navigation was spot on. They landed directly behind Raiding Forces Headquarters.

"Nice job, Colonel," ex-Sgt. Rawlston said, sounding slightly embarrassed as he tried to re-light the wet stub of his blunt cigar with shaking hands.

In the back of the jeep, the two Zar priestesses, Rita and Lana, were in borderline cardiac arrest.

Lady Jane leaned over and planted a huge kiss on Lt. Col. Randal's cheek.

"Now I understand what you mean when you say 'surf's up,'" Lt. Mandy said. "Knew you could do it, John."

Lt. Col. Randal said, "I thought we were goners."

James "Baldie" Taylor was standing on the beach a few feet from where the DUKW ground to a halt. There was a lot on his mind.

Ultra intercepts confirmed that the Germans had canceled their plans to invade Cypress. The A-Force deception OPERATION CYPRESS DEFENSE PLAN had worked.

He had returned only that evening from Persia, where he had been conducting a post-invasion intelligence assessment of what was now being called the Anglo-Persian War—one of the shortest in history. It had only lasted four days. OPERATION COUNTENANCE/ BISHOP had succeeded beyond anyone's wildest dreams.

But he was worried. Colonel Dudley Clarke was not at A-Force when he went there to report.

Col. Clarke was officially missing. No one knew where he was. A-Force staff was in full panic mode. Could enemy agents have kidnapped him? Had he gone over to the other side? Anything was possible.

"Perfect sea conditions to conduct your exercise, Colonel," Jim said, when the DUKW rolled to a stop. He was not ready to discuss the Dudley Clarke problem. Not until he had more information.

"Nice and calm tonight."

LIEUTENANT COLONEL JOHN RANDAL WAITED UNTIL HE WAS SURE Captain the Lady Jane Seaborn was sound asleep. Then he carefully inched out of bed, put on his swimming trunks and canvas-topped raiding boots, then went downstairs and outside to the motor pool.

The DUKW fired up on the first try.

Lt. Col. Randal drove across the beach into the water, clicked on propeller drive and putt-putted a half mile out, turned around and came back to the shore. Within thirty minutes, he was back upstairs at RFHQ stealthily slipping back into bed—he thought.

Lady Jane threw a tawny thigh over his chest and put her hand on his shoulder. "Better luck this time?"

"Negative," Lt. Col. Randal said.

17
COWBOYS DON'T SURF

THE LANDING CRAFT TANK KING DUCK WAS STEAMING OFF THE COAST of Libya fifty miles west of Benghazi. At this point along the Mediterranean, the Via Balbia ran about fifteen miles inland. The time was 2145 hours.

Waldo Treywick and Skipper Sub-Lieutenant Warthog Finley were standing on the bridge, smoking Waldo's custom-rolled cigars.

Lieutenant Roy Kidd's Duck Patrol was mounted in six jeeps that were sitting perched in the back of six DUKWs. Each of the amphibious trucks had an RNPS coxswain at the wheel. The patrol was ready to go ashore.

For tonight's raid, Lt. Kidd had his Squadron Commander, Captain Jeb Pelham-Davies, riding in his jeep, with James "Baldie" Taylor in the back. The Raiding Forces Demolitions Officer, Captain Pip Pilkington, MC—along to supervise mining the road—was in the jeep behind them. Lieutenant Butch "Headhunter" Hoolihan was a passenger aboard the third jeep. Captain Hawthorne Merryweather was aboard the fourth jeep.

Two more DUKWs with cranes—each commanded by a Royal Navy Patrol Service coxswain with two RNPS ratings to operate the lift—were going ashore with the patrol to unload the jeeps. Practice had reduced the operation of unloading down to minutes.

A ninth DUKW transporting a seventh gun jeep was attached to Duck Patrol tonight. It was driven by Vice Admiral Sir Randolph "Razor" Ransom, with his grandson Lieutenant Randy "Hornblower" Seaborn in the passenger seat. Lieutenant Colonel John Randal, ex-Lieutenant Billy Jack Jaxx and King were sitting in the jeep.

A lot of straphangers were tagging along as observers tonight.

Lt. Col. Randal and Lt. Kidd had carefully worked out the composition of Duck Patrol. The Table of Organization and Equipment (TO&E) was designed for maximum flexibility.

Standard Operating Procedure for Desert Patrol jeep operations called for gun jeeps to always operate in pairs.

However, for Lt. Kidd's Sea Squadron jeep patrol, that SOP had been modified.

Duck Patrol was a "light patrol" consisting of twelve men instead of the standard eighteen of RFDP. It was intended to operate as a single unit or a pair of three gun jeep sections, though nothing forbade Lt. Kidd from breaking his command into three two-jeep elements if he chose to.

The patrol had two 20mm Breda gun jeeps, giving it an extra heavy machine gun. Duck Patrol did not carry a mortar.

There were two Phantom radio teams assigned.

The idea was that Lt. Kidd could go ashore on a beach and have one element mine the road while the other raided a roadhouse or shot up a truck park. Or, Skipper Finley could drop off one section of Duck Patrol, then sail to another beach and drop off the other.

The DUKWs would transport the gun jeeps to shore. The crane DUKW would unload the jeeps. Then, Duck Patrol would proceed on its mission.

VAdm. Ransom and Lt. Seaborn were along to determine if the best plan was for the DUKWs to laager on the beach in concealment and wait for the jeep patrol to return—or to stand offshore until the gun jeeps completed their mission, then come in and pick them up.

There were a number of questions that needed to be resolved. For example: Skipper Finley commanded at sea. His RNPS coxswains were at the helm of the DUKWs. When did Lt. Kidd take command—at the time Duck Patrol launched, or when it landed on shore?

In the event Duck Patrol was ever unable to make the rendezvous with the DUKWs, it could drive inland, link up with RFDP and return to Raiding Forces Headquarters, then the *King Duck* through Oasis X.

Nothing prevented a RFDP from doing the reverse: driving to the coast and linking up with the DUKWs after a mission, loading on and sailing home aboard the *King Duck*.

A Raiding Forces team could drop by parachute, raid a coastal target, then exfiltrate by DUKW.

There were a lot of possibilities. Lt. Col. Randal was running combinations through his mind as he waited for the ramp to go down.

"Sir," Lt. Col. Randal said to VAdm. Ransom, who was sitting in front of him at the wheel of the DUKW, "I'd like to move Sea Squadron out of Tobruk. Randy tells me there aren't any offshore islands along the Egyptian or Libyan coastline that Raiding Forces can use as a forward operating base."

"Not a single solitary one," Lt. Seaborn said.

"What about," Lt. Col. Randal said, "converting a Royal Naval Patrol Service vessel into a troop ship, Admiral? Station Sea Squadron on board and let it rove up and down the coast."

"Now, there's a thought," VAdm. Ransom said. "Worthy of Bootnecks. The Marines have four battalions being held in reserve in the U.K. to be deployed in the event the Germans invade the Irish Republic. Might motivate the Royal Marines to relax their prohibition on us recruiting more of their light infantry people to Raiding Forces."

"That'd be good," Lt. Col. Randal said. "We only have two Marines."

"Fit fuel bunkers aboard the RNPS troop ship … then it could do double duty as an oiler," VAdm. Ransom said. "Randy's MAS boats would be able to top off at sea without needing to return to port … capital idea, Colonel.

"What say you, Randy?"

"Any plan that transfers Sea Squadron out of Tobruk," Lt. Seaborn said, "meets my approval, sir. Besides, a floating patrol base will afford the squadron considerable flexibility it does not currently have. I should have thought of it."

"Consider it done, then," VAdm. Ransom said. "The Patrol Service should have a hulk we can requisition. If not, I shall have the RNPS launch a priority search to locate a suitable scow and commandeer it."

"All we need is a sea-worthy transport capable of sleeping sixty Sea Squadron Raiders."

The ramp went down and the column of DUKWs started rolling forward. The *King Duck* was standing three miles off the coast—a long way behind enemy lines. Lt. Kidd's Duck Patrol was preparing to conduct the first amphibious truck/gun jeep raid in history.

Sitting in the back of the DUKW in his jeep, Lt. Col. Randal was enjoying the ride, even though the Mediterranean was considerably choppier than on the night of his initial amphibious truck assault training at RFHQ.

The little craft rolled and swayed, the motion accentuated by being perched up high. However, with VAdm. Ransom at the helm, Lt. Col. Randal could relax and take in everything that was going on from his position of dead last in line.

Duck Patrol was snaking its way toward shore in an undulating column formation.

The objective was to land on a deserted beach, unload the seven gun jeeps, then have them travel approximately fifteen miles inland to mine an isolated black-topped stretch of the Via Balbia.

Tonight's operation amounted to a live-fire training exercise behind enemy lines.

The nine DUKWS would set up a perimeter on shore, wait for Duck Patrol to carry out its mission and return, then transport them back out to the LCT.

While Lt. Col. Randal did not have any leadership position in the patrol, he was well aware of the inescapable fact that he could delegate authority but not responsibility.

Lt. Col. Randal was in command. Period.

The trick was to not act like it and let Lt. Kidd lead his patrol.

Which was not easy. Lt. Col. Randal liked leading patrols. Tonight he was going to have to force himself to stay out of the way.

Lt. Kidd needed to be left free to act as if he were alone and unencumbered by an army of Raiding Forces special operations observers along—who all out-ranked him—looking over his shoulder, critiquing his every move.

Ex-Lt. Jaxx racked a round into the chamber of his new 9mm Beretta MAB-38 submachine gun. He had traded in his .45 Thompson once he fired the Beretta.

"Sir," ex-Lt. Jaxx said, "might it be possible for me to ship a couple of these M-38s back home to the Sheriff's Department?"

"Talk to Jane," Lt. Col. Randal said. "She has a stash of captured M-38s in a warehouse."

"The Sheriff will love these little carbines, sir," ex-Lt. Jaxx said. "Full auto 9mm is like squirting a water hose compared to the .45 Thompson submachine gun."

"Tell your grandfather," Lt. Col. Randal said, "compliments of Raiding Forces."

"I believe you could shoot an M-38 out the window of your car at a fleeing felon one-handed while you're driving, sir," ex-Lt. Jaxx said.

"Can't do that with a Thompson … I've tried."

"Hot times in Texas," Lt. Col. Randal said, sticking one of Waldo's thin, unlit cigars between his front teeth.

"Friday nights."

"That would be a Rodge, sir," ex-Lt. Jaxx said.

The DUKW swept into the surf zone. The amphibious truck bobbed, skidded and fishtailed. Up on a crest one second, then dropping down into a trough the next. VAdm. Ransom seemed to be enjoying himself.

He was steering with one hand.

The Admiral and his grandson were engaged in a technical debate over the merits of various types of RNPS craft that might serve as a Raiding Forces troop ship. Neither appeared to notice the fact the DUKW was in a death battle with the current, waves and the looming beach.

Lt. Col. Randal was not so sanguine.

Ex-Lt. Jaxx looked green.

"For a second," Lt. Col. Randal said as the DUKW plunged over the peak of a wave, "I thought we were going shoot the curl."

"I wouldn't know, sir," ex-Lt. Jaxx said. "Cowboys don't surf."

The DUKW cast up on the beach as light as a feather. VAdm. Ransom switched to wheel drive, then drove up and assumed his position in the perimeter.

Ex-Lt. Jaxx said, "I'm not a real cowboy, sir."

"You grew up on a ranch, Billy Jack."

"I don't really like cows."

One of the DUKWs w/crane pulled alongside. Lt. Col. Randal, ex-Lt. Jaxx and King jumped down onto the sand. The RNPS ratings climbed up and placed chains on the gun jeep—front and rear.

Within two minutes the jeep was lifted out of the bed, swung around and set on the ground ready for action.

"Good teamwork, men," Lt. Col. Randal said to the RNPS crew. "Outstanding."

Lt. Kidd was holding a leader's conference at his command jeep. Assistant Patrol Leader Frank Polanski, the jeep commanders, the RNPS coxswain who was in command of the DUKWs and the attached observers who would be traveling to the Via Balbia were gathered in a semicircle as he sat sideways in the driver's seat and gave a crisp recital of the patrol's order of march, actions on the objective, actions on enemy contact, signals, etc. one final time.

Lt. Col. Randal was last to arrive.

Lt. Kidd conducted himself as Duck Patrol Leader the way he had been taught at the Commando Castle in Achnacarry, Scotland, the way he had seen Lt. Col. Randal do it with the Strike Force at RAF Habbaniya during the siege and with Violet Patrol.

He left nothing to chance.

Capt. Pilkington began his demolitions briefing on road mining when Lt. Kidd wrapped up.

He kept it 'Short and Simple' as per Raiding Forces' Rules for Raiding.

"Each jeep crew will be responsible for planting two General Service Mark II mines containing 4 pounds of TNT. Bury your mines no closer than 5 feet together to prevent simultaneous detonation," Capt. Pilkington said.

"The Mark II has a thin brass plate cover supported by four leaf springs. Sufficient pressure on the cover causes the springs to contract, pressing down on the striker. This, in turn, pushes aside ball bearings beneath it, releasing the striker that plunges into the C.E. pellet, triggering the exploder and then the main charge.

"Any questions … no?" Capt. Pilkington said. "Now, the idea is to plant the mines across the black-topped Via Balbia in a wide belt, hoping a wheeled—or possibly even a tracked—vehicle will drive over one of them.

"I shall come by and inspect your work," Capt. Pilkington said, "then you cover up your two mines. Throw sand over them, doing your best effort to make it look as if the wind simply blew the sand and it drifted across the road."

"We're moving," Lt. Kidd said, "in zero five."

Back at his gun jeep, Lt. Col. Randal said, "You drive, Billy Jack. Brandy says you're a pretty fair wheelman."

"Mrs. Seaborn in rolled-up khaki shorts, sir, teaching me how to do a wheelie in a jeep like Roy Rogers on Trigger, straight up a sand mountain …," ex-Lt. Jaxx said. "that's what I call training.

"Hard to believe she's Randy's mother, sir."

"Yeah," Lt. Col. Randal said.

Gun jeep starters began whining, engines catching, motors racing. The metal on metal sound of twin .303 Vickers K and 20mm Breda machine guns being charged put an examination point on the seriousness of the night's business.

This was more than an exercise. Duck Patrol was behind Afrika Korps lines. The enemy, if any were encountered, would be firing live ammunition.

Lt. Kidd pulled out on schedule.

The moon was three-quarters full. Brilliant silver-white, it seemed to be illuminated from within. Visibility was not a problem.

From dead last in the column, Lt. Col. Randal could see the line of little cars winding their way inland in the moonlight, trying to stay in the tracks of the jeep to their immediate front while maintaining ten-yard spacing.

The thousand-mile stretch of the Afrika Korps Line-of-Communications, *aka* the Via Balbia that Raiding Forces was most interested in, ran from Tripoli to Tobruk. The blacktop, the only hardball Rommel had, kept to the coast, skirting the desert except in places where the soft sand stayed farther inland. Where that occurred, the paved road cut in as far as twenty-five miles from the coast.

While that distance made it out of reach of a traditional Commando raid by Sea Squadron operating out of the MAS boats, Duck Patrol would be able to land from the sea, drive to the Via Balbia, mine the road, return to the coast, load on the DUKWs and motor out to the LCT. And then, to do it all over again somewhere the next night.

Driving cross-country was not going to be difficult tonight. Except for isolated patches, Duck Patrol would not need to be concerned with soft sand. Lt. Kidd had briefed that where soft patches were encountered, the patrol would find a way around.

Dust *was* a problem. Lt. Col. Randal and ex-Lt. Jaxx had parachute cloth scarves tied over their faces. Oversized Italian tanker goggles covered their eyes.

Ex-Lt. Jaxx had asked Captain the Lady Jane Seaborn where he could get a cover like Lt. Col. Randal's. Lady Jane inquired about size. She obtained an Australian bush hat, took measurements of Lt. Col. Randal's brim and had a local millinery shop professionally trim it to the same pattern.

While she was at it, Lady Jane had a new hat done for Lt. Col. Randal. He had originally cut his down with a pair of mule shears prior to jumping into Abyssinia.

His old headgear had seen long, hard service.

Both officers had their new hats pulled down low to the edge of their goggles.

"Sir," ex-Lt. Jaxx said, "why is it you want to concentrate on Afrika Korps wheeled vehicles? Wouldn't we be getting more bang for our buck going after enemy airfields?"

"We're guerrillas, Billy Jack," Lt. Col. Randal said. "We have to think like 'em."

Ex-Lt. Jaxx said, "Wouldn't guerrillas attack airfields, sir?"

"Sometimes," Lt. Col. Randal said. "Active airfields are well-defended. We have to travel a long way to reach them. There's no assurance any aircraft will be waiting at the landing ground when we get there.

"And, the bad guys fly in new planes the next day to replace the ones we destroy.

"Think of it this way, Jack," Lt. Col. Randal said. "Guerrillas can't win a war. Can't win big battles or hold ground against a determined conventional enemy like the Afrika Korps, the world's premiere counterattack army.

"And, this is important—they can't afford to take unnecessary casualties.

"What guerrillas *can* do," Lt. Col. Randal said, "is exploit a conventional opponent's weakness, tie down his troops and degrade his morale."

"How do we do that, sir?" ex-Lt. Jaxx asked. "Raiding Forces only has about 200 operators ... and this is a BIG country."

"We have spies scattered all across the desert preparing a target list of hard targets for RFDP to raid," Lt. Col. Randal said. "We go after those and the Via Balbia."

"When you initially briefed me," ex-Lt. Jaxx said, "you said Raiding Forces only raids soft targets, sir."

"Know the difference between a hard target and a hardened target, Jack?"

"No, sir."

"A hard target is one where we have 'hard' or 'eyes on' intelligence," Lt. Col. Randal said.

"A hardened target is one where the enemy has defenses in place and is expecting to be attacked at some point."

"Hard intelligence," ex-Lt. Jaxx said, "soft targets, Roger."

"In Raiding Forces we don't attack hardened targets unless we have a specific strategic mission we are tasked to carry out by higher headquarters," Lt. Col. Randal said.

"What we do is arrive out of the blue at one of the targets on our list, hit our objective, do a lot of damage quick, and be gone," Lt. Col. Randal said.

"Then we go do the same thing somewhere else.

"Pretty soon, with a little help from our Political Warfare mastermind, Capt. Merryweather, word gets around that the desert Raiding Forces is out there in the dark … everywhere."

"Sort of like Comanches," ex-Lt. Jaxx said, "in the old West, sir?"

"Exactly," Lt. Col. Randal said.

"Rommel has to ship all his supplies from Italy to Tripoli by air or sea. Then, using wheeled transport, he has to deliver it to his fighting troops at the front by pushing it down a single, hard-topped coastal road, the Via Balbia.

"Truck transport is Afrika Korps' weak link," Lt. Col. Randal said. "The chink in Rommel's armor."

"It was a bad day for the Desert Fox," King said, "when the Chief came into possession of *that* piece of information."

"Raiding Forces, being a guerrilla outfit looking to exploit our enemy's weakness," Lt. Col. Randal said, "we know enemy traffic on the Via Balbia is where our guerrilla style—small-scale pin-prick raiding—can cause the enemy maximum pain.

"Raiding Forces' primary mission is to damage or destroy Rommel's wheeled vehicles, which he will have to repair or replace to stay in business."

Lt. Col. Randal continued, "The Desert Fox has only the one paved highway."

"Is it actually true, sir? There's only *one* black-topped road from Tripoli to Tobruk?" ex-Lt. Jaxx said.

Lt. Col. Randal said, "And we know where it is."

"Makes it simple for us," ex-Lt. Jaxx said.

"Sooner or later, on every patrol, Raiding Forces arrives at the Via Balbia under cover of darkness—unannounced and unexpected," Lt. Col. Randal said, "mine the road, ambush the convoys, and shoot up the roadhouses, truck parks or some isolated enemy refueling installation.

"Then we disappear back into the desert or out to sea, causing the bad guys to tie down troops searching for us after we're long gone, and securing the places we've shot up against future raids we will probably never carry out."

"So, in the big picture," ex-Lt. Jaxx said, "the Great Sand Sea—and now the Mediterranean—are sanctuaries for Raiding Forces to strike out of, then retreat back into, not obstacles."

"There you go," Lt. Col. Randal said. "What you and I are going to do, Billy Jack, is design missions based on what hard intelligence we have against pinpoint targets in the middle of nowhere and hammer the Via Balbia along the coast non-stop. Our concept of Raiding Forces operations is to slip in, take down the objectives fast and get out with a minimum of casualties—hit and run—guerrilla war and plenty of it."

"Colonel," ex-Lt. Jaxx said, "I'm going to like this job. We're here, we're there, we're everywhere, we're nowhere."

"Stick with the Raiding Forces' Rules for Raiding, Billy Jack," Lt. Col. Randal said. "Plan carefully. Execute meticulously. Take no unnecessary risks."

"That's not exactly," ex-Lt. Jaxx said, "the way troops describe how you do it, sir."

"Really?" Lt. Col. Randal said.

"Word is," ex-Lt. Jaxx said, "sooner or later, sir, on every patrol you end up strapping a bomb with the fuse lit on the back of a fuel truck you're sitting in or joyriding down the Via Balbia with all guns blazing—the troops claim you're a hellraiser, Colonel."

"That what the men say, King?" Lt. Col. Randal said.

"No comment, Chief."

After an hour of driving, Duck Patrol halted and set up a perimeter while Lt. Kidd led a four-man reconnaissance patrol forward on foot to determine the exact location of the hard-topped road. The Via Balbia was close. Several dirt roads paralleling it had been crossed en route. Based on the odometer, the patrol had traveled to within a quarter of a mile of the main highway.

The dust kicked up by the jeeps settled as Duck Patrol waited.

Lt. Kidd was back in twenty minutes and called another leader's conference around his gun jeep.

"The hardball is two hundred yards straight ahead," Lt. Kidd said. "You all know what to do. I want your mines placed and us to be rolling out of here in thirty minutes.

"Let's go."

All the gun jeeps drove up to the edge of the black-topped Via Balbia, but did not cross it. The crews dismounted and began placing their mines.

Lt. Col. Randal's jeep was on the extreme right flank. Ex-Lt. Jaxx and King took a pick and shovel out of the jeep and started digging holes for their two mines. Lt. Col. Randal went in search of Capt. Pilkington.

He found the Raiding Forces' Demolitions Officer on the extreme left flank, supervising the installation of the mines from Lt. Kidd's jeep.

Lt. Col. Randal, Capt. Pilkington and Lt. Kidd then strolled back down the length of the area being mined. As they went along, Capt. Pilkington was pointing out to the jeep crews the best places to bury their mines.

As they came past where Capt. Merryweather was standing beside his mine, the Political Warfare Executive (PWE) officer said, "After we do these mining raids for a while, Colonel, all I shall do is hire Arabs to sneak out at night and throw sand on the pavement up and down the Via Balbia. Bring traffic to a standstill. The convoys will be forced to stop and check it out.

"If they choose not to, sooner or later the truckers will find themselves driving over one of our real mines ... trifle with their minds."

"Good idea, Hawthorne," Lt. Col. Randal said. "I knew there was a reason we let you come along tonight."

Duck Patrol was working with a will.

The plan was to place the mines and be away before anyone was the wiser.

Everything went like clockwork. Unless a convoy was running at night, which did happen from time to time, there was not much of a chance of enemy contact.

The patrol was mounted up and moving out back to the beach in less than the thirty minutes allowed. Driving to the Via Balbia had been easy enough. The patrol simply dodged any terrain that might pose an obstacle.

However, Duck Patrol had not driven to the Via Balbia in a straight line. The patrol was going to intersect the road no matter how much they deviated from the original azimuth. Finding it was guaranteed.

Now the patrol had to navigate its way back to the beach. The perimeter where the DUKWs were parked was a pinpoint target.

Getting back to the Extraction Rally Point was going to be tricky. The DUKW perimeter concealed in the sand dunes at the beach was a tiny spot to locate after driving the fifteen miles cross-country in the dark.

Lt. Col. Randal wore his Bagnold Model compass on an OD cord around his neck, tucked into his left breast pocket. In addition, his wrist compass was strapped next to his Rolex. The pocket compass had been designed by Colonel Ralph Bagnold, the founder of the Long Range Desert Group, and was different from British Army-issue.

What Lt. Col. Randal liked most about the Bagnold compass was its simplicity.

Duck Patrol had been traveling for twenty minutes when the sky flared behind it, followed by a rolling *KAAAAABOOOOM!*

Everyone on board the gun jeeps craned their necks to look back. But the initial explosion was it. Nothing else happened.

An enemy convoy traveling at night had hit a mine—no one had hoped to be that lucky.

"Scratch one truck," ex-Lt. Jaxx said.

It took an hour to reach the beach. It took another hour to locate where the DUKWs were parked. Finding them was not easy.

Navigation had to be almost perfect, which is hard to do from a rolling jeep.

Lt. Col. Randal said, "We need to work on our link-up procedures."

King said, "Finding an Extraction Rally Point laagered in hiding on a deserted beach at night, deep behind enemy lines, is a formula for disaster every time, Chief."

"Militarily speaking," Lt. Col. Randal said, "making a fast getaway while having to search for your taxi home is not good."

"That's a definite Rodge," ex-Lt. Jaxx said. "I was wondering if we were lost.

"MIA my second mission …"

"King," Lt. Col. Randal said, "get with Roy when we get back, see what you two can do to make the linking-up problem go away."

"Wilco."

"Don't make it sound like I was criticizing his navigation," Lt. Col. Randal said. "I didn't have a clue where the DUKWs were parked."

"Neither did I, Chief."

"I thought," ex-Lt. Jaxx said, "maybe the DUKWs got tired of waiting and went back to the LCT."

"Never even crossed my mind," Lt. Col. Randal said, "that could happen. We need an SOP to cover that contingency.

"That's why we ran this pioneer patrol … to discover problems."

"Pioneers," ex-Lt. Jaxx said, "aren't they the ones with the arrows in their backs, sir?"

"You're not the first person to point that out to me, Billy Jack," Lt. Col. Randal said.

As the DUKW carrying Lt. Col. Randal's gun jeep rolled across the beach into the water, VAdm. Ransom said, "Profitable night's endeavor, Colonel.

"Gleaned a lot of useful information."

"So did I, sir," Lt. Col. Randal said.

18

NO SUBMARINES IN THE GREAT SAND SEA

LIEUTENANT COLONEL JOHN RANDAL GAVE THE COMMAND, "PREPARE to move out as soon as you return to your jeeps."

At Captain the Lady Jane Seaborn's suggestion, Violet Patrol had been renamed Ranger Patrol after Lt. Col. Randal's former Territorial Regiment, "The Rangers" (he wore their regimental crest on his green beret). The name change was needed because Raiding Forces Desert Patrol, now under the command of Major Sir Terry "Zorro" Stone, had been reorganized into Wing Squadron and Regiment Squadron.

The patrols in Captain Taylor Corrigan's Wing Squadron were named after colors: Red, White, Blue and Gold.

Major Jack Black's Regiment Squadron was made up of the Lancelot Lancers Yeomanry Regiment *aka* Lounge Lizards. Regiment Squadron patrols were named after lizards: Gecko, Chameleon, Iguana and Horny Toad.

Lt. Col. Randal's Ranger Patrol was not part of either the Wing or Regiment Squadron.

The name changes were taking a bit of getting used to. They were slightly confusing—which was the point.

It never hurt to keep the enemy guessing.

Raiding Force was a constantly evolving special operations unit. Reorganizations and name changes within the outfit went with the territory.

Ranger Patrol had a new 20mm Breda heavy machine gunner to replace Frank Polanski, who had been transferred to Sea Squadron to be Duck Patrol's sergeant.

The new man, "Guns," was a Royal Naval Patrol Service rating, a veteran anti-aircraft gunner on Royal Navy Patrol Service minesweepers from the days of the Norwegian campaign. He was credited with shooting down seven Luftwaffe aircraft and having been sunk four times.

Guns volunteered for duty in the Middle East Command because he'd had enough of serving in a semi-arctic climate where ships kept getting blown out from under him. He claimed to have grown tired of swimming to the nearest lifeboat in freezing water.

Skipper Sub-Lieutenant Warthog Finley recruited him for Landing Craft Tank *King Duck* because of his unparalleled anti-aircraft gunnery skills.

During Duck Patrol's first mission, Guns overheard Lt. Col. Randal mention the need for a replacement heavy machine gunner for Ranger Patrol, and he immediately applied for the job.

"Why would a sailor," Lt. Col. Randal asked, "volunteer for duty in gun jeeps?"

"Can't get mucking torpedoed, Colonel," Guns said. "Ain't any submarines in the Great Sand Sea."

"Good point."

Lt. Col. Randal hired him on the spot, which violated every principle of Raiding Forces troop selection except one: Right Man, Right Job. He needed a heavy machine gunner, and good ones did not grow on trees.

Although Guns was the RNPS's titleholder as an airplane shootdown artist, all his experience had come with the Oerlikon. He proved to be a quick study on the captured Italian Breda.

After working with the weapon, he reported to Lt. Col. Randal, "Italian 20mm is definitely superior to our ammunition, sir."

"Why might that be?"

"Eyties have an explosive tipped round. We don't," Guns said. "Mucking beautiful, Colonel."

Guns was on probation until he proved he had the right stuff to serve in Raiding Forces. And he had to agree to complete parachute training.

Ranger Patrol would be operating under the new RFDP Standard Operating Procedure for what action to take in the event of an enemy air attack.

The Long Range Desert Group's SOP was simple and inflexible. LRDG patrols were under strict orders to never, under any circumstance, return fire if they came under air attack.

Having seen what happened when a patrol followed that SOP, Lt. Col. Randal and Maj. Stone had been working together to develop a different response to enemy air for RFDP.

In the event an RFDP unit came under aerial attack, the machine gunners were to dismount their machine guns, move them to a location away from the jeeps and return fire.

When a patrol halted, machine gunners were instructed to dismount their machine guns, move to a location away from the jeeps and set up a camouflaged air defense perimeter.

The new SOP was well-received by the officers and men of RFDP. The idea of sitting it out while being shot to pieces by enemy aircraft did not sit well with Raiding Forces troopers.

Ex-Lieutenant Billy Jack Jaxx was at the wheel of Ranger Patrol's command jeep. Captain Pip Pilkington was riding in the back seat. King was on the twin pedestal-mounted Vickers K .303 machine guns.

Every jeep in Ranger Patrol was equipped with one of the Bren guns captured in Persia, giving it a highly mobile light machine gun that could be easily deployed by a dismounted Raider.

All the jeeps were freshly painted in the pink, yellow and pale green pattern specified by The Great Teddy.

Having lectured ex-Lt. Jaxx on the perils and pitfalls of raiding enemy airfields, Lt. Col. Randal was headed out to do exactly that. Royal Air Force photo reconnaissance had spotted a cluster of hidden landing grounds with a heavy concentration of enemy aircraft, located in the vicinity of Sirte. They were beyond the range of Allied bombers, which the Luftwaffe had every reason to assume meant they were out of the reach of the British.

The Royal Air Force had requested that Raiding Forces raid them. In the interest of inter-service cooperation, Lt. Col. Randal had agreed.

Ranger Patrol was raring to go. The troops viewed attacking Axis airfields as glamor missions. Enemy airplanes on the ground were the targets of choice of Raiding Forces.

Lt. Col. Randal knew he had a problem on his hands. It is never good when what should be a unit's primary target is not the one the unit's men want to go after. Rolling down a runway under cover of darkness in their gun jeeps, shooting up an Afrika Korps landing ground with enemy aircraft parked wingtip to wingtip, was his men's idea of a Hollywood-type glory mission.

Shooting up trucks? Not so cool.

Lt. Col. Randal was planning to go to work on changing the troop's attitude when he returned from this patrol. Though, to be perfectly honest, he was not exactly sure how to do it.

Ranger Patrol traveled for three days. Late on the fourth day, the patrol came over a rise in the desert and found Mr. Zargo and Joker sitting beside a rock formation that looked like an upside-down ice cream cone.

A map was broken out, and Mr. Zargo gave Lt. Col. Randal a briefing on the airfields the RAF wanted attacked.

"There are five landing grounds in the immediate area of Sirte," Mr. Zargo said. "We have reconnoitered all of them. Only two are worthy of your attention, Colonel.

"For simplicity's sake, let's call them Target A and Target B. There are approximately thirty Ju-88s stationed on Target A and about the same number of Ju-52s on Target B. The troops guarding both landing grounds are Italian. The aircraft are German. The best of both worlds for us."

"Yeah," Lt. Col. Randal said, "the worst sentries and the best airplanes."

"I recommend you consider breaking Ranger Patrol down into two elements," Mr. Zargo said. "I will guide one party. Joker will lead the way for the other."

"How do you suggest," Lt. Col. Randal asked, "we go about executing our raids?"

"By stealth," Mr. Zargo said. "The enemy are not expecting an air attack, knowing they are out of range of the RAF, and the only thing they have to fear on the ground is the odd Arab slipping on base trying to steal something.

"Infiltrate on foot, place bombs on the aircraft with delayed time fuses and exfiltrate with no one the wiser."

"There's bound to be guards on the airplanes," Lt. Col. Randal said.

"There are," Mr. Zargo said. "You, King, Joker, and I will have to deal with them discreetly."

Lt. Col. Randal said, "We can do that."

Mr. Zargo and Joker began building mock-up terrain tables of Target A and Target B out of rocks and broken sticks on the ground. Lt. Col. Randal reorganized Ranger Patrol for the night's mission.

"Billy Jack," Lt. Col. Randal said, "are you prepared to command your first raid?"

"Roger that, sir."

"You'll tackle Target A with Mr. Zargo and King. Corporal Pompedous will be responsible for the three-jeep section which will transport you to your Objective Rally Point. He'll wait with the jeeps while you four infiltrate the landing ground, eliminate the sentries guarding the Ju-88 aircraft parked there, place bombs on the airplanes and exfiltrate back to the ORP."

"Once back at your ORP, you'll then drive to a location to be designated, where you'll rendezvous with the three jeeps I take to attack Target B."

"Is that clear?"

"Clear, sir."

"I'll be carrying out the identical mission on Target B," Lt. Col. Randal said, "with Joker, GG, the two Lovat Scouts Fenwick and Ferguson and Mr. Treywick, plus the AVG drivers in my three-jeep section."

Lt. Col. John Randal gave a Patrol Order to Ranger Patrol. He broke it down into two elements, stacking the deck as heavily in ex-Lt. Jaxx's favor as he could without it being obvious what he was doing.

Mr. Zargo and King gave the Target A team a decided edge.

It was the best Lt. Col. Randal could do 800 miles behind enemy lines. Every officer has to lead his first combat mission sooner or later. Tonight was ex-Lt. Jaxx's moment.

Without anything having to be said, Mr. Zargo and King understood what was expected of them. Their assignment was to keep ex-Lt. Jaxx out of trouble and to see that his mission succeeded.

Immediately following the order, the two elements of Ranger Patrol—Team A and Team B—moved out independently. Night was falling by the time the jeeps were rolling. The idea was for Ranger Team A and Ranger Team B to strike their objectives at 0100 hours.

The two Ranger Patrol elements needed to complete their mission, link up at their post-mission ORP and move before sunrise to a safe location, where they could lay up in concealment under their camouflage netting. It was a sure thing the Luftwaffe would be out searching for them at first light.

Lt. Col. John Randal drove his command jeep. They wound through the desert with Joker navigating. As they approached the Target B landing ground, its lights came on.

"Well, that tore it," Lt. Col. Randal said. "Looks like we're expected."

One of the reasons he did not like attacking landing grounds: once alerted, they were dangerous.

"Possibly not," Joker said. "Those are the field's landing lights, Colonel."

Up in the sky, a flight of Ju-52s turned on their lights as they lined up in trail astern to land.

Lt. Col. Randal stopped his jeep as Waldo Treywick and the 20mm gun jeep driver jogged over for a conference.

"Those lights are going to ruin the night vision of everyone on the airfield, so let's take advantage of the situation," Lt. Col. Randal said.

"Instead of infiltrating on foot, we'll loop around and follow the last plane on to the tarmac in our jeeps. Brief your gunners to fire short crisp bursts. Conserve your ammunition. Make every shot count.

The Ju-52 transports are primary targets—but shoot up any airplane or truck you see. There's a group of Ju-52s sitting parked next to the control tower, as briefed.

"Let's do it," Lt. Col. Randal said. "Follow me."

"I knew somethin' like this was goin' to happen," Waldo said as he turned back to his jeep. "Colonel, you can't ever stick to the nice safe plan."

The three gun jeeps raced around to the end of the runway as the big Junkers transports came in for landing, props thundering as they passed low overhead. There were five Ju-52s in the flight.

The noise of the planes was deafening. The big transports made a keening scream as they came over, lowering their landing gear.

Lt. Col. Randal drove up onto the hard surface of the airstrip. From the jeep behind him, Guns fired a burst of explosive-tipped 20mm rounds into the belly of the last big airplane in the formation as it sailed overhead. The result was instantaneous. The Ju-52 nosed over to the right and crashed headfirst into the airstrip about twenty yards in front of Ranger Patrol.

KAAABOOOM! A giant fireball went up, followed by a massive explosion that deafened everyone in the gun jeeps.

Lt. Col. Randal barely managed to avoid driving into the burning airplane. As soon as the jeep cleared the sea of fire caused by the fuel on the tarmac, he began firing the twin .303 Vickers K machine guns mounted on the center of the hood at the last Ju-52 of the four that had already touched down.

Joker was working his pair from the right seat, and Scout Fenwick, manning the pair on the pedestal mount in the back, was putting out short, professional bursts of six.

The next Ju-52, now last in line of the four remaining enemy aircraft, ground-looped, ran off the runway into the sand, then flipped.

It blew up.

Just ahead, the next German transport veered hard to the left as the six machine guns from Lt. Col. Randal's jeep vectored in on it. The pilot may have been killed, or at least wounded, because the Junkers slammed into a large aircraft hangar.

There must have been airplanes parked inside the hangar because it erupted like a volcano, turning night into day. The parked planes cooked off one by one as their fuel tanks detonated.

The next transport in line ran off the runway, and its wheels collapsed in the sand. It nosed in, skidding on its belly and caught fire as the six machine guns from Lt. Col. Randal's jeep turned it into a cheese shredder.

The pilot of the lead plane, seeing what was going on behind him, tried to lift off to escape, but he did not have enough air speed to make it back into the air. The fifth Ju-52 managed to get its nose up before it crashed tail first, slamming down and exploding.

Behind Lt. Col. Randal's jeep, the other gun jeeps were weaving in and out around the crashed, burning Ju-52s, firing on the airplanes and buildings along the side of the tarmac as they sped past.

Surprise and violence of action were working to Raiding Forces' advantage. The Italians guarding the landing ground were caught off guard. The Blackshirts did not, however, go to ground without a fight.

A Breda 20mm began firing from the roof of the HQ complex, and a Blackshirt team manned a mortar in a circular pit. The combined firepower of the guns on the three-jeep element of Ranger Patrol snuffed out the heavy machine gun by killing the crew—or at least convincing them that discretion was the better part of valor.

The 20mm ceased fire.

The Italian mortar team fared better, getting off a single round. The muzzle flash gave away its position, and it was instantly torn to pieces by the massed Raiding Forces machine guns.

Unfortunately, that one mortar round went up and came down with unerring accuracy directly in front of Lt. Col. Randal's lead jeep. For the second time on operations, the only mortar round fired by the enemy found its target. Italians were excellent mortar men when they chose to be.

Lt. Col. Randal's command jeep took steel splinters through the radiator. The engine was knocked out.

"Abandon ship," Lt. Col. Randal ordered. He slung his 9mm Beretta MAB-38, along with his 45mm Brixia, over his shoulder, removed the twin Vickers K .303 machine gun from its mount on the hood and tossed it in Waldo's jeep.

Joker and Scout Fenwick were doing the same thing with their weapons. Capt. Pilkington was unloading his prepared explosives from the back. The gear was distributed between the remaining two gun jeeps. Lt. Col. Randal climbed in behind the wheel of Waldo's jeep.

Scout Fenwick threw a thermite grenade into the shot-up command jeep, then jumped aboard the gun jeep where his partner, Scout Ferguson, was manning the pedestal-mounted twin Vickers K .303 machine gun.

In less than a minute, Ranger Patrol was back on the attack.

Joker directed Lt. Col. Randal to the area of the landing ground where the Ju-52s were parked wingtip to wingtip. Guards might have been posted there at one time, but they were no longer present.

"Hop out, Pip," Lt. Col. Randal said. "Work your way down the line. I'll drive up to the other end, then do the same back this way."

"Meet you in the center, sir," Capt. Pilkington said. "Remember, place the bomb at the joint of the wing and the fuselage."

GG went with Capt. Pilkington to carry the pack containing the prepared explosives.

When he reached the end of the line of airplanes, Lt. Col. Randal stepped out of the jeep, and Waldo took over the wheel. Joker left his jeep, ran over and picked up the pack with the demolitions.

He and Lt. Col. Randal jogged to the first aircraft, placed the small explosive device and set the time pencil. There was a thirty-minute delay on the fuse. Since the pencils were being squeezed at different times as the explosives were placed, the detonations would be staggered.

The two worked fast, going from plane to plane until they encountered Capt. Pilkington and GG coming from the other direction.

Without ceremony they climbed back in their respective jeeps, Lt. Col. Randal behind the wheel of his with Waldo in the front seat. The two jeeps ran up the airstrip, intending to exfiltrate the landing ground and drive to the Rally Point.

Lt. Col. Randal spotted two Lancia fuel tanker trucks parked by a farm of above-ground aviation fuel storage tanks. He cut off the tarmac and drove cross-country straight to the trucks.

"Blow those fuel tanks," he ordered Capt. Pilkington.

"Joker, get the trucks."

While they were working, Waldo said, "Colonel, looks like some more airplanes over on the other side of the field."

The fires from the burning Ju-52s they had shot down while they were landing were providing a considerable amount of illumination. When Lt. Col. Randal looked to where Waldo was pointing, he saw what appeared to be Ju-88 bombers in the flickering light.

"We're done out of explosives," Waldo said.

"Take the wheel, Mr. Treywick," Lt. Col. Randal ordered. "When we're finished here, drive over and both jeeps can strafe 'em with our machine guns.

"I'll see what I can do with my 45mm Brixia."

"We could be running low on MG ammo too," Waldo said, as he and Lt. Col. Randal were exchanging places.

"We're going to go shoot up those airplanes," Lt. Col. Randal called to the other jeep, as he pointed across the airstrip. "Short bursts, gas tanks and engines. Conserve your ammunition."

Capt. Pilkington piled in the back of the jeep. "One would not want to be anywhere in the immediate area when those tanks go off, Colonel."

"OK, Mr. Treywick," Lt. Col. Randal said. "Let's roll.

"Pip, see if you can get a pair of those Vickers Ks we removed from my jeep working back there to help out."

"Wilco."

As the two Ranger Patrol jeeps drove toward the parked Ju-88 bombers, Lt. Col. Randal pulled open his pack containing forty rounds of 45mm mortar rounds for the stubby little Brixia.

"How long was the fuse on those fuel tanks?"

"Short, sir," Capt. Pilkington said. "Five minutes."

KABOOOOOM! A charge on one of the Ju-52 transports exploded prematurely. The detonation set off a chain reaction, as other planes began blowing up.

That was not part of the plan, but it did not change anything. It did contribute mightily to the confusion going on at the Target B airfield.

Before the two Ranger Patrol jeeps could make it across the tarmac to reach the parked JU-88s, the first of the six fuel storage tanks erupted in a massive fireball that shot up over 300 feet. One after the other, the rest of the fuel tanks in the farm blew, turning the night into a mellow yellow.

The two Lancia tanker trucks exploded.

Now illuminated by the conflagration, the Ju-88s could be seen clearly. Like the transports, they were parked wingtip to wingtip. The main concern of the Italians was Arab infiltrators trying to sneak in and loot—not an air or ground attack by British Forces.

Not at night.

Not this far behind the lines.

Mr. Treywick drove slowly down the line of deadly-looking German bombers, staying to the center of the airstrip about fifty yards away. The distance was point-blank range for the combined firepower of the machine guns in the jeeps.

Lt. Col. Randal swiveled sideways in the seat, trying to balance himself to fire the 45mm Brixia over Waldo's head. The little modified shoulder-fired mortar was a single-shot weapon, slow to load. He was cycling it as fast as he could. There were no sights on its stubby barrel, but the targets were big and the short range perfect.

Waldo cruised, barely touching the accelerator, allowing Lt. Col. Randal to get off a round at each Ju-88.

The massed fire of Ranger Patrol's machine guns tore into the airplanes. The bombers were being reduced to scrap metal, and some began to catch fire as the patrol drove past with all guns blazing.

Target B was burning—crashed Ju-52s littered the strip. Other Ju-52 transports that had been parked were exploding as the demolitions cooked off and fuel fires from the storage tanks were erupting.

The twelve machine guns from the two Ranger Patrol jeeps were spewing lead into the Ju-88 bombers.

Lt. Col. Randal's 45mm mortar rounds were booming.

As Waldo reached the end of the parked Ju-88 bombers, Lt. Col. Randal sat back down, having fired off thirty rounds.

"Let's get the hell out of Dodge."

As the two jeeps raced for the end of the airstrip and then headed out in the darkness, the first bomb load onboard one of the heavily-damaged Ju-88 bombers cooked off behind them, with a massive thunderous explosion so powerful that the blast caused all the others to go up simultaneously.

The shock wave from the detonation rolled over Ranger Patrol as it drove into the night.

Hit and run.

EX-LIEUTENANT BILLY JACK JAXX WAS WAITING WITH THE TEAM A element of Ranger Patrol at the link-up point when Lieutenant Colonel John Randal's two jeeps arrived.

"There weren't any enemy aircraft at Target A, sir," ex-Lt. Jaxx reported. "We hit a dry hole."

"That's one of the problems attacking airfields," Lt. Col. Randal said. "The airplanes fly away from time to time."

"Rather than alert the Italians," ex-Lt. Jaxx said, "once we realized there weren't any Ju-88s we decided to pull out and head to the link-up point, sir."

"Your planes relocated to our target," Lt. Col. Randal said. "We had a turkey shoot."

"Just my luck," ex-Lt. Jaxx said. "What's our next move, sir?"

"I'm going to let you take charge of Ranger Patrol, Lieutenant," Lt. Col. Randal said. "Redistribute ammunition—we used up most of ours."

"Yes, sir."

"Then," Lt. Col. Randal said, "you take the entire patrol minus one jeep back to Target A and shoot the place up. That wasn't part of the original plan, but no plan should ever be so inflexible you can't take advantage of an opportunity when one presents itself."

"That's a Rodge, sir."

"While you're reorganizing, Mr. Zargo and I'll be doing a map study to select a Laying Up Position where we can hide out tomorrow.

"I'll accompany Ranger Patrol as far as your Objective Rally Point, you'll lead the raid from there. After completing your mission, return to the ORP, link back up with my jeep, and we'll move out to the Patrol LUP."

"Yes, sir!"

"Don't get tied down in a firefight, Jack," Lt. Col. Randal said. "Just let the Italians stationed on the base know they're not safe from Raiding Forces. One flashy pass, shoot the lights out and be gone."

"Can do, Colonel."

"Let me show you," Lt. Col. Randal said, "how to operate my 45mm Brixia.

"Might come in handy."

Ex-Lt. Jaxx gave his patrol order—called a frag order because it was a fragment—a short, concise, abridged version of the full order. The only things covered were the elements needed to carry out the mission. The troops paid close attention.

Ranger Patrol was going into action.

Time was short. The patrol needed to hit the objective, carry out the raid and be gone fast to the LUP where they would hide the next day under camouflage netting in deep concealment from the inevitable aerial search the Luftwaffe and the Regia Aeronautica would be conducting, looking for payback.

"OK, boys," ex-Lt. Jaxx said, "Let's go break things and kill people."

RANGER PATROL ROLLED OUT. EX-LIEUTENANT BILLY JACK JAXX LED the way. Lieutenant Colonel John Randal, Mr. Zargo and Waldo Treywick brought up the rear. The patrol only had to travel ten miles to reach the ORP.

Since he had already been to Target A, ex-Lt. Jaxx led the way through the night at a fast clip. Half the Raiders had already conducted a successful raid, and the other half were eager to.

Ex-Lt. Jaxx's plan was simple.

Ranger Patrol would cross the single strand of barbed wire that the Italians had strung around the landing ground, drive onto the tarmac, drop Captain Pip Pilkington off at the tank farm with the explosives originally intended for the JU-88s that had flown out to Target B, and roll on down the strip strafing everything in sight. Then they would turn around and drive back the way they had come, repeating the process, pick up Capt. Pilkington and return to the ORP.

Target A was laid out like all Regia Aeronautica landing grounds—tarmac airstrip, aviation fuel tank farm, hangars along the strip, barracks, and headquarters/air control center. Ranger Patrol was going to focus on the hangars, troop barracks and the two-story building that appeared to be a combination headquarters and air control center.

Ex-Lt. Jaxx already knew from his earlier reconnaissance that since the JU-88s were absent from the base, guards were not stationed in the six flak towers that surrounded the perimeter of the airfield—not that guards ever were stationed there after dark when the airfield shut down. And he thought the Regia Aeronautica ground personnel, living on an isolated post 800 miles from the nearest British Forces, had most likely called it a night and gone to bed.

There were not even any sentries posted at the headquarters complex. A junior officer and an NCO were on duty, but the officer was asleep on a folding metal bed in a back office.

Lt. Col. Randal, Mr. Zargo and Waldo Treywick were sitting in a jeep at the ORP located on a high point in the desert a mile north of Target A. From their position, they could observe the airfield in the distance and dimly make out the tiny Ranger Patrol jeeps winding their way to the target.

"Any fool can be uncomfortable in the field," Waldo said, handing out cigars.

"That is a fact," Lt. Col. Randal said, sticking one of the thin cigars between his front teeth.

"One a' the things I admire about Raidin' Forces," Waldo said, "is we don't feel no remorse in enjoyin' small pleasures when we can get 'em."

The three were waiting for the show to get started.

Ex-Lt. Jaxx did not disappoint.

For a while, nothing happened. Then tracers lit up the night from the fourteen machine guns mounted on the gun jeeps. The tracers looked like solid green beams of light. It was hard to imagine that in between each tracer was a mixed combination of five rounds of ball, incendiary and armor-piercing ammunition. Tracer rounds were ricocheting off the tarmac into the sky as streams of bullets were directed into the hangars along the side of the strip. Others seemingly disappeared in midflight when they slammed into the hangars, as if swallowed up.

It took a while for the hammering of the automatic weapons to drift to the ORP. The trained ear could easily detect that all the firing was one way. There was no opposition from the Italians.

Guns, Royal Navy Patrol Service ace on the Breda 20mm, was keeping up a steady *Pocka, Pocka, Pocka …*

There came the occasional flash of a small detonation, followed by a hollow *Cruuuuumph…* Ex-Lt. Jaxx was firing the modified 45mm Brixia shoulder mortar.

Ranger Patrol made its way slowly down the tarmac, working over each building it passed with massed machine gun fire. Tracers probed every nook and cranny. When the patrol reached the headquarters/air control complex, it paused while all guns were concentrated on the two-story structure.

Then, with parade ground precision, Ranger Patrol executed a slow turn while continuing to maintain its rate of fire, then marched back up the landing strip in echelon, guns blazing.

"Lt. Jaxx," Mr. Zargo said, "has the patrol well in hand."

The night turned white as a blinding flash and then a massive explosion occurred. It was so powerful that Lt. Col. Randal, Mr. Zargo and Waldo could feel the shock wave a mile away.

Ranger Patrol's machine gun fire ceased.

"What was that?" Waldo nearly bit his cigar in half. "Somethin' big!"

No more firing came from Target A. After a while, Ranger Patrol motored into the ORP. Behind it, a mile away, a series of soft detonations began taking place on the airfield. The aviation fuel tanks began exploding as the time pencils on Capt. Pilkington's demolitions cooked off, one by one.

In the distance, the Regia Aeronautica airfield was bathed in dancing yellow flames.

King walked over to Lt. Col. Randal's jeep and tossed his gear in the back. He appeared shaken. Lt. Col. Randal had never seen the Merc rattled.

"Do you know what is to be found on a JU-88 bomber airfield, Chief, even when the planes are not present?"

"What might that be?"

"Bombs."

"That explains the blast," Lt. Col. Randal said.

"Jack Cool," King said, "fired your Brixia 45mm at a hangar, missed and the round sailed over the roof.

"Must have landed in a bomb dump behind the buildings."

"Anyone hurt?"

"I would surmise," King said, "we all are, Chief."

Ex-Lt. Jaxx arrived. He handed the modified Brixia shoulder mortar to Lt. Col. Randal.

"Any chance I could get one of these, sir?"

"I don't see why not."

"Most satisfying weapon," ex-Lt. Jaxx said, "I've ever fired, Colonel."

Ex-Lt. Jaxx did not seem shaken or rattled.

19
RANGER PATROL

RANGER PATROL WAS UNDER CAMOUFLAGE NETTING IN A LAYING UP position thirty miles south of Target A. Not very far, but it was the best Raiding Forces could do in the short amount of darkness remaining after ex-Lieutenant Billy Jack Jaxx's raid.

Lieutenant Colonel John Randal was following The Great Teddy's Standard Operating Procedure for camouflaging a jeep patrol to the letter. The pale green and faded pink gun jeeps were dispersed in a wadi below an escarpment and covered with netting. Local "flora and fauna" (as specified by Teddy) were added to the netting to make it even more difficult to spot from the air.

Not far away, another LUP consisting of rubber blow-up jeeps under netting with smoke pots was in place. The sham patrol base was not quite as well camouflaged, intentionally. If one of the positions were discovered, it would hopefully be the phony location.

In the event enemy air made a gun or bomb run on the actual LUP, a smoke pot would be ignited at the fake location in hopes the pilots would see the smoke, believe it was coming from something burning on the ground, and shift the point of their attack.

The deception might work.

Ranger Patrol's machine guns had been dismounted, cleaned after a night of hard use and positioned around the wadi near the fake LUP in accordance with Raiding Forces Desert Patrol new SOP to provide air defense. Under no circumstances was anyone to fire on an enemy airplane unless it attacked the gun jeeps in the actual LUP.

The plan was for Ranger Patrol to lay up all day, then move out after dark, heading toward the Via Balbia on the coast. Lt. Col. Randal intended to work his way back to Oasis X, ambushing convoys and attacking truck parks, fueling stations and roadhouses as they went.

Lt. Col. Randal, Mr. Zargo, Waldo and ex-Lt. Jaxx were sitting in canvas folding chairs under the netting covering Ranger Patrol's command jeep.

Lt. Col. Randal knew he had a problem convincing the hard-charging fire-eaters in RFDP that Axis trucks had top priority over airplanes; enemy aircraft parked on the ground were the Raiders' personal target of choice. So he decided to try his hand at exercising command guidance by converting ex-Lt. Jaxx to his way of thinking while waiting for the day to pass.

If the logic of his argument worked on Jack Cool, then he stood a fair chance of getting the rest of the men of RFDP on board.

Lt. Col. Randal took out his Fairbairn Commando knife and drew the outline of Italy in the sand, then sketched Tripoli—which he marked with a big T—and the Libyan and Egyptian Mediterranean coastlines, putting an X at Tobruk.

Mr. Zargo and Waldo observed as he worked.

"The object, Billy Jack," Lt. Col. Randal said, "of all military commanders has always been to threaten the security of their opposite numbers' lines of communications.

"That's particularly true out here in Africa. Without the lifeline of supplies that has to flow out of Germany, travel down the length of Italy, across the sea to Tripoli, and then along the Via Balbia on the coast to reach the Axis armored tip at Tobruk, Rommel and the Afrika Korps wither on the vine and die."

Ex-Lt. Jaxx said, "That's a long haul, sir."

"In days past," Lt. Col. Randal said, "attacks on enemy lines of communications fell into two categories: Flanking movements by large, conventional elements in the main battle area and long-range raiding parties of horsed cavalry operating in the enemy rear, independent of the main forces."

"We would be," ex-Lt. Jaxx said, "today's long-range raiding parties of cavalry, sir?"

"Affirmative," Lt. Col. Randal said. "What we're fighting, Billy Jack, is a logistician's war. The winner will be the side that can get the most stuff to fight with to the men at the sharp end of the stick."

"Never heard the situation broken down that way, sir," ex-Lt. Jaxx said. "Makes perfect sense."

"The bad guys have their work cut out," Lt. Col. Randal pointed with the silver tip of his double-edged fighting knife.

"The RAF is attacking rolling stock on the mainland as it makes its way down the boot of Italy to ports of embarkation and shooting up every Axis ship it can locate at sea. The Royal Navy is interdicting enemy convoys bound for Africa with submarines and surface warships.

"In this part of the world, rail lines are few and far between. Percy Stirling's hard at it making sure the opposition's railroads never run on time. He's the best train buster in the business, so Rommel's out of luck on rail transport.

"Afrika Korps has to load trucks with every stick of military material that survives the journey to Tripoli and then drive 1,500-plus miles down the Via Balbia along the Mediterranean coastline to reach the front," Lt. Col. Randal said.

"Truck transport of all types is Rommel's weak link. And, it's Raiding Forces' Number One Top Priority target. We hunt trucks. We kill trucks.

"Trucks are the biggest military threat."

"If you say so, sir," ex-Lt. Jaxx said. "But right this minute we're burning daylight sitting in this LUP under camouflage netting concealed in a wadi—sweating bullets hiding from enemy *airplanes*."

• • •

RANGER PATROL POSTED AN ALL-DAY LOOKOUT ON A RISE ABOVE THE escarpment. Everyone took turns standing watch. Staring through binoculars, scanning a full 360 degrees, they were hoping not to see anything. The heat was shimmering. Mirages danced in the distance.

Occasionally there was a lizard to check out.

The duty was only one hour per man; however, it was nerve-wracking work—the principal fear being that they would spot the enemy aircraft everyone knew were out looking for Ranger Patrol. No one wanted to see an airplane. An hour seemed like a long time. It was hot. The sun blazed, and there was not even the hint of a breeze.

The air seemed burnt.

The day was too hot to walk, so most of the time the sentry simply sat or lay, gazing out into nothingness through the migraine-inducing glare, for a long sixty minutes until relieved by the next Raider.

"If we depart at sundown, we can reach the *casa cantoniera*—or roadhouse as you call it—located approximately here," Mr. Zargo said, pointing to the map he and Lieutenant Colonel John Randal were studying.

"We have no way of knowing if there will be any trucks there, Colonel."

"That's fine," Lt. Col. Randal said. "We keep knocking off these isolated roadhouses, the bad guys will be forced to divert a lot of people defending against future raids."

"There is no shortage of targets," Mr. Zargo said. "The Italians have established *casas cantoniere* every fifteen miles along the entire length of the Via Balbia."

"The more the merrier," Lt. Col. Randal said. "I want to hit 'em all sooner or later."

"Lt. Jaxx," Lt. Col. Randal ordered, "Ranger Patrol will pull out at dark. We'll travel to the Via Balbia where we'll set up an Objective Rally Point. From there, you'll lead a reconnaissance patrol consisting of yourself, King and Joker to check out the roadhouse.

"Based on your report, we'll craft a hasty plan to attack it."

"Roger that, sir!"

"Pass the word to the men," Lt. Col. Randal said. "Be ready for a raid tonight."

"Yes, sir."

However, after discussing the situation with Mr. Zargo, Lt. Col. Randal made a change of plans.

"It was decided that Lt. Jaxx's jeep would leave the LUP with King and Joker independently an hour before sundown. That would give them time to perform a reconnaissance of the *casa cantoniera* by the time Ranger Patrol reached the ORP.

"Are you up to another mission with Lt. Jaxx?" Lt. Col. Randal asked King.

"Asking a lot," King said. "Jack Cool may be a bigger danger magnet than you are, Chief."

"Well," Lt. Col. Randal said, "see to it that he doesn't get into any trouble he can't get out of."

"Like I said, that's asking a lot."

Mr. Zargo and Joker made final coordination on the location of the ORP.

The rest of the men in Ranger Patrol spent their time working on their jeeps, cleaning their vehicle-mounted machine guns, then checking and re-checking their personal weapons.

Once they had been alerted for a mission, time passed much more quickly.

There was one concern—and it was a big one. The gun jeeps that had been with ex-Lieutenant Billy Jack Jaxx when he shot up Target A were running rough. The massive explosion when the bomb dump went up must have damaged their electrical systems and/or timing.

While the Ranger Patrol American Volunteer Group drivers were reasonably good shade-tree mechanics, as one of them said, "Ain't no shade trees round-abouts."

The mechanical problem was more than the drivers were capable of repairing in the field.

Lt. Col. Randal intended to press on, but he was concerned. The desert was hard on transport. RFDP always wanted the advantage of finely tuned vehicles.

Speed gave them an edge.

Not so easy to shoot up a target, then try to make a fast getaway in a sputtering jeep.

Ex-Lt. Jaxx pulled out as the sky turned scarlet, and the glowing ball of the sun began to sink out of sight on the horizon.

When the desert began to cool an hour later, Lt. Col. Randal led Ranger Patrol out, with Mr. Zargo riding shotgun in his jeep, navigating. If all went well, the patrol had a four-hour trip ahead of it.

The cross-country drive to the ORP was uneventful except for a number of flat tires that required the patrol to halt while the crew changed them. The jeeps were continuing to run rough. Lt. Col. Randal was more than a little concerned by the mechanical problems.

Ex-Lt. Jaxx, King and Joker were waiting when Ranger Patrol arrived at the ORP. The mission brief began immediately.

"Small squat stucco, two-story structure," ex-Lt. Jaxx said. "Two above-ground gas tanks for refueling. There were no trucks present when we pulled our recon of the objective. There were about twenty motorcycles parked outside.

"However, while we were waiting here for you to show up, we heard the sound of vehicles arriving at the roadhouse in the distance."

"Any idea how many?"

"Negative."

"What's your plan, Lieutenant?"

"I'm thinking, sir," ex-Lt. Jaxx said, "let's do this the easy way.

"We've been hauling that three-inch mortar around, towing a trailer full of ammo on board. With our jeeps not in the best of shape, why not lighten up the load while we have the chance?"

Lt. Col. Randal said. "Good idea."

"Set up the tube line of sight, sir," ex-Lt. Jaxx said. "Mortar the hell out of the target area. Do a slow-speed drive-by with all guns blazing. Keep on going."

"You give the order, Jack," Lt. Col. Randal said.

Ranger Patrol had two functions: to carry out special missions and to act as a training patrol for new officers and NCOs.

"Lt. Jaxx," Lt. Col. Randal said, doing it by the book. "Take command of Ranger Patrol."

"Yes, sir!"

Ex-Lt. Jaxx briefed the Raiders. He gave a detailed explanation of exactly what was going to take place—up to a point.

After the patrol shot up the roadhouse with the jeep's machine guns, they were going to drive down the Via Balbia looking for targets of opportunity. There was no way to plan for the unexpected—except to expect it.

Last, ex-Lt. Jaxx gave Ranger Patrol an unorthodox instruction.

He said, "Take the cat's eye dimmers off your jeeps. When we depart the *Casa Cantoniera*, we'll have our lights turned off.

"I'll be driving the lead jeep and turn on my lights every ten seconds or so, then back off. You men follow suit.

"The chain-of-command is me, Colonel Randal, Captain Pilkington, Corporal Pompedous.

"Questions?"

"Why're we taking the dimmers off," Lt. Col. Randal asked, "then flicking our lights now and again?"

"The idea is to make it look like we're coming over a hill to oncoming traffic, sir," ex-Lt. Jaxx said.

"Roger," Lt. Col. Randal said, wondering why the Lieutenant wanted the patrol to appear to be coming over a hill.

Ranger Patrol departed the ORP, with the three-inch mortar under Corporal Ned Pompedous moving out first. The mortar team would loop around out in the desert to reach a point past the roadhouse to set up, conduct its fire mission, then swing in last in the column when the patrol drove past after shooting up the roadhouse.

"You know how to operate a mortar?" Lt. Col. Randal asked before they pulled out.

"Yes, sir," Cpl. Pompedous said. "Not very good, though. There is not a single school-trained mortar crewman in the patrol, Colonel."

"I've been thinking," Lt. Col. Randal said, "maybe we should ditch the tube for another 20mm Breda."

"I shall make it happen," Cpl. Pompedous said, "when we repair to X. Dragging the trailer of mortar ammunition all over the Great Sand Sea has been a strain, sir."

"Keep ten rounds in reserve," Lt. Col. Randal said. "Shoot up the rest."

"Sir!"

Lt. Col. Randal said, "Put up another stripe when we get back.

"You've been doing a good job, Sergeant."

"Sir!"

"Congratulations, Sgt. Pompedous," Waldo said, handing the brand-new sergeant one of his cigars. "Colonel Randal's compliments."

Ex-Lt. Jaxx gave Sgt. Pompedous thirty minutes to get the mortar into position, then he led the four remaining jeeps of Ranger Patrol up to the Via Balbia, made a right-hand turn on the blacktop and cruised along at fifteen miles per hour with their lights off. It was easy to see the road since the pavement stood out starkly against the desert sand.

Up ahead, the occasional beam of light flashed as the door to the roadhouse opened and shut. Not good blackout discipline, but then, 800 miles from Tobruk no one in the small remote building even considered the possibility that it might be the target of an enemy attack.

Ex-Lt. Jaxx's plan called for the gun jeeps to pull off the road 500 yards from the *casa cantoniera* and wait for Sgt. Pompedous to initiate his mortar barrage.

Everyone had synchronized their watches.

The attack would begin at 2415 hours.

The unmistakable sound, *BLOOOOP, BLOOOOP, BLOOOP,* came right on time. Three-inch mortar rounds rained out of the sky, slamming down on the target—rapid-fire, sounding like the grand finale at a Fourth of July celebration—only louder.

The night lit up with the flash of detonations that were occurring too fast to count, but the barrage was all over within seconds. The result was stunning, though the actual material damage caused by the mortar rounds was not all that much.

Ex-Lt. Jaxx had the jeeps rolling before the last round crashed down. Up ahead, panicked men could be heard shouting. One of the aboveground fuel storage tanks was blazing.

Per orders, Ranger Patrol drove up on the target with its lights out. Ex-Lt. Jaxx initiated the strafing attack by opening on a dozen Lancia fuel tanker trucks parked on the gravel lot next to the roadhouse.

Each of the five gun jeeps in turn commenced firing as they came to bear. The armor-piercing rounds punctured the huge trucks' fuel tanks; then the incendiary rounds and the tracers slammed in and ignited the fuel. Trucks began exploding.

Guns pumped explosive 20mm rounds into the undamaged above-ground fuel storage container, and it went up with a *WHOOOOOOF.*

In the mellow dancing light of the flames, from the wheel of his jeep, Lt. Col. Randal caught sight of five tank carriers with what he thought to be Panzer Mark IIIs on their flatbed trailers. Two of the panzers were already on fire—either from fuel splattered from the above-ground storage tanks or from the explosions of the fuel carrier trucks.

In front of the roadhouse, the parked motorcycles were turned into junk metal by the combined fire of thirty-four .303 Vickers K model machine guns.

Then the combined weapons of the gun jeeps were turned on the roadhouse. As the jeeps rolled past, Lt. Col. Randal managed to get a 45mm mortar round from his shoulder-fired Brixia through one of the front windows, firing one-handed while he drove.

It detonated inside, blowing out all the remaining windows on the ground floor.

In less than a minute, Ranger Patrol had shot up the *casa cantoniera,* rolled past it, and was gone in the night. Ex-Lt. Jaxx sped up, turning his lights on every ten seconds or so in accordance with the plan. The rest of the jeeps followed his lead.

Ranger Patrol ran down the road for approximately thirty minutes, then came around a curve in the Via Balbia and met a convoy coming from the opposite direction. Ex-Lt. Jaxx had given firm instructions for no one to open fire until he did.

Lt. Col. John Randal, driving the second jeep, had his twin Vickers Ks locked, loaded and trained on the passing enemy column rumbling by at a matter of inches.

Mr. Zargo, riding shotgun, and King, on the pedestal-mounted Vickers K in the back, were both on their guns—impatient to engage.

Orders were orders. They had to wait.

Ex-Lt. Jaxx was no longer switching his lights on and off. The enemy convoy was an unusual combination of captured Chevrolet and Ford trucks painted with German identification symbols. The Axis convoy was a gypsy caravan that reminded Lt. Col. Randal of Abyssinia.

Without any advance warning, once he could identify the last truck, ex-Lt. Jaxx opened fire on the tail end of the column. When he did, the Ranger Patrol jeeps, running with about twenty-yard spacing between each other, all engaged. In the last jeep, Sgt. Pompedous' pedestal gunner swung all the way round and fired on the lead Nazi trucks.

The continuous roar from thirty-four Vickers K .303s and Guns' big 20mm Breda was staggering. The flames from the muzzles of the machine guns lit up the convoy, but it also blinded everyone on the jeeps. Unfortunately for the enemy truckers, the range was point-blank.

The result of the massed fire was as if the Germans had driven into a steel-jacketed hailstorm.

Drivers panicked. Some braked, causing the truck behind to crash into their tail end. Some ran off the road, flipping when they hit the soft sand at speed. And some, with the drivers dead at the wheel, failed to negotiate the slight curve in the road and sailed over and down into the wadi on the far side, crashing head-first fifteen feet below.

Ex-Lt. Jaxx never slowed his speed. There was no going back to check on what damage had been inflicted. He continued running down the Via Balbia.

Ten minutes later, he braked, pulled off the road and lined up Ranger Patrol in an ambush position, facing the blacktop from a hull-down position.

Then the patrol waited.

Three Fiat 611 Model Armored Cars came racing down the road from the direction of the roadhouse.

"OK, boys," ex-Lt. Jaxx shouted, "commence fire!"

Counting the guns taken off Lt. Col. Randal's command jeep—damaged during the raid on Target B—that were now being propped up on the hoods or over the side of Ranger Patrol jeeps, thirty-four .303 caliber Vickers K Model machine guns opened on the armored car's tires.

Italian military designers had neglected to place armored plates over the wheels. The intense volume of concentrated fire shredded the Italian's hard rubber tires in an instant.

Guns, on the Breda 20mm, fired short, crisp, professional bursts into the turret of each of the Fiat 611s. The Italian designers had also failed to install armor for the turrets capable of defeating their own 20mm rounds.

The three enemy armored cars rolled to a stop on flat tires. The Royal Naval Patrol Service gunner continued to pump round after round into the Fiats, turning their turrets into cheese shredders. The 20mm rounds penetrated the cars' thin armor and exploded inside the interior compartment.

The Vickers K .303 tracer and incendiary rounds were ricocheting off the tortured steel, screaming into the night. At such point-blank range, the tiny black-tipped Armor Piercing (AP) rounds were slicing through the Fiat's thin armor.

The ambush was over in a matter of seconds. Not one Italian in the Fiat 611s survived the initial onslaught.

Ex-Lt. Jaxx led the way back out on the blacktop and continued driving, flicking his lights on and off from time to time.

Whatever that was about, Lt. Col. Randal thought, it sure had confused the bad guys. Ranger Patrol drove for another twenty minutes. In the distance, the next roadhouse could be seen coming into sight.

When Ranger Patrol arrived, a group of enemy personnel was standing outside in the parking area, looking back up the Via Balbia in the direction from which they were coming.

Since King had taken the precaution of cutting the telephone lines when ex-Lt. Jaxx had made his initial reconnaissance of the first roadhouse, there was no way for word about what had happened to have reached this new target.

However, the sound of the gunfire and explosions had clearly alerted the Italian staff, and the truckers who had stopped there realized something was up. So they had come outside to see for themselves what the commotion was about.

Ranger Patrol rolled up. Ex-Lt. Jaxx opened on the crowd immediately. The rest of the Ranger Patrol gun jeeps followed his lead. Taken completely by surprise, Italian *casa cantoniera* staff and German truck drivers went down like bowling pins.

Guns worked the building over with explosive 20mm rounds, while the other gunners on the jeeps shifted their fire to the rows of trucks parked next to the roadhouse.

If there were above-ground fuel storage tanks at this location, no one saw them as Ranger Patrol drove by, all guns blazing.

A mile past the second roadhouse, ex-Lt. Jaxx turned off the Via Balbia and headed out into the desert.

The jeeps were running very rough at this point. It was time to put as much distance as possible between the patrol and the scene of the action. With luck, they could lose themselves in the vastness of the wide open spaces.

Three hours later, Ranger Patrol was working its way around a series of deep wadis as the sun was beginning to come up pink in the distance. The jeeps were sputtering. Drivers were having a hard time keeping the little cars going.

The patrol was going to have to go into a laager shortly to hide from the inevitable enemy air that would be out looking for them and try to figure out how to repair the damage to the jeeps' engines. The gun jeeps were on their last legs.

Two riders on camels appeared right in front of the patrol. They were wearing Italian uniforms. When they saw the jeeps, the camel riders attempted to flee but a short burst of Vickers K rounds from ex-Lt. Jaxx's guns brought them up short.

GG hopped down and ran up to the lead jeep to interrogate the men. The two Italians were policemen. They surrendered their 6.5mm Carcano cavalry carbines and 10.35mm Glisenti revolvers.

The policemen informed GG that they were en route to a small Italian outpost neither Mr. Zargo nor Joker knew about.

A hasty conference was conducted around Lt. Col. Randal's jeep.

220

GG said, "The *carabinieri* say there are less than a dozen Italians stationed at the outpost, Colonel."

"What in the world are they doin' out here in the middle a' no-where?" Waldo said.

"Guarding an auxiliary Regia Aeronautica landing ground, Mr. Treywick," GG said.

"What's at the airstrip?" Lt. Col. Randal asked.

"They say nothing, Colonel," GG said. "Almost no one ever comes around. The strip is only used as an alternate location to divert a damaged plane in an emergency."

"Why don't we ride over," ex-Lt. Jaxx asked, "capture the place and park in the shade while we pull our maintenance, sir."

"Enemy air will never suspect our presence if we put the jeeps under camouflage inside the Italian compound," Mr. Zargo said. "Not likely to bomb their own establishment."

"Do the Italians have a radio?" Lt. Col. Randal asked.

"Telephone, sir," GG said. "No wireless."

"Jack," Lt. Col. Randal said. "Take my jeep, one of the *carabinieri* as a guide, and GG. Go find that line and cut it."

"Can do, sir."

"Make it quick," Lt. Col. Randal said. "We need to get this done before full daylight."

Sgt. Pompedous went around to each jeep redistributing ammunition. The men did what they always did when they had a few minutes before going into action—checked their weapons and personal gear, re-checked, then checked it again.

Ex-Lt. Jaxx was back in less than ten minutes.

"Mission accomplished, sir."

"That was fast."

"Knocked the telephone pole down with the front bumper, sir," ex-Lt. Jaxx said. "Clipped the wires."

"Let's roll," Lt. Col. Randal ordered.

He drove his command jeep with GG and one of the policemen sitting on the hood. They approached the Italian position from the west.

The mud fort stood out against the sunrise looking like a scene out of *Beau Geste*. The village next to it included fewer than a dozen hovels.

Lt. Col. Randal pulled up to study the place through his Zeiss binoculars captured from the 10th Panzer Division at Calais.

The complex was surrounded by a six-foot mud wall with a big wooden gate.

"Send your policeman in," Lt. Col. Randal ordered GG. "Tell him that if the Italians don't surrender in ten minutes we're going to attack and kill everyone inside, including him."

The *carabinieri's* eyes bulged when he heard the translation. He jumped off the hood of the command jeep and jogged toward the fort.

Ten minutes later nothing had happened.

"Sgt. Pompedous," Lt. Col. Randal ordered, "set up your mortar and stand by."

"Sir, we had a miscue about the mortar," Sgt. Pompedous said. "Fired up all the rounds at the first roadhouse."

"No problem," Lt. Col. Randal said. "I'll let Lieutenant Jaxx work 'em over with my Brixia 45mm."

A confused stir of noise came from behind the wall.

Lt. Col. Randal wondered, *had the policeman lied about the size of the garrison? Was this a counterattack?* Stranger things had happened.

"Stand to your guns," Sgt. Pompedous ordered unnecessarily. Every man was locked on his weapon, staring over open machine gun sights awaiting developments.

A small throng of people left the fort's western gate. With banners flying, symbols smashing and drums beating, the *mudir* and the village elders were marching out to surrender the village in traditional medieval style.

Trailing along behind were a dozen sheepish-looking Italian *carabinieri* with their carbines at slope arms.

While GG held court by the village well, Mr. Zargo, Joker and King went through the papers in the commandant's office looking for anything of intelligence value.

Sgt. Pompedous brought the jeeps inside the wall and parked them beside the two-story main building, which was immediately christened

the "Mud Fort." The Raiders put up camouflage netting on poles commandeered from the village market. In minutes, Ranger Patrol was
invisible from the air.

"Best LUP we have ever had, Colonel," Sgt. Pompedous reported.
"Security's posted for a full 360 degrees, with a Lovat Scout in the
tower on the roof with a scoped Boys .55."

Ex-Lt. Jaxx disarmed the *carabinieri* by having them stack arms.
Then he conducted an inspection of the fort's small armory.

Waldo found the safe.

"Send me the Wop headman in here, GG!" he shouted out the door.
"On the double!"

When the senior Italian officer, the fort's commandant, arrived,
Waldo produced his private-purchase N frame Smith & Wesson .38
revolver. He placed the muzzle against the startled Captain's head.

He cocked it.

Inside the safe were thousands of lire.

"Mr. Treywick," Lt. Col. Randal said. "I didn't know you spoke
Italian."

20

FIRE IN THE HOLE

THE WORD ON THE JEEPS WAS NOT GOOD. WHATEVER HAD HAPPENED TO the engines when the bomb dump exploded at Target B, it was outside the range of repairs the Ranger Patrol drivers were able to make. Eight hundred miles behind enemy lines, with the bad guys looking for them with a vengeance—it could be a problem.

Lieutenant Colonel John Randal drafted a short message for the Phantom team to transmit. He was up in the tower with Lovat Scout Fenwick when one of the radio operators brought him the response. Two American Volunteer Group mechanics from the Light Repair Section that ex-Technical Sergeant Hank W. Rawlston had established at Oasis X would be flown in to effect the necessary repairs.

Raiding Forces Desert Patrol's Avro Ansons were en route and would arrive before sundown. Standard Operating Procedure called for all desert flights to travel in pairs in case one plane went down for any reason.

Lt. Col. Randal had another situation he needed to resolve—what to do with the Italian policemen. He did not want to leave them behind when he finally departed the fort. The men had too much detailed information about Ranger Patrol. However, the patrol was one jeep short, and it did not have room to transport prisoners.

Another message was dispatched to the Long Range Desert Group, asking if it would be able to assist.

A reply came back promptly. G Patrol was passing fifty miles south of their position, returning from a classified deep-desert strategic reconnaissance mission. It would alter course, drive over and pick up the Italians.

The LRDG would arrive prior to sundown also.

Lt. Col. Randal did not like the idea of Ranger Patrol simply sitting doing nothing all day. He met with Mr. Zargo and Joker in the Mud Fort's commandant's office. They broke out maps.

Joker had the target list he had prepared.

Ex-Lieutenant Billy Jack Jaxx arrived to sit in on the meeting.

"We only have one jeep fully operational," Lt. Col. Randal said. "What have you got that we can hit with one gun jeep, Joker?"

"We could send a Boy's sniper team back down to the Via Balbia to snipe trucks from long range," Joker said.

"As much as I'd like to take out more trucks," Lt. Col. Randal said, studying the map, "I don't want to run the chance. If the Lovat Scouts stir up trouble and end up being pursued, we might be discovered here.

"What else do you have?"

"A massive tire dump," Joker said, pointing to the map. "A juicy target. But to get the mountain of tires burning will require a major demolitions effort. Work best done at night, Colonel."

"Good target," Lt. Col. Randal said, lighting a cigarette with his old, battered 26th U.S. Cavalry Regiment Zippo from his Huk guerrilla hunting days. Now *he* was the guerrilla.

"May take a crack at it later if we can get our jeeps running.

"What else?"

"There is an abandoned Regia Aeronautica landing ground about thirty miles from here," Joker tapped the map. "No guards. No buildings. A small emergency fuel cache."

"That'll work," Lt. Col. Randal said. "Anything else?"

"The Germans have a six-man radio relay post located in this vicinity," Joker said, indicating a position approximately forty miles from the Mud Fort.

"Big radio antenna, six technicians living in a cellar-like bunker carved into the side of a hill. The men claim to be a Luftwaffe meteorological reporting station."

"Technicians," Lt. Col. Randal said. "Might have code books."

"What do you like, Lieutenant—landing ground or weather station?"

"If I'm going to drive all day through the desert," ex-Lt. Jaxx said. "I'd prefer the chance to shoot somebody when I get to my objective, sir."

"Yeah," Lt. Col. Randal said. "You and Joker saddle up and move out. Take anyone you want with you.

"Try not to kill 'em all, Jack. Bring me back at least one prisoner."

"Roger that, sir," ex-Lt. Jaxx said. "Can I borrow your 45mm Brixia?"

"Don't lose it."

EX-LIEUTENANT BILLY JACK JAXX DEPARTED WITHIN THE HOUR. He drove, with Joker in the right seat navigating and Captain Pip Pilkington in the jump seat in the back, in case there were any demolitions that needed to be carried out. He was armed with the vehicle's .303 Bren gun—one from the stash captured in Persia.

A Phantom operator was manning the twin .303 Vickers K machine guns on the pedestal mount.

Having a trained radio specialist would come in handy when sorting through any signals documents captured at the German meteorological station. One of Phantom's fortes was collecting and evaluating enemy wireless/telephone (W/T) equipment, operating manuals, traffic logs, etc.

"Two of my operatives 'accidentally' stumbled on the German station," Joker said. "The Nazis were talkative."

"Really?"

"They claim to be Air Force meteorologists. A weather crew based out of Benghazi," Joker said.

"The Germans claim they were dropped off by an aircraft that landed them on the makeshift airstrip next to the hill. The Nazis say they stay on site for ten days before being relieved by the next shift.

"Hate the duty."

"Sure seem to be a lot of Italian landing grounds," ex-Lt. Jaxx said, "round about."

"There are," Joker said. "Building them all had to have taken the Regia Aeronautica an incredible number of man-hours. Drives the Italians absolutely glass-house-crazy when Raiding Forces destroys one."

"Why so many, Joker?"

"While we tend to describe them as 'abandoned'; actually the landing grounds were built as alternative airfields. Italian airmen are deathly afraid of going down in the desert. To offset their fear, the Regia Aeronautica has established auxiliary airstrips everywhere to use in an emergency," Joker said.

"Each one has a small cache of aviation fuel, water and food, so that any crew that has to ditch can hopefully either land at one or walk to it."

"Don't the Arabs steal everything?"

"They do if they can find it," Joker said. "The Italians bury the water and foodstuffs, with instructions on where it's hidden posted on the aircrew's escape maps.

"Aviation spirits are of little value to an Arab. Does not work very well for heating or cooking because of the fumes it produces.

"When the Italians catch any of the locals with their military fuel, even in small amounts, the Blackshirts shoot them out of hand."

"Ever plant a little," ex-Lt. Jaxx said, "on bad actors you wanted shot?"

"Might be a future for you, Lieutenant," Joker said, "in counterintelligence."

The Ranger Patrol jeep was averaging better than ten miles per hour through rugged desert terrain. Very few vehicles could have negotiated it. The German weather station was located in a truly remote, difficult-to-reach corner of a very big desert.

At 1645 hours, the target swam into view through the mirage caused by the intense desert heat. Ex-Lt. Jaxx had not been expecting to see an Italian Savoia Marchetti-82 tri-motor transport parked outside of the vault carved in the side of the hill.

He thought the structure looked like a west Texas tornado shelter.

"Let 'em have it, boys," ex-Lt. Jaxx ordered. "Light 'em up!"

Ranger Patrol hit hard and fast.

Six .303 caliber machine guns plus the .303 Bren gun onboard the jeep opened fire at maximum effective range, in hopes of pinning the Germans inside the dugout while they closed on the target. The Vickers Ks had such a high cyclic rate that when fired it sounded like canvas being torn.

The SM-82 returned fire with the machine guns mounted onboard.

"Shift to the airplane," ex-Lt. Jaxx commanded, changing targets as he spoke.

All guns on the Ranger Patrol jeep immediately transitioned their fire to the aircraft, and the incoming rounds ceased as if snuffed out.

Two men jumped out of the SM-82 transport with their hands up, wigwagging wildly.

"Check fire," ex-Lt. Jaxx ordered.

Ranger Patrol closed on the objective, continuing to engage the dugout carved in the side of the hill. As soon as he was in range, ex-Lt. Jaxx launched a round from the 45mm Brixia. It landed outside the front door, making an impressive *KRUUUUMPH!*

The shell did not do any damage. However, it had an immediate effect. Six men immediately came out of the bunker waving a white cloth.

In their confused state of mind, caused by the surprise of being attacked with no warning, the German weathermen believed the weather station had been fired on by a tank. All eight enemy personnel were captured unharmed.

The bullet-riddled SM-82 was flickering flame, but undeterred, the Phantom operator piled out of the jeep, raced to the tri-motored airplane, climbed onboard and managed to secure the charts, signals book and a pair of 9mm Beretta MAB-38 submachine guns from the cockpit before the plane burst into flames.

The operator proceeded to the dugout where he took possession of the W/T equipment, codebooks and the traffic tables.

While Joker was helping search the place for anything else of intelligence value and Capt. Pilkington was arranging for the destruction of the 2,500 gallons of aviation fuel on the airstrip (all it was going to take was striking a match), ex-Lt. Jaxx was dictating a message for the radio operator to transmit to the Mud Fort for instructions about what to do with the prisoners.

When Lieutenant Colonel John Randal received the message, he re-contacted LRDG's G Patrol. The patrol leader agreed to divert two of his new Australian-assembled Canadian pattern 15cwt 4X2 Chevrolet gun trucks—custom-fitted with the Indian Army model body—to ex-Lt. Jaxx's location to pick up the POWs.

"Not much here, Lieutenant," Joker said. "We have recovered everything of interest."

Ex-Lt. Jaxx gathered up the weapons in the dugout. There were two MP-40 submachine guns, four Mauser 98 rifles (two with scopes) and six 9mm Walther P-38s belonging to the German troops.

The two Italian airmen were armed with standard-issue Regia Aeronautica Beretta M1934 .380 pistols.

The fact that each of the German "meteorologists" was armed with a state-of-the-art personal sidearm in addition to their primary weapon was a clue that they might be more than simple weathermen.

"What do you think, Joker?"

"Lieutenant, my guess is that we have no idea what is actually going on here.

"Keep the Germans separated from each other," Joker said, "so they don't have an opportunity to organize a story. SIME can sort it out when we get them back to Cairo."

"Roger," ex-Lt. Jaxx said.

LRDG gun trucks from G Patrol arrived two hours later. The bearded, sun-bronzed desert brigands attired in shorts and sandals herded the prisoners on to their trucks. They were experienced at being a desert taxi service.

Handling prisoners was not a novel exercise for the LRDG. First thing, they blindfolded the men. The POWs were threatened with being gagged if any attempt was made to talk to each other.

The LRDG operators formed a chain to load the tins of water out of the dugout on to the trucks. Fresh water was always a welcome commodity.

Capt. Pilkington said, "Fire in the hole!"

He fired a flare from a Very pistol inside the dugout. Half a dozen fifty-five-gallon barrels of aviation fuel had been rolled inside. Several cans had been poured out on the floor.

The bunker gave a soft *WHOOOOOF!*

Capt. Pilkington proceeded over to the stack of fifty-five-gallon drums containing the aviation fuel. A small charge had been placed on one of the cans in the middle of the dump. He lit the fuse.

As the fuse burned, Capt. Pilkington stood back at a distance, took one of the captured Breda M-38s and shot holes indiscriminately in the stack of fuel cans. Then he switched submachine guns and emptied the second weapon's magazine into the drums. Aviation fuel squirted out onto the ground through the 9mm holes.

"Fire in the hole!" he said, seconds before the charge went off.

The explosion sounded like a large firecracker, but the aviation gas was highly flammable. In an instant, the pile of drums was a roaring inferno.

Capt. Pilkington had the foresight to soak the base of the wooden frame of the radio antenna on top of the hill with fuel.

As the two LRDG gun trucks and the RFDP's Ranger Patrol jeep pulled out, the antenna on top of the hill was burning merrily.

"Nicely done, Jack," Capt. Pilkington said. "Roll in, shoot up the place, capture an enemy force that outnumbers you two-to-one without a single casualty.

"Quintessence of efficiency."

"I've had practice, sir," ex-Lt. Jaxx said.

"So I hear," Capt. Pilkington said. "What exactly is a 'panty raid'?"

LIEUTENANT COLONEL JOHN RANDAL GLANCED AT HIS ROLEX—A GIFT from Captain the Lady Jane Seaborn. The sun was beginning to arch toward the horizon. Once it started down, the flaming ball of fire always seemed to pick up speed.

Night came on fast in the desert.

Lt. Col. Randal knew three elements were closing on the Mud Fort, but as of yet there was no sign of any of them. A pair of Avro Anson aircraft were airborne—inbound from Oasis X. G Patrol of the LRDG was en route. And ex-Lieutenant Billy Jack Jaxx was returning to base with two LRDG gun trucks after his successful raid on a German meteorological station.

A Phantom operator brought Lt. Col. Randal a message. Ex-Lt. Jaxx was requesting permission to divert in order to raid the abandoned landing ground Joker had briefed during the morning strategy session.

From outside the wall of the Mud Fort, a shout went up as some of the men lounging in the shade near the airstrip heard the sound of an approaching aircraft.

"Tell Lt. Jaxx," Lt. Col. Randal said, "to send the two LRDG trucks ahead to the Mud Fort with the prisoners. Give him my permission to break off and carry out his attack on the landing ground."

"Roger, sir."

Lt. Col. Randal and Waldo strolled outside the gate and down to the airstrip. A tiny speck could be seen approaching in the sky. Raiders were standing, waving at the inbound aircraft.

Mr. Zargo walked up.

"Lt. Jaxx and Joker are going to divert to take out that abandoned landing ground we discussed this morning," Lt. Col. Randal said. "The two LRDG trucks transporting the POWs from the weather station will be continuing on here."

"Excellent," Mr. Zargo said. "My men like to see the targets on their list raided. Motivates them to work harder preparing their next one if they know something is going to come from the effort."

"Nothing we like better," Lt. Col. Randal said, "than working through their lists."

"Colonel," Waldo said.

"If we can get the jeeps tuned up," Lt. Col. Randal said, "I want to craft a plan to go after the tire dump Joker showed us. That's a really good target."

"Colonel ..."

"We will have to work out an incendiary demolitions plan," Mr. Zargo said. "Not easy to light off that many tires."

"*Colonel*," Mr. Treywick shouted, "that ain't one of our Avros!"

"What—?"

On closer examination, it became apparent the high-winged single-engine aircraft (Avro Ansons were twin-engine) was sporting mottled desert pattern camouflage of the kind found on Italian aircraft. The airplane was touching down on the end of the strip, and it clearly was not RFDP.

"IMAM Ro.63 liaison plane," Mr. Zargo said. "Probably bringing the Mud Fort its mail."

"Keep waving," Lt. Col. Randal called to the Raiders who were beginning to get the picture.

Italian policemen wore khaki. Afrika Korps soldiers wore khaki. Raiding Forces wore khaki. It was little wonder the pilot of the Ro.63 did not see anything out of the ordinary about men in khaki on the landing strip.

The sleek little aircraft taxied up to the crowd, slewed around and cut its engine. The Regia Aeronautica aviator stepped out of the airplane.

GG came running up.

Lt. Col. Randal said, "Explain the situation to the pilot, GG—once we make sure he's disarmed."

"Allow me," Mr. Zargo said. He walked over to the Italian officer with his 9mm Browning P-35 in hand behind his back.

The Regia Aeronautica pilot's friendly smile changed to a look of horror when the pistol came up and pressed against the bottom of his chin. Mr. Zargo reached out and extracted the Beretta M1934 .380 from the shoulder holster on the Italian's chest.

While GG was informing the Ro.63's pilot that for him the war was over, the pair of RFDP's Avro Ansons made their approach. The twin-engine RFDP aircraft touched down, one behind the other.

Squadron Leader Paddy Wilcox was piloting the lead Anson with Lieutenant Penelope "Legs" Honeycutt-Parker acting as his navigator. Brandy Seaborn was napping in the back seat.

Lieutenant Pamala Plum-Martin was flying the second Anson with James "Baldie" Taylor aboard for her navigator.

"Ro.63," the Vargas Girl-looking Royal Marine pilot said to Lt. Col. Randal who was there to greet her as she stepped onto the runway.

"Lovely machine, John. Italian design, German engine. Renowned for its short landing and takeoff capabilities. Did you seize it when you took the Mud Fort?"

"Flew in and landed," Lt. Col. Randal said, "while we were standing here waiting for you to arrive, Pam."

"For a sleepy little village no one even knew existed," Lt. Plum-Martin said, "seems to be a lot of excitement going on."

Sqn. Ldr. Wilcox walked over, wearing his trademark black eye patch over one perfectly good eye.

He said, "That Ro.63 is a valuable capture, Colonel. RFDP can put it to good use."

"She is a beauty," Jim Taylor said, "I can fly it back."

Brandy walked over in rolled-up khaki shorts and desert boots. Golden tan. There was a web belt around her waist carrying a holstered Colt 1911 .38 Super automatic.

"Hi, John."

"Sightseeing, Brandy?"

"Business, actually," Brandy laughed. "Always a thrill to see you, handsome.

"Have the German meteorologists that Billy Jack captured arrived yet? We want to interview them before the shock of finding themselves POWs wears off."

"Should be here shortly," Lt. Col. Randal said. "Plenty of time to break out your rubber hoses."

"Parker and I never resort to rubber hoses," Brandy said with a big white-toothed smile, but not sounding 100 percent convincing.

"We have other means."

"G Patrol of the LRDG diverted a couple of their trucks to pick up the prisoners. They're transporting them to the Mud Fort as we speak," Lt. Col. Randal said.

"Perfect."

"Jack Cool won't be with 'em. He's decided to stay out and go raiding again tonight."

"Too bad," Brandy said. "Love Billy Jack—fabulous accent. My favorite student."

"I thought I was your favorite student."

"You are my favorite *person*," Brandy said.

"We flew over the main body of G Patrol driving this way," Jim said, "about half an hour out.

"Saw two other trucks coming in from the south. Must have been the G Patrol detachment with the prisoners."

"Care to explain," Lt. Col. Randal said, "all the interest in weathermen?"

"'Need to Know,' John," Brandy said. "What I am at liberty to divulge is that one remote weather station in the desert probably does not mean much of anything.

"A series of clandestine 'weather missions'... now that would be what one might expect Count László Almásy to set up to have a dual purpose: gather weather intelligence and to use as waystations across the Great Sand Sea to infiltrate Abwehr agents into Egypt.

"Parker and I are hot on his trail."

"I see," Lt. Col. Randal said. Which meant he did not have a clue what she was talking about.

Jim and Mr. Zargo rummaged through the cockpit of the Ro.63. They located the flight logs and the pilot's charts. The two men spread the maps out on the ground beside the airplane.

"Bring the pilot over here," Jim ordered GG.

After a brief discussion, they folded the maps and strolled over to where Lt. Col. Randal was standing with Brandy and Lt. Honeycutt-Parker.

"Bingo," Jim said.

"We have the coordinates to virtually every Italian landing ground in this quarter of Africa. Zargo has a wealth of new targets to add to the list for his men to inspect.

"And Mrs. Seaborn, you will be interested to know the pilot admits he delivered mail earlier today at the weather station Lt. Jaxx raided, but it's *not* marked on the map."

"Intriguing," Brandy said. "Did he mention if there were any more locations that happen not to appear on his chart?"

"We did not get into details," Jim said. "Thought you and Parker would prefer to handle that aspect of the questioning."

"Definitely," Lt. Honeycutt-Parker said. "No time like the present, actually."

"John, do you have a place," Brandy said, "we can have a private *tête-à-tête* with the Italian pilot?"

"The commandant's office should work," Lt. Col. Randal said. "I'll have King sit in to be the heavy in case you ladies decide to play good cop, bad cop."

"Wonderful; always hate to break a nail," Brandy said.

"At least my own."

THE LRDG's G PATROL, MINUS THE TWO GUN TRUCKS DISPATCHED TO assist ex-Lieutenant Billy Jack Jaxx, arrived within the half hour.

The G stood for Guards Patrol. The unit was made up of volunteers from the bluest of blue-blooded regiments in the British Army serving in Middle East Command.

Captain Michael Crichton-Steward, Scots Guards, commanded G Patrol. He was an archetypical by-the-book Brigade of Guards officer who believed that the best desert operators were Guardsmen who were the best "squarebashers." His number two was Lieutenant Martin Gibbs, Coldstream Guards.

LRDG patrols consisted of two officers and thirty-six other ranks. Most contained at least a dozen trucks. They were the unquestioned masters of deep desert reconnaissance. When G Patrol returned to base, it would wrap up a 3,500-mile roundtrip mission behind enemy lines without having fired a shot in anger.

The motto of the LRDG was "Not by Strength by Guile." And they lived up to it. In the first year of desert operations, the LRDG had the enviable record of having lost only two men killed in action.

G Patrol had been hastily formed a few days before OPERATION BATTLEAX and sent off straightaway on an operation, with the LRDG having virtually no desert training or even having the time to familiarize themselves with the Lewis guns they were armed with.

Even though G Patrol had not been in existence as long as RFDP, as members of the mystical LRDG, the Guardsmen tended to look on RFDP as very much the junior partner in desert operations.

They also viewed Raiding Forces as having a tendency to shoot first and ask questions later...an opinion that may have been influenced by the book *Jump on Bela* in which it was claimed that Lt. Col. Randal had ordered his troops to, "Kill 'em all and let Allah sort 'em out."

The two units enjoyed an excellent working relationship.

While G Patrol was climbing down from their trucks, the detachment sent to transport the prisoners for Ranger Patrol drove up. The blindfolded Germans and Italians were helped out of the back, segregated, separated and seated on the ground in the shade.

Raiding Forces personnel took over responsibility for guarding the prisoners and ensuring that they did not attempt to communicate with each other.

All the LRDG trucks were moved into position against the wall and concealed under camouflage netting.

The Italian pilot of the Ro.63 was escorted to the commandant's office.

Jim, Mr. Zargo and Lt. Plum-Martin started setting up in a separate room. When Brandy and Lt. Honeycutt-Parker finished an interview, the three planned to take the POW and conduct their own interrogation. The idea was that everyone could later compare notes.

Any discrepancies, and the party telling different versions of the same tale was going to have to do some explaining.

Just for fun while waiting for their first interview, Jim had GG and Mr. Treywick sneak in with a stretcher. Outside the window where the group of POWs had been moved, the enemy personnel were sitting, leaning up against the wall of the building waiting their turn to be questioned. The men were at a distance so they would not be able to hear what was going on inside.

That is, unless someone screamed.

From the makeshift interrogation center, Mr. Zargo started shouting questions in Italian, only to be greeted with silence—no prisoner being present in the room to answer.

Jim nodded to Mr. Treywick. Waldo pulled out his five-inch Smith & Wesson N frame .38/44. He fired a shot into the ceiling.

GG climbed on the stretcher. Jim covered him up with a blanket. Mr. Zargo and Waldo trotted outside, carrying it past the astonished prisoners, most of whom had figured out a way to peek out from under their blindfolds.

No interviewer experienced any problems eliciting a response during the interrogations.

Four hours later, the questioning was complete, and Jim, Mr. Zargo, Brandy and Lt. Honeycutt-Parker met to review notes. Lt. Col. Randal asked, "Learn anything?"

"We did," Brandy said. "*Kampfgeschwader* 200. Let's just call it KG 200."

"Never heard of it," Lt. Col. Randal said.

"Neither have we," Jim said. "Apparently it's a super-secret Luftwaffe special operations unit. An element of indeterminate size has arrived in the Middle East to commence operations.

"KG 200 specializes in extreme, long-range missions for the Abwehr. Works closely with the Brandenburg Commandos."

"Those I have heard of," Lt. Col. Randal said. "What's it mean?"

"Almásy," Brandy said.

"Nazi pervert," Lt. Honeycutt-Parker said. "We shall run him to ground."

"We will," Brandy said. "Delicious fun."

21
RAIDING FORCES WAS HERE

THE THREE AIRPLANES DEPARTED THE MUD FORT AN HOUR BEFORE daylight. The Italian pilot of the IMAM Ro.63 and the German identified as the officer-in-charge—he was not wearing any rank—of the weather station destroyed by ex-Lieutenant Billy Jack Jaxx, were on board the Italian plane being flown by Jim Taylor.

One of the Raiders from Ranger Patrol was also on board to make sure the prisoners did not cause any trouble during the flight, which would be difficult since the two were firmly tied to their seats, then strapped in by their safety belts.

As they flew out of sight, Lieutenant Colonel John Randal had a quiet word with King.

"How did Brandy and Parker perform in the interrogations?"

"I always had the sense," King said, "that Mrs. Seaborn and Lieutenant Honeycutt-Parker were bored upper-class ladies playing at spy catching."

Lt. Col. Randal asked, "You telling me they're not?"

"Surprised me, Chief," King said, "Highly skilled professionals."

Ex-Lt. Jaxx drove in shortly after sunrise. He had raided the abandoned Regia Aeronautica landing ground. Captain Pip Pilkington had blown up the small 500-gallon aviation fuel dump. The patrol had knocked down the windsock.

Not a lot to report. There had been no contact with enemy forces. Materiel damage was negligible.

Lt. Col. Randal was pleased.

The raid was guerrilla war at its finest. Ex-Lt. Jaxx had taken down both his targets and brought all his men home safe and sound. Raiding Forces let the enemy know they could strike when and where they chose.

And there was nothing the Axis Forces could do about it.

GG had breakfast ready for the patrol. Lt. Col. Randal discussed future plans with Capt. Pilkington and ex-Lt. Jaxx while they ate.

"The mechanics got the jeeps running," Lt. Col. Randal said. "I want to pull out of here as soon as you finish your meal. We've been stationary entirely too long to suit me."

"Roger that," ex-Lt. Jaxx said. "I'll need to redistribute ammo, refuel and refill our water; then my boys will be ready to roll, sir."

"I'm planning to raid the tire dump," Lt. Col. Randal said. "Turns out the Italians have been hauling their worn-out tires to this one location just off the Via Balbia for decades.

"Joker says it's the Mt. Everest of used tires."

"I thought he was talking about new tires, sir," ex-Lt. Jaxx said, "when he briefed us."

"So did I," Lt. Col. Randal said. "Doesn't matter. The psychological impact is what counts—not the material damage.

"A tire dump on fire puts out a thick cloud of black smoke. We light off Joker's mountain—Raiding Forces will leave a calling card in the heart of Afrika Korps that nobody can ignore."

"Tires can be difficult to light off," Capt. Pilkington said. "You have to heat the rubber to 400 degrees for several minutes.

"That said, sir, once on fire, tire dumps have been known to burn for years. Virtually impossible to extinguish a big one."

"What makes 'em so hard to put out, sir?" ex-Lt. Jaxx asked.

"Tires burn from the inside out, Jack," Capt. Pilkington said. "You can spray them with water but they will continue to smolder unless you bury the entire dump."

"No one's going to be spraying water out here in the middle of the desert," ex-Lt. Jaxx said. "That's for sure."

"Agreed," Capt. Pilkington said. "The trick is starting the fire in the first place."

"What's the plan, Captain?" Lt. Col. Randal said. It was not really a question.

"Shredded tires work best as an igniter, sir."

"How do we shred tires?"

"Small charges of explosives should do the job," Capt. Pilkington said. "Set them around the dump with the idea to shred a certain number of tires in strategic locations, add a generous dose of petrol, then light it off, sir."

"We don't have any gas to spare," Lt. Col. Randal said.

"But there's a stockpile of aviation fuel the Ro.63 used to top off its tanks when it landed here to deliver the Mud Fort's mail."

"Aviation spirits will do nicely," Capt. Pilkington said. "Detonation cord and a small amount of explosives mixed with a liquid combustible to act as an accelerant are all the components we require, sir."

"We've got that," ex-Lt. Jaxx said. "Let's do it."

"Every tire will generate two gallons of gasoline as it burns down," Capt. Pilkington said. "Once the pile is burning, the fire will become self-sustaining.

"The toxic smoke will be jet-black, thick, oily, extremely heavy, and it's not going to disperse, sir. The cloud will lie on the ground, and the prevailing breeze could push it a hundred miles—maybe more."

"That's what I want," Lt. Col. Randal said. "A giant billboard: 'RAIDING FORCES WAS HERE.'

"We'll put Captain Hawthorne Merryweather on the case. Make sure there's not any question who's responsible. He's a genius at that sort of thing."

"Sir," ex-Lt. Jaxx said, "this bonfire may turn out almost as good as those squirrels you painted orange.

"A gift to Rommel that keeps on giving."

"We can hope," Lt. Col. Randal said.

"I'm really loving RFDP guerrilla tactics, Colonel," ex-Lt. Jaxx said. "Joy riding in gun jeeps, blowing things up, setting fires that never go out.

"Raising hell and getting paid for it."

"Guerrilla war—cavalry style," Lt. Col. Randal said. "Arrive unannounced, hit, run, ride out.

"Let everybody know you did it and will be coming back at a later time and place of your choosing."

WALDO TREYWICK SAID, "THERE WAS A BIG TIRE FIRE OUTSIDE A' ADDIS Ababa that burned for over twenty years. Shifta bandits set it off hopin' to get at the scrap metal they thought was buried underneath the pile."

"I had a report," Mr. Zargo said, "about one in China that's been burning since 1912."

"There's a tire dump burning on Madagascar," Guns said. "See it fifty miles out to sea.

"A mucking giant black smudge over the water by day—some say it kills fish under the cloud, glows at night."

"You weren't kidding, Joker," ex-Lieutenant Billy Jack Jaxx said. This really is the Mt. Everest of bald tires."

Ranger Patrol was at the dump located approximately three miles off the hard-topped Via Balbia. The size of the place was overwhelming. What seemed like millions of tires were piled up.

The men were unloading steel drums of aviation gas from the back of the two Long Range Desert Group trucks attached to Ranger Patrol to haul the accelerant to the tire dump.

The Raiders had been working for hours to get the drums in place. It was not easy manhandling full barrels of fuel up a pile of tires. Placing the steel fifty-five-gallon drums higher than a third of the way up was proving extraordinarily difficult.

No one had any experience climbing a mountain of tires.

None of the conventional rules of mountaineering, which Raiding Forces had trained for extensively, applied. Eventually they settled on having a team scale fifty feet up the pile of tires (a hundred or more feet from the top), then haul the drums up with ropes.

The idea was to have the flammable fuel spill down inside the base of the rubber mountain all around, then set the pile ablaze.

G Patrol had donated all of their explosives, but Captain Pip Pilkington still did not have enough detonation cord to link all the charges together. The massive size of the tire dump made it impossible to shred the tires, connect all the cans and evenly distribute the accelerant with a single shot.

Capt. Pilkington strung out all the cord he had. Then he set time fuses with a tiny charge on the barrels not linked up until he ran out of time pencils.

In order to set off the steel drums studded up the sides of the rubber mountain that were not connected to the main charge or primed with individual explosives, the Raiders loaded magazines full of tracers in their 9mm Beretta MAB38 submachine guns and stood by around the base of the pile, awaiting the command to shoot the cans.

The tracers would penetrate the steel drums and ignite the fuel. The hope was that the flaming liquid would spurt out, flow down inside the mound, catching tires on fire internally as it went. Then, as the fire burned, the tires would yield the desired two gallons of gasoline each and the fire would feed itself.

It should work.

Through a Herculean effort, one fifty-five-gallon drum of aviation fuel was muscled to the very apex of the mammoth pile of tires. When they stumbled back down, the shattered Raiders who had dreamed up the feat claimed that getting the steel can to the top of the tire mountain was the toughest challenge they had faced in all their training or on any operation—ever.

Lieutenant Colonel John Randal was accorded the honor of taking on the top drum with his 9mm Beretta MAB-38 submachine gun.

"Fire when ready, Colonel," Capt. Pilkington said. "I shall blow the main charge immediately after you have your target alight."

Lt. Col. Randal aimed at the drum and squeezed off a short, crisp burst. The tracers streaked into the can, sparkling on the steel—but the result was less than inspiring. The burning fuel ran out the bullet holes as the lid popped off showing flames. That was about it.

The peak of the mound was on fire, but it was not much of a blaze.

"Fire in the hole!" Capt. Pilkington shouted and pulled the igniter on the daisy chain.

"Commence firing."

The popping sound of the string of small firecracker-sized explosions ignited by the detonation cord intermingled with the time fuses cooking off, blowing the individual charges. Simultaneously, Raiders opened up on the cans in their assigned sector with their submachine guns. The magazines were loaded all tracer.

Soon the fifty-five-gallon drums were flaming. The entire operation was over in less than thirty seconds. The troops stood looking up at the mountain, unimpressed.

The most exciting part had been shooting up the barrels. The tire dump was on fire, but there were not a lot of flames. Little smoke. Nothing had blown up after the initial blast.

Everyone was exhausted from his efforts placing the heavy barrels of aviation fuel.

But no one had been scared out of their wits like nearly always happened when Captain "Pyro" Percy Stirling blew something up. It was a let-down, the Raiders having come to expect massive explosions when demolitions were involved.

Privately, Ranger Patrol was disappointed.

Assured by Capt. Pilkington that the mountain of tires was burning internally, Lt. Col. Randal had the Phantom team send a coded message to Captain Hawthorne Merryweather to execute his psychological warfare campaign taking responsibility for the attack that caused the fire.

The gun jeeps pulled out. The patrol had a long way to go before daylight. They needed to put as much distance as possible between the mountain of tires and their next Laying Up Position.

"That was a lot of work," ex-Lt. Jaxx said to Mr. Zargo, riding in his jeep. "Sure didn't get much bang for our buck."

"Anti-climactic," Mr. Zargo said. "I must admit."

Fifty miles away, when Ranger Patrol went into a camouflaged LUP in a wadi as the sun came up, that attitude changed. Back on their line-of-march, the horizon was black. The sky looked like the mother of all thunderstorms was developing.

The Raiders stopped what they were doing and stared, open-mouthed. The enormity of the low, dark cloud was alarming. The formation seemed to be alive.

It was growing.

Had they caused that?

"Would you look at that monster," Waldo said to ex-Lt. Jaxx, "broiling up like that!

"Like it's coming after us."

"Avoid the front line," ex-Lt. Jaxx quoted Lt. Col. Randal on guerrilla tactics. "Strike fear and terror in the enemy's rear."

"We sure done that, Lootenant," Waldo said. "At least I hope we did. Cause if that's a *khamseen* a-brewin' and headed this way, we're dead men."

"Oh, that's our fire all right," ex-Lt. Jaxx said. "Read 'em and weep, Mr. Desert Fox."

"In that case, Rommel's just got the message," Waldo said. "Raidin' Forces own his sandbox."

"Hit and run," ex-Lt. Jaxx said. "Always on the move.

"What a way to fight a war."

"Too bad," Waldo said, offering ex-Lt. Jaxx one of his cigars, "you wasn't with us in Abyssinia, Lootenant.

"Now there was some serious guerrilla operatin'."

"Nice job, Pip," Lt. Col. Randal said.

"You have your billboard, Colonel."

"Roger that, stud," Lt. Col. Randal said, "A real Picasso. Your masterpiece."

"Sir, ranger patrol has a frogspawn prefix message," the Phantom operator said.

"What's it say?"

"You are instructed to move to the abandoned Italian auxiliary landing ground located at these coordinates for aerial pick up tomorrow morning at 0700 hours, sir."

The Phantom operator handed Lieutenant Colonel John Randal a slip of paper with the grid coordinates written on it. Waldo Treywick and Mr. Zargo were sitting with him, on folding canvas chairs smoking Waldo's cigars, while enjoying the view of the black cloud on the horizon.

"Are you familiar with this airstrip, Mr. Zargo?" Lt. Col. Randal passed him the flimsy.

"Approximately forty miles from our LUP," Mr. Zargo said, tracing the coordinates on a map with his finger.

"The landing ground is one of the objectives on our target list. Ranger Patrol should be able to reach it in the time specified even if we wait until nightfall to move out."

"Wilco the message," Lt. Col. Randal said to the Phantom operator.

"Have Lieutenant Jaxx report to me."

"Sir."

"I know you were planning to drop off at some point to work with one of your Intel teams," Lt. Col Randal said to Mr. Zargo, "but these orders change things.

"Lieutenant Jaxx is going to have to take command. He could use your counsel. I'd appreciate it if you would stick with Ranger Patrol."

"My pleasure."

"Don't let Jack get in over his head."

"Do not concern yourself, Colonel," Mr. Zargo said. "We will complete the mission."

"What's your thought on Lieutenant Jaxx?" Lt. Col. Randal asked Mr. Treywick.

"You're askin' me for an opinion on one a' your officers?" Waldo said. "You ain't never done that before."

"Well, I'm asking now."

"Lieutenant Jaxx reminds me a' me," Mr. Treywick said, "with a little a'

'Geronimo' Joe and a touch a' you thrown in."

"He reminds you of you?"

"Barely twenty years old," Waldo said. "Done been arrested twice—once for murder."

Lt. Col. Randal said, "Some track record."

"Judge in Texas was smart to keep Jack away from his granddaughter like that, makin' him join the paratroopers," Waldo said.

"Beat the rap a' gunnin' down some major at Fort Bennin', too."

"I heard it was a colonel," Mr. Zargo said. "Shot in the back."

"Lieutenant Jaxx shot a captain—a fleeing felon," Lt. Col. Randal said. "Justified."

"Blew the hell out of him with a forty-five," Waldo said. "Jack Cool."

"I was more interested," Lt. Col. Randal said, "on how you think Lieutenant Jaxx will do as Ranger Patrol leader, Mr. Treywick."

"Make a good officer," Waldo said, "if he don't get killed first."

When ex-Lt. Jaxx arrived, Mr. Zargo and Waldo decided they had business elsewhere.

"You wanted to see me, sir?'

"Ranger Patrol has been ordered to move to a location tonight where I can be picked up by air at first light in the morning.

"Lieutenant Jaxx, take command of the patrol, work through the remainder of targets on Joker's list and lead it back to Oasis X."

"Roger."

"I'm giving you a big assignment, Jack," Lt. Col. Randal said. "We're 700 miles from X; there are a number of objectives to tackle, and you're the least-experienced officer I have ever let lead a patrol.

"Think you can handle it?"

"Yes, sir."

"Well, we're getting ready to find out, Lieutenant," Lt. Col. Randal said.

"Ranger Patrol is made up of hand-picked men from a pool of picked men, and some of them, like Sergeant Pompedous, have been with me since Swamp Fox Force at Calais. Don't get any of 'em killed."

"I thought Pompedous was a corporal, sir," ex-Lt. Jaxx said.

"He got promoted," Lt. Col. Randal said. "Make sure you call him 'Sergeant.'"

"Wilco."

"Mr. Zargo is going to stay with Ranger Patrol for the duration of the mission. Use him as your military as well as your intelligence advisor," Lt. Col. Randal said. "If he says no, that means you don't do it.

"Is that clear?"

"Clear, sir."

"Mr. Treywick has a built-in danger barometer," Lt. Col. Randal said. "Keep your eye on him like I do.

"The minute he quivers, you get nervous."

"Understood, sir."

"When you're in command, Jack," Lt. Col. Randal said, "*command.* Is that clear?"

"Perfectly, sir."

RANGER PATROL SPENT THE DAY UNDER CAMOUFLAGE NETTING IN their lup. The two mechanics from the Light Vehicle Section had remained with the patrol. They spent the time tuning up the jeeps.

The men worked on their weapons and personal gear. Everyone stayed busy. Word had gone around that Lieutenant Colonel John Randal would be turning over command of the Patrol to ex-Lieutenant Billy Jack Jaxx and flying out on the morrow. Ranger Patrol would continue the mission.

Lt. Col. Randal, Mr. Zargo and Joker went over the catalog of potential objectives in detail. The list was pared down to eliminate any target that could result in Ranger Patrol getting into a prolonged firefight.

Then ex-Lt. Jaxx was briefed on the modified target list.

"You understand what's going on here, Jack?" Lt. Colonel Randal said.

"Yes, sir," ex-Lt. Jaxx said. "Hard intelligence. Soft targets.

"You only want me to hit cream puffs."

"Operating behind enemy lines," Lt. Col. Randal said, "there are no sure things. Nothing wrong with only swinging at the perfect pitch if you have the luxury—you do."

"Understood, sir."

"I'm having a navigator flown in on the plane that's picking me up," Lt. Col. Randal said. "That'll leave you free to concentrate on command and tactics."

"Thanks, Colonel," ex-Lt. Jaxx said, sounding relieved.

"Expect the unexpected," Lt. Col. Randal said, quoting Raiding Forces' Rules for Raiding.

"I will, sir," ex-Lt. Jaxx said. "I know your rules by heart."

"It's good to be confident, Jack," Lt. Col. Randal said, "but never hold the enemy or this desert terrain in contempt. That can come back to bite you when you least expect it."

"That's pretty close to what my grandfather, the Sheriff, used to say, sir," ex-Lt. Jaxx said, "serving warrants."

"According to Mr. Zargo, in the fifth century BC," Lt. Col. Randal said, "a King Cambyses marched his 40,000-man army into the sand sea somewhere in this general area. Disappeared to a man. Vanished without a trace."

"I'll keep it in mind, sir," ex-Lt. Jaxx said.

"You do that."

RANGER PATROL MOVED OUT AFTER DARK. LIEUTENANT COLONEL John Randal waited because he did not want to run any chance of being spotted by the Regia Aeronautica and Luftwaffe aircraft that were crisscrossing the desert looking for the raiders. Enemy airplanes would not be searching after last light.

As long as they traveled at night and went into a camouflaged LUP during the day, it was going to be very difficult for enemy air to find them. It was a big desert. Ranger Patrol was very small—half the size of the normal LRDG patrol—and their jeeps were smaller than the LRDG trucks.

Lt. Col. Randal actually wanted to leave earlier to make sure Ranger Patrol reached the rendezvous on time, but this was his last opportunity to set the example for Lieutenant Billy Jack Jaxx not to take unnecessary chances.

The night was bright. There was a full moon. Morale of the troops was high.

The tire fire had turned out to be more impressive than their wild-est imagination once the burning rubber started smoking. There was nothing the Raiders liked more than slipping in deep behind enemy lines, carrying out a mission and leaving their calling card. Not going to be any question that Raiding Forces had been here and gone.

The jeeps arrived at the Italian landing ground before sunrise. As expected, it was abandoned. The place was the typical auxiliary airfield. A windsock hanging limply on a pole, a scraped-out strip, a small cache of aviation fuel, food, water—and that was it.

The trick was finding the hide. Ranger Patrol cheated. It carried a mine detector on board one of the jeeps.

Using the detector, it did not take long to locate where the emer-gency supplies were buried. Ranger Patrol took what they wanted, dug a new hide in another location and reburied what they did not need in case they might be passing by at some later date. Any German or Ital-ian who landed on the strip was going to be disappointed to discover the information on their map indicating where the hoard was hidden was not accurate.

Ranger Patrol was sitting parked beside the landing ground when the two Avro Ansons came in for landing.

"Pip, since we don't have any explosives left, you can come out with me," Lt. Col. Randal said.

"If it is all the same to you, sir," Captain Pip Pilkington said, "I shall stay and finish the patrol. One never knows what Jack Cool is going to do next. Could be interesting."

"Your call," Lt. Col. Randal said, slinging his gear over his shoulder.

As Lt. Col. Randal was walking out to board the plane with King, who would be flying back with him, he ordered ex-Lt. Jaxx, "Send me a Situation Report every time Ranger Patrol stops long enough for the Phantom team to set up their aerial."

"Yes, sir."

"You can ambush the Via Balbia or attack roadhouses—but no joy riding looking for targets of opportunity. Is that clear?"

"Are you worried about me, Colonel?" ex-Lt. Jaxx asked.

"I sure as hell am."

22

FULL DRAG

LIEUTENANT COLONEL JOHN RANDAL WAS SITTING IN THE LIVING ROOM of the suite Captain the Lady Jane Seaborn retained at the posh Mena House Hotel, reading a Phantom message that had been delivered to his room while he was still traveling to Cairo from Oasis X. He was wearing his King's Royal Rifle Corps dining-out uniform. Four hundred yards beyond the wall of windows, the Great Pyramid was a shadow in the night.

"*1630 hours Ranger Patrol engaged two (2) Italian tank carriers transporting two (2) German Mark III Panzers. Both carriers and tanks destroyed.*"

Lt. Col. Randal passed the message to Major Sir Terry "Zorro" Stone. Now that he had all four of the Regiment's patrols ready to take the field, Maj. Stone would be taking command of Raiding Forces Desert Patrol.

"You have to be a head of state or a major movie star to rate this particular room in these digs," Captain "Geronimo" Joe McKoy said. "Lady Jane seems to get it every time."

"Jane keeps this one year-round nowadays," Vice Admiral Sir Randolph "Razor" Ransom said. "The Mena has a reciprocal agreement with her Bradford Hotel in London."

"Fit for a Pharaoh," Maj. Stone said.

"She agreed to allow the Prime Minister the use of it on his trip out," VAdm. Ransom said.

"I'm almost ready, John," Lieutenant Mandy Paige called from the bedroom.

"Does everyone understand tonight's drill?" VAdm. Ransom asked.

"You and I are going to go get us a steak," Capt. McKoy said. "Might stop in and have a drink at Shepard's.

"Zorro and Travis are headed out on the prowl. They ain't saying where. My guess is the Kit Kat Club is in their future.

"John and Mandy are taking Rocky out to dinner at the Gezira Club.

"Then we're all meeting back up at Raiding Forces Headquarters at 2400 hours. Lady Jane and Baldie, who'll have Field Marshal Auchinleck in tow, will link up with us there.

"Right now, Jim and Lady Jane are tied up in an urgent meeting having to do with Dudley Clarke who, as I understand it, is still missing, causing a big flap."

"Correct," VAdm. Ransom said. "From RFHQ, we shall drive out to a cove approximately five miles from the compound to observe a landing of Roy Kidd's patrol from three Landing Craft Vehicle Personnel."

"What's the difference between a Landing Craft Assault and the Landing Craft Vehicle Personnel?" Lt. Col. Randal asked.

"Basically the same," VAdm. Ransom said. "We British call it an LCA and the Americans call it the LCVP. Designed by Higgins out of New Orleans for oil field workers to get to their rigs in the Louisiana swamps.

"You can carry them on the deck of a ship and lower them into the water with block and tackle or have davits fitted that will swing out and lower the boats with the troops and cargo on board.

"The original Higgins did not have a ramped bow. Called a Eureka, it is still in use by the Commandos. The men have to jump over the sides when they storm ashore," VAdm. Ransom said.

"We've trained on the Eureka," Maj. Stone said.

"A U.S. Marine officer showed Higgins a photograph he had snapped while stationed in China of a Japanese barge with a ramped bow that could be lowered," VAdm. Ransom said. "Higgins incorporated the design, and now it's possible to load two jeeps plus their crew on one, drive up on the beach, lower the ramp and have them roll off.

"Tonight we are planning to observe Lt. Kidd," VAdm. Ransom said, "landing his Duck Patrol from three LCVPs provided by U.S. Lend-Lease.

"FM Auchinleck has asked to be included in our party tonight to evaluate for himself Raiding Forces' ability to strike the coastline from the sea. Operations Division staff has been telling him that amphibious Commando raids are a nonstarter out here in Africa."

"Now, that's a real colorful story, Admiral," Capt. McKoy said. "Exceptin' it ain't exactly true."

"No? Which part?"

"Higgins didn't design his boat for oil field workers. He mighta got a picture from a China Marine, but as a law enforcement officer of some experience, that whole yarn sounds a little too cute to me."

"When I was at the Infantry School at Fort Benning," ex-Captain Travis McCloud said, "I heard the story about the Louisiana swamps, oil fields and the Jap photo."

"What is the truth, Captain?" VAdm. Ransom asked.

"Andy Higgins was a broke boat builder down in New Orleans," Capt. McKoy said.

"Then Prohibition got voted in. Rumrunners needed a way to get their booze off ships out in the Gulf of Mexico on to land, loaded on trucks and not get caught doing it.

"Higgins designed 'em a shallow draft boat the bootleggers could winch crates of illegal alcohol onto from the decks of trawlers, run ashore on an isolated beach someplace and load up quick into a waiting convoy.

"The whopper about swamp boats for oilfield roughnecks ain't nothin' but a cover story," Capt. McKoy said. "But it's a dang good one."

"Personally," Maj. Stone said, "I favor the bootlegger version, Captain. Seems more appropriate for what we intend to use Higgins boats for—clandestine missions by moonlight."

"Another fine example," VAdm. Ransom said, "where truth and legend fail to marry up."

"Seldom do," Capt. McKoy said.

"Hate it," Lt. Col. Randal said, "when that happens."

KING CAME IN AND GAVE LIEUTENANT COLONEL JOHN RANDAL another Phantom message delivered by courier from RFHQ.

"1925 hours Ranger Patrol carried out raid on an Italian overnight truck park. Twenty-nine trucks damaged believed destroyed."

"Jack Cool," Major Sir Terry "Zorro" Stone said, after Lt. Col. Randal handed him the note as he and ex-Captain Travis McCloud were leaving for their night on the town.

Captain "Geronimo" Joe McKoy and Vice Admiral Sir Randolph "Razor" Ransom had already departed the suite at Mena House.

Lieutenant Mandy Paige was still not finished getting ready.

"Lieutenant Jaxx is a natural raider. Seems to have the magic touch," Maj. Stone said. "Not every patrol leader does."

"No," Lt. Col. Randal said, "they don't."

"Raiding's what got him here," ex-Capt. McCloud said. "Hit the Tri Delta Sorority House in Austin."

"I shall have to put him in the queue," Maj. Stone said, "to fill in when one of my patrol leaders is sick, injured, or goes on leave—satisfactory with you, old stick?"

"Go ahead," Lt. Col. Randal said.

After the two officers left, Lt. Mandy Paige came out of the master bedroom adjusting an earring. She was wearing one of Captain the Lady Jane Seaborn's simple black sheath dresses and six-inch heels.

Lt. Mandy looked ten years older than the twenty-year-old horse girl Lt. Col. Randal had first met a few months earlier at RAF Habbaniya.

She was a knockout.

"Has everyone already gone?"

"Got tired of waiting for you," Lt. Col. Randal said. "Their loss. You look good in that dress, Mandy."

"Thank you, John," Lt. Mandy said. "You have been very patient."

In Lt. Col. Randal's experience, beautiful women and being patient went in tandem.

"I tried to talk Jane into letting me wear the diamond ear studs you gave her, but she drew the line on that idea."

King came in. He did a double take when he saw Lt. Mandy. She rewarded him with a magnificent smile.

"Flanigan's here, Chief. Car's standing by."

Lt. Col. Randal clapped on his green Commando Beret sporting The Rangers Regiment badge, slipped his 9mm Browning Hi-Power around back under the short King's Royal Rifle Corps jacket and was ready to go.

King said, "I will see you at the restaurant."

"Roger," Lt. Col. Randal said. "If any man so much as looks sideways at Mandy when I'm not physically present—kill him."

"With alacrity, Chief."

Walking out, Lt. Mandy said, "For a cold-blooded mercenary, King uses big words."

"You noticed that," Lt. Col. Randal said.

From the back seat of the car where he and Lt. Mandy were sitting, Lt. Col. Randal asked, "Know where we're going, Flanigan?"

"Miss Runborg's apartment, then to the Gezira Club, sir."

"Let's do this."

Lt. Mandy said, "John, are you up to speed on what's going on tonight?"

"Not really."

"Rocky agreed to work for MI-5 as a double agent," Lt. Mandy said, "but she does not trust British Intelligence."

"That I do know," Lt. Col. Randal said.

"Her arrangement with R. J. was that she was to be seen in a public place with you once a month. That is the reason why you were called in from your patrol, John."

"That part is new news."

"You are her protector; you gave your word she will not be harmed or compromised as long as she cooperates," Lt. Mandy said.

"Rocky has been throwing a fit because we have not honored the deal."

"Doesn't make sense."

"Does to Rocky; perfectly good tradecraft too. Not something an amateur would think of," Lt. Mandy said.

"Lady Jane is not about to let the two of you go out on the town alone. Since she was unexpectedly called away on an emergency tonight, I am her stand-in."

"*You,*" Lt. Col. Randal asked, "are my chaperone?"

Lt. Mandy said, "How am I doing so far?"

Flanigan cruised into downtown Cairo en route to Rocky's apartment. The night was sultry. After the solitude of the desert, being in the teeming city was like landing on another planet. No one was paying any attention to blackout restrictions.

"John," Lt. Mandy asked, "have you heard the stories going around about the Admiral you shot during OPERATION COUNTENANCE?"

"No."

"The Persians are claiming Admiral Bayandor was aboard his flagship at his duty station when the invasion started. He exercised command afloat for the first part of the battle. Then the Admiral went ashore to personally man a machine gun where he was killed at his post, heroically fighting to the last round.

"True?"

"Negative," Lt. Col. Randal said. "Billy Jack shot him."

"I thought you did."

"The two of us were clearing the radio station," Lt. Col. Randal said. "Lt. Jaxx entered the Admiral's office, found the man sitting at his desk and shot him.

"All I did was back him up."

"Is Billy really 'Jack Cool' like everyone says?" Lt. Mandy asked. "I thought Westcott Huxley was Raiding Forces young gun."

"Lt. Huxley's an aristocrat born to be a 10th Lancer," Lt. Col. Randal said. "To Westcott, killing enemies of the Crown is like shooting clay pigeons.

"Billy Jack—he's a gunfighter. Every move thought out.

Lt. Col. Randal said, "He's Jack Cool."

As the Rolls Royce pulled up in front of Rocky's apartment building, Lt. Mandy said, "Remember, light subjects only tonight. Our assignment is to be seen in public. We are not to try to learn anything about Rocky's past. The idea is to cultivate her trust."

"Turning into a real counterintelligence agent, Mandy," Lt. Col. Randal said as he stepped out of the car.

"I liked you better when you were a simple horse girl."

"You told me that before," Lt. Mandy laughed.

"Keep your mind on business, John. Make Rocky keep her hands to herself. Be back in ten minutes or Flanigan and I are coming in after you two."

"Well, that doesn't give me time," Lt. Col. Randal said, "to do a strip search."

"Ten minutes, John."

"How," Lt. Col. Randal said through gritted teeth as he was getting out of the car, "did this happen?"

Inside the building, Lt. Col. Randal took one look at the elevator and decided to take the stairs. Getting stuck in an Egyptian elevator was not his idea of a good time.

Rocky lived on the fifth floor in a modest apartment paid for by British Intelligence.

Lt. Col. Randal came out of the stairwell around the corner into the hall on her floor to see a man bending down unlocking the door to Rocky's apartment.

He was not using a key.

The man looked up, made eye contact, produced a wicked-looking knife seemingly out of thin air and came for Lt. Col. Randal at a dead run.

The 9mm Browning High-Power came out, up, and fired with no conscious thought on Lt. Col. Randal's part. Hit in the forehead, the knife-wielding assailant crumpled so fast his head hit the floor before his feet left it.

The report reverberated in the enclosed hallway, but it sounded more like a door slamming hard than a gunshot. Typically, it being Cairo, no one came out to investigate.

Lt. Col. Randal reached down, seized the dead man by the back of his collar, dragged him over to Rocky's door, knocked and identified himself. When she cracked it open, he hauled the body inside.

"Grab your purse, Rocky," Lt. Col. Randal said. "Car's waiting downstairs.

"Need to use your phone."

Lt. Col. Randal and Rocky came out of the building. Flanigan held the door as they slid in the back of the Rolls Royce with Lt. Mandy. As the limousine pulled away from the curb out into traffic, police cars with sirens screaming and red lights flashing were racing past, screeching up to the apartment complex.

Policemen with weapons drawn began running inside.

Lt. Col. Randal said, "Step on it, Flanigan."

"There goes Sammy Sansom's car," Mandy said. "Was something happening back there?"

"The Colonel shot a man breaking into my apartment," Rocky said.

"Left the body in my living room."

"It'll be gone," Lt. Col. Randal said, "by the time you get home."

LIEUTENANT COLONEL JOHN RANDAL WAS STANDING AT THE BAR IN THE Gezira Club talking to Captain A. W. "Sammy" Sansom when Captain the Lady Jane Seaborn walked into the restaurant.

"My meeting concluded," Lady Jane said. "Thought I would join you."

"Glad you did," Lt. Col. Randal said.

Lady Jane's eyes flashed pleasure, realizing he meant it. She *had* been anxious about Rocky.

"Why are you two at the bar?"

"Colonel Randal killed an intruder attempting to break into Rikke Runborg's apartment earlier tonight," Capt. Sansom said.

"Burglar tools, no ID, sterile clothing. We still have no idea who or what he is."

"Really?" Lady Jane said. "Coincidence?"

"I don't believe in coincidences," Capt. Sansom said. "The dead man is either a thief, an aspiring rapist or enemy agent."

"I do not believe in coincidences either," Lady Jane said, "which eliminates the first two options."

"If the deceased was employed by the other side," Capt. Sansom said, "the actor was trying to get into Rocky's apartment to search the place or attempting to make contact for some nefarious reason.

"Conceivably, he was attempting to deliver new instructions from Berlin."

"If he wanted to talk," Lt. Col. Randal said, "why not knock on her door?"

"Agreed," Lady Jane said. "Do you have reason to think Rikke is blown, Captain?"

"Not likely," Capt. Sansom said. "The Nazis have no cause to suspect she's flipped, Lady Jane.

"It's fairly common practice in the intelligence world to arrange a break-in to toss one of your own operatives' living quarters. Good way to keep tabs on your spy.

"I do it all the time."

One of the waiters brought a silver tray with an envelope on it to Lt. Col. Randal. He opened the sealed flap. Inside was a Phantom situation report.

"*2100 hours Ranger Patrol executed attack on Regia Aeronautica Landing Ground 317. Nine Fiat G-50 fighter aircraft destroyed.*"

LIEUTENANT COLONEL JOHN RANDAL RETURNED FROM WALKING RIKKE "Rocky" Runborg to her apartment. Flanigan, Captain the Lady Jane Seaborn and Lieutenant Mandy Paige were waiting in the Rolls Royce. The evening had turned out more entertaining than he had expected.

Major Sir Terry "Zorro" Stone and ex-Captain Travis McCloud had joined the party with a couple of dancers from the Kit Kat Club in tow.

Lieutenant Pamala Plum-Martin arrived with an RAF fighter pilot.

A young captain from the legendary 11th Hussar Regiment flirted with Lt. Mandy.

Every officer in the Gezira Club with even a passing acquaintance to anyone in their group had dropped by the table.

Rocky attracted men like moths to a flame.

Flanigan drove out of town to RFHQ.

Lt. Mandy retired to her room.

Lady Jane and Lt. Col. Randal went upstairs to their suite. She was going to bed, and he was changing into battle dress.

Maj. Stone and ex-Capt. McCloud arrived—minus their dancers.

Vice Admiral Sir Randolph "Razor" Ransom and Captain "Geronimo" Joe McKoy drove up at the same time.

James "Baldie" Taylor and Field Marshal Claude Auchinleck appeared at 2400 hours on the dot. They stepped out of their car and into the Rolls Royce. Flanigan came inside RFHQ to announce their arrival.

Lt. Col. Randal and VAdm. Ransom got into the limousine.

Maj. Stone, Capt. McKoy and ex-Capt. McCloud climbed into a jeep. They followed Flanigan as he drove down the coast road. Off to their right, the Mediterranean was black.

The night was pitch-dark.

Jim and Lt. Col. Randal rode in the front seat with Flanigan. FM Auchinleck and VAdm. Ransom sat in the back. The Admiral kept up a running commentary about the demonstration they were going to observe.

"Under our normal operating rules," VAdm. Ransom said, "the three LCVPs would be transported on a mother ship to a distant location farther up the coast toward Tripoli than our Landing Craft Tank will generally operate because of speed time constraints. They would launch a minimum of three miles off the coast.

"The LCVPs will have a gun jeep patrol or a Commando raiding party onboard."

"Why so far from shore, Admiral?" FM Auchinleck asked.

"We intend to carry out these coastal Commando/gun jeep type raids for as long as British Forces are engaged in operations in this part of Africa," VAdm. Ransom said. "Therefore, it is imperative that we always work under a cloak of secrecy. We never want the opposition to understand whence the raiders come nor how they retire.

"Three miles is over the horizon—a safe distance to preserve our elements of anonymity and surprise."

"A joint tactical misinformation campaign shall be opened in conjunction with the coastal raids," Jim said. "Parachutes left on shore to make it appear our Raiders dropped in on the beach—little tricks like that to mystify and mislead.

"Raiding Forces has one of the best Psychological Warfare men in the business attached to orchestrate it."

VAdm. Ransom said, "The addition of the LCVPs to our mix of swift Italian MAS boats and the LCT equipped with the DUKWs provides Raiding Forces maximum amphibious flexibility for short-, medium- and long-range amphibious raiding operations.

Jim said, "Sea Squadron's motto is 'No beach out of reach.'"

"Innovative," FM Auchinleck said. "I wish all my people were as eager by half to get at the enemy."

"Tonight," VAdm. Ransom said, "we shall not be dropping the LCVPs from a ship offshore. Lieutenant Roy Kidd, our Duck Patrol leader, loaded his gun jeeps onboard them at RFHQ, and they are going to simulate being dropped off by sailing out to sea and coming back in to land on our target beach.

"I believe you will be suitably impressed with how stealthy the LCVPs are at getting Lt. Kidd's patrol ashore, Field Marshal."

"Sounds impressive," FM Auchinleck said. "Lady Jane tells me Raiding Forces is entirely equipped with vehicles, aircraft and boats that no one else seems to want.

"Is that actually the case, Admiral?"

"Absolutely," VAdm. Ransom said. "We also use captured enemy weapons and equipment when they fit our requirements. Virtually everything we have is a castoff or has been rejected. If anyone on your staff or the army line commanders makes the claim that Raiding Forces is drawing off essential kit they need, know that this is simply not the case.

"I will be delighted to go over Raiding Forces' table of organization with you item by item if you would like, Field Marshal."

Flanigan drove up and parked on a rise overlooking a small inlet with a thin slice of beach where the LCVPs would be coming ashore. The night was black. It was difficult to see much farther than the winged goddess ornament on the hood of the Rolls Royce.

The conditions were perfect for raiding.

"Colonel Randal," FM Auchinleck said, "your most ardent advocate, Lady Jane, and Mr. Taylor both inform me you are the army's best authority on unconventional irregular warfare.

"Commando, for reasons not quite clear to me, is an inflammatory word to my Operations Division staff. They tell me that amphibious raiding is an impossibility in this theatre, quite adamant about it, yet you are proposing to do precisely that.

"Tell me, Colonel, how do you intend to prove my staff wrong?"

Before Lt. Col. Randal could answer, VAdm. Ransom said, "Anyone who says we cannot raid from the sea along the Mediterranean coastline is either a liar with an agenda or a bloody fool, Field Marshal."

Jim said, "The Via Balbia runs from Tripoli all the way down the coast. Rommel has to push every item of his equipment, all his military supplies, fuel and foodstuffs down the 1,500-mile length of its narrow corridor to the front. Raiding Forces is developing the capability to raid the coastal road along its entire length from both sides, desert and sea."

"Raiding Forces," VAdm. Ransom said, "consists of less than 250 men all up, including rear echelon maintenance personnel and female support staff, as I pointed out earlier.

"Our size is insignificant in comparison to the rest of the army. That said, our Raiding Forces Desert Patrol has already destroyed more enemy aircraft than most RAF fighter squadrons. Sea Squadron has mined the Via Balbia over fifty times. Stationing a Commando-type element at sea to rove up and down the coast will greatly improve our ability to chip away at the enemy."

"Trucks," Lt. Col. Randal said, "are our primary …"

"John is experiencing some difficulty," VAdm. Ransom interrupted, "convincing his troops to focus on attacking wheeled transports, Field Marshal, enemy airplanes being seen as the more glamorous target."

"Lady Jane," FM Auchinleck said, "has broached the subject with me. I believe there may be a way for me to encourage your men to concentrate on attacking trucks, fuel carriers and tank transports for you," FM Auchinleck said.

"Any help," Lt. Col. Randal said, "will be appreciated, sir."

"You were going to give me your views on guerrilla war," FM Auchinleck said, "as it pertains to the desert environment."

"Sir, my patrols arrive unexpected at a remote location—preferably under cover of darkness—achieve fire superiority at the point of contact with massed machine guns and are gone before the enemy can react," Lt. Col. Randal said.

"We pick our targets based on intelligence gathered by our operators in the field. Plan meticulously. Then, utilizing the elements of surprise and violence of action, we strike and inflict as much damage as fast as possible before moving on to do it all over again somewhere else."

"What is your goal?" FM Auchinleck asked. "What specifically are you trying to accomplish with your private army?"

"Our intent is to damage or destroy enemy equipment difficult to replace, sir," Lt. Col. Randal said. "Overload the opposition's maintenance system with material that has to be repaired. Cause Rommel to divert combat troops from the battlefield to guard installations of no military value …"

"Raiding Forces," Jim said, "also conducts an ongoing Psychological Warfare campaign to degrade enemy troop morale.

"Y-Service intercepts report that the toxic smoke from the tire dump fire Lt. Col. Randal started is now drifting across the Via Balbia. Turned day into night, and anyone traveling down it has to wear their gas masks along a five-mile stretch of the road," Jim said. "PWE is working full bore to let everyone on the enemy side know who caused the fire.

"Colonel Randal," VAdm. Ransom said, "made a bold statement that Raiding Forces can operate at will in Rommel's backyard with his tire dump fire."

Lt. Col. Randal said, "We'd like the Desert Fox and all his people worried that Raiding Forces is hiding behind every sand dune."

"I should like that also," FM Auchinleck said.

Lt. Col. Randal glanced at the lime green hands on his Rolex. He was not happy. The LCVPs were scheduled to have landed ten minutes ago.

It became quiet in the car.

Time seemed to stand still. There were no boats gliding into shore from the sea. It was becoming uncomfortable in the Rolls, the atmosphere strained.

Finally, FM Auchinleck said, "Those craft are very stealthy. I never saw or heard a thing. Quite the ghosts."

"Yes, they are," VAdm. Ransom said. "Stealthy indeed."

"Flanigan," Lt. Col. Randal said, "run the Field Marshal and Admiral Ransom back to Cairo."

"Sir!"

"I'll hop out here," Lt. Col. Randal said, "debrief Lt. Kidd, then ride back to RFHQ with Major Stone."

"Capital idea, Colonel," VAdm. Ransom said.

"Do not take overly long," Jim said. "We need to discuss a late-breaking matter of some urgency—a recent development."

"Roger."

Lt. Col. Randal walked over to Maj. Stone's jeep.

"Where are those bloody LCVPs?" Maj. Stone said. "Twenty minutes behind schedule."

"Lost," Lt. Col. Randal said. "Let's go try to find out where Roy came ashore."

"Of all the nights," Maj. Stone said. "Typical."

"The Field Marshal," Lt. Col. Randal said, "complimented Duck Patrol for landing on time on target. We just couldn't see 'em."

Capt. McKoy said, "Hate for the man to find out those boys hit the wrong beach."

"Nothing useful could come from that," Maj. Stone said.

"You reckon the Field Marshal really believes those boats were invisible, John?" Capt. McKoy asked.

"Negative," Lt. Col. Randal said. "He let us off the hook."

After searching for a half hour, Duck Patrol was finally located farther down the beach. The Royal Navy Volunteer Reserve Sub-Lieutenant in command of the three LCVPs had landed in the wrong place. He was not looking forward to explaining his navigation to VAdm. Ransom.

The Admiral was not known throughout the Service as "Razor" for his gentle disposition or for suffering fools lightly.

Lt. Kidd said, "It was dark."

Lieutenant Colonel John Randal arrived back at rfhq to find James "Baldie" Taylor and Captain the Lady Jane Seaborn waiting for him.

Lady Jane said, "Frogspawn."

Lt. Col. Randal had had a long day but he instantly clicked on.

"Dudley Clarke has surfaced," Jim said, "under arrest in Spain."

"Spain?"

"No one has any knowledge of why Colonel Clarke went to Spain," Jim said. "None of the intelligence agencies ordered the trip. No one authorized his travel."

"What's he arrested for?" Lt. Col. Randal asked.

"Espionage," Jim said.

"Dudley was apprehended in full drag," Lady Seaborn said, "to include makeup, bra, panties, garter belt and silk stockings."

"You're kidding."

"No, unfortunately not. The Gestapo is pressuring the Franco government to turn him over to them for interrogation," Jim said.

"Dudley is in possession of certain state secrets that, if divulged, would pose a grave danger to British National Security. The intelligence community is in full-blown crisis mode.

"The Nazis cannot be allowed to get their hands on him."

"And you don't know why Colonel Clarke is in Spain?" Lt. Col Randal asked. "You would tell me, right?"

"It's a mystery. Dudley was not acting for British Intelligence," Lady Jane said. "That much is confirmed.

"No British authority sanctioned the mission; no one has an inkling what his motive was, who he went to Spain to see or why he would travel incognito."

What Lady Jane did *not* say was that she and Jim were in possession of a mug shot of Col. Clarke taken by the Spanish police at the time of his arrest. And she was never going to allow the photo to be shown to Lt. Col. Randal.

Not ever.

Lady Jane knew that if Lt. Col. Randal saw the photograph he would realize this was not the first time Colonel Clarke had dressed up in women's clothing. The photo was classified Need to Know, and no one other than the Prime Minister or C, the Chief of MI-6—the Secret Intelligence Service, had that need.

Jim said, "Colonel, are you prepared to accept a mission?"

Lt. Col. Randal stared at the two of them without comment. Jim's question was not really a question. It was, in fact, a formal statement—a preparatory order—and it did not require an answer.

"Place Raiding Forces on alert," Jim ordered. "Stand by to launch an operation to rescue Colonel Clarke—or in the eventuality that is not possible—prevent him from falling into German hands.

"Begin pre-positioning your troops."

"You want me to invade Spain," Lt. Col. Randal said. "Spring Colonel Clarke out of jail?"

"Or silence him," Jim said, "should you, in your sole discretion, determine extraction is not a practical solution."

"Kill Dudley Clarke?"

"Exactly," Lady Jane said.

And she did not bat a drop-dead gorgeous eyelash.

King came running up the stairs and burst into the suite. He was waving a flimsy from the Phantom radio room.

"Read this, Chief."

"0315 hours Ranger Patrol ambushed. Two gun jeeps destroyed. Capt. Pilkington killed. Lt. Jaxx, W. Treywick and five men missing presumed captured.

The Raiding Forces mission continues in *Africa 1941* coming 2016.

Made in the USA
Middletown, DE
27 November 2016